YOU
KNOW
WHAT
YOU
DID

YOU
KNOW
WHAT
YOU
DID

A NOVEL

K. T. NGUYEN

DUTTON

DUTTON
An imprint of Penguin Random House LLC
penguinrandomhouse.com

LIBRARY OF CONGRESS CATALOGING-IN-PUBLICATION DATA

Names: Nguyen, K. T., author.
Title: You know what you did : a novel / K.T. Nguyen.
Description: [New York] : Dutton, 2024.
Identifiers: LCCN 2023022638 (print) | LCCN 2023022639 (ebook) |
ISBN 9780593473856 (hardcover) | ISBN 9780593473870 (ebook)
Subjects: LCGFT: Thrillers (Fiction). | Novels.
Classification: LCC PS3614.G887 Y68 2024 (print) | LCC PS3614.G887 (ebook) |
DDC 813/.6—dc23/eng/20230920
LC record available at https://lccn.loc.gov/2023022638
LC ebook record available at https://lccn.loc.gov/2023022639

Printed in the United States of America
1st Printing

Dedicated to mothers, daughters,
and the daughters who mother

Evil is unspectacular and always human,
And shares our bed and eats at our own table.

—W. H. AUDEN

YOU
KNOW
WHAT
YOU
DID

PART 1

PROLOGUE

Annie Shaw held her mother's hand one last time. She wrapped her own bloody fingers around the old woman's fist, which now clutched a rusty dao bào knife.

"Mẹ." Annie babbled the Vietnamese word for "mom" over and over again. "Mẹ, I didn't mean it. We struggled but . . . I-I never wanted to hurt you." She wasn't sure if she'd said the words out loud or just thought them. Regardless, her mother's crepe-paper eyelids remained shut, her mouth frozen in a gummy, rictus grin.

Just then, a strange sensation crept over Annie. Was any of this real? The small hand, grasped in hers, felt too light, as if the bones were hollow like a bird's. Bright red blood on the blade and on Mẹ's neck suddenly looked as fake as cherry Jell-O. A gurgling sound rose in the back of Annie's throat. Uncertain if it was a sob or a giggle, she swallowed, embarrassed, though it was just the two of them.

How long had she been crouched over the body—seconds, minutes, maybe more? Tall stacks of mildew-stained books and newspapers blocked out the daylight, creating perpetual dusk inside the carriage house. Field mice had marked the perimeter of the room. The unmistakable ammonia odor of their urine hung in the air.

Slowly, as if in a trance, she let go of her mother's hand. She rose to her feet, knees cracking. Her legs felt heavy and numb. She took her first step but stumbled and crashed into a wall of empty juice bottles and rancid carryout containers. A fishy stench invaded her nostrils.

She landed on all fours, palms down on a carpet of soggy paper towels and mildew-blackened newspapers. She squeezed her eyes closed. How had she lost control? She loved Mẹ. Didn't she?

Just then, a gray blur whizzed past her cheek. Jolted to her senses, Annie sprang to her feet. Get out. Run!

L et me help with the funeral stuff," Tabby says, grabbing a cold kombucha from the fridge. "I could find the caterer for Grandma's wake or whatever. Like when Papa died last summer."

After Annie's father-in-law passed away quietly at the Shaw family estate in Boston, Tabby proudly assisted with telephone calls and vendor arrangements. Duncan Shaw welcomed his daughter's involvement even though the thirteen-year-old's constant questions about how and what to do ultimately created more work for him. He confided in Annie, "Any inconvenience is well worth it, if it helps Tabby to process her grief."

Now Annie flips through a stack of mail on the counter, buying time as she struggles to craft a tactful response to her daughter's offer. There will be no funeral for Mẹ. Annie, riddled with guilt, couldn't even bring herself to attend the cremation. Duncan had taken care of it for her, disappearing for several hours one morning then returning with four and a half pounds of cremains in a black plastic tub.

Fortunately, something on the kombucha label has caught Tabby's eye and distracted her from the topic of funeral plans. The girl's nose, freckled from a decade of riding lessons, crinkles. "This says 'Made in San Francisco,' but locally brewed is *so* much better for us and for the environment. Do better, Mom." At that, she raises the bottle to her rosebud lips and chugs the entire thing.

Six dollars gulped down in fifteen seconds. At times like this,

Annie can't help but notice how much Tabby takes for granted. She'd never wanted her daughter to grow up as she herself did—and perhaps had overcompensated as a result, buying trendy brands and ignoring Duncan's penchant for lavishing expensive gifts on his little girl.

Tabby swipes her lips on the sleeve of her crisp white hoodie, then tosses the empty bottle into a stainless steel recycling bin built into the custom cabinetry. Again, she fixes a pair of expectant brown eyes on her mother. "So what can I do?"

Annie clears her throat nervously and attempts to level expectations as gently as possible.

"We're not doing a funeral. Just the cremation. I thought you knew . . . there's nobody to invite anyway. Grandma didn't have any friends left, and there aren't any other relatives that I know of."

This was completely true. Annie hadn't even met her father or her older brother, nor did she know the particular circumstances of their deaths. Mẹ had never been willing to share much, only vaguely alluding to the fact that they both died during the war.

"Um . . . well, what about the ceremony to spread the ashes or the wake?" Tabby's voice is growing precariously thin and nasal. With the fragile pride of a teenager, she's taken the rejection of her help, so rarely offered, personally. "I mean, if we don't do *something*, Grandma's ghost won't be able to rest."

Her daughter's presumptuousness grates on Annie. As soon as Tabby grew old enough to be embarrassed by her grandmother's missing teeth, broken English, and odd ways, she avoided the old woman as much as possible. What right did she have to dictate the terms of Mẹ's burial?

"Tabby, I appreciate the offer—I do, but Grandma wouldn't want anything fancy."

Her mother scorned American funerals, deriding them as a foolish waste of money with their shiny lacquered coffins and expensive floral arrangements. In fact, with each passing year, Mẹ eschewed more and more material comforts. By the time she reached her eighties, she even refused to sleep on a mattress, opting instead for a frayed tatami mat.

"Wow. Just wow . . . so no service at all for your own mother?" Tabby says, waving her hands around melodramatically. "Is it really what *Grandma* would've wanted? Or are *you* just too busy with your painting, your gardening, your precious dog? If Daddy or I died, would you ignore us too?"

"Of course not . . . Tabby!" The thump of her daughter's feet stomping up the stairs drowns out the rest of Annie's words. A minute later, anguished wails of pop-punk music seep down from the girl's bedroom. Lately, this is the norm. Tabby, like every teenager, has developed the uncanny ability to shift moods from zero to sixty in seconds.

Drawn out by the commotion, Duncan emerges from his study and shuffles into the kitchen, coffee mug in hand. "Hurricane Tabitha, I presume?" he says, cocking his head toward the ceiling.

Annie nods. As she fixes lunch, she fills him in on the kerfuffle. Duncan responds as he does every time their daughter acts out.

"She's exploring boundaries, testing out her emotional safety net. Tabitha needs to know we love her unconditionally. You're the adult. Try to be patient."

"You always give her a free pass," Annie says, dumping a bag of mesclun into a big white bowl. She plucks a fennel bulb from a basket on the counter and rinses it. "It's not good for her to always get her way."

"Well, I think she has a point this time. We *should* have some kind of service for your mom. For closure."

"She would've hated a service. You don't know her like I do." Her voice cracks in frustration. How can she make Duncan and Tabby understand? She and her mother aren't like them.

In search of the right tool to cut the fennel, she slides open a shallow drawer and lifts out the mandoline slicer. *Mẹ would have used the dao bào.* The image of the old woman's fingers wrapped around the bloodstained knife flashes into Annie's mind. The thought paralyzes her, and she freezes.

At that moment, Duncan wraps his arms around her waist from behind and kisses the top of her head. Startled, she drops the mandoline. It clatters onto the pale green enameled countertop.

"Watch out! Are you trying to make me cut myself?" Her words are drenched in accusation.

Exasperated, Duncan throws up his hands and retreats to the breakfast bar.

Annie waits until he's situated safely across the room before she picks up the mandoline again. Suddenly realizing how much the kitchen tool resembles a rat-sized guillotine, she grimaces. Her cheek twitches, and she can almost feel the gray blur scurrying past her face again. She rubs her cheek against her shoulder, brushing off the sensation.

As she positions the fennel bulb along the chef-sharp steel, Annie thinks about her life before the medication, the pale yellow pill she now takes daily. Back then, riddled with self-doubt, she couldn't trust herself to be near sharp blades.

Her hands tremble as she slides the bulb back and forth across the mandoline. Has she somehow forgotten to take her prescription today? Not likely—but possible. Her mind combs through her actions from the moment she woke up, seeking some detail that will erase the doubt. Nothing comes. After twelve years, swallowing the small oblong tablet is an action done on autopilot, as difficult to recall as taking her first breath in the morning.

Creamy white fennel shavings pile up on the cutting board. Their sweet licorice aroma fills her lungs, pushing out the tightness in her chest and pulling her from her mental quagmire. Exhaling slowly through her mouth, she scoops up a handful of the paper-thin shavings and tosses it into the salad bowl.

"I'm sorry I snapped at you," she says, glancing over at Duncan with genuine remorse in her eyes. "I've been preoccupied with my mom, and there's just so much to do before the *SouthernHer* interview Tuesday." As soon as the words leave her mouth, she wishes she could take them back.

Annie had been thrilled when the lifestyle magazine approached her last month, but the article, which promised to feature her as a rising local artist, had become a tender subject in the Shaw household. Duncan had suggested Annie postpone the interview given her mother's recent death. She'd refused—the thought of putting off the interview hadn't even crossed her mind. For days, they'd squabbled on and off about it.

Her husband pounces on the opportunity to revisit the debate. "It's only been a couple of weeks since your mom died. It won't hurt to reschedule or even cancel if need be. You have to give yourself a chance to mourn."

"Duncan, I told you the editor has already slotted the story. Besides, a big opportunity like this might not come along again. *SouthernHer* has a national reach. You know how important this is to me." But she can never tell her husband—or anyone—the real reason why it matters so much. As if her success as an artist now will help justify what she did all those years ago.

Duncan slides off the barstool. He approaches her slowly, using the time to choose his words. "You've been handling her death so well—I haven't even seen you cry once. But you know you can lean on me, right? Let me take care of you, Annie." With his palm, he alternates between stroking and patting his wife's back as if she's a newborn. "I'll take a few bereavement days."

"I appreciate the thought, but that won't be necessary. I'm fine. Really."

"C'mon, Annie! It's not like there's some stiff-upper-lip award being given out. You're putting on a good show, but I heard your voice that afternoon. When you called me, you sounded hysterical. Now, suddenly you're 'fine'?"

In a cold sweat, she'd called Duncan at work that afternoon. Of course her husband would help her. He'd be able to move her mother to the front porch—this absolutely needed to be done. She couldn't risk having the police discover the truth. As expected, Duncan did rush home, but to Annie's dismay, he refused to disturb the body.

"We shouldn't. How can you ask me to do such a thing? It's not right."

She pleaded with him, panic rising with each word. "I can't have the police poking around there, they might . . . Of course, I'd be charged . . ." Too ashamed to continue and unable to communicate the full story, she let her words hang in midair. Eventually, responding to the raw fear in her eyes, he complied.

Annie jams the fennel trimmings down the garbage disposal with unnecessary force. She wants to move ahead with her life, rather than dwell on the one that's already ended. If she tells Duncan the truth—that despite her guilt, a huge burden has been lifted off her shoulders—he'll think she's a monster. He'll *know* she's a monster. She shuts down instead, offering him a clipped response.

"I can't do this right now. We need to eat before the fennel turns brown."

CHAPTER 2

O MG I'm *obsessed!*" Millie Rae says, twirling around the foyer. The bubbly blond intern from *SouthernHer* magazine drinks in every detail, from the vintage milk glass chandelier down to the Virginia oak plank floor gleaming out from between cozy woolen scatter rugs. "Your home is spectacular, Mrs. Shaw. A Pinterest board come to life!"

Millie Rae pauses to admire a delicate pastoral painting. Ink-dappled cows bathed in golden sunlight; rows of field corn rippling toward a cloudless sky. She leans in and squints at the artist's signature, partially hidden in the brushstrokes that create the illusion of grain. "Ooh! One of yours?"

"Why, yes." There's a note of surprise in Annie's voice. She passes by this plainly framed canvas a dozen times a day, but she hasn't *seen* it in years. "A relic from college," she murmurs, momentarily transfixed by the bucolic world she fabricated decades ago, a world almost entirely divorced from her reality.

"College? You went to RISD, right? Is this a painting of a place in Rhode Island?" The chirpy journalism student takes a step back and snaps several pictures with her phone.

"Ohio. Believe it or not, I grew up in the boonies, working farm country. This field was just up the road from me." Registering the mild surprise on the young woman's face, Annie explains, "My family escaped Vietnam by boat during the war. We were fortunate enough to build a new life in America."

The line has rolled off her tongue so many times, the words barely register anymore. But it serves its purpose—to curtail questions. Most listeners automatically fill in the blanks with reassuring "pull yourselves up by the bootstraps" fairy tales. Refugee success stories that allow them to celebrate the American dream, without sharing in any of the culpability of war.

Eager to change the subject, Annie clears her throat and ushers Millie Rae into the formal sitting room. "Shall we?"

Once the two women are seated comfortably in a pristine pair of Hepplewhite wing chairs, the budding reporter takes charge.

"Like I said in my message, your profile will be part of our 'Rising SouthernHers' series. My editor wants a short Q&A and lots of photos since the piece will live on digital." Having thoroughly raked over the home's interior design, Millie Rae's bright blue eyes now appraise her interview subject.

Annie self-consciously smooths her hair and presses her lips together. The soft pink gloss she swiped on earlier has already disappeared, leaving her feeling naked. Glancing down at her simple olive sack dress and vintage combat boots, Annie reminds herself that a full face of makeup wouldn't suit the breezy artist persona she's so carefully crafted. In her younger days, she would have shriveled under the scrutiny of a pretty, popular girl like Millie Rae. But marriage, motherhood, and a burgeoning art career have bolstered her confidence.

Besides, she can't let this opportunity slip through her fingers. The article will be a launchpad, earning her broader recognition and a chance to be viewed as a serious artist, not just as hired help. No longer will her artistic choices be dictated by the color of a client's new ottoman, nor will she have to paint the screaming toddlers and uncooperative pets of the local one-percenters. Swallowing her insecurities, she flashes a broad smile and announces in a voice that's just a little too loud, "A visual spread makes perfect sense. My home, my studio, the work, *me* . . . snap away!"

Satisfied, Millie Rae nods and checks off a note on her pink legal pad. "And how about some exterior shots? From what I could see from the porch, your native plant gardens are stunning."

"Of course," Annie says, her voice faltering. Even though she tells herself everything will be okay, her thoughts instantly spiral. *Turn back as soon as you reach the old white oak—the carriage house won't be visible yet. Nobody can know what went on there.* She lowers her head, feeling her cheeks flush hot with shame. Her right palm zings as if she's received a low-voltage shock. She flips it over, exposing the mental image of Mẹ's lifeless hand enclosed in her own. The day her mother died Annie had washed her hands over and over again. Bloody water pooled at the bottom of the basin before sinking down the drain. Even after the water ran clear, her brain cast a bloody pink filter over everything.

The urge to wash her hands right now overtakes Annie. But feeling the weight of Millie Rae's gaze on her, she folds them tightly onto her lap. Her eyes drop to the reporter's feet, ensconced in peep-toe mules, toenails painted scarlet. *Fake red like cherry Jell-O.* Annie's mouth goes dry, and she coughs. There's a buzz in her ears growing louder by the second.

Just as the wave of panic threatens to swallow her whole, a familiar high-pitched yap pulls her back from the brink. The Shaws' long-haired dachshund bursts into the room. Determined to sniff the new visitor, he springs up, forepaws resting on the young woman's expertly spray-tanned thigh.

"Down, Deja. Down!" Annie says, relieved by the interruption. "I'm so sorry. I hope he didn't scratch you. He's due for a nail clipping."

"*So* cute! We must get a pic of you, little guy," Millie Rae coos, scratching the dog behind the ears. Deja wags his tail, soaking up the attention, until the thud of footsteps in chase sends him guiltily scurrying toward Annie.

Millie Rae's attention pivots to the open door. Duncan hovers just outside in the hallway.

He clears his throat before speaking in a confident yet soft-spoken voice. "My apologies, ladies. I tried to keep Deja out of your way, but he doesn't listen to me."

Now ignoring the dog, Millie Rae flips her shiny golden hair back and stands, giving the hem of her short skirt a tug that only draws more attention to its brevity.

"Hi there. You must be Mr. Shaw. I'm Millie Rae." Her eyes, narrowed and deepened to violet, remain fixed on Duncan even as her words address Annie. "You didn't tell me your husband was *so* handsome, Mrs. Shaw."

Having regained her composure, Annie swivels around. Though she rolls her eyes at her husband, she can't help but view him with fresh appreciation. Like the pastoral painting, she's stopped seeing the strapping, sandy-haired man after fifteen years of marriage.

Following brief introductions, Millie Rae maneuvers from the wing chair to a love seat. She pats the cushion directly beside her, beckoning Duncan to join the interview. But he brushes off the vivacious blonde with a polite nod and stands behind his wife, his strong hands gently massaging her shoulders as he speaks.

"It's a pleasure to meet you. Unfortunately, I have to get back to my work. As long as Deja isn't bothering you, Annie?"

The old dog, having exhausted himself with his brief burst of enthusiasm, has collapsed into a warm puddle of silky caramel fur next to Annie's feet. He lets out a ragged snore.

Smiling, Annie shakes her head. "No bother at all . . ." Then she tilts her face up toward Duncan and adds, ". . . my *so handsome* husband." Before she can wipe the sarcastic grin from her face, he dips his head down and kisses her long and deep, his fingertips resting lightly on her throat. Then with a gallant bow, he exits the room.

This sudden show of passion renders both women speechless. The soft thud of a door closing somewhere down the hall releases Millie Rae from the spell. She leans forward, wide-eyed and serious. "Mrs. Shaw, your life is *so* perfect. I'm *obsessed!*"

CHAPTER 3

Annie turns her head from side to side, scrutinizing her reflection. She fingers the silvery strands that have cropped up along her temples and frowns, remembering how precipitously her mother's raven-black hair went white by her midforties.

Duncan materializes behind Annie, his six-foot-four frame dwarfing hers. For a moment, the good-looking couple stand together framed in the Celtic standing mirror, an heirloom passed down through generations of Shaw men.

"You look fantastic, as always," he says, with a reassuring squeeze of her narrow shoulders.

Buoyed by the compliment, Annie relaxes, and the furrow between her brows dissolves. She spins around and rests her cheek against Duncan's broad chest, murmuring, "Mmm—you smell fantastic."

"New aftershave. Notes of the bergamot orange. Like in Earl Grey." After each phrase, he pecks her lips playfully.

"I like that. You be the Earl of Grey, and I'll be your wench." Annie flashes him a wicked grin.

Duncan waggles his eyebrows, playing along with the joke, but also clearly excited. Then catching sight of his wristwatch, he clears his throat and takes a step back.

"As much as I'd love to, we should get going. Tabby's riding lesson doesn't start until ten, but we're dropping you off first for your meeting with Byrdie."

Miss Byrdie Fenton has lived her entire life at Pinewood Manor, located twenty minutes away from the Shaws' hilltop home in the bucolic town of Mount Pleasant, Virginia. The eighty-six-year-old art patron has been Annie's steadiest client over the years.

"Hey, why are *you* allowed to call her Byrdie to her face, but to *me*, it's Miss Fenton?"

"Because I'm such a good-looking guy. Chicks dig me."

"Oh, honey," Annie says, letting a note of false pity creep into her voice, "something tells me you aren't her type."

The never-married heiress lived with her longtime companion Claire for decades until her tragic death in a drunk driving accident.

"So maybe our thing isn't purely physical," says Duncan. "I'm witty too, and charming, did I mention that . . ." He ticks off each attribute on his fingers.

Deja, who has been silently curled up on a rug near Annie's feet, snorts.

"Our dog has perfect comedic timing." Annie laughs.

"*Your* dog," Duncan says, raising his chin in mock umbrage.

In truth, Deja does belong to her more than to anyone else in the family. Tabby prefers horses, and Duncan is a people person, a diplomatic way of saying he doesn't love animals. Most of the canine care and feeding falls on Annie, but she's never minded. For the most part, kibble and a kindly belly rub are more than enough to satisfy the little dog. Annie even finds ways to make mundane chores, like nail trimming, more fun. While clipping the dog's alternately dark and clear claws, she makes a goofy show of singing the Michael Jackson song refrain, "It's black, it's white."

Duncan checks his watch again and sighs. "Welp, we are officially late." He strides into the hallway, calling out, "Tabitha! Time to hit the road. Like ten minutes ago."

"Since when do we call Tabby Tabitha?" Annie whispers, not realizing her daughter has come up behind them with paddock boots, riding helmet, and gear in tow.

"Everyone calls me Tabitha, Mom, because that's my name.

'Tabby' sounds like an OnlyFans handle," she says with the sting-
ing sarcasm of an oversensitive teenager.

"That's awful, Tabby! How do you even know about that stuff?"
Annie can barely hide the disgust in her voice, but Tabby isn't listening, having already raced halfway down the stairs toward
the car.

Even with her daughter out of earshot, Annie lowers her voice
into an accusing whisper. "Makeup, new clothes, now *porn* sites?
You don't think she's having sex, do you?"

"Now that's a major leap of logic! Besides, I think, or at least I
hope, we'd know." All of a sudden looking very tired, Duncan sighs.
"Let it go, Annie. Tabitha's nearly fifteen. That's not exactly a kid
these days."

No, fifteen is a stone's throw away from a learner's permit. The
thought sends a cold chill down Annie's spine.

On the ride to Pinewood Manor, the Fenton family estate, nobody talks.

In the back seat, Tabby avoids her parents by pretending to
sleep—arms crossed, eyes squeezed shut, earbuds ever present. Annie eagerly buys into the ruse. She's experienced enough friction
with her daughter for the day. As rolling hillsides and grassy lawns
slide past her window, she daydreams about throwing herself into
a big project, the kind of professional challenge she couldn't possibly have taken on when her mother was alive. The feature in
SouthernHer, scheduled to post next month, will hopefully garner
respect for her artwork and drum up fresh opportunities. Existing
clients like Miss Fenton will have to view her in a new light.

Behind the steering wheel, Duncan listens intently to Al Jazeera,
a frontline report on border skirmishes and power grabs. His boss
at the Body Politic, a politics and international affairs site, recently
offered him a hotshot assignment in Syria, a job he promptly
turned down. Twenty years ago, he'd have killed for that kind of
high-risk, high-reward gig. Then, fresh out of Columbia Journalism, he'd landed an assignment as an embedded journalist in

Kabul. The army unit adopted Duncan, with his razor-sharp mind and rugby player build, as one of their own. He got more access, took more risks, and saw more than any other embed. His military reportage earned him a Pulitzer, as well as the nickname "Blood and Guts" Shaw, borrowed from General Patton. But he despised the macho epithet, which romanticized the atrocities he'd witnessed in the desert.

Afterward, he wouldn't talk to Annie about the emotional toll it took, nor would he share personal details with the many cable news outlets that interviewed him. He even resisted his nerdy colleagues' repeated attempts to extract battle stories from him. Instead, Duncan channeled the violence and horror of war into tidy political pieces and neatly packaged narrative features. Emotionally, he shut down for months. The emptiness in his eyes had scared Annie, until her unexpected pregnancy revived him. Fatherhood gave Duncan purpose.

On the radio, a reporter interviews a mother with young children in a refugee camp. "Feeling terror, it is a permanent state of mind. I never know if I will wake up the next morning."

The translated words echo traumatic stories Annie heard in Vietnam War documentaries—documentaries because her mother had never shared much about her own experience escaping the war-torn country. Rather than listen to history replicating itself like a gross malignancy, Annie turns away from the radio. She rests her cheek on the cool glass of the passenger-side window and watches the painted white line race by. Soon her eyes start to swim.

The news report has transported Duncan back to the Registan Desert. His mind is somewhere in the barren red sand dunes. His adrenaline is pumping. He's driving too fast.

Annie shoots a worried glance at her husband, sees the vein throbbing above his right eyebrow. She considers saying something to snap him out of it. Street signs whiz by. She's afraid now but doesn't know what to do. Any action she takes to intervene, a hand on his arm or a sharp word, could distract him further.

In the passenger-side mirror, she glimpses Tabby, oblivious to the change in speed. A slight flutter of the child's paper-thin eyelids suggests she actually has fallen asleep. With every millimeter Duncan's foot depresses the gas pedal, Annie's heart rate rises exponentially. Paralyzed, she does nothing. Instead, like her sleeping daughter, she closes her eyes. Her husband is an excellent driver, she reminds herself, and despite his speed, he's in full control of the vehicle. She takes slow, deep breaths and, gradually, her pulse steadies.

Duncan has made Annie feel safe from the moment they met in college. It wasn't necessarily a head-over-heels romance, but after fifteen years of marriage there's a lot of love between them. As she breathes him in, the tension drains from her neck and shoulder muscles.

Suddenly, tires screech, their high-pitched wails echoed by human screams. Annie lurches forward. Her seat belt catches, slamming her against the seat back. Instinctively, she swivels around to check on her daughter. Tabby's eyes are riveted on something straight ahead, her mouth frozen in a silent scream. Annie follows her stare.

A thin, ashen-faced woman leans against the hood of Duncan's car. Clutching at her waist is a flaxen-haired girl no more than eight, eyes ballooned with fear.

Bones snap. Steel crunches. The sick thud of a skull slamming against the dashboard.

An auditory memory—then Mẹ's voice rings out clear and close: *"You get what you deserve, Anh. You know what you did."* With the sound of blood rushing in her ears, Annie barely hears her husband swear, barely gets the door open in time before she's sick.

◆

Tabby's shouts finally break through. "Stop it, Mom! Chill out!"

She tugs at her mother's sleeve, but Annie doesn't move. She's paralyzed by the sound of a child's sobbing. "Don't cry, Tabby,"

Annie mutters in her confusion. Duncan wraps his wife in a bear hug, picks her up, and sets her down on the curb. Only then does she notice the red satin headband in her hand. Golden strands cling to the black plastic teeth and flutter in the breeze.

"What are you doing, Annie? What the hell's gotten into you?" Duncan yells, his voice uncharacteristically harsh. He snatches the hair accessory from her fingers and returns it to the little girl, who immediately pops it back onto her head and shoots Annie a dirty look.

Annie blinks at the towheaded child in disbelief. Then the sun emerges from behind a cloud, and the red satin glistens in the light like a bloody gash.

"I'm s-sorry," Annie whispers. "I thought . . . I thought it was blood. It *was* blood."

◆

"What the actual fuck? It was like you were possessed, Mom. You ripped the headband off that kid's head," Tabby says once they are safely at home.

"I was trying to help her. I thought she was bleeding. The car crash . . ."

"There was no actual crash," Duncan snaps defensively. "I braked. It was just a close call."

"What happened, Dad? I fell asleep; next thing I know . . . *screech!* . . . and I'm tasting breakfast again."

Before answering, Duncan shoots Annie a disapproving look that confuses her. He turns to Tabby, his voice soothing. "I must have been distracted. Sorry, honey. Anyway, the woman insisted they were okay. She said her daughter was more upset about the headband being taken than anything else. She has my number in case they experience any ill effects later that require medical treatment."

Tabby nods and hugs her dad, clinging to him for several seconds. Excitement replaces fear, and she races upstairs, eager to message her friends. She knows there's social currency in a story that's so eminently "shareable."

After Tabby leaves, Duncan pulls Annie aside, gesturing toward the barstools in the kitchen. "We need to talk." He sits down, but she glides past him to the sink and starts loading the dishwasher.

Undeterred, he raises his voice above the clatter of silverware. "Your mom's death is still fresh. Understandably, you're shaky. You're not yourself, but what happened today—what you did— something is clearly very wrong."

"I told you I was trying to help the girl. My eyes played a trick on me."

"I think you need to take a break. A real break to deal with your mother's death. You haven't stepped foot inside the carriage house since it happened. Going through her things could help you sort through your emotions. Maybe think about checking in with Lily Patel."

"Dr. Patel? The psychiatrist? Don't be ridiculous. I'm not crazy!" Annie pounds her fist on the counter, then whirls around to confront her husband. But the deep disappointment on his face extinguishes her outrage. Duncan doesn't need to volley harsh words at her; his silence is the sharpest jab yet.

When Annie speaks, her tone is eerily calm, her words measured— as if the break is entirely her idea. "Fine. I'll slow down. I was planning to postpone the meeting with Byrdie until Tuesday, but I can put it off until next month. Anyway, I could use the time to take care of my mother . . . my mother's belongings."

CHAPTER 4

The next morning, Annie wakes to the sun streaming through her window. Duncan's side of the bed is cold. It's late, but she doesn't move, paralyzed by the bad dreams that rocked her sleep. In all of them, she's behind the wheel, sees a collision coming, hits the brakes—but her car won't stop. She sideswipes a row of parked cars, turns the wrong way on a one-way street.

Bones snap. Steel crunches. The sick thud of a skull slamming against the dashboard.

Suddenly aware that her pillow is damp, her eyelashes wet, Annie props herself up on her elbow and throws her legs over the edge of the bed. Everything hurts. She has no visible injuries after yesterday's close call, but hundreds of minor muscles that were stretched, strained, and swollen scream at her.

Propelled by a fresh resolve to get rid of Mẹ's things, she shoves her arms into a sweatshirt and steps into an old pair of jeans. Duncan was right—she has been avoiding the carriage house, but continuing to do so will only invite more questions about what happened there. She has to act as if everything is normal. Clean out the space so she can have it converted into an art studio.

Her mother annexed the six-hundred-square-foot outbuilding almost fifteen years ago. At the time, they were still counting Tabby's age in months. Annie, mired in a fog of postpartum depression, could barely take care of herself and her baby, much less another person.

"I can't do it, Duncan. Can't you see I'm struggling? We can find another facility for her."

"There isn't one. At least, nothing decent that's within a forty-five-minute drive. Your mom has . . . issues. She's already been kicked out of a half dozen of the finest retirement homes in the D.C. metro area. We've run out of alternatives. The carriage house is the last, best option. You'll be able to keep an eye on her without having to drive to another town."

Despair blossomed on her face, but he continued. "Money isn't an issue. We can hire a nurse. You won't have to do everything yourself."

Annie had stopped listening. She lay down on the bed, struggling to breathe. It felt like a grown man was sitting on her chest pinning her down. She knew Mẹ would never agree to a nurse. She also knew how difficult it had been to separate from her mother the first time. What if she couldn't do it again?

Now, as she plods along the wooded path to the carriage house, her mind wanders. She imagines what life would have been like if Mẹ hadn't moved in with them all those years ago—if Duncan hadn't insisted. Without the daily demands of elder care, she wouldn't have had to divide her attention between taking care of her mother and her own daughter. Professionally, she would have been able to accept that adjunct lecturer position at the fine arts college in D.C.—an offer she'd received after successfully advancing through four rounds of interviews. Maybe then her paintings would be hung in galleries rather than hawked at local art fairs. Most important, she'd have something of her own, outside of her life as a daughter, mother, and wife.

She rounds the final bend, where the path is flanked by aromatic spicebush—one of the few shrubs unpalatable to the surging local deer population. When the carriage house comes into view, Annie's chest tightens. She pauses, leaning against the thick trunk of a black walnut tree. Beneath her rubber boots the soil is barren, a dead zone. She'd read that the tree poisons competing plants by exuding a toxin called juglone from its leaves and roots. Her spine tingles. She forces herself to keep walking.

Leaf sludge and dead branches litter the front walkway. A shingle hangs from the roof like a loose scab. Mẹ refused to allow basic maintenance. The closer she gets, the more she wants to turn around, run home, and throw herself into bed. *Don't be a coward. Nobody's inside.* A shot of adrenaline surges through her body, driving her feet forward.

Two severed tree stumps guard either side of the front door. Her mother preferred them to chairs. Annie had sat here, across from Mẹ, the day before it happened. They'd talked—and they'd argued.

Annie traces her index finger in circles along the unfinished wood grain like a needle on a record, the memory playing in her mind.

◆

"You've let this go on too long. That girl is out of control," Mẹ said through pursed lips, fringed with fine, silver-gray whiskers. Thick fog coated her glasses, obscuring the disapproving look Annie knew was there, because it was always there.

She wished she hadn't bothered to check on her mother, but she'd had no choice. Northern Virginia would see unseasonably cold temperatures tonight. She needed to make sure the heater was in working order and that there were plenty of clean blankets, especially since her mother insisted on leaving the windows cracked open at all times "for fresh air." But as soon as Annie arrived, Mẹ shooed her out. "Go! Go! More comfortable outside."

They perched on the tree stumps. Even in her down coat, Annie had to clench her teeth to keep them from chattering. Her mother, inured to the cold, wore a pilled beige sweater and moth-eaten watch cap, knitted before arthritis had gnarled her fingers. The old woman's cheeks were rosy. She'd launched into one of her favorite tirades—the corruption of her granddaughter.

"You need to get Tabby on your side. Do it while she's young. The girl is spoiled. Too American."

Annie gritted her teeth harder but said nothing. She'd heard Mẹ's criticism a thousand times over, but it still managed to cut. Especially since she'd been second-guessing her own mothering skills lately. Just this morning, she and Tabby had a dust-up over whether the teenager could post to TikTok. Annie hadn't even realized her daughter had her own account.

"Last week, I see Tabby go to school—to study . . . or to fish for boys? Tight shirt showing her boobies. Dirty, black makeup around her eyes like a whore!"

Annie winced. Nasty criticisms came to Mẹ as naturally as breathing.

"That's not nice!" Annie knew her retort was weak. She wanted to defend her daughter by extolling her virtues—clever, kind, brave!—but the words stuck in her throat. It was easier to attack. "This is a waste of time." She stood up to face her mother. "You don't listen to anyone else. I might as well be talking to that stump."

Annie derived no satisfaction from hurling the insult. Her words were too pathetically close to reality—shrunken with age, wizened with bitterness, Mẹ could have been mistaken for part of the lifeless tree stump. Annie felt sick to her stomach.

The old woman glared past her daughter into the middle distance and spit out a warning. "I try to help. You shit on me. You get what you deserve, Anh. You know what you did."

GRACE FALLS, 1984

"Frère Jacques, Frère Jacques, Dormez vous? Dormez vous? Din, din, don. Din, din, don." Mẹ sang softly to herself as she opened the old yellow Frigidaire. The song was a remnant of her childhood when French soldiers still roamed Vietnam's cities and countryside.

Lying on her belly in the living room, Anh strained her ears to hear. She drank in every note whenever her mother was happy enough to sing. The five-year-old understood this meant it had been a good week at the nail salon where her mom worked—enough hours, enough tips, enough to eat.

Her mother wasn't great with money; she'd never had to be before. She was the daughter of a prosperous, politically connected merchant, and her life in Saigon included Catholic boarding schools, fragrant gardenia-lined paths, maids, and chauffeured Mercedes. But her luxurious lifestyle had ended as the Communists seized control. Suddenly, she found herself alone and pregnant in a refugee camp. In America, she landed a job filing calluses off the feet of rich ladies—the chubby ones who, Anh noticed, spoke louder, never slower.

More often than not, Mẹ struggled with her demons, but Anh learned to treasure the bright spots. And something truly amazing had happened earlier that week. Her mom had splurged, bringing home the sixty-four-count Crayola crayons box—the big one with the built-in sharpener. Anh had been virtually inseparable from it ever since.

As she stroked raw umber on a page of newsprint, the aroma of toasted star anise warmed her nostrils. Mẹ was making a big pot of Saturday phở. Expertly wielding both blades of the dao bào, she peeled a finger of ginger and chopped a white onion in half. Then she held them directly against the gas flame until a familiar smokiness filled the house. Charred aromatics gave the broth its distinctive flavor, a complexity that created the illusion of substance even when there wasn't enough meat.

In a few hours they'd sit together at the folding card table, slurping steaming bowls of noodle soup. A happy family. *Just the two of them.*

As her mom floated around the kitchen, Anh wriggled her toes into the shaggy, moss-green carpet and sketched. She felt full even though she hadn't eaten yet.

CHAPTER 5

Annie watched the artificial burger patties sizzling in the cast-iron pan. The faux meat smelled and charred like the real thing—even bled like actual flesh. She switched off the heat and resumed telling Duncan about the harsh exchange she'd had earlier in the day with her mother.

"She said Tabby looked like a whore! Can you believe that?" Annie secretly hoped her husband would say something to justify her own unkind words, for which she felt a growing remorse.

Duncan thought for a moment before responding. "It's tough. Your mother has mental problems. But engaging like that only makes the situation harder on *you*. She needs you, Annie."

She cast her eyes down at the pan, listening as the sputtering slowed to a quiet. "You're right. I'll smooth things over in the morning. For my own peace of mind—and because I know Mother will never change. She's from the 'I criticize because I care' culture."

"Well, thank god you can be here for her twenty-four-seven, basically. That's a gift."

"*You're* a gift." Annie caressed his cheek, reminding herself not to take her husband's generosity for granted. It was his ample trust fund that afforded her the flexibility to work from home.

Duncan finished setting the table, then shouted up the stairwell. "Taa-bitha! Dinner!" The booming voice he used at work to commandeer the newsroom yielded no response at home.

"Why do you bother?" Annie asked, wiping her hands on a tea towel. "She's probably gaming with those monster headphones you gave her for Christmas. Just message her."

"I refuse to text someone in my own home. Another human being, no more than a furlong away." Duncan puffed his chest out while nudging up his horn-rimmed glasses at the bridge, his brawn incongruous with the nebbishy mannerism.

"What the fu . . . *furlong*?" Impatient with her husband's high-hatted stance because she knew it was only partially in jest, she whipped out her phone.

"Furlong. An eighth of a mile, a unit of distance dating back to early Anglo-Saxon times . . ." Duncan continued his rant but stopped abruptly when he saw the choked expression on his wife's face. "Something I said?"

"Duncan, look at Tabby's new profile pic!" She pointed to the open messenger app on her phone. Barely recognizable beneath thick coats of bronzer, mascara, and gloss, their child stared back at them. Lips parted, shoulders bare, filtered to high heaven.

"What the . . ." Duncan turned his face away, not wanting to look at the sexualized image of his little girl, but quickly steadied himself. "It's okay—we can fix this. Let's not read too much into it. She's fourteen. Kids that age always want to look older."

Annie barely heard him above the hum in her ears as she recalled Mę's words from earlier in the day: *like a whore*. What would her mother say if she saw *this*? Annie's cheeks grew hot. Without thinking, she sputtered, "What is she trying to do? It looks like kiddie porn!"

A voice floated down from the landing where their daughter had been eavesdropping. "Thanks, Mom. I thought I looked pretty too. Always count on you not to be j-judgmental." Gulping sobs swallowed up the last word, and then Tabby's door shut with such force Annie felt her spine rattle.

The teenager skipped dinner entirely and refused to open the door when Annie brought up a plate. Duncan and Annie picked at their meal, consumed by a conversation that rapidly devolved into whispered bickering.

"If we overreact, we'll push her away," Duncan said.

"*We?* Just say what you really mean—*me!*" Annie hissed. "Why do I always have to be the bad guy while you're Daddy Dearest?"

"Bad guy, good guy—it doesn't have to be so black and white. She took a—an *interesting* selfie but characterizing it as 'kiddie porn'? That was uncalled for."

"My god! You think I knew she was listening? It was a mistake. She would have been just as upset if she'd seen the horrified look on your face."

Unlike her own mother, Annie would never dream of saying such awful things to her daughter. At least she tried to resist replicating her mother's constant criticisms.

"You should apologize anyway," Duncan said, frowning at his wife. But after a moment, he appeared to see through Annie's defensiveness to her contrition, and his face softened. "Look, I've got to get into the office early tomorrow. Overseas conference call. Drive Tabitha to school, and you'll have a captive audience. She'll have cooled off by then." He reached across the table and put his hand on top of Annie's. "I'm sure you can smooth things over."

CHAPTER 6

Annie peeked at her daughter in the rearview mirror. Tabby slouched in the back seat, earbuds implanted. A fuzzy rainbow fleece one size too large hung off her shoulders, and blue cell phone light illuminated her bare face. She looked young. Just a couple years ago, Tabby begged to sit in front with her mom, "like a big kid." These days, Annie wouldn't be surprised if she'd prefer to hide in the trunk.

Annie blamed the rejection, in part, on her dingy Toyota, which, unlike Duncan's shiny black Beamer, stuck out in the sea of luxury cars at Park Waldorf Academy. She'd gotten her driver's license only out of necessity after Tabby was born, and thanks to a combination of superstition and nerves, she drove that first Corolla for twelve years until it gave out. Only then did she purchase a replacement—of the exact same make, model, and color—and vowed to drive it to the death.

"Hey, Tabby. Can we talk a second?" Receiving no response, she wondered if Tabby's earbuds were even switched on or if they merely served as a conversational deterrent.

"Tabitha!" Annie hadn't meant to shout, but it worked.

With a sigh, Tabby pulled out one of the earbuds. "Yes?"

"I didn't mean anything last night. I certainly didn't know you were listening. I-I just think you should tone down the makeup and tight clothes. You don't want to give people the wrong idea." Annie hated herself for stammering, and, catching the flash of annoyance on her daughter's face, she regretted not planning her words in advance. "I'm not expressing myself well."

They reached the school drop-off zone and she slowed the car to a stop.

"Don't worry, Mom. I hear you loud and clear. Look, not a drop of makeup!" Tabby pointed to her own face, a smidge too earnestly.

Annie nodded her approval. Maybe she hadn't done such a bad job explaining herself. "Have a good day—"

But Tabby had already shot out of the car. From the crowded sidewalk, she clasped her hands together as if in prayer and bowed her head. "Under his eye, Mother." Then she flipped her middle finger at the car and disappeared into the throng of teenagers. The morning monitor, a busybody parent, gawked and shook her head at Annie disapprovingly.

Embarrassed, she pulled away from the curb quickly, telling herself Duncan could handle it tonight. The girl respected her father.

Besides, Annie still had to apologize to her own mother. The more she thought about yesterday's argument, the more she regretted her unkind remarks. On the way home, she stopped at the market to pick up Mẹ's favorite pickled radishes. After the disappointing talk with Tabby, she savored the dopamine rush that came with shopping and lost track of time. It was late morning when she pulled into her driveway.

While unloading the groceries, the rice cooker, permanently stationed on the counter, caught her eye. Its warming light glowed orange as usual. The plastic serving paddle, white and glossy, lay beside the cooker. As she lifted the lid, a blast of hot steam escaped. Inside, the rice glistened, its surface completely unbroken.

Mẹ, unless she felt poorly, came by weekdays, rain or shine, for the soft, sticky rice. She considered the trek to be her morning constitutional and often bragged that others her age couldn't manage the journey. Too proud to be seen taking food, she'd wait until Duncan and Tabby left the house before secreting a Tupperwarefull back to her lair, which was equipped with a microwave and mini fridge but nothing that could catch fire if left unattended.

Annie picked up the rice paddle. Habitually, in the afternoon, she'd soak the paddle in warm water to loosen any shards of dried-on rice. As she slowly twirled the pristine utensil around, a knot formed in her stomach. *Something isn't right.*

Peering out the kitchen window, she craned her neck in the direction of the carriage house but could only make out the contours of the roof. A quarter-mile expanse of dormant trees, an army of black skeletons clad in hoarfrost, obscured her view.

She threw on her jacket and boots, then slipped out the back door. Underfoot, the paving stones were slick with ice. She had to tread carefully, and with every measured step, her concern grew. But as soon as she saw the carriage house, her legs broke into a run. It felt like she was chasing ghosts—each exhalation clouding in front of her eyes, then disappearing into the frigid air.

She knocked on the front door. When there was no response, she pressed her forehead against the transom. Almost instantly, the smudgy pane fogged, throwing her coffee-stale breath back in her face. She wiped the glass with the sleeve of her jacket, but all she could see was her own reflection. Beyond that, only darkness.

Circling the six-hundred-square-foot outbuilding, she stared into the small windows but discerned no movement on the other side of the dirty glass. Her boots cracked the frost-crusted ground and sank into the mud. Their rubber soles made an ugly sucking sound every time she lifted her feet.

Was her mother playing a trick on her? A childish attempt to manipulate her emotions, to scare her after their argument—she'd done that sort of thing before. But the lump expanding in Annie's throat, the one making it hard to breathe, told her this was not the same.

She raced back to the front. This time she pounded on the door. Chips of peeling blue paint scattered across the cement stoop.

"Mẹ!" she called out. "Mẹ! Mẹ!" Nobody answered.

CHAPTER 7

Now—three weeks later—Annie hovers in the exact same spot. Dots of pastel blue still cling to the stoop. *There's nothing to be afraid of now.* She lifts her fingers from the lined surface of the tree stump and grabs the doorknob. Her clammy palm sticks to the frozen metal. If she pulled her hand away, would it take her flesh?

Slowly, she turns the knob, feels the impact of her boot hitting the threshold. But she doesn't go any farther. She can't. Falling backward, she catches just enough of her footing to pivot and run. Behind her, the carriage house door swings back and forth, taunting her with the squeal of its rusty hinges.

She doesn't stop running until she reaches her back door. Then she buckles at the waist, a sharp cramp splitting her in two. After she catches her breath and steps inside, Deja greets her with an ecstatic yip and frantic tail wags as though she's returning from a long journey.

"I'm back. It's okay. It's okay," she says, half to the dachshund and half to herself.

As she makes herself a cup of chamomile tea to steady her nerves, Deja races around her socked feet. Failing to get her attention, he clowns around with a noisy squeaker toy shaped like a hot dog. In the warmth of her kitchen, with her dog by her side, Annie feels foolish. She should go back out. But every time she considers returning to the carriage house, her stomach churns. "That stuff's not going anywhere—is it, Deja? We'll give it a day," she says, shivering despite the hot tea.

She'll use the time to finish a tabletop landscape. Commissioned by a local family-owned restaurant, it's the last thing on her calendar until next month's rescheduled meeting with Byrdie Fenton. She would honor the promise she made to Duncan by taking a rare sabbatical.

Deja tracks her every movement as she loads a handful of treats into his puzzle ball. "You work on this for a bit, while I work on my painting." Agreeing to the deal, he snatches the toy from her and absconds with it to the privacy of his crate.

She spends the rest of the morning upstairs in her attic studio. Painting provides a respite from the mental cage of her anxieties. Everything dissolves when she abandons herself to the interplay of color and light. But today's escape is brief. She completes the work before lunch. Then, not wanting to risk overworking the piece, she leaves it to cure.

Descending the narrow staircase from the attic to the second floor, she grimaces. Her neck has stiffened up considerably. Duncan had warned her to take it easy, explaining that delayed physical reactions were common after car accidents. She tries to turn her head to the side but stops, groaning in pain.

"Now you've done it," she mumbles. If only she'd stayed in bed this morning and rested. She grabs an ice pack from the freezer then gingerly lowers herself onto the sofa, lies back, and shuts her eyes. *Just a few minutes. Not long enough for a nightmare.*

◆

The steering wheel slips from Annie's grasp. The brake pedal is suddenly just out of reach. By sliding down in her seat and stretching her leg, she manages to depress the brake with the toe of her sneaker. The car doesn't stop.

Three thousand pounds of steel and aluminum plows into a

crosswalk, teeming with schoolchildren. A small head crowned with curly brown hair smashes through her windshield and rolls into the footwell. Shards of blood-smeared glass shoot past Annie's cheek, piercing her cornea. Inches in front of her nose, a torso lodges in the thick glass. Backpack strapped on, a purple gorilla charm dangling from the zipper pull.

Bones snap. Steel crunches. The sick thud of a skull slamming against the dashboard. You know what you did.

"No!" Annie's eyes fly open. She sits up straight, the searing pain in her neck and shoulders wrenching her back to reality. Heaving sobs rack her body. Her clothes are soaked with sweat. She scrambles to orient herself by recalling specific details from the morning. Deja's treat ball, the chamomile tea, the tabletop landscape—the carriage house door.

A fog of guilt envelops Annie. This is how her mind will punish her. By transporting her beyond the door with the peeling blue paint, back to the last time she saw her mother.

CHAPTER 8

Mẹ!" Annie shouted, pounding on the old wooden door until her knuckles bled. "Mẹ! Mẹ!" When there was still no response, she heaved her body against the door. It gave way with a sharp snap, leaving two halves of the tarnished chain dangling.

Heart thudding in her chest, she darted inside. Her shin knocked against the empty jelly jars her mother set up each night as a makeshift security alarm. She didn't hear the glass clattering over the sound of blood whooshing in her ears. Boxes of mildew-stained books and free newspapers rose in columns so tall they blocked out the daylight. She had to turn her slender frame sideways to squeeze past them. The farther she waded in, the more she could taste the bile rising in the back of her throat. The sour stench of rotting food assaulted her nostrils.

Annie realized too late that she'd planted her foot on a rusty can. Her leg shot out from underneath her. She felt her stomach drop. She landed on the plush pile of a velvety Korean comforter. Her eyelids fluttered closed as she expelled a tense breath. *Pull yourself together.*

Just then, she saw it. Something protruding from underneath the blankets. A hand. It looked like her mother's hand, but the skin was purple and mottled. Annie, the wind knocked out of her chest, fell backward onto her haunches. Rising to her knees, she hurled the blanket aside, revealing a child-sized figure huddled in a fetal pose. Clutched in her mother's right hand, as it had been every night for the past forty years, a rusty dao bào knife guarding against imagined enemies.

"Mẹ?" She heard herself babbling. Without fully realizing what she was doing, Annie reached down and held her mother's stiffened hand in hers. For a moment, they stayed that way, just the two of them. Warm blood from Annie's battered knuckles trickled onto Mẹ's icy fist, like an attempt at supernatural revivification. She watched as her own blood dripped onto the knife and onto her mother's cheek.

"I'm sorry we argued yesterday. I didn't mean it. We struggled—" Her words came out haltingly. "—we struggled in Ohio. I had to get away from all that. But I-I never wanted to hurt you. I'm so sorry."

Annie was unsure how long she'd knelt there, pleading with the lifeless body. It must have been a while, though, given the stabbing pains that shot through her legs when she finally rose to her feet. Taking her first step—the first step without her mother fully alive on the same planet—Annie stumbled. She didn't try to get up right away, forcing herself instead to inhale the rank odor of spoiled takeout. Only when the mouse brushed against her cheek did she come to her senses.

She clambered out of the carriage house as quickly as she could. *When had things gotten so out of control?* At some point, the compulsive hoarding had consumed her mother. It was almost as if she had no individual force of will. Obeying the commands of her obsessive disorder had become more important to Mẹ than her own physical needs, more important than her own child. Eventually, Annie had accepted failure. Her mother wouldn't allow herself to be helped—in fact, it enraged her.

As Annie raced home through the woods, she began to panic. If the police saw the conditions in the carriage house, they would arrest her. Elder neglect. Never mind that Mẹ fought tooth and nail whenever Annie tried to make the place more livable. Each old newspaper, each empty bottle thrown in the trash seemed to rip out a chunk of her mother's soul. Annie knew she had no choice. She'd have to ask Duncan to move the body.

◆

She waited until she heard the paramedics pull out of the gravel drive. Only then did she emerge from the bedroom. Her face was drawn. Water dripped from the ends of her just-washed hair.

When she encountered Duncan in the hallway, she asked, abruptly, "Is it done? Did they see?"

"They just took her. She's gone. I'm so sorry." Duncan's brow furrowed in confusion, as an emotion more akin to relief than grief passed over Annie's face.

Then she threw herself into his arms, burying her head against his chest. She breathed in the bergamot orange of his expensive Italian aftershave, only to pull back sharply a moment later.

"Dammit! My hair is wet. I messed up your shirt." She pointed at the dark blotches now marring the starched oxford.

"Don't worry about it." Duncan gave her a strange look. "You lie down for a bit. I'll pick up Tabby from study hall and break the news to her about Grandma."

"Take the shirt off. I'll press it first." Fixated on rectifying her error, she fumbled with the buttons until he clamped one large hand on top of hers. "Your mom just died. I understand you're in shock, but—" He gestured toward his shirt in confusion. "—*this* doesn't matter."

"It'll just take a minute." Undeterred, she unbuttoned the shirt, slid it off his stock-still frame, and disappeared down the hall as her husband watched in dismay.

HOTEL

It takes everything she has left to open her eyes. Annie's head feels heavy and thick, and the rest of her is just numb. She concentrates, trying to lift her eyelids, but the muscles refuse to cooperate. *Something tells her she should keep them shut.* You won't like what you see.

Lying motionless in a pool of sweat, she slips in and out of consciousness. Where are you? *Her ears strain for clues, but she hears nothing above her own raspy breathing and pounding heart. Suddenly, an AC unit whirs to life. A frigid blast assaults her bare shoulders, back, hips.* Where are your clothes?

The icy shock revives her long enough to realize she's on a bed. The sheets smell faintly antiseptic, citrusy. Aftershave, maybe cologne.

You're not alone. *A wave of nausea crashes over her, knocks her back into oblivion.*

How long were you out? *Her lids flutter, then finally flick open. But the light is too bright, blinding. She shuts her eyes, lets her trembling fingers probe her surroundings. Damp pillow, hard jawline, stubble. But there's no response to her touch—only cold, stiff silence.* You know what you did.

◆

CHAPTER 9

Annie wakes up thrashing in a pool of sweat. She lies still, afraid to move—even to turn and glance at the clock. Since the near collision last week, her nightmares have grown more vivid, more violent. Every night, she awakes sick with guilt from the carnage her unconscious mind has wrought.

Duncan never notices; he sleeps like a dead person. Hearing his measured breaths, she allows her head to tilt slightly, just enough to see him in her peripheral vision. It relaxes her. She hears her own breathing start to keep pace with his. Then the gentle rhythm is drowned out by screams.

Bones snap. Steel crunches. The sick thud of a skull slamming against the dashboard. You know what you did.

Annie claws her way back from sleep and stumbles into the bathroom. She splashes her face with cold water and sees the digital clock in the smart shower. Only one o'clock. She's so tired she could cry. Leaning against the wall, she grabs a fistful of her own hair by the roots, as if to yank out the thoughts. "The nightmares, the blame—it all has to stop," she mutters, addressing the vanity where she's stowed her mother's ashes.

A knock at the door startles her. Duncan's sleep-sluggish voice filters through. "Everything okay in there, Annie?"

Until now, she hasn't realized she's been talking out loud. She checks her face in the mirror, then opens the door with an attempt at a smile. "Sorry if I woke you. I had a nightmare. I went in there to . . . read."

He yawns, too drowsy to notice she has no book or tablet. "Come back to bed." He grasps her hand and leads the way. Within minutes, he's fast asleep. During the interminable hours until dawn, she listens to the cadence of her husband's breath and vows: No more bad memories. No more bad dreams. This is the day she will attack the carriage house and throw out everything belonging to her mother. It's the only way to exorcise the demons once and for all.

◆

Annie twists the cap off the orange plastic bottle and tilts out a single, pale yellow pill. She slips the tiny oblong onto her tongue and chases it down with a gulp of water. She has no appetite but, after all these years, she knows her stomach will turn if she doesn't take the medication with food. Still, she can't fathom it being much worse than the way her sleep-deprived body feels now.

Downstairs, she grabs a banana from the kitchen but can only manage eating half. She offers the rest to Deja, who snaps it up eagerly. Just as she's grabbing her coat, Duncan enters with a big stretch and a raucous yawn.

"Man, I could not get out of bed this morning. TGI-Saturday." He kisses Annie on the cheek on his way to the espresso machine. "It's gorgeous out. Going for a walk?"

"No. I-I'm going out to the carriage house. I've had a few days off. If I don't get started now, I'll never get my new studio."

"You really should've let me hire a cleaning crew, honey. It's too much for one person."

"It's okay. She hates having strangers touching her things, going through her stuff."

"True. Your mother wouldn't have wanted that . . ." Duncan pauses, fresh concern clouding his face. "Well, at least let me help. Just give me a few minutes to get caffeinated and changed."

"No!" Annie's objection comes out much sharper than she intended. "I-I mean, you don't have to. It's your day off. Uh . . . TGI-Saturday, right?"

He turns back to the espresso machine, but not before she catches his injured expression.

He forces a chipper voice as he measures out coffee beans. "Suit yourself. But I'm here if you need me." He presses a switch and the grinder whirs and catches.

Dodging further discussion, she darts out the back door, listening as the rumble of the grinder fades into the distance.

Annie's increasingly desperate desire for a clean slate drives her over the threshold this time. Capitalizing on the momentum, she works straight through her growling stomach and throbbing head. For hours, she bags empty milk jugs, tin cans, and juice bottles, each clinging to just enough of their contents to sour and stink. Noon comes and goes before she steps outside to take a break.

Blinking in the sunlight, Annie slips off her latex gloves and wiggles her cramped fingers. She sucks in the cool, clean air. *Thank god this is the last time.* No more begging. No more battling Mẹ for the "privilege" of dumping just enough junk to clear a pathway. Throwing away *anything* triggered hysterics in her mother.

Wary of the ache growing in her chest, Annie wriggles on the gloves and trudges back inside. She surveys the room, struggling to envision the space as her new studio. The mess is discouragingly massive. A dresser stacked with outdated bus schedules and coffee-stained coupon circulars. Half-open drawers overflowing with tangles of cheap costume jewelry, lightly used paper towels, and pinecones. Stacked-up containers of molding food.

These were the conditions she was too ashamed to let outsiders see. As if she had any control over her mother. Annie's throat tightens as the familiar feelings of helplessness and shame take hold. She tells herself she had good reason to ask Duncan to move the body.

Her mother's hoarding started innocently enough. Shortly after

Annie was born in a California refugee camp, a resettlement program relocated them to Grace Falls, Ohio. Here, Mẹ discovered the joys of garage sales. Having come to the United States with nothing but a couple of silk áo dài, the dao bào, and an unborn baby in her belly, she got a rush out of being able to buy things for a nickel or a dime. It gave her the illusion of power after war had left her powerless. Midcentury cookie tins, Bakelite jewelry, crispy copies of *Gourmet* magazine; and for Annie, picture books and miniature porcelain animals with *Made in Japan* stamped on the bottom.

"They don't know what they have. *I* know," she said, bringing home another haul. "One day, I die, you sell this stuff. Or keep for *your* daughter. Very valuable."

As the years progressed, it mattered less and less *what* her mother collected, just that she *had* to collect. She amassed towering stacks of VCR cassettes, which persisted long after the advent of the DVD. During one attempt at a cleanout, Annie found four duplicate copies of *Wookiee Cookies: A Star Wars Cookbook* despite her mother never having seen the movies.

Avoiding her mother's wrath, Annie let the time between cleanings grow. Left unchecked, her mother's disorder took on a life of its own. Once Mẹ grew too old to drive to rummage sales and flea markets, she collected oily sardine cans, blackened banana peels, and rain-soaked branches. Her increasingly disordered mind imbued them with special value.

"She needs therapy, medication," Duncan insisted early in their marriage—in the years before he gave up.

"Old Vietnamese people don't believe in that stuff," Annie tried to explain. "She'll just freak out if we mention it."

"Of course, I'll pay for it. As many sessions as she needs," he offered, before secretly approaching Mẹ on his own. Sure enough, his mention of a psychiatrist outraged her. "That's for crazy Americans," she sputtered. From then on, she never looked at her son-in-law the same way. Though she grew more distrustful and paranoid the older she got, she never quite reached the point of losing "decisional capacity."

"This is how I choose to live. Do not harass me. Just leave me alone!"

Mẹ finally got her wish—in death, she'd be left alone.

Maybe she could have found a way to have her mother forcibly medicated—if you visited enough doctors, enough lawyers—but city streets were full of patients whose families had tried and failed to force treatment on them. "Annie? Are you there?" Duncan's shouts drag Annie into the present, where she's holding a half-eaten box of Ritz crackers. When she tosses it into the trash, mouse droppings fall like sprinkles.

"Just a minute. Be right out!" She squeezes through columns of trash, hastily making her way outside.

Only the top of Duncan's sandy head sticks out above the enormous pile of black contractor bags in front of the cottage. He lets out a low whistle.

Seeing his concern, she lies, "It's not so bad. I'm making good progress."

"Let me help. You can't go on pretending like everything's fine. Let me *in*. I'm your husband."

"*He's your husband, but he's still an outsider.*" Caught off guard, Annie turns, almost expecting to see her mother. But, of course, she isn't there. She's dead. Yet the statement rings true. Even fifteen years of marriage couldn't dissolve the barrier that separated her and Mẹ from the rest of the world.

Annie could never explain this to Duncan—he'd never understand what it was like to have nothing and be treated like nothing. Her husband's insistence on helping stirs up the raw shame she harbors about her mother's hoarding. Annie's face darkens, an argument brewing in her belly.

Just then, the wind shifts. It sends a foul, fishy odor curling up their nostrils—garbage bags baking in the afternoon sun. Duncan covers his nose with his forearm and stifles a gag. Annie stares at her feet. Hot tears roll down her cheeks and splatter on the ground.

"Hey, I'm sorry. I just didn't want you to overdo it. You're supposed to be taking a break," Duncan says. "Come in for lunch."

When he reaches out, she relents. Locked in her husband's tight embrace, nose pressed against his breast pocket, Annie can hardly breathe. Yet she doesn't move. Instead she lets herself drift—dizzy and lost in the heat of his body. The comforting saltiness of his sweat almost drowns out the fetid stench of trash.

◆

It's late by the time Annie trudges home, dejected by her lack of visible progress. Her expectations had been unreasonable—at this rate, it will take her over a week to empty out the carriage house.

She leaves her shoes outside and undresses in the mudroom, dumping her clothes directly into the hamper. *Who knows what could be stuck to them?* Then she washes her hands, arms, and face in the utility sink, taking care not to brush against the sides of the steel basin. *Dirty water splashed on there.* After bubbles coat the bottom of the sink and the smell of antiseptic soap fills the room, she pats her skin dry with a paper towel.

At the door to the kitchen, she stops and listens before scurrying inside. Her mind readies an excuse in case she encounters Duncan or Tabby. If they saw her racing around in her underwear, goose bumps prickling her bare skin, they might ask questions. This would only slow her down.

The fierce urgency driving her to bathe unsettles Annie. She justifies it by telling herself *anyone* would want a long, hot shower after delving into the moldy food and mouse droppings. But a worry nags at her. This is different—because it's familiar. She'd felt this way before the medication.

Only when she enters her private bath does she start to relax. Off-limits to the rest of the family, the spa-like room was a gift, a concession, to Annie when early in their relationship Duncan's journalism career required that they relocate from Manhattan to Northern Virginia. The move meant sacrificing her beloved studio space in a Lower East Side artists' collaborative and giving up her job as a Soho gallery assistant. In turn, Annie had free rein to select every feature of the remodeled bathroom, which took the place of two existing bedrooms. It featured dark granite from floor to ceiling, sleek Boffi fittings, a floating vanity molded from concrete, and a spacious wet room separated by a frameless glass partition. The modern, minimalist design stood in stark contrast to the rest of the Colonial Revival home, which Duncan had restored with total fidelity to historical detail. To Annie, this made her space even more separate. More of a sanctuary.

"Set light ten percent bright. Set my shower to one hundred degrees. Start my shower."

The smart shower responds to Annie's voice commands. No knobs or handles to touch. Its pulsating spray massages her tired muscles and warms her to the core. She lathers her scalp with shampoo, then washes her skin from ears to toes. Jets of hot water help to quell the questions churning inside her head. *What was that brown splotch on the telephone book she tossed out? Could it have been feces? Dried blood?* Doubt spirals in her brain, like the dirty suds circling the drain.

CHAPTER 10

Annie squints at the receipt in her lap. Twelve dollars for a paper cup filled with purple mush! At best, the stuff resembles baby food; at worst, the aftermath of Grimace trapped in a Vitamix. Thinking about what her mother would say about the cost of the açai bowl, she crumples up the receipt and hides it in her pocket.

Soul Bowl, with its rainbow-painted elephants and rhinestone-studded mandalas, is the current favorite of yoga moms and the cycling set. Annie would never have chosen this café, save for the fact that it's walking distance, a straight shot downhill from her house to the Mount Pleasant town square. The near collision in Duncan's car took place more than three weeks ago, but ever since then, Annie has been avoiding driving whenever possible.

She thought purging the carriage house would help her banish the bad dreams and memories, but they—along with her worries—have only grown more persistent with time. It took ten days to clear out everything, and that was with the concession of a junk hauler helping outside the building. Deep, blue crescents appeared under her eyes, and after the long hours, Annie often forgot to eat. The waistband of her jeans had begun to grow slack. Out of concern, Duncan begged off work to supervise the team charged with redesigning and renovating the space. Annie protested at first but quickly gave in, too tired to put up a fight. But loitering around the house left her feeling more drained, so she had agreed to meet her friend Danielle Park this morning. It was a chance to get dressed, put on makeup, and get back into the swing of daily life.

Annie glances over at the counter, where Danielle is gossiping with the cashier while deftly executing a quad stretch, balanced on one leg and holding the other behind her sculpted rump.

She's the only real friend Annie has made in Mount Pleasant. Initially, their daughters' friendship pushed the two moms together, but after a few years of obligatory birthday parties and school events, the two women started socializing sans kids. There's an ease to their relationship bred by familiarity. Danielle's bold personality draws Annie out of her bubble. Conversely, Annie's quiet introspection helps ground her friend.

"You're the size of one of my thighs, you skinny bitch!" Danielle's brash proclamation reaches the table before she does. Her wide hazel eyes gawk at Annie for a few seconds, and then she plops onto a chair and continues chattering without pausing for air. She's pure stream of consciousness in yoga pants. "You definitely don't need to work out, but if you want, I'll share my Peloton subscription with you. I've found the hottest instructor, Cody. He has the sweetest butterscotch hair and is probably hairless everywhere else, not that I've seen firsthand . . . yet. I'd totally leave Ray for him if he weren't gay—Cody, not Ray."

Exercise is the last thing on Annie's mind. Eating and sleeping like a normal person would suffice. Beyond not having an appetite, she's started finding many foods disgusting. Meat is particularly off-putting. She can't look at it without being consumed by thoughts of the animal being killed. As she glances down at her untouched açai, Annie's stomach turns. She couldn't help but notice that the teenager who prepared it had dandruff, fingernails bitten to the quick, and ragged cuticles.

"Doesn't taste good?" Danielle asks.

"Er—no. I mean, it's not bad. I'm just not very hungry." Annie smiles apologetically but doesn't elaborate. She doesn't have the energy to engage in a wellness conversation with Danielle, who unfailingly dishes up the same advice, "Listen to your body."

She wouldn't like some of the things your body tells you to do.

Danielle stares into her cold-pressed juice, stirring it so vigorously with a paper straw that her ponytail swishes. "I've been thinking a lot about you since your mom died, but Ray told me not to intrude. You kind of disappeared. How are you doing, *really?*"

Surprised by the sudden emotional intimacy, Annie isn't sure how to respond. She views masking vulnerabilities as a means of self-preservation. Her response is guarded. "I'm fine. Thanks. I just needed time to get all her stuff sorted out. You understand."

"I do understand. My mom is my rock. I'd be a mess without her."

The words are meant to comfort, but they make Annie feel more alone. Danielle's relationship with her doting mother is nothing like Annie's relationship with Mẹ. She can't possibly understand. So before Danielle can probe further, Annie cuts her off. "As a matter of fact, everything's finally coming together for me careerwise. I'm getting a new studio space and, believe it or not, *SouthernHer* magazine is doing a profile on me!"

The ploy succeeds in distracting Danielle. Eyes wide, lash extensions like daddy longlegs, she exclaims, "What? That's amazing! I'm so proud of you, sweetie!"

Excited, Annie grins broadly. "The reporter took tons of photos of me and my work. I'll let you know when it's out."

A shadow passes over Danielle's face. "Not gonna lie. Part of me is totally jelly." Last year, she launched an Etsy storefront to sell her jewelry designs. As far as Annie could tell, she hadn't sold many pieces but loved handing out expensive linen business cards embossed with her name, title, and tagline: *Danielle Park / Bead Babe Founder & Designer in Chic / Breathe, Believe, Bead.*

In truth, Annie doesn't feel too sorry for Danielle, whose husband Ray Park is a ridiculously wealthy investment banker with family ties to a powerful Korean chaebol. The Parks aren't exactly hurting for money. Annie is attempting to craft a tactful reply when a muffled rapping catches their attention. Danielle's daughter Aimee, a popular tenth-grader one year ahead of Tabby in school, knocks on the glass, her knuckles covered by the sleeves of a boyfriend-sized hoodie. Shoulder to shoulder with her, Tabby sticks out her tongue, crosses her soft brown eyes, and giggles. Annie basks in the silliness—unguarded acts from the self-conscious teenager are rare nowadays.

Annie can't believe only a few years have passed since the time her daughter raced out to the garden to find her. Face white as a sheet, eyes brimming with tears, the girl whispered, "Look." Then she opened her fist and thrust forward a pair of Hanes girls' size 10–12 briefs, the kitten-print cotton stained with blood. Though she was too embarrassed to say the words, Tabby had gotten her period. She'd learned about the biological process in school and from the books her parents discreetly stocked on the shelf, but, in that moment, she needed Annie. Nowadays, Tabby seizes every opportunity to push her mother away. How had it all changed so quickly?

The café door jingles, announcing the girls' entrance. Danielle waves them over to their table.

"Howdy, ladies! What are you two up to this morning?" she asks. "Cruising the mean streets of downtown Mount Pleasant?"

"Just going for a ride. I need to get my practice hours in," Aimee says, then yips in pain as Tabby elbows her in the ribs.

Annie's eyes widen in disbelief. "You two *drove* here by yourselves? What were you thinking?" Her voice is unnaturally shrill and grows embarrassingly loud. Panic stricken, she's oblivious to the cashier and the other customers turning around to stare at them. "What if you got into an accident? I'd be responsible."

Nausea overtakes Annie. She sees her daughter's lips moving but can't hear the words above the audio memory replaying in her head.

Bones snap. Steel crunches. The sick thud of a skull slamming against the dashboard. Screams. A child cries.

Tabby snaps her fingers directly in front of Annie's face. "Hello! Are you even listening? We just came down the hill and around the block. Five minutes! Aimee's already got her learner's permit. And you know I'm going to get mine later this year. Can you *please* not overreact for once!"

Danielle interjects before a full-blown shouting match erupts. "I agree. It's not a good idea, girls. Aimee is supposed to have a licensed adult in the car with her. You two meet me back here in twenty, and I'll take you both back in the Range Rover."

"Whatever, Mom." Aimee rolls her eyes and snickers, hooking elbows with Tabby and pulling her out of the café. As they leave, Annie hears Tabby say, "Sorry my mom's so lame. Seriously, she can fuck right off."

The comment hits Annie hard. Even though she suspects Tabby is just trying to save face in front of the older girl, there's a part of her that believes her daughter really does despise her—and that maybe she should. Only two people knew what Annie did on that frigid afternoon, and one of them is dead.

"Spoiled brats," Danielle says matter-of-factly. "Don't know how good they have it, right? When I was their age, I had to wake up at three A.M. to milk the cows and churn the butter . . ." She says the last part in a funny old geezer voice to lighten the mood.

Even though she still feels sick to her stomach, Annie can't help but smile. She appreciates how Danielle takes everything in stride.

"By the way," Danielle says, taking a last sip of juice. "I kind of signed us up to run the arts and crafts booth at the spring festival. This Saturday . . . but before you kill me, you have to know it counts as five full volunteer credits!"

Annie stares down at her hands. She doesn't feel up for forced small talk and unfamiliar faces. "I don't know . . ."

"C'mon. We'll bring the guys. Make it a double date. It'll be a blast. Hey, you remember dunk Duncan?"

"How could I forget?" Annie leans back in her chair, a wide grin spreading across her face as she recalls the happier time, well before Tabby became a teenage nightmare. That year, Duncan volunteered to sit in the dunk tank. Annie and Tabby bought dozens of tickets and got in line again and again to drench him. Later that night, they made hot chocolate, ordered pizza, and fell into hysterics looking at the pictures together.

Family moments like this were few and far between these days. Tabby glued to her devices, Duncan preoccupied with work, and with Annie's mother requiring so much emotional capital—maybe she had shortchanged her daughter and husband. Vowing to make more of an effort, Annie accepts the invitation before she can have second thoughts about strangers and dirty public bathrooms.

"Count us in. The spring festival is just what our family needs."

CHAPTER 11

You've got to be fucking kidding me!" Tabby shouts, pounding the kitchen counter with her fist. "I'm not going to an event for babies. How do you not understand I'm turning *fifteen*? Does that not register in your psycho brain?"

"That's out of line, Tabitha," Duncan says quietly but sternly. "Your mother was just trying to engineer a way for us to spend time together. She meant well. Cut her some slack."

Annie bends over the gardening catalog that she's pretending to read, the pages soggy from her tears. When she accepted Danielle's invitation at the café, she thought she was being a good mother. She never dreamed her daughter would react this way.

"*Fuck* that! It's so embarrassing. *She's* so embarrassing!" Tabby says.

"Tabby, enough!" Duncan says. But his stern expression dissolves into a half smile. "When, exactly, did you start swearing like a sailor?" He rests a hand on his daughter's forearm. "Listen, spring festival may be an event for younger kids, but you'd be doing me a huge favor by taking care of my volunteer hours." He looks at Annie apologetically. "Jonah asked me to fill in last minute. I have to moderate a panel in Georgetown this weekend." Jonah is Duncan's longtime editor, an editor of editors.

Tabby stares at her feet but doesn't say no. She scampers upstairs, thumbs tapping furiously on her phone, no doubt running it by Aimee.

"We'll see if that works," Duncan says with a tired sigh.

"Thank you. You always find a way to save me—*us*."

As she says this, Annie can't help but wince slightly, her gratitude tinged with resentment. Duncan can do no wrong in Tabby's eyes, whereas Annie can only ever mess up.

◆

Saturday morning, Annie's eyes are glued to the road, but she barely sees it. She's too distracted. When she pulled out of the driveway a few minutes ago, a ginger cat darted in front of the car.

"That cat! Did I hit it?" she shouted to Tabby in the back seat.

"Huh? I didn't see a cat. Um . . . why couldn't Dad drop us off?"

"What? He left for his panel at six A.M. I can't answer your questions now, okay? I'm driving."

She didn't hear Tabby's muttered response. Too many doubts cycling through her brain.

How far in front of the car was the cat—twenty yards, ten, five, even less? Did it make it across the road to the ditch? *What if you killed it without knowing?* Soft flesh, fine bones—silently crushed under one and a half tons of metal. *Maybe you should go back and check.*

Glancing at the impatient teenager, Annie knows she can't backtrack now. She drives the remaining ten miles to the spring festival at a snail's pace. When they arrive, she parks far away from the other cars. She'd rather walk than risk even dinging another vehicle. Before the engine's off, Tabby is halfway out the door.

"Finally! I'm going home with Aimee after," she says, slamming the door and disappearing to find her friend.

Once Tabby is out of eyesight, Annie paces around the dusty blue Corolla, checking the tire treads for bits of ginger fur, blood, entrails. She circles the car several times, doubt swirling in her brain. *Did you hit it? Check the tires one more time to make sure. One more time won't hurt.*

Her phone pings with a text from Danielle asking where she is. Annie casts a weary glance toward the already crowded soccer field and tries to summon enough courage to face the snobby parent cliques of Park Waldorf Academy, where the annual tuition rivals the GDP of a small island nation. Though the elite school's marketing materials tout "charting your own course," the parents are remarkably similar—Tesla dads and Peloton moms.

Annie breathes a sigh of relief when she spots Danielle's familiar face across the parking lot. She's engaged in an animated conversation with a high school student. It isn't until Annie is right next to them that she realizes the pretty blonde clad in a form-fitting lime-green tank dress is actually a parent. Danielle introduces her as Nina, the chairperson of this year's festival.

Annie can't help but stare enviously at Nina's expertly shaped eyebrows, trendy manicure, impossibly toned legs, and smooth, bronzy skin. She's suddenly conscious of the ever-deepening bags under her own eyes and of her cheeks, which recently developed a constellation of age spots.

They exchange information about their kids—Nina has one boy in Park Waldorf's lower elementary. Then with a cheerful smile and a slight Eastern European accent, Nina asks Annie, "And you do what, girlie?"

"I'm a painter," Annie says. Then feeling the need to qualify her statement, she adds, "I mean I do it on the side. Part time. I'm not famous or anything."

"Don't be so modest," Danielle interjects. "Annie is crazy talented. She's going to be featured in *SouthernHer* magazine. They're doing a whole profile on her."

Nina's face lights up. "An artist! That's so amazing. My father played violin in the Sarajevo Philharmonic Orchestra." She adds wistfully, "I have such respect for creative genius."

Blushing, Annie shakes her head modestly, but being *someone* in this sea of successful strangers relaxes her. She strides across the soccer field with her shoulders squared and a lightness in her step.

◆

The arts and crafts booth proves to be so popular that hardly an hour passes before they're out of clean palettes and water. Danielle has her hands full with a pair of rowdy twin boys who are attempting to paint a wind chime, as their mother coos, "Noah's the color *savant!*" Annie wonders which one she's referring to—the boy trying to stab his brother in the eye with a paintbrush, or the one ducking.

"Going on a supply run. Be right back," Annie says, jumping on the opportunity to flee. She fills a shopping bag with dirty palettes and slings it over her shoulder, then stacks buckets inside one another and slips their collective handles over her wrist.

"Thanks, sweetie," Danielle says. "And if you see Ray, tell him I'm looking for him. He's supposed to be helping, but he's wandered off somewhere. If only every husband were as reliable as dear, old Duncan."

There's a sharpness to Danielle's tone that makes Annie look back. Could it be jealousy? But Danielle's smiling face betrays no signs of bitterness.

On the way to the art studio, Annie passes by the musical chairs game run by Tabby and Aimee. Annie's hands are too full to wave, and the girls don't seem to notice her. They're busy laughing their heads off as they start and stop an Olivia Rodrigo song. Annie frowns, observing that Tabby has applied a full face of makeup since leaving the car. Did she do this every time Annie dropped her off at school?

A pale, lanky boy dressed in a button-down and chinos attends the prize table. It's stacked high with brownies, cookies, and cakes. Annie resists the urge to call out and warn Tabby against eating anything. Four out of ten Americans surveyed admitted to not washing their hands after using the bathroom at home—and that was just counting the honest ones. Bake sales, potlucks, you could never be sure what you were putting in your mouth. When the round ends, Tabby runs over to the prize table. Even with her daughter's back facing her, Annie can tell Tabby's thankfully not picking up any of the desserts.

The buckets and palettes shift awkwardly in Annie's hands, and she's about to continue on to the art studio when she sees the boy slide his hand into the back pocket of Tabby's jeans—and she lets him. The intimacy of the gesture so casually executed triggers a chain of emotions in Annie. Confusion. *Why didn't she tell you she has a boyfriend?* Anger. *Is this pimply-faced boy a bad influence? Is he the reason Tabby's turned against you?* Fear. *What else have they done?*

Annie doesn't want to confront her daughter. Afraid to see anything more, she turns away and disappears into the crowd.

CHAPTER 12

B y the time she reaches the fine arts building, Annie has calmed down. She's convinced herself that Tabby and the boy were probably just showing off, mimicking older high school kids. That was the extent of it. Besides, she knows her daughter. If she's confronted, Tabby will go on the offense and accuse Annie of spying and being a helicopter mom.

Still debating her next move, Annie pushes the swinging door open with her hip. She stops halfway, alarmed by a strange gurgling noise coming from somewhere inside the classroom.

Ray Park, Danielle's husband, stands behind a wide butcher block table. Backlit by huge floor-to-ceiling windows, he has his eyes closed. For a moment, Annie thinks he's praying, and then his face twists into something between a grimace and a grin. She opens her mouth to say hello but shuts it when she sees a flash of lime green and realizes he is not alone. Nina's head bobs up.

Ray's infidelity isn't the first thing to register in Annie's brain. What if semen gets on the table or the floor? Innocent children could touch it or step on it. Even a drop could spread around the school and be tracked home on the soles of their shoes. The ever-spiraling train of thoughts disgusts her.

With the steely deftness of someone who's been caught in the act before, Ray rearranges his face into an unnaturally calm smile. "Annie! Nina was giving me a tour of the art facilities," he says, zipping up his jeans as though nothing's happened. "My family is considering some new investments."

The Park Family Endowment holds two permanent seats on the school's board of directors. Their surname, rather than any leafy green space, put the *Park* in Park Waldorf Academy. With sleek black hair and rippling muscles, Danielle's husband resembles the chisel-jawed doctor in one of the medical dramas Annie follows. The thought of spoiled Ray, with his notoriously low attention span, in an actual medical school forces Annie to stifle a nervous giggle.

"Annie? Are you feeling okay? Is something amusing to you?" he asks.

"I . . . I was just looking for the utility sink to wash these things out."

"Oh! It's right over there," Nina says, gesturing to the corner of the room. "Sorry, the water runs really cold, but there are paper towels under the sink if you need them."

Or if you *need them.* Annie makes a mental note to avoid the spot where they're standing.

As he leaves, Ray shoots Annie a nasty warning look—one he probably saves for the interns at his private equity firm—but she's already made up her mind not to get involved. *Nothing good can come from seeing that.* Ray's dalliances were an open secret among the parents of Park Waldorf—because he'd slept with many of them. Danielle seemed willfully oblivious to her husband's cheating.

On the way back to the arts and crafts booth, Annie's head swims. She tells herself it's better to stay out of the Park marriage. *You know what happens to the messenger.* Besides, she's not sure she'd want to know if Duncan cheated. Sometimes it's better to look away.

Absorbed in her thoughts, Annie stumbles over a divot in the soccer field. She wobbles and regains her balance, but the too-full water bucket in her hand slips. Just before it falls and explodes onto the grass like a bomb, rough hands and a mop of wavy brown hair materialize in front of her.

"Whoa, lemme get that!" The friendly baritone belongs to a short but devastatingly handsome man. He takes the bucket and flashes her a brilliant smile.

"Th-thanks. I lost my grip . . ." She trails off, grateful for his help but embarrassed by her carelessness in front of the other parents.

"Eh, no problem. Happens to the best of us. My name's Gabe." He cocks his head and lifts the bucket in greeting as she introduces herself. Though he's dressed in a nondescript button-down and navy flat-front slacks, he's distinctly unlike the Mount Pleasant Tesla dads. Broad shoulders flow into a compact waist, flanked by solid, well-muscled limbs. Thick, dark stubble hugs his jawline. Annie surprises herself, imagining the coarse hair rubbing against her fingertips, her lips.

But before she can fully process the thought, a little girl jumps out from behind the man's legs. Her hair is a tangle of fiery, carrot-colored curls. Her lips are circled in red, no doubt from the Popsicle that drips in her hand. She resembles a baby Pennywise.

"*No!* I wanna go *there!*" she screams, jabbing a sticky finger impatiently at the pony rides.

"We're going to help out this nice lady first." He speaks with a quiet command that even the brattiest child wouldn't dare protest. Then he turns to Annie with an apologetic look and answers her unasked question. "Annabelle is my niece. My brother's kid."

They realize simultaneously that they are still just standing there taking each other in, saying nothing. It only takes a few seconds for the silence to become unseemly, and both rush to speak at once.

"Where can I—"

"Thanks—I'm right over there at the art booth," she says, pointing to the far end of the field. "I'm Annie. Annie Shaw."

Seeing them approach together, Danielle raises a mischievous eyebrow.

Gabe sets the water gallons down on the grass. He's rolled up his sleeves and his bare forearm brushes hers. It's unseasonably warm, and his cologne mingles with sweat. Annie remembers reading that when you smell something, it contains actual molecules from whatever it is you're smelling. At the time, her mind had gone straight to public bathrooms. Today, the thought sends a current of electricity rippling through her body.

"Are you a teacher here?" he asks, glancing at her left hand.

There's no wedding ring—well, there is, but it doesn't look like one. It's just a regular piece of costume jewelry that Duncan bought for Annie at a Hong Kong night market. Really rich people found those kinds of not-spending-money gestures romantic.

Before Annie can correct him, a couple in hemp shirts, shorts, and matching neoprene toe shoes approaches the booth, shepherding their daughter toward the table. "Arrow, would you like to color a puppy or a fire truck?" The child points to a princess picture instead. The parents grimace, barely managing to hide their disappointment.

In a low voice, Gabe says, "To be honest, I don't know how people have kids. Or how kids have parents. Well, I *physically* get that part. But I'm pushing forty and still a bachelor, much to my mother's chagrin."

Annie grins. "You get used to them, and you don't have to like them. That goes both ways, for the parents and the kids." She immediately regrets her response, stealing a glance at him to see if he's offended, and is relieved by his bemused expression.

"That's a refreshing response coming from someone in your profession, but look, I get it. My mom was a teacher and so's my sister back home in Queens, so yeah, I totally get it."

Annabelle runs over with her freshly painted caterpillar and shoves it against his white shirt. "Hold this, Uncle Gabe. I need to go potty."

"Nice," he groans. "Okay, let's go for the *fifth* time."

Annie hands him a paper towel for his shirt, and when he grabs it his hand brushes against hers. "Let's get a drink if you ever want to talk more about teaching, not liking kids, or, uh, getting rid of paint stains," he says, looking down ruefully at his shirt.

"I'd like that." Annie hears the words but doesn't quite believe she's the one saying them. She's never been—or seriously considered being—with anyone besides her husband. But in that moment, she sees herself through the eyes of this stranger and likes what she sees. An image of perfection that can be derived only from newness and unfamiliarity, in the fleeting moments before flaws and anxieties reveal themselves.

Looking directly into Annie's eyes with an intensity that makes her heart race, Gabe slips his business card into her hand. Then he scoops up the child, who has begun to wiggle suspiciously, and dashes toward the port-o-potties.

Annie sneaks a glance at the card in her hand. *Gabriel Correa, CPA.*

"What in holy heck was that?" Danielle asks the second there's a lull at the booth. She hooks her slender arm into Annie's and leans in close to talk. "I thought you guys were gonna clear the table and go at it right here. We're doing arts and crafts, not chemistry, sweetie!"

"Shhhh! Was it that obvious? I just met him outside the art studio. It was nothing."

"Whatever. He was definitely hot for teacher," Danielle whispers in an exaggerated breathy voice that makes them both laugh.

Annie sobers suddenly, seeing Ray step out from the shadow of a nearby refreshment stand. He'd been watching them all this time. Annie clocks the irritation on his face and realizes he might suspect her of telling Danielle what she saw in the art room.

Her cheeks flush red and hot. She turns away, crumpling the business card in her hand before jamming it into her pocket. Ray hates her now—and he's seen her flirting with Gabe.

HOTEL

Annie recoils as though she touched a hot cast-iron pan rather than cold, lifeless flesh. She swallows, trying to force back the tide of sour acid rising in her throat. The world looks like she's viewing it from underwater, sunlight refracting against the surface. Jagged shards of light pierce her eyes.

Don't call out. Don't say a word. They could still be here. *Who? She's doesn't hear anyone else in the room, but how can she be sure there isn't someone behind her? The back of her neck tingles.*

She tries to shift her lower body, but nothing happens—it's as though the line from her brain to her leg muscles has been severed. A bitter taste lingers on the back of her tongue. Did you black out?

Sharp pain pulsates behind her eye sockets. She squeezes her eyelids shut, trying to force order onto her thoughts.

Disturbing images flash into her mind. Jumbled snippets. Ray Park's sneering face inches from her own. The blade stained with rust and blood. A long tongue, not human, dangling like a strip of red meat. No, no, no!

◆

CHAPTER 13

The morning after the spring festival, Annie wakes at dawn, having just fallen asleep an hour earlier. She spent the night staring at the ceiling worrying about Ray Park. She told herself that because she hadn't actually done anything with the handsome stranger, Ray had no leverage over her. But in the same way Danielle had seen through her and sensed the chemistry with Gabe, maybe Ray had detected her betrayal too. Though Annie strayed in *thought* only, it felt almost as wrong as physical betrayal. How she wished she'd never gone to the spring festival! Then she'd never have met Gabe, and she wouldn't have witnessed anything untoward with Ray or Tabby.

If only Annie could erase the image of the pimply-faced boy stroking her daughter's bottom. It might as well have been yesterday that Annie had to apply diaper cream to an angry red rash there, given the way time seemed to fold over on itself lately. She casts a jealous glance at Duncan, snoring loudly beside her. He'd come home late last night from his panel in Georgetown, too exhausted to talk with Annie about Tabby.

Annie gives up on sleep and steals downstairs. Maybe she can assuage her conscience by making Sunday breakfast for the family. One by one, she cracks eggs into a bowl, taking care to wash her hands after each to avoid getting any potential contaminant from the eggshell into the omelet. Then she sprinkles in frozen spinach and a couple tablespoons of pre-grated cheese—a vision of her knuckles scraped raw against the microplane deterred her from grating.

As Annie melts butter in the skillet, she tries to formulate a plan for asking Tabby about the boyfriend without alienating her. She has no road map to talk to her daughter about sex, having grown up with Mẹ's incessant warnings about boys and her shaming for any display of sexuality. She doesn't want to transfer this burden onto Tabby.

Maybe she should get Danielle's advice. Her friend has never been prudish about sex, speaking freely about her annual pilgrimages to Mama Marissa's Self-Pleasure Bootcamps. She even tried to get Annie to attend once. But the thought was abhorrent to Annie— paying ungodly sums of money to be locked in a Carpinteria cabin with a group of wealthy white women telling her to surrender herself to "the womanly arts."

Roused by the aroma of eggs and butter, Deja trots into the kitchen. He sits down at her feet, tail wagging, soft brown eyes gazing up hopefully.

"This stuff is too rich for your old arteries, Deja. Let's get you your senior chow." She changes his water and pours a half cup into his slow feeder bowl. At the sight of the little dog blissfully chomping on kibble, Annie feels her heart melt.

Deja entered her life as a cure for her condition but quickly became so much more. Having never had a pet, she was completely unprepared for her loyal companion's unconditional love. When, as a young mother, she was stressed, Annie stroked his silky, dappled fur and smelled the top of his warm head. This tactile stimulation, then and now, provides a quick hit of oxytocin, a naturally occurring hormone that eases anxiety. She feels the tension in her jaw ease. All of a sudden, she hears Duncan tramping down the stairs. He races into the kitchen.

"What's burning?" he asks.

Before Annie can act, Duncan swoops in and snatches the pan

from the burner, using the spatula to scrape the eggs directly into the trash.

"I just left them for a minute to feed Deja. How . . ." It seemed like a minute but thinking back, Annie remembers washing out Deja's water bowl, rinsing—*how many times?*—to make sure there were no traces of soap.

"A minute? They were like charcoal, Annie." Irritated, Duncan rubs sand from his eyes. Still in flannel pajamas with his hair sticking up every which way, he looks like a giant little kid.

"I'm sorry. I must have lost track of—"

Suddenly, an earsplitting wail interrupts her. The disembodied voice of a woman repeats, "Attention: smoke warning. Guardian Angel Sentry system detects smoke. In the kitchen. Attention: smoke warning." Each phrase strung together robotically, making the warning all the more unsettling.

Sounding his own alarm, Deja races around their feet barking and whining. Then Tabby stumbles in, groggy and clad in an oversized tee. "What's happening?" But after just one look at the charred remains in the pan, she turns to Annie. "What did you do, Mom?"

Annie turns away, embarrassed by the redness she knows is creeping over her cheeks. She can't seem to do anything right lately.

Duncan returns from opening the windows and replies, "She was just trying to make us a nice breakfast." He punches something into his phone app and the robotic voice quiets. Then he puts his arm around his wife and squeezes. "Since we're all up, let's eat together. Frozen waffles, anyone?"

Twenty minutes later, they're seated at the dining table. Sated by his meal, Deja rests with his nose between his paws beside Annie's feet. She cuts up her waffle in silence, pushing the wedges around with her fork to make it look like she's eaten. Between gulps of coffee, Duncan glances from his wife to his daughter before asking, "So how was the spring festival?"

Annie stares at her plate, leaving Tabby to reply.

"Uh, fine. Aimee and I were swamped at the musical chairs station, though. You owe me big-time for those volunteer hours, Dad. I'm sure you'll keep that in mind when it's time to buy me my first car." Tabby exchanges a wink with her father.

The split-second action leaves Annie feeling excluded. With her confidence at an all-time low, the unintentional slight lands harder than it should. What's more, the topic of Tabby's driving terrifies her. Desperate to change the subject, Annie blurts out, "Was it just you and Aimee running the game? I thought I saw some boy there."

"'Some boy'?" Tabby mockingly repeats the words, narrowing her eyes and rising to the bait. "There were a lot of kids around. Our friends stopped in to help. Like I said, we were busy."

"Sounds like it. Thanks for helping, honey," Duncan says, casting a warning look at his wife.

But Annie won't let it drop. She knows what she saw. "When I walked by, I saw a tall boy with terrible skin. He had his hands on your . . . on you." Despite herself, disapproval oozes from every word.

"Oh my god, Mom. Don't you have other things to do in your pathetic life than spy on me?" Tabby rises to her feet.

Annie shrinks back, stung by the unkindness of her daughter's statement, even though she could have anticipated the reaction.

"Tabitha! Stop right now," Duncan interjects, holding his palm out. "Let's all take a deep breath. I think what your mother is trying to say, in her own way, is that you can talk to us about your friends, your relationships, *boyfriends*, whatever is going on in your life. We just don't want to be shut out."

Refusing to look at her mother, Tabby answers. "I don't have a *boyfriend* if that's what you guys think. We were all just hanging out." She adds in a syrupy-sweet voice directed at her father, "May I please be excused now?" Duncan nods and the fourteen-year-old turns on her heel, leaving behind her dirty plate for Annie to clear.

Duncan turns to his wife. "It didn't have to go like that, you know."

"I tried . . ."

"You sounded disgusted, like you were accusing Tabby of doing something shameful," Duncan says, his endless patience waning. "She's just acting like a normal teenager!"

She flails, unable to respond. How can she explain that she has no idea what that means? At Tabby's age, Annie had no leeway—in the same situation, her mother's reaction would have been to berate her, even ridicule her. That was one of the many differences that formed a gaping divide between Annie and her husband and daughter.

When she was thirteen going on fourteen, Annie received an invitation to Chrissy Miller's slumber party. This had never happened before, but the birthday girl's mother had insisted on including *all* the girls in the class. Annie, having just rejoined the public school, was hungry to fit in. She sheepishly asked Mẹ for permission. Not only did her mother forbid it, but she humiliated her for even wanting to attend. Ignoring her daughter's tearful pleading, Mẹ called Chrissy's mother. Clearly disgusted, she said, "Anh is not allowed to sleep over anywhere until she is eighteen."

"How can you turn this around on me?" Annie asks. "You always take her side."

Duncan sighed. "My loyalty is to this family. We sink or swim together. It's not about sides."

Annie stares out the window toward the carriage house, listening to the familiar voice in her head. *"It's always about sides. Us and them, Anh. Where do your loyalties lie?"*

CHAPTER 14

Wrought iron scrapes against asphalt as the gates of Pinewood Manor close behind Annie. She casts a nervous glance over her shoulder, hoping to see Duncan's reassuring smile, but he's already sped away. He'll be late for work, as if his Monday mornings weren't hectic enough already.

Regret and shame gnaw at Annie. She purposely left her own car's headlights on overnight to sabotage the battery. She wanted it to die. But she had to be careful. Her husband seemed to have picked up on her reluctance to drive, her excuses and requests for rides. Duncan made a few half-joking comments about being an Uber driver on the side, asking if he should display his Pulitzer in the windshield. She didn't want to try his patience, especially after yesterday's burned breakfast and botched discussion with Tabby. That's why she had to get creative with the car battery. Having already missed last month's meeting with Miss Fenton, she can't afford another mistake.

Now that she's arrived at Pinewood, a sense of unease creeps through her body. She keeps walking, tells herself it's just nerves. Towering above Annie's head, rows of Italian cypress flank the estate's long, curving drive. Beyond these lie terraced gardens, stone fountains, and sprawling lawns. Despite the manicured greenery, there's a dead quality to the estate. A bizarre absence of chirruping birds or buzzing insects. Wind slices through the trees, carrying with it a faint, metallic smell like blood.

Shuddering, Annie lowers her head and quickens her pace. Her nerves won't settle, even with Pinewood's antebellum façade now in sight. She can't shake the feeling she's being watched, eyes boring into the back of her head. Before she can turn around, a hand hooks her shoulder, yanking her backward. She jerks away, stumbles. Her throat is so tight, her scream comes out as a choked gasp.

"Annie, are you okay? You walked right past me."

She swivels around, surprised to see the bemused face of her old friend Ike Oteh. They met in RISD's freshman sculpture studio and quickly bonded as the only two first-generation scholarship kids in the sea of moneyed dilettantes. Today, he looks as dashing as ever. His low fade is peppered with a little more silver than when she last saw him, but he's smartly dressed in consignment-store Thom Browne, tailored and pressed, and white gum-soled sneakers.

"Sorry. I . . . uh . . . don't know what's gotten into me," she stammers, having regained her composure enough to be thoroughly embarrassed.

"Good. So it is not me. I did not think I was looking so scary today," Ike says with an impish grin.

"My god, it's really good to see you." Annie clasps his hand between hers. "But I had no idea you were still doing projects for Miss Fenton." Seeing his face fall, she instantly regrets her comment.

At the top of his class, Ike graduated with honors from RISD's rigorous architecture program. While those below him took internships at prestigious firms or went on to pursue their master's, Ike took the train back to D.C. to be a cashier in the family convenience store. Right before graduation, his dad, a heart surgeon in their native Nigeria, had been held at gunpoint, shot, and killed while tending the register. Ike's mom needed him. It was only supposed to be for the summer, but each year he talked about grad school less and less. Recently, he'd stopped mentioning it altogether.

Annie had introduced Ike to Byrdie years ago. The old woman wanted someone to redecorate her guest room, and he needed the money. His talents lay in structural analysis and environmental design, but Byrdie didn't know the difference. Plus, none of her friends had a "gay African" decorator, as she described Ike. She found this desperately exotic and tripled his rate as if he were a high-priced escort.

"Yes, Miss Fenton has decided to replace the red carpet in the dining room and seeks advice about which shade of red to update it with," he says.

Annie groans in sympathy, fully aware that this sort of project could entail weeks of back-and-forth with the eccentric heiress.

"It is okay, though. I chose the exact same shade that existed prior, and she has hailed me as a creative genius. It works every time. People want to feel like they're getting something different, but they like what is familiar."

Annie laughs and wraps Ike in a warm embrace. Usually, she shies away from unnecessary physical contact. This is a rare case when the kinship she feels overrides her discomfort. Ike even smells welcoming, exuding the same Jo Malone lime-and-mandarin cologne he's worn since college. She rests her head on his shoulder, perhaps for a moment too long. Then the unmistakable twang of Miss Byrdie Fenton cuts through their reunion.

"Yoo-hoo! You there?"

A moment later, a plump, round figure emerges. Juxtaposed against the tall, classical columns of Pinewood Manor, Byrdie looks like a bowling ball barreling toward a set of pins.

"Whatcha lovebirds doing? I'm not payin' y'all good money to make out. Smooch on your own time."

Giggling, Annie bids Ike a hasty good-bye with the promise of getting together soon.

Byrdie beckons her to the portico. "Anh Le! *Anh Le!* Over here, darlin'." She calls Annie by her full Vietnamese name, and always, inexplicably, says it twice.

"You've gotten so skinny, sweetie. Good thing you already got a man, 'cause there's no danger of you landin' one looking like that.

And if you did, those bones'd stab him to death!" She cackles at her own joke, feigning an overhanded stabbing motion. "But you still got that silky China-doll hair, Anh Le, Anh Le. Now don't you let it go coarse and gray or you'll be lost!"

Annie doesn't respond because Byrdie talks enough for the both of them.

Christened Elisabeth Fenton, the socialite descended from a proud, unbroken line of Daughters of the Revolution and considered herself quite worldly despite having never ventured north of the Mason-Dixon. She's lived alone in the cavernous mansion for over a decade, ever since her longtime companion Claire's death by drunk driver. After the tragedy, Byrdie's contributions to the arts grew considerably as she tried to fill lonely days with charitable auctions and galas. Annie suspected her patron paid as much for her companionship as her artwork.

In the foyer, Annie pauses as Shug, Byrdie's Siamese cat, weaves around her ankles mewing.

"Step lively! We've got so much to do and so little time," the heiress says. She places a hand on Annie's elbow and steers her toward the study. Suddenly, Byrdie reaches out and strokes Annie's hair, clearly delighting in the satiny texture so different from her own.

Back in Grace Falls, everyone from classmates to substitute teachers and grocery clerks used to "pet" Annie's hair. Sometimes they asked first; sometimes they didn't. She was used to it. But today, she bristles at Byrdie's touch. The old woman's fingers smell of stale cigarettes and her breath of decay. Annie recoils in disgust but immediately regrets her reaction when she sees Byrdie's heavy-lidded eyes widen in surprise.

"Miss Fenton, I'm so sorry. It's . . . I've been a little on edge since my mother passed."

Byrdie knew about the death, yet she never acknowledged it directly to Annie. Even now, she pretends not to hear. "What's that, dear? Bless your heart." Like Ike, Annie was invited to Pinewood to play a part, and gay decorators and China dolls needn't have troublesome backstories.

Byrdie waves Annie toward a chaise longue, lavishly upholstered in golden Shantung silk. She plops herself down on a saggy, tufted armchair. Almost immediately Byrdie's longtime housekeeper Lydia enters carrying a silver tray laden with frosty glasses of unsweet tea, a pitcher of ice water, and dainty nut-filled dishes.

As soon as Lydia excuses herself, Byrdie springs up like a rotund jack-in-the-box and shuts the door. Then she pulls something out from behind a dusty tome on the bookshelf. Eyes glittering with mischief, she brandishes an unlabeled glass jug.

"This, my dear, is the last of the Fenton family moonshine. Made by my papaw, the Colonel himself." She chuckles. "He must be fit to kill looking down—or up, more like it—on a lady drinking all his precious brew. I'd never dare touch it while he was alive."

Having sworn off alcohol since her partner Claire's death, Byrdie calmly registers the shock on Annie's face. "Aren't you a picture sitting there all scandalized? It may have been a while since I've imbibed, but there's nothing wrong with taking a kip now and again. Nothing 't all." She pours a jigger-shot into an empty glass and offers it to her guest. When Annie declines, Byrdie downs it. "Ah, that's bracing! The older I get, the more I understand you only live once. No time to sit around being scared of life, my dear," she says, waggling a finger at Annie.

Byrdie freezes, still as a hyena ready to pounce. She stares at Annie, raking over the younger woman's features as if searching for the answer to some unknown question. A long silver nose hair flutters with each of the spinster's jagged breaths.

Annie shifts in her chair, clears her throat, and waits.

Byrdie leans forward, unblinking, and whispers, "Young lady— I know your secret."

Time stands still, for how long Annie's not sure. Her body is frozen, but her mind races. *Is it possible? Does she know?*

CHAPTER 15

Miss Fenton's shrieks of unhinged laughter bounce off the walls of the study, sending a startled Shug leaping from her perch atop a dusty gramophone stand.

"You look white as a ghost, my dear!" Byrdie howls, the tension instantly broken.

"Is this some kind of joke? I don't understand," Annie says. The booze must have gone straight to the old woman's head.

"I know all about your star turn, little Miss Saigon!"

"What? I'm not . . . there must be some mistake."

"Assure you there is not." With a mischievous grin, Byrdie continues, "My niece Millie Rae brought her machine over. Wanted to show me a preview of the *SouthernHer* story."

"Oh! Yes, of course." Annie says, her relief immediately supplanted by confusion. "The reporter is your n-niece? You always say you're the last of your line."

"Technically, yes. By blood, but some things are more important, I've learned," she says with a hint of sadness in her voice. "Millie Rae is Claire's niece. I told her she simply *had* to write about you."

Annie's stomach sinks. She thought she was being featured based on her own merits. Why hadn't anyone told her Miss Fenton arranged the whole thing? Annie can't help but be insulted by Byrdie being shown the article before she herself caught a glimpse of it.

Then curiosity gets the better of Annie, and she swallows her pride. "Could I see it? Did she print out the story for you?"

"Of course! I can't stand to look at those evil machines for more than a minute. Too, too bright. Gives me a headache every time," Byrdie says, shaking her head. "It's why so many little ones wear glasses these days."

Annie shifts impatiently on the chaise, silently willing Byrdie to get to the point.

"Well, I said to that girl, 'I'm no robot! You give me a piece of paper to look at, Millie Rae!'" Nudging her own glasses up the bridge of her nose, Byrdie chuckles. Then she lunges toward an end table, stretching so the soles of her taupe orthopedics rise up off the floor. "Oof, here you go." Beaming with pride, she hands over an orange folder.

The article inside features a hero shot of Annie lovingly cuddling Deja on her lap. The dachshund, doted on by Millie Rae, grew increasingly hungry for attention during Annie's portion of the photo shoot. A collage inset includes a few pieces of her artwork, the largest, by far, an oil painting of a socialite's schnauzer appearing comically serious atop a blue velvet cushion. A casual reader would assume Annie is a pet portraitist.

"Isn't it just darling?" Byrdie gushes.

Annie barely manages a weak smile. This was supposed to be her big break. The thing that would earn her respect and esteem— enough clout so that Mount Pleasant's one-percenters, the snobby parents at Tabby's school, wouldn't dream of approaching her for landscapes to complement the color of their newest living room sets. The printout falls from Annie's limp fingers onto lap.

"I didn't know you paint *creatures*!" Byrdie exclaims. "You've never done Shug! Let me set you up with some of the girls from the garden club. Most have dogs or cats—and, well, one keeps angora goats. I suppose you do farm animals too."

Frowning at the printout, Annie barely listens but bobs her head periodically in agreement.

Oblivious, Byrdie continues, ". . . but her Doberman is taxidermized, so you shan't worry about it moving during the sitting . . ."

Annie's humiliation swells with each word that tumbles carelessly out of Byrdie's mouth. To distract herself, she focuses her keen artist's eye for detail on the surrounding décor. Polished mahogany bookshelves lined with leather-bound tomes; thick, intricately patterned Persian rugs; deep wine-colored velvet drapes secured with antique brass holdbacks. Shug.

Still miffed at being disturbed from her nap, the Siamese cat stalks to a sunny spot across the room and begins to groom herself next to a large Ming-style floor vase. A dramatic arrangement of cotton-tufted branches and long-stemmed lotus pods juts out the mouth of the vase. The black-brown lotus pods' flat faces are pitted with densely packed, asymmetrical holes, the rims ridged in sick emphasis. A dark, round seed is embedded in each of the cavities.

The deep pockmarks fill Annie with intense disgust, but she can't tear her eyes away. She mentally transposes the irregular pattern of pits onto the soles of her feet, her palms, the inside of her cheek, the folds of her labia. Squirming, she crosses her legs and runs her tongue across the inside of her cheek in need of reassurance that everything is smooth and intact. The urge to destroy the lotus pods is almost unbearable.

The study has grown inexplicably hot. With the back of her hand, Annie wipes the sweat off her forehead. Just then, Shug catapults onto the window ledge. The cat paws at one of the lotus pods and then, fixing her icy blue eyes on Annie, flicks her small pink tongue across the embedded seeds. Annie watches in horror, her throat closing up.

". . . as I was saying, *Anh Le, Anh Le*! The vase is made in China. You probably recognize that, and the striking dried bits are lotus pods. From the *Orient*! Somethin' Southern and somethin' Oriental. That's what I told the florist. I knew you'd adore it! Why, you can't hardly take your peepers off of it, can ya?"

She toddles over, grabs Annie's hand, and attempts to guide her toward the vase. "Don't be shy. Let's get a closer look. Maybe you can do a still life."

The room starts to spin. Clinging to the armrest, she resists Byrdie's tight grasp, which has no doubt been strengthened by the shot of moonshine. Pure panic grips Annie. In that moment, she is desperate, trapped, and afraid of what she might do to get away . . . push, kick, grab a fistful of hair. Luckily, Miss Fenton relents just enough for Annie to shake her off. "I . . . I'm not feeling well. Excuse me. Need some—some air."

Annie stumbles out onto the portico and, without stopping, runs all the way to the road, only stopping once she's beyond the gate. There, she calls Duncan's cell. He isn't expecting her call until lunchtime, and it goes to voicemail. Forcing the words out in measured syllables, she lies. "Had to cut the meeting short. Byrdie's drinking again. And the cat . . . allergy attack. Can you pick me up early? Anytime. Now?"

Little lies weave in and out of every marriage, and, after fifteen years, this is no exception. Their relationship is a carefully choreographed routine, their parts long since memorized. Every time Annie falls, Duncan is there to catch her, more tender, more thoughtful than before.

◆

"Go inside and lie down. I'll be back in thirty with your allergy mist," Duncan says, sticking his head out the car window. He left work and rushed over to pick her up without a word of complaint. When she's at her worst, he's at his best. His sandy hair flops onto his forehead, giving him the look of a giant sheepdog. He shakes it off and smiles at his wife. "Just relax, okay? You don't look so good."

"I don't know what I'd do without you," she says, with a sniffle and a tremble she doesn't need to fake. Once his car has disappeared down the driveway, she stations herself on the front porch, takes a deep breath, and telephones Byrdie. Thankfully, the art patron is more amused than offended when Annie apologizes for her abrupt departure.

"We all have spells. Especially when goin' through the change o' life," she says, whispering the last few words. "With our meeting cut short, I called my hairdresser to see if he could fit me in for a quickie. Well, gossipy Jasper—that's the front desk boy—he told me you can't tell how old Orientals are. And that sure is the truth!"

After Annie hangs up, she feels a cloud of despair descend upon her. Between Byrdie and "gossipy Jasper," how long before word of her instability spreads around Mount Pleasant?

She clutches her knees, rocking back and forth to calm herself. Annie can still feel the old woman's fingers clawing at her skin. *What were you capable of doing to get away?* She tries to dismiss the question, but it throbs in her head like a toothache.

GRACE FALLS, 1986

Anh wiggled the metal rabbit ears on the old black-and-white television in the back room of Mrs. Ingold's beauty shop. When the wavy horizontal lines condensed into one equatorial band, she scooted back just a few inches. Her mother would be mad at her for sitting so close. "You'll make your eyes weak. Need ugly glasses."

But Mẹ wouldn't know. She was busy in front doing nails. Today's *Twilight Zone* episode was one of Anh's favorites. It was about a six-year-old boy with godlike powers who could read minds. By blocking communication signals and disabling cars, he isolates his Ohio town from the rest of the world. He brings grotesque figments of his imagination to life to terrorize the townspeople and banishes anyone who displeases him. Everyone is under his control.

Anh watched, mesmerized and hungry with want. She longed to *be* him. That way, the other kids in her class would be too afraid to stare at her, make her feel like an alien. The dirty-faced little boy who made singsong "Chinese" noises at her and laughed—well, he'd disappear.

She waited until the episode ended, reading each of the names as they rolled down the screen. If she shut it off before the credits finished, there was a chance something bad would happen. The television set could break entirely.

Anh quickly grew restless when the program finally did end. She tried to occupy herself reading the miniature labels on the bottoms of the polish jars. It was how she taught herself to read years ago, but it bored her now that she was seven. Instead, she crept toward the door and turned the knob slowly, noiselessly. She slunk down the short hallway, smashing her small frame against the wall and peeking out between the curtains that separated the staff area from the front. Her mom didn't like her coming out where customers could see, so she had to be careful whenever she decided to spy. Anh drew in a breath and held it, inhaling a noxious cloud of acetone. She pressed her lips together hard to prevent any sound from coming out.

Hair pulled back in a sleek chignon, her mother bent over a pair of flaking feet.

From her vantage point, Anh was close enough to see the customer's unpainted toes. Ragged, yellow nails, ridged and speckled with blue-black fungus. She watched in fascination as the veneer of mauve lacquer consumed the underlying disease and decay.

"No lumps. See? So smooth." Mẹ didn't like her job, but she took pride in her work, meticulously applying thin coats of polish until the nails gleamed. Her mother was an artist.

"Could you just not talk? Cannot understand a word you're saying. I don't speak Chinese." The woman's response to Mẹ's commentary was rough and dismissive. She punctuated her statement by sticking her unfinished foot close to Mẹ's face and wiggling her dirty toes.

As she observed her mother recoiling into silent compliance, Anh's face flushed hot with rage. She hated the stupid customer. If only she could make the woman's head explode—just by thinking it. If only she could protect her mother from the monstrousness that lay in wait just beneath the surface.

CHAPTER 16

In the two months since Duncan brought her mother's ashes home from the crematory, Annie has done nothing with them. Whenever she tried to select an urn, she heard Mẹ finding fault with each one. *"Too round, too bright, too cheap, too expensive."* Nothing was suitable.

Impulsively, Annie decides she will evict the ashes from her home once and for all—tonight. Away from the judgmental eyes of her husband and daughter, she will attempt to lay her mother to rest. She lies awake until two o'clock in the morning, then slips into her bathroom and extracts the black plastic tub from deep inside her vanity. As she steals into the gardens under cover of darkness, the ashes feel surprisingly light in her hands. Her mother's overbearing presence weighed so heavily on her in life and in death—would this final act release Annie?

Ashes to ashes, dust to dust. Roses were Mẹ's favorite, so Annie stops beside a bed of pasture roses, kneels down, and dumps out the powdery gray remains. Her thin fingers, sickly white in the moonlight, rake the ashes into the soil. Her nail snags on a sharp fragment of limestone, and she swears at herself for neglecting to bring a spade or fork. A biting wind cuts through her sleep clothes as she ferries pails of water from two rain barrels, installed outside the carriage house as part of the studio conversion. She takes care to thoroughly dampen the ashes, so they'll sink deep into the earth.

By the time she gets back to the house, her socks and the hem of her pajama pants are drenched with dew. The fabric clings to her skin, chilling her to the bone, but it's the only thing she feels. She hasn't shed a tear. At the back door, she presses her thumb onto the biometric reader of the Guardian Angel Sentry security system. When it flashes green, she reaches for the door handle, but something stops her midair.

Like a bullet, Mę's sneering voice rips through her head: *"You can't protect your family from the danger. You can't erase the ugliness inside."* Annie whirls around, but nobody, nothing, obstructs her view of the dark woods.

As Annie washes her trembling hands in the mudroom, Deja enters, ears pricked. The sound of water running in the dead of night disturbed his sleep. She pats her hands dry on a paper towel, then bends down to stroke his head. The dog's half-closed eyes focus on hers for a moment, and then, reassured, he putters off.

In the morning, Annie wakes with the sun shining brightly on her pillow. Its warmth makes last night's cold sojourn feel like a dream—so unreal that she's startled to see crescents of soil embedded in her fingernails. She washed her hands so many times last night—how did the dirt, the ashes, cling to her?

In the bathroom sink, she scrubs her fingertips with hot water, soap, and a bamboo nail brush until the skin is red and puffy. Blood trickles down from where she snagged the nail during the night. She stares at it, mesmerized by the wicked red stripe escaping down the length of her index finger.

Then the clatter of pots and pans downstairs rouses her. She bandages her hand and dresses hastily. She's due downstairs for brunch. It's Mother's Day.

◆

"The seat of honor, milady!" Duncan says as he pulls out a heavy maple dining chair for Annie. Uncomfortable at the head of the table, she feels her left eyelid spasm uncontrollably. Hopefully, it isn't noticeable. She takes a bite of French toast for show, but the gummy mass sticks in her throat. Chasing it down with a gulp of water, she says, "D-delicious. My compliments to the chef."

"Painting and putting the finishing touches on your studio was our real gift, but we still wanted to do something to celebrate today," Duncan says. The bulk of the carriage house renovation was completed expeditiously in a matter of weeks, but interior details lagged behind—especially once Duncan had gone back to work.

Tabby sullenly scarfs down fried eggs and fruit. Refusing to forgive Annie for spying on her at the spring festival, the teenager has ignored her mother for the past week.

You get what you deserve, Anh. Your daughter wants nothing to do with you.

Annie shakes her head. How can this be the same child who couldn't fall asleep unless her parents read to her? Annie remembers the tattered book of nursery rhymes, stamped on the inside cover with *Friends of the Grace Falls Library*. It held a place of honor beside Tabby's bed for the better part of a decade. Like many small children, she had a favorite that had to be read at least once before bed.

> *Ladybird, ladybird, fly away home,*
> *Your house is on fire and your children are gone,*
> *All except one,*
> *And her name is Ann,*
> *And she hid under the baking pan.*

Tabby liked it because she thought "Ann" was the same as her mom's name, and the image of her mother hiding under a baking pan delighted her. The illustration accompanying the nursery rhyme was charming and the page bordered by pretty red ladybugs—enough for the little girl to overlook the fire reference.

Both parents grew sick of the rhyme, but Annie particularly disliked it, having learned it dated back to the 1700s and referred to either Catholics being burned at the stake or the superstition that killing a ladybug brings bad luck. Either way, it was not *Goodnight Moon*. She especially hated reading it on the nights when Duncan worked late in the newsroom, leaving her and Tabby alone in the lonely hilltop house.

"Care for a refill?" Duncan offers to pour Annie cranberry juice.

She declines, glancing up at her husband and daughter but seeing them through the walls of the heavy Depression glass pitcher, the dark red juice distorting their faces.

Annie imagines a watcher, observing her handsome family through the dining room window. Broad-shouldered Duncan, natty in his plaid button-down. Tabby with her big brown eyes, creamy complexion, and graceful limbs. A pretty picture. Annie knows she has much to be thankful for this Mother's Day. But she can't shake the feeling that something is very wrong.

Tabby's long, slender legs swing back and forth under the table, casting spindly shadows on the wall that look like spider legs. For the first time during the meal, the girl speaks—having previously relied on grunts, shrugs, and nods. "Where's the dog?"

During family meals, Deja could always be found scurrying underfoot in search of table scraps. Reflexively, all three look under the table. Nothing but a wisp of dog hair floating in the air, propelled by the force of their pushed-back chairs.

Annie leaves the table in search of her little friend. "Deja, Dejaa!" Not in his crate, not anywhere on the first floor. She chastises herself. "Why didn't I notice sooner? I hope he's not sick."

Duncan's shouts carry down from the second floor. "Deja, Dejaa!" No dog nails scuffling against the floor planks, only her husband's plodding steps.

A tight pit forms in Annie's stomach. Deja always comes when she calls.

CHAPTER 17

Duncan flies down the stairs shaking his head. "Not on the second floor, and the attic's locked so he couldn't have gotten into your old studio."

"I'll look in the garage," Annie says out of desperation. Afraid of cars and loud noises, Deja rarely ventures out there.

Just as Annie is about to check, Tabby shouts, "Hey, the back door is open!"

"How the heck . . . he must've slipped out," Duncan says. In response to Annie's gasp, he adds, "Don't worry. He can't have gotten far with that bum hip."

With a bag of grain-free dog treats and Deja's leash in hand, Annie races past Tabby, who stands awkwardly in the doorway as if she's uncertain whether she should join her parents or wait at the house. Outside, Annie and Duncan agree to split up to cover more ground. Heading in opposite directions, each will weave around the perimeter of the property, eventually meeting up behind the carriage house. Annie glances over her shoulder and observes Tabby, having overcome her moment of indecision, darting straight into the heart of the woods.

When Annie reaches the carriage house, she doesn't see anyone at first. "Deja! Deja!" Her eyes scour a thicket of thorny wineberry. But instead of toffee-colored fur, Annie spies her daughter crouched down in the underbrush. Sunlight creeps through the vines casting weird shadows. It merges the teenager's body with a shrub, creating a deformed hunchback. Despite the day's warmth, a chill shoots up Annie's spine.

She hears Duncan shout Deja's name as he approaches the carriage house from the rear. Immediately, from the tone of his voice, she knows he's found something. Tabby also emerges, racing toward Duncan's voice at the same time as Annie.

In the distance, Deja lies on his side, next to the bed of pasture roses. It's where Annie spread Mę's ashes. The rose shrubs, recently thriving, show signs of decay. Leaves mottled with ugly black spots; early blooms shriveled like a hag's claw—as if her mother's poisonous reach shot up through the soil. The old woman hated Deja. *Filthy rat-faced dog. You treat it better than me.*

Duncan cuts off Annie, his forearms extended like a crossing guard. "Stay back! You shouldn't look . . ."

"Let me go!" Annie darts underneath his arm. "Deja!"

The dachshund's limbs are unnaturally stiff; his mouth lies open as if gasping for a last breath that will never come.

Duncan grabs Annie around the shoulders, but she shakes him off, falls to her knees, and cradles her little one. Suddenly, her stomach drops. She sees.

Scores of lady beetles have burrowed into the grooves on the roof of Deja's mouth. The entire expanse of wet, pink tissue is encrusted with the invasive, parasitic insects. A few, unable to latch, roam the cavity, exploring the dog's tongue. It dangles like a strip of raw meat.

Annie is paralyzed by the realization that she's somehow seen this image before. "G-get them out of there!" she shrieks. "You have to help him."

"Honey . . . he's gone," Duncan says.

"Leave it, Mom!" Tabby shrinks back into the shadows.

"No! No! Get rid of them! Disgusting," Annie shouts.

When she realizes that Duncan isn't going to do anything, she grabs a stick and jabs at the beetles, but they're latched onto the dog's pink flesh. She scrapes harder, more erratically. Shells crunch, and bits of the dachshund's gums fly out along with the parasitic beetles.

Her husband is saying something, but she doesn't hear. Obsessed with getting rid of the disgusting sight, Annie stabs wildly. The beetles release a noxious odor that chokes her, snaps her out of her violent frenzy. She covers her nose with her sleeve and stumbles home to safety.

◆

Crumpled on the sofa, Annie can't expunge the image of Deja's beetle-encrusted mouth from her brain. Every time she closes her eyes, she sees them, *feels* them, on the inside of her eyelids. Duncan hovers over her with an expression of tender concern clouding his pale blue eyes. Looking up at him, Annie envisions the beetles attached to his scalp and clinging to his throat in red, scaly patches.

"Hello? Dr. Davis?" Duncan has called the veterinarian's office. He puts the phone on speaker and the doctor's kindly baritone fills the living room. "What happened to Deja was an unfortunate accident. There have been other recorded incidents of the beetles clustering in the mouths of domesticated dogs." He explains that when threatened, the Asiatic lady beetle secretes a rank, poisonous fluid laden with corrosive chemicals, which can cause severe burns in the mouth and gastrointestinal tract. "Death is an unexpected outcome, but not entirely surprising given Deja's advanced age."

After Duncan hangs up, he caresses Annie's cheek. "I'm so sorry, honey. There was nothing we could do."

She avoids his eye, not commenting on Dr. Davis's assessment—because she already knew. Last month, she saw a flyer at the vet's office warning about Asiatic lady beetle toxicity in canines. The accompanying photo of a dog, mouth caked with beetles, had distressed her to such an extent that she immediately checked inside Deja's mouth. At the time, she wondered if such a thing could really happen.

"Did you get rid of it?" Annie asks abruptly.

It's the tenth time she's asked this question. She's desperate for reassurance that the disgusting thing, the thing that is no longer Deja, is gone. It needs to be burned to ashes, rendered as unrecognizable as her mother's cremated body.

Exhausted by the repetition, her husband's response is curt. "I said I'd handle it."

Tabby sits on the floor, clutching her knees to her chest, eyes teary. "Dad will take care of everything. It's all so, so awful. I-I'm sorry, Mom."

Annie nods, accepting the condolences as an olive branch. Tragedy mends many a familial fracture.

"I just don't understand how Deja got out," she says. "Wouldn't the security app have pinged your phone, Duncan?" Annie ordered the Guardian Angel Sentry system last year, after she'd been rattled by a news report detailing how easily intruders could hack into standard four-digit security codes. The biometric readers were her version of the dao bào that her mom clutched each night for peace of mind. Guiltily, she now recalls deleting the app from her phone just a month after it was installed—too many annoying notifications.

"It sent me a 'door open' message, but I didn't catch it in time. Left my phone upstairs—there's a lot going on at the office. I didn't want work messages to interrupt your celebration."

"But who left the door open? I was in bed until you called me down for brunch. I just saw Deja . . ." Annie pauses, unwilling to confess to distributing the ashes in secret in the small hours of the morning ". . . last night."

"It wasn't me. I was in the kitchen cooking all morning," Duncan says. "Hadn't even stepped outside."

Annie glances over at Tabby. Catching her mother's eye, Tabby pops up. "Don't look at me—I didn't touch the back door!"

Annie should say, *Of course not!* but she says nothing, distracted by the flurry of memories swirling in her grief-stricken brain. A young Tabby, jealous of the attention Annie lavished on Deja, stuffing the dog in the dryer—thank god the toddler couldn't reach the dials yet! Ten-year-old Tabby collecting ladybugs in a jar, hiding them under the bed for months, until a foul smell filled the room. Today, Tabby alerted them to the open back door. Why had neither Annie nor Duncan noticed it was ajar? Her mother's warning echoes in her head: *"That girl is out of control!"*

Now, Annie stares at her daughter's face, but in her mind's eye she sees the creamy complexion pockmarked with beetles. Involuntarily, she flinches but tries to suppress her disgust.

It's too late—Tabby has registered Annie's expression. Tears trickle, then stream down her cheeks. "How can you look at me like that?" Tabby asks, her voice choked. She runs to the stairs but trips on the bottom step, just catching herself with an open hand.

Annie springs up. "Tabby! Are you okay? Let me help—"

"Don't touch me! Just go away," Tabby says. Each word drips with teenage misery, the sentence punctuated by the slam of her bedroom door.

Duncan leans on the sofa's armrest, clutching his forehead in his hands. What starts as a low growl rises to a shout. "Have you lost your mind, Annie? Our daughter did not . . . your paranoia is out of control!"

"It's not paranoia. You saw that what happened to Deja was *real!*"

"What happened to Deja is tragic, but it is not anyone's fault." Duncan stalks into the kitchen to put space between them. "How could you even *think* our daughter could have done this?" he shouts as he hurls his favorite Santoku knife into the sink.

Hiding from the violent clang of metal on metal, Annie buries her head against the sofa cushion and mutters a weak apology: "I didn't say Tabby did . . . I didn't mean . . . ." She listens to her husband's footsteps retreat up the stairs in pursuit of their daughter. Tabby isn't capable of hurting Deja—at least, Annie doesn't really think so—but her mind scrambles to devise a scenario other than the one lurking in its depths. That she herself is somehow responsible.

◆

"Set light ten percent bright. Set my shower to one hundred ten degrees. Start my shower."

Annie methodically lathers her skin from head to toe, using strong eucalyptus soap. She stands with her feet planted directly beneath the shower head, being careful not to brush against the shower walls. If she touches anything, she'll have to start over again.

Did Tabby change clothes after riding the Metro to the city with her friends yesterday? A serial killer, rapist, or pedophile could have sat in the same train seat right before her. Semen, blood, or other taint of his sick acts could have transferred to the seat and then to Tabby's jeans or jacket. *Did you touch a chair Tabby sat on afterward? What if she lay down on your bed? What if she snuck in and used your bathroom or shower?*

No matter how improbable the chain of events, there existed a possibility. In that possibility lay doubt. Questions gnaw at Annie's brain, burrowing in like tapeworms. Uncertainty devours her from the inside out. The pale yellow pill, which for so long reined in her intrusive thoughts, grows weaker by the day. The only way to quiet the parasitic thoughts is to obey them.

CHAPTER 18

A hostile silence emanates from Tabby's room. Outside in the hallway, Annie presses her ear against the cold wooden door. She's hungry for a sigh, a yawn, any sliver of contact with her daughter. She didn't mean to accuse Tabby, even if indirectly, of harming Deja, and her weak attempt to explain herself later only resulted in the silent treatment from her daughter. After he calmed down himself, Duncan advised Annie to give Tabby time to stew.

Imagining Deja writhing in pain, remembering the revolting state of the dog's corpse, sinks Annie. It's only a quarter to nine, but she's ready to collapse under the burden of grief and guilt. Abandoning hope of communicating with her daughter tonight, she goes to bed and climbs in next to Duncan. His nose is buried in the print edition of *Foreign Affairs* magazine, which to her relief arrives monthly in a clear plastic bag that can be easily discarded, leaving the contents pristine and untouched.

"All quiet on the Tabitha front?" he asks, setting the magazine down and lifting his arm to receive Annie's head. He never stayed angry for long.

"You're lucky she's such a Daddy's girl. I wish she understood I'm doing my best."

"You doubted her—I'm sure that hurt. She wants to hurt you back." He holds his thumb and index finger up in a near pinch. "Just a little bit."

"When it rains it pours," Annie says. "I don't know how much more I can handle."

"Well, that's something we need to discuss. It's happening again. I know it, and I'm sure Tabby senses it too. You undress in the mudroom after you've gone to the grocery store or even just to get the mail. The washing machine is constantly running. You lock yourself in the bathroom for hours. Annie, we've had this thing beat for so long, but you have to face it—your OCD is back."

Annie freezes. Her husband's words give shape and substance to the anxieties she's been unwilling to articulate, the symptoms she's denied. For weeks, she's engaged in mental contortions, convincing herself that every flare-up was a blip, a one-off, and that she had the disorder more or less under control. Even now, confronted by her husband, the disease fights to conceal itself.

She hears herself lying: "It's not that bad."

"Not that bad? Look at this." He grabs her hand, which is red and cracked from overwashing. "I love you, and I can't stand to see you hurting yourself. You need to see Dr. Patel."

Lily Patel went to college with Duncan at Brown. After completing her psychiatric residency, Dr. Patel joined a private practice specializing in anxiety disorders. Before realizing that she preferred clinical research, Dr. Patel treated Annie for several months after Tabby's premature birth. She diagnosed Annie with postpartum depression and obsessive-compulsive disorder.

The latter came as a shock to Annie, whose only knowledge of OCD came from television. The quirky germophobic detective, the neat freak with a color-coded closet, the lovable sitcom neighbor who knocks three times fast and two times slow before entering a room. None of these lighthearted portrayals bore any resemblance to the debilitating disorder that consumed her or the intrusive thoughts that held her hostage at times. Annie wasn't afraid of catching a disease, nor was she especially organized or tidy. How could she have OCD?

Dr. Patel described a lesser-known type of the disorder, a form of contamination-based OCD characterized by intense *disgust*. The human brain, as a means of self-preservation, is hardwired to be repulsed by "disgusting" stimuli—the caveman who discovers a rotted carcass thinks, *Don't eat that*. However, in people with disgust-driven OCD, this reaction is magnified. The brain panics when faced with images others might find mildly unpleasant, such as repetitive patterns of holes, raised bumps, skin disorders, blood, urine, feces, semen. Exposure to, or even just thinking about, such things can make the person feel "dirty" and trigger increasingly elaborate decontamination rituals.

For Annie, Dr. Patel prescribed a combination of medication—sertraline taken daily to correct the chemical imbalance in her brain—and cognitive behavioral therapy, which included adopting a pet. A puppy would physically interrupt the punishing loops of intrusive thoughts that cycled through her head, and picking up after the animal would be a form of exposure therapy. The regimen worked for Annie, so that eventually the unwanted thoughts quieted to whispers that she could readily dismiss—until recently.

Annie straightens up and turns around to face her husband. "Why do I need to see Dr. Patel now? Her treatment plan worked for years, and I'm still following it chapter and verse. At least, I was until my dog died today." Reminded again of Deja's death, Annie feels her lungs turn to concrete. She finds it physically difficult to breathe, much less continue conversing. *When you saw Deja last night, he was fine. Wasn't he?*

Duncan interrupts her thoughts. "I think we need to consider this, Annie. Your mother died a couple months ago. Instead of grieving, you've thrown yourself into your work. If you continue to keep your feelings bottled up, it's only a matter of time before there's an explosion." He reaches out and clasps Annie's hand. "Since you can't seem to confide in me, maybe a professional can help."

"Well, I don't think Dr. Patel even sees private patients anymore. She runs big clinical trials now."

Duncan drops his wife's hand and crosses his arms in disapproval. "These all sound like excuses. Why can't you just try? I'll make the appointment with Lily for you."

Annie's skin crawls at the thought of visiting Dr. Patel's clinic, housed in a major research hospital in the city. Bedpans, bloody syringes, medical waste stuffed into rusty step cans, unwashed strangers with oozing wounds.

"I'm perfectly capable of making my own appointments," she snaps, instantly sorry when a mixture of hurt and anger clouds his face. "I'll think about it, okay? You have to know I *am* trying, in my own way, to cope. Just give me some time."

Duncan nods. He lifts Annie's chin gently and leans in for a kiss.

Her husband is so close that she can smell his aftershave, but in the razor-thin space between them a face appears. Gabriel Correa. A man whose image of Annie is still pristine, not yet marred by the realities of raw, cracked skin; teenage resentment; and troubled in-laws.

Before Duncan's lips touch hers, she looks down. His kiss lands awkwardly on her brow. Neither acknowledges the disconnect. Yet it underscores the painful fact that they again haven't been intimate in months. Duncan picks up his magazine, his expression obscured by *Foreign Affairs* once more.

Exhausted, Annie lies down on her side and pulls the covers up over her ear. For so many years, her life was structured around elder care, catering to Me's physical needs and mental illness. Spending time with Duncan had been Annie's escape hatch, just like marrying him had been. With her mother gone, she's not sure how they fit together anymore.

GRACE FALLS, 1987

The picture, torn from *National Geographic*, was stained with grease and foxed at the edges. Anh counted to twenty as she stared at the photo of a French Quarter townhome, draped in fuchsia bougainvillea, set against a turquoise sky. She shut her eyes tight for a count of twenty and then repeated the process. Her mind had to be blank. She thought of nothing other than that photo. If she really concentrated this time, the yelling on the other side of the wall would stop. It had worked before.

Mẹ had suitors despite being a single mother in her thirties. She was slender with high cheekbones and shining black hair, which she kept in a stylish, shoulder-length cut. When she wasn't working, she dressed in satiny blouses with pussy bows like Anh had seen Jane Fonda wear in *9 to 5*. Anh knew her mother was the most beautiful woman in the world. She spoke three languages; she went to college; she cooked delicious food.

For these reasons, Anh was perplexed when none of Mẹ's relationships lasted. Her mom blamed it on her financial misfortunes: "Nobody wants to marry a poor woman," or "Who wants to raise another man's child?"

But Anh had overheard the arguments, and they weren't often about money or kids. The men shouted words like "crazy, nuts" and ones she didn't understand like "paranoid." Though each boyfriend treated Anh kindly—Mẹ wouldn't have allowed anything less—they secretly poisoned her mother and put chemical irritants in her clothes and shoes. Her mother only shared this with Anh after the fact. If the girl had known at the time, she would have done something—she would have made them stop one way or another.

Anh wondered if the current boyfriend did these bad things too. He had seemed so nice, reading to her and bringing her small gifts—a koala bear sticker that actually felt fuzzy, a chocolate-brown-and-black rabbit's foot, a brand-new spiral-bound notebook.

Her gaze fell back to the photo, and she forced herself to concentrate on tracing circles on the satiny cover of her twin-sized mattress as she counted. But her chewed-up fingernail snagged one of the polyester threads. This made her mad. The ritual wouldn't work now. Anger surged through her small body.

Shut up! Shut up! Anh wanted to make him stop shouting. She kicked the wall hard. Chips of plaster rained down onto the large red flowers printed on the mattress.

The voices on the other side of the wall quieted for a moment, then grew loud again. A door slammed, a car engine revved, tires spit gravel. Anh was familiar with this sequence of sounds indicating the departure of a man and the onset of deep depression in her mother. Mẹ would be away more, trying to scrape up more hours, and they'd resume the juggling act to keep the electricity, gas, or phone from being shut off.

At least it would be just the two of them again. No more shouting. No more fighting—as long as Anh didn't cross her mother.

Just then, a loud knock on the door made Anh jump. Several softer knocks followed. Not waiting for an answer, her mother pulled the wood-laminate accordion door open and stuck her head in. "Anh? You okay?" She added in Vietnamese, "Mẹ ở đây," meaning "Mother is here."

Facing the wall, Anh lay in a ball, knees pulled tight to her chest. She didn't want to talk to her mother—inevitably the blame for the man leaving would fall on Anh, "another man's child." So she pretended to sleep, breathing slowly in and out of her nose.

Wanting to believe the lie because it was easier than accepting her daughter's pain, Mẹ closed the door softly and left.

CHAPTER 19

In the week after Deja's death, Annie found herself slipping—when she sliced an apple, she expected to hear the quick tap-tap of the dog's paws on wood. At the dining table, her heart plummeted whenever she glanced under the table and saw emptiness where the droopy-eared dachshund should've been. For over a dozen years, Deja had served as a steady source of unconditional love and nonjudgmental support.

The dog's death left her feeling bereft and pining for the lost joys of companionship. In contrast, her mother's passing had overwhelmed Annie with guilt and shame. *"Everything you touch suffers."* More and more, Mẹ's words dominated Annie's thoughts. Though she'd spread the ashes herself, Annie felt as if her mother somehow was not really gone.

Compounding the hurt, today is Tabby's fifteenth birthday, but she's chosen to spend it away from her parents. Ever since ten-year-old Tabby decried birthday parties to be "baby stuff," the Shaws have celebrated at home with a buffet of Tabby's favorite dishes—Hawaiian pizza, falafel, tom yum soup, and birthday-cake-flavored frozen yogurt—a comically dissonant menu that highlighted Tabby as the only common thread. Duncan made the same joke each year, setting a Costco-sized container of Tums on the counter along with the food.

Instead of continuing the family tradition, Tabby had announced earlier that week that she'd be attending a concert, then sleeping over at Aimee's house Thursday night—Friday being a teacher in-service day. If Duncan was disappointed, he masked his feelings well, breathing a huge sigh of relief as he rubbed his belly. Annie, on the other hand, couldn't stop the onslaught of tears. It was the last straw in a very bad week.

Tabby had exchanged glances with her father across the dinner table. "It's okay, Mom. I know you've gone through a lot recently with Grandma and Deja." Then she'd gotten up and hugged Annie. "We can do the birthday buffet another day."

The kindness made Annie feel worse. Her own child pitied her.

When Tabby leaves for the concert, Annie pretends to be busy at the computer and offers a clipped good-bye, lest she embarrass herself by bursting into tears again.

Alone in the house, she mindlessly scrolls through tabloid news and gossip. Until now, she's resisted viewing the *SouthernHer* feature that went live last night. But, desperate for a distraction, she searches for it, then clicks on the link. Although the digital layout is identical to Byrdie's printout, the schnauzer painting looks even sillier, more prominent in HD. She doesn't even remember sending that photo image, but it must have been among the dozens of files she dropped into the shared folder. And then, unable to bear the sight of Deja cuddled on her lap, Annie clicks on a random link, a clickbait article attached to the bottom of the page.

The headline flashes in front of her: *Are deadly spiders lurking in your produce?* The article tells the story of a UK teenager who bit into a banana completely unaware of the egg sac attached. *"It was like a horror movie. Dozens of spiderlings spilled down my chin. Some crawled up my nose and into my eyes. I couldn't stop them. I had no idea something like this could happen."* The piece concludes with a quote from an arachnologist: *"Though extremely rare, there have been reports of these highly venomous spiders making their way in shipping containers from Brazil to your neighborhood produce aisle."*

Annie can't tear her eyes away from the image of spider bites on skin. Red, inflamed, some filled with pus. Visualizing the hordes of squirming spiders makes her skin crawl. She reaches down to scratch the spot on her calf where she cut herself shaving this morning. *You didn't put a bandage on it. What if a spider or a flea laid eggs inside? The sac might look like a mosquito bite—a lump that would erupt when you scratched it. Just in case, you should clean the cut with peroxide and seal it with a liquid bandage. Kill whatever might be inside.*

Transfixed, she jumps when Duncan speaks.

"Annie? Didn't you hear me come in?" He sounds concerned. "What are you reading?"

Annie knows she shouldn't let the article rattle her. It's silly. But even if there's a little chance . . . maybe Duncan can reassure her. She points to the screen. "This can't really happen, can it?"

Duncan leans over her shoulder to peruse the story. "Well, I mean, technically speaking, it seems as though it *has* happened. Clearly, it was a freak accident, though. One in a bazillion. I wouldn't exactly lose sleep over it." He casually tosses a copy of *The Paris Review* along with the day's mail onto the desk beside her. "That tabloid stuff isn't good for you. Try this instead."

She shies away from the magazine as though it's covered in excrement. *Who knows who touched it before Duncan brought it into the house?*

Confiding in her husband rarely helps—when she mentioned her driving nightmares he dismissed them: "Everyone has the occasional anxiety dream about fender benders or speeding tickets. Try not to worry too much."

Though she knows he doesn't understand, she's compelled to seek reassurance from him. *Did I step in that? Did I brush against that trash can?* Every reassurance, every ritual, eventually begets more need—like an addict's dependence on increasingly harder drugs to blunt the pain. Nothing will ever placate the insatiable doubt, but she has to try each time. The futility of her actions tortures her.

Annie scoots her chair away from the desk and follows her husband into the kitchen. "It's only five. You're home early?"

He finishes rinsing his coffee thermos and dries his hands on a towel. When he replies, there's a sparkle in his eye. "I've got a hot date tonight." Seeing her bewildered expression, he takes her in his arms. "I pulled some strings, nabbed a reservation at that hip Japanese French fusion restaurant in the city."

Trudging along filthy city streets is the last thing Annie wants right now. However, her protests of "perfectly good leftovers in the fridge" fall on deaf ears, and she soon finds herself made up, dressed up, and seated at a table for two.

CHAPTER 20

As they study the menu, a diaphanous sheet of washi paper affixed to a slab of slate, Duncan reaches over and grabs Annie's hand. "Tell me this doesn't beat the birthday buffet."

Annie nods but can't muster a convincing smile. Her daughter's latest rejection, piled on top of Deja's death and the disappointing magazine article, have depleted the last scraps of her emotional capital. Spent, she wants nothing more than to be buried in her bed, suffocating beneath impenetrable high-thread-count sheets.

"Listen, I'm sad about Tabby too, but she's not going anywhere—not quite yet anyway. This can be a new chapter for *us.*"

Before she has to answer, a young waiter with tattoo sleeves and a handlebar mustache approaches to take their orders. He carries a bored expression but no pen and paper. When he leaves, Duncan clears his throat. "So I have another surprise. Jonah offered us the use of his cabin on the Chesapeake Bay. Week after next. Let's get away. Just the two of us."

Annie's throat constricts, her speech strained. "How can you think . . . I can't deal with staying in your boss's timeshare or whatever it is right now. You know how I feel about those rental places." Swimming in strangers' dead skin cells, stray pubic hairs, bodily fluids carelessly wiped off by an indifferent housekeeper.

"But it's not some random rental. The place has been in Jonah's family for decades. It's on the historical register, for god's sakes."

"It's a really nice thought. I don't mean to sound ungrateful, but I'm exhausted. It all just feels like so much work."

Duncan winces as though she slapped his face. He snaps, "By *'all'* do you mean our marriage? Because I'm pretty sure that comes with the territory. Relationships take work . . . and I can't do it all myself."

The couple at the next table have taken notice of the Shaws' squabble. The men exchange smirks, savoring the friction more than their wakame consommé. Conscious of eyes on her, Annie flushes red. She shushes Duncan. He doesn't register any of it, intent on proving his case as the injured party.

"It didn't exactly look good—me leaving the office at three o'clock in the afternoon today. There have been cuts. The Body Politic laid off eight reporters last week. But I still made the effort to beat the traffic so we could have a special dinner." He waves his hands around, indicating the glass tables and minimalist dark gray décor. "I chose this artsy place for *you*. I only wanted to cheer you up . . ." His voice trails off. Now that he's said his piece—and in the process, verbally announced his failure to make his wife happy—all the bluster is gone.

In the early years of their marriage, Annie's mom encouraged her to compromise and do everything possible to nurture the relationship. Initially, this surprised Annie as it ran counter to her mother's possessive tendencies. But the canny old woman had picked up on something useful in Duncan's nature.

"One day, I won't be here to look after you. This one will. He needs you, Anh. He will never leave."

"He needs me? Or *you* need him?" Annie's response was especially cruel because it was, in part, true. Her mother had no way to support herself, and they both knew that a lot of men wouldn't take on the burden of an elderly mother-in-law. Duncan had done so without complaint. But now, without the distraction of caring for her mom and with Tabby growing more independent by the day, Annie finds it increasingly difficult to ignore the not-so-fine lines between gratitude and love, love and passion.

Her mother's sneering voice reverberates in her skull. *"This is a good, kind man who has taken care of us all. You are a stupid, selfish girl. You don't deserve him."* Annie presses her index fingers against her temples, angrily rubbing in circles, as though this will erase the words.

Now more irritated than embarrassed, Annie turns her head sharply to catch the neighboring couple in the act of gawking. She shoots them a nasty glare.

Their waiter returns and ceremoniously sets tiny entrées on the table. The row of frog legs glistening on Duncan's plate compounds Annie's lack of appetite. The crisp skin, separated from its flesh, disgusts her. She stares at Duncan's dish, transfixed by the ambiguity—not fish, not fowl—even as he speaks.

"Look, I should have known cabin life wasn't your thing. But I still think it's a good idea for us to get away, to reconnect for a week or even just a long weekend. I'll book a hotel suite—the cleanest, most luxurious hotel in whatever city you choose."

Given the edge in his voice, Annie knows she can't say no. Not now, especially with the couple at the next table hanging on their every word, so she punts. "Okay. I'm sorry. Everything's been so crazy lately. I'm not sure what projects I have coming due and when, but let's check our calendars, then fix a date."

Whether they end up going or not, Annie vows to snap out of her funk. Her husband has been more than patient with her. During the rest of the meal and on the ride home, she makes a concerted effort to appear animated and engaged.

By the time she undresses in the mudroom, the adrenaline has faded. She listens to the swoosh of the pipes carrying dirty water away from Duncan's shower. Her mind likens them to veins carrying away blood waste. The thought of blood traces on city streets—the result of some violent or perverse crime—spreading to her shoes, to her—compels Annie to wash her hands again.

Just as she considers repeating the ritual, her phone buzzes. She doesn't answer, doesn't want to talk to anyone. But a minute later, she lifts the phone, worried it could be Tabby. Reading the missed-call notification banner, she does a double take and nearly drops the phone in the utility sink. *Gabriel Correa.*

How did he get her number? She didn't give it to him at the spring festival. Of course, she did take his card when he offered it—it would've been rude not to do so. He must have searched on-line, but she can't remember if she told him her last name.

Then the voicemail badge appears. With a confusing mix of excitement and terror, she presses play.

"Hi, Annie, this is Gabe. We bumped into each other at the Waldorf school thing last month. Thought maybe we could grab that drink sometime? Call me back when you get a chance. Take care."

Annie hears the shower turn off upstairs. Her pulse races. A cold draft slithers in from the garage, rakes over her bare skin. She wraps her arms around her chest, suddenly feeling vulnerable in her underwear. Her mind spins. This handsome stranger materialized at just the right moment to come to her aid at the spring festival. A Hallmark movie scenario, a fantasy . . . too good to be real?

Casting a doubtful eye over her stretch-mark-riven belly and pale, dimpled thighs, Annie lets her suspicions run wild. *Why would he be attracted to you? What is he after? Could he be some kind of a scam artist or stalker? Maybe the red-haired kid isn't even his niece; they looked nothing alike.*

Not only does the possibility that Gabe might have bad intentions rattle her, the mental image of Ray glaring at her from across the soccer field rushes into her head. His eyes—black, soulless holes—were pitfalls, traps into which she'd plummet if she weren't careful.

Annie rifles through her purse until she finds Gabe's business card. For a split second, she hesitates before tearing the card to pieces, then crumpling the bits up in her fist. Once she's upstairs in the private bath, she decides against flushing the evidence of her emotional betrayal down the toilet. It could clog. Instead, she stuffs the remains of the card in the wastebasket, careful to hide them under her used sanitary pad.

After a long, hot shower, Annie settles into bed beside her husband. The mattress, imprinted with her form, cups her body in welcome. Duncan rolls over in his sleep and wraps his arm around his wife as he always has. Any friction seems to have dissolved into the ether, the invisible yet volatile solvent that courses through every marriage—melting away differences, corroding individuals.

CHAPTER 21

The next morning, before Duncan leaves for work, he gives Annie a kiss on the cheek along with a printed list of open dates
he's available for their getaway. "No pressure. Just wanted you to
have these."

But pressure is exactly what Annie feels. Right now she's crum-
bling underneath a freightload of responsibility, guilt, shame. As
Duncan's taillights disappear down the drive, she thinks about all
the changes that have happened in the last couple of months—
losing her mother, Deja—and the ones that are still happening:
Tabby growing up so quickly, the evolution of her marriage. Overwhelmed, Annie wishes she could stop the world from spinning
and halt the perpetual doubt looping through her brain.

She fills a thermos with hot coffee and trudges toward the carriage house. She still thinks of it that way, even though the conversion is complete—aside from a final few boxes she needs to unpack.

At a high point along the stone path, she pauses to survey the
native plant gardens sprawling below. A show of white fringe trees,
electric-yellow pops of witch hazel, and the rolling blush of eastern
redbud—the result of fifteen years of painstaking landscape resto-
ration. When they purchased the hilltop property, invasive box-
woods, barberry, nandina, and English ivy crowded out the
ecosystem, starving native fauna. Despite practically taking a
flamethrower to it all, Annie had to be vigilant. Invasive seeds

were known to lie dormant in the soil for decades before emerging in times of weather-induced stress.

Her view shifts from the vista to the trail directly in front of her, where a charm of goldfinches feeds from a stand of dead sunflowers. Annie knew that left untouched over winter, the sunflowers' hollow stems would shelter hibernating bees, and the seed heads would act as natural birdfeeders. Nature is exquisite by design until tainted by human hands.

The finches scatter suddenly, disturbed by Annie's cell phone. Rummaging through her backpack, she extracts the phone and answers hastily without checking the caller ID. In the instant before the phone reaches her ear, her heart leaps. Could it be Gabe?

The voice on the other line hits her like a bucket of icy water.

"Anh Le, Anh Le!"

"Oh—good morning, Miss Fenton. How are you?"

"Busy! As usual. No time for chitchat. Can you swing by later? Got a big, big project with your name on it."

Annie shudders, remembering Byrdie's recent suggestion to do a portrait of the taxidermy Doberman. Before she can reply, the heiress plows on.

"The long and the short of it is, I'd like you to create a mural of Lake Gaither. Claire and I met there when we were kids. It's time to memorialize it on the walls of Pinewood Manor. She's as much a part of the family as any Fenton."

Taken aback by the depth of emotion in her patron's voice, Annie stammers, "A mural? I've never . . ."

Reverting back to her jovial self, Byrdie says, "Aren't you a dear! Come by this afternoon—say two-ish—and I'll fill you in on the details. Bye now."

Annie considers the project as she unpacks boxes of supplies in the studio. Pinewood Manor is listed on the register of historic landmarks. The mural would certainly be a step up from silly dog portraits. It could even land her coverage in a respectable architectural or interior design journal. The challenge of such a large-scale project excites her.

Prestige, professional development, and a hefty commission, no doubt—these were all positives, but the assignment would also require her to spend long hours away from home both at Lake Gaither and at the Fenton family estate. Though she's never produced a mural, she did study the mezzo fresco technique at RISD and understood the process to be a massive commitment of time and energy with little room for error. Out of habit, she thinks of her mother and Deja before dismissing each obstacle, in turn, as obsolete. And with the school year wrapping up, Tabby will be off to summer equestrian camp soon. Annie's heart beats a little faster. This could work. She'll consult Ike—he has experience with community murals.

She sits down at her drafting table to jot a few notes, but Duncan's list of dates stares up accusingly. She brought the piece of paper along to cross-reference with her schedule. A weeklong couple's getaway would be out of the question. *"You are a stupid, selfish girl. You don't deserve him."* She knows she's being disloyal for treating the trip like a chore, for hoping Gabe will call again. A week away would be tough, but surely she could find a weekend?

She stands up and paces the room. As she does, she's reminded of her husband's generosity in taking time off to oversee the carriage house renovations. High-tech insulation installed, electricity and plumbing brought to code, wood floors refinished, dingy yellow wallpaper stripped. Annie runs her fingers over the smooth, freshly painted wall. The shade she'd selected was out of stock, but Duncan found an excellent match with Farrow & Ball. Annie loved the quiet gray-brown until she discovered its name: Mouse's Back.

Nauseated by the new-paint smell, she covers her nose with the back of her hand. She stumbles backward, shaking her head in confusion. It's not paint fumes but the telltale ammonia odor of mouse urine. But how? The renovation team completely stripped the carriage house, extirpating every physical trace of her mother's rodent-infested existence. Annie drops to her knees, desperately scanning the floor for signs of droppings. But the wood, newly sealed and polished to a sheen, is so spotless it reflects the contours of her face.

◆

"You committed to this massive project?" A mixture of shock and disappointment play out on Duncan's face as he regards Annie, his fork suspended in midair.

"Byrdie didn't really give me a chance to refuse. Besides, the Pinewood mural could open up a lot of doors for me. I've never done anything like it," Annie says.

"So which is it, Annie? You *couldn't* say no, or you didn't want to?" Duncan's eyes fix firmly on his wife.

But she stares miserably at her plate, not even pretending to mask her lack of appetite. Duncan's already upset, and with Tabby at the movies, there's no need. "We could still go away for a weekend or maybe one night," she says, her voice barely above a whisper.

"I don't ask a lot of you, but the one time I do, you offer me one night?" He shakes his head in disbelief, finally breaking his gaze. As he speaks his hands wave wildly in the air. "I thought you'd lean on me when your mother passed away. Instead, you pulled away. When I try to help with your OCD, you push me away. This trip was supposed to bring us closer together, make our marriage stronger. Do you even want that, Annie?"

Her head feels like it's stuffed with cotton wool, her disconnected thoughts stuck in the fibers. Playing for time, she stands up and takes their dishes to the sink. "Closer together? I don't know what you're talking about. We've been together for fifteen years. Why are you making this out to be such a big deal?"

Duncan follows her into the kitchen. "Our marriage is a big deal to me." Then he pauses for a beat too long, and she turns to look. Tears heated by a flush of anger steam up his glasses. He takes them off and wipes the lenses on his chambray sleeve. They've left angry red indentations on the bridge of his nose that, in contrast, make his pale blue eyes look cold. "This family is everything to me. If only you felt the same, Annie."

Overcome with guilt, she leans over the sink and turns on the tap. But she doesn't hear the water rushing or the dishes clattering. Instead, she hears *the violent thud of a head on a dashboard, bones snapping, steel crunching, screams.*

HOTEL

The paralysis in Annie's limbs gives way to a prickling tingle. She props herself up on one elbow and forces her eyes open despite the harsh light flooding in from the window wall. As her vision adjusts, the figure next to her begins to take shape.

A white hotel bedsheet wraps around his body, but, of course, she can tell—it's him. The realization sets off an explosion of neurotransmitters. Clean citrus, his scent, permeates her nostrils and triggers a flood of memories. Last night, she laughed at his jokes; he hung on her every word. She felt comfortable enough to be reckless, more reckless than she'd been in years.

Now, memories hit her like body blows. Her tongue on his shoulder. The taste of his sweat. Then nothing . . . a blank. She falls back onto her pillow.

Annie sits up, her stomach lurching at the sudden movement. He could be asleep. There's still a chance.

Her throat is dry, raw. It hurts to talk, but she's desperate to elicit a response. "Wake up! Can you hear me?"

But his body lies rigid. The only motion comes from the flashes of light that flicker and fall in front of her eyes. They haven't fully adapted to the harsh daylight. She blinks once, twice, to clear her vision. She stares in disbelief.

It's not just the floating specks of light, something really is moving.

Annie hoists herself onto her knees. She grips the piped edge of the sheet and yanks it off. Sour acid surges in her throat. She clamps her jaw shut and bites down hard on the inside of her lower lip. Right now, the familiar, metallic tang of blood is the only thing that makes sense.

◆

CHAPTER 22

W"hy bother with the pita?" Duncan asks. "Let's just put the falafel on top of the Hawaiian pizza. Then we dip that into the tom yum soup and wash it all down with birthday-cake froyo." He leans back in his chair, sighs, and pats his belly.

"Gross, Dad!" Tabby says, with a giddy shriek. Despite her teenage self, she's genuinely excited to dig into her belated birthday buffet.

Annie can't help but smile. In the two days since she and Duncan argued, neither wanted to risk another emotional blowup. They filled every encounter with anodyne conversation, signaling an unspoken détente. "Oh! I forgot to take out the kombucha. A local, small-batch microbrew," she says, getting to her feet and smiling at Tabby.

"I'll get it," Duncan says.

For a moment, they both stand hovering over the table, too careful, too polite. Then, assessing the awkwardness, Duncan sits down again and clears his throat. "Thanks. We'll need some of those probiotics to wash down the Tums."

Annie proceeds to the kitchen. Along the way, her phone buzzes, and Danielle's name flashes on the screen. After Annie witnessed Ray Park's indiscretion at the spring festival, he's been finding ways to insert himself into their plans. When Danielle brought over wine to wash away the tears after Deja's death, Ray tagged along. When they met for coffee, Ray happened to stroll in just as the two women sat down. Annie stopped calling Danielle, hoping the awkwardness with Ray would die away on its own. The guilt of not being honest with her friend propels Annie to answer the phone now.

"Hi, what's up? We're just getting ready for Tabby's birthday buffet."

"Ooh! Enjoy! I'll let you go in a sec, but I was calling to see when you could take a look-see at my new bead designs. You said you would, then I didn't hear from you. BTW, the kids had an absolute blast the other day!"

"At the concert? Yeah, Tabby said it was fun. Thanks for driving."

"The concert was good. The afterparty at our house was even better. We missed you guys. Tabitha said you two had dinner plans. Half the class was there. Tabitha and Austin were inseparable. So sweet."

Danielle's words land like a kick in the gut. For a moment, Annie feels too betrayed to speak. Her daughter said she was going to a concert and sleepover with Aimee and a couple other girls. From Danielle's description, they had an actual birthday party. What's more, Tabby attended with a boyfriend. Annie wants to ask Danielle to describe him—was it the pale, pimple-faced boy from the musical chairs game? But she's too embarrassed that Tabby introduced him to Danielle and not her. Why hadn't Danielle told her about the party beforehand?

"Anyway, I won't keep you. When's good for me to bring my bead stuff over? I'm not sure the colorways pop."

Jealous and confused, Annie lashes out at Danielle—the mother her daughter seemed to prefer. "Sorry, I'm too busy with my artwork right now. A serious commission for a large-scale fresco. There's a chance I could look at your *baubles* in a month or two."

There's an audible gasp on the other end of the line, followed by an uncharacteristic silence. Already regretting her remark, Annie tries to extract herself from the conversation before she can make things any worse.

"Okay. We're about to sit down for dinner . . ." She knows she should apologize right now but hesitates. How can she explain her recent mood shifts? The irritation and anger that would overtake her suddenly.

Roused from her shocked stupor, Danielle unleashes. "Why do you have to act so superior all the time? Like your 'artwork' is so freaking important, Annie. News flash—it's not."

Annie struggles to formulate a response, but Danielle has already ended the call.

A burst of raucous laughter erupts in the dining room, an inside joke between father and daughter. As she returns to the table, Annie's eyes flash from Tabby to Duncan. The two have always been so alike. When Tabby—with her fair, freckled skin and coppery hair—was younger, other Park Waldorf parents assumed Annie was the nanny. She feels more alienated than ever now. *"It's always about sides. Us and them, Anh. Where do your loyalties lie?"*

"Who were you talking to?" Duncan inquires, slathering hummus onto a round of pita.

"Danielle called," she says, watching her daughter's reaction. Eyes downcast, Tabby is suddenly absorbed in the contents of her plate.

Duncan talks between bites of falafel. "Anything exciting at Casa de Park?"

"Well, actually it seems they threw a party Thursday night. For Tabby's birthday?" Annie's eyes shift back and forth from Tabby to Duncan. Did her husband already know?

But Duncan raises his eyebrows, genuinely surprised. "Are you talking about the concert?"

Tabby silently glares at her mother.

Annie speaks directly to Duncan now. "After the concert, the Parks had a huge birthday celebration for Tabby at their house. One that you and I were regrettably unable to attend due to 'dinner plans.' Go ahead and tell your father about it, Tabby."

Beet red, the girl sets down her glass, slowly and softly. "I didn't lie. You did end up having dinner plans. Besides, I knew it wasn't your kind of thing. All those strangers."

"But Tabitha, why didn't you mention it to me?" Duncan asks, frowning.

"Because you'd tell *her*! I didn't want her acting weird. Since the car accident when she went nuts on the kid, she zones out all the time. Like she's listening to something or watching a movie nobody else sees. She barely goes anywhere, doesn't eat. You think I want her around my friends? It's embarrassing!"

It doesn't matter that Tabby employed Annie's difficulties as cover for her own fibbing. The truth of the girl's words sharpen their brutality. Deflated, Annie sinks back in her chair.

"That's why your mother agreed to resume therapy." Duncan lies, shooting daggers at his wife. "She's doing it for the benefit of the family."

Ashamed and backed into a corner, Annie nods. She pushes her plate away, suddenly disgusted by the slice of Hawaiian pizza. The ham—who slaughtered the pig? A degenerate who enjoyed the animal's squeals of pain? The cardboard pizza box—who handled it? Jeffrey Dahmer worked in a candy factory.

◆

"Set light ten percent bright. Set my shower to one hundred twelve degrees. Start my shower." Annie pumps bodywash into her cupped palm. After dinner, Duncan took Tabby for a "heart-to-heart" walk, so thankfully, nobody's home to note the duration of her shower. Beginning at the top of her head and inching down to her feet, she lathers, then lets the hot water jet blast away the nagging thoughts cycling through her brain. *Was the seal broken on the top of the frozen yogurt carton? What if someone opened it in the grocery store? Smelled it or licked it, then put it back. It happened last year—that story on the news.*

"Stop my shower." Annie carefully steps out directly onto her flip-flops. *Did your bare foot brush against the ground? Maybe you should wash it again, just in case.* Naked, shivering, she stares down at her feet. Fat water droplets fall from her hair onto the granite. *It'll be easier if you shower one more time.*

◆

It's only eight o'clock, but Annie puts on her pajamas and draws the curtains. She climbs into bed but doesn't sleep. If she closes her eyes, the nightmares come.

Annie is a master of creating worlds—in her paintings, her gardens, her identity. Like many with contamination-based OCD, she's learned to cope by mentally carving out separate, distinct spaces. Inside and outside. Clean and dirty. She can function in the external, dirty world because it's all "contaminated" anyway. Only by decontaminating herself—undressing, shampooing, showering—can she reenter her clean world. Calamity strikes when the two worlds collide—inside-outside, clean-dirty. The blurring of borders triggers punishing uncertainty.

Did your sock brush against the curb? Before you showered, did your elbow bump into the doorjamb? Seemingly meaningless questions precipitated an agonizing mental review of everything she'd done before and after the incident in question. But these churning thoughts only left her with more doubt.

Now, Annie's clean world is closing in on her. Hunched over, knees curled up to her chest, paralyzed on the middle of the mattress. Nothing to touch. Nothing to set off a cascade of intrusive thoughts.

CHAPTER 23

Annie lets the old-fashioned door knocker fall from her hands. The anchor-shaped brass fixture lands with a thump, triggering a flutter of anticipation in her stomach. She hugs the leather portfolio against her chest. It contains hundreds of detailed sketches, more than three weeks' of worth of dedication, sacrifice, focus, and creativity.

Though it was difficult, and her progress halting, she'd driven herself to Lake Gaither many times over the past couple of weeks. She immersed herself in the hot, humid environs, capturing the ripple of water, the sway of branches. At night, she returned to the carriage house studio, and with Byrdie's childhood stories dancing in her head, she re-created the world on paper. Even without color, she succeeded in bringing the spirit of the lake to life via a combination of technical precision and creative license.

The biggest challenge loomed ahead: transferring the composition to a large-scale, three-dimensional space. Intimidated by the scope of the project and her relative inexperience, she'd called Ike.

"Remember freshman studio?" he said. "Neither one of us knew what we were doing. We figured it out along the way: one step, one decision at a time. Don't give up on yourself."

He was right about RISD. Though Annie started freshman year clueless and confused, she finished it winning the school's prestigious Adler Prize for Emerging Artists. This was a chance to right her career, which had somehow devolved into pet portraiture.

She left Duncan and Tabby largely to their own devices, reasoning neither wanted much to do with her lately, and sequestered herself in the studio. She spent long hours researching and experimenting with the mezzo fresco method of producing murals. The technique, popular in the sixteenth century, involved painting on slightly wet plaster. For this reason, the artist had to work quickly. Annie discovered she could extend the play time of the paint using an old trick she'd picked up in college. Back then, she'd found herself short on cash at the front of a long checkout line. The RISD store clerk, a fellow starving artist, suggested using windshield wiper fluid as a medium instead of the expensive stuff they stocked. Sold in bulk by the gallon, it was much cheaper but just as effective.

Annie raises her hand to knock again just as the door flies open. Byrdie's housekeeper greets her in a harried mix of English and her native Bulgarian. "Ma'am. Molya. Miss Fenton sees you here."

Lydia leads Annie upstairs to Miss Fenton's private quarters. A strange feeling of dread begins to take hold of Annie. She's never been invited inside Byrdie's bedroom for any reason, much less a business meeting. Shug sprawls across the runner, guarding her master's door. She hisses at Annie's approach, warning her she does not belong. Lydia smooths her gray curls with one hand and knocks softly with the other. Then she opens the door just wide enough to pop her head in. After a muffled exchange, she waves Annie in with the caveat: "Very tired. You stay not long."

Unlike the rest of Pinewood Manor, this bedroom hasn't been updated in decades, not since Claire's demise. The wallpaper, a swirly pattern of moss-green leaves with tarnished gold swirls, peels away from the wall in places. Fingers of paper stick out, pointing to the owner's neglect. An antique canopy bed upholstered in gaudy burgundy brocade dominates the room.

The enormity of the bed dwarfs its elderly occupant and seems to swallow up her boisterous voice. "Is that you, Anh Le, Anh Le?" With much grunting, Byrdie hoists herself into a sitting position.

Annie is shocked to see her benefactor's rosy complexion turned the same shade of sickly gray as her pajamas. The old woman's signature lilac perfume mingles with the unmistakable smell of bottom-shelf liquor and stale tobacco. On her head, patches of yellow scalp show through greasy white strands.

"My dear, I've been worrying after you ever since you rushed out the other day like your knickers were on fire!"

Annie blinks in confusion. That disastrous meeting in the study took place weeks and weeks ago. She's visited Pinewood and spoken with Byrdie numerous times since. But deciding there's little to be gained from correcting Miss Fenton, Annie ignores the odd comment.

"How are you, Miss Fenton? Lydia mentioned you're under the weather?"

"May have been feelin' poorly, but I'm on the mend now." She takes a crumpled-up tissue from inside the cuff of her nightgown and dabs the corners of her eyes and blinks. "Can't see a thing without my specs. Claire's always movin' them. You'd think she *wanted* me to trip and kill myself!"

Claire? Dead Claire? Annie scans the nightstand. She catches a glimpse of pearly-framed bifocals behind the jug of Fenton family moonshine. Annie lifts the jug, which is surprisingly light, reaches back, and grabs the glasses with her fingertips. Byrdie snatches them out of her hand and slips them on. Thick, round lenses magnify her bloodshot eyes, giving her the look of a creepy Halloween owl.

"Ah, so what can I do for you today, my dear?" Byrdie asks.

"I brought the sketches of Lake Gaither for you to review." Annie carefully slides out the stack of drawings. "If you're happy with these, I'm ready to start the mural immediately."

Byrdie raises an eyebrow as she accepts the stack of pages. She riffles through, looking increasingly perplexed. Suddenly the unease Annie has long associated with Pinewood rushes over her. She stammers trying to fill in the silences between Byrdie's periodic *hmms.* "I-I can change the perspective, adjust the composition, if you're not happy."

"That's all fine . . . but what are these for exactly? I wish you would consult me before starting such a big project, dear. I can see you put a lot of time into these, and they *are* nice, so let me ask Claire what she thinks. Just hold your horses, and don't do any more work without permission, for heaven's sakes. Money doesn't grow on trees."

Annie flinches at Byrdie's disapproval; her chest tightens. The butterflies that fluttered in her stomach dissolve in gastric acids.

Gradually, Byrdie's scowl fades, replaced by a distant, dreamy expression. "Claire and I need to watch our accounts. You see, she's been planning a grand tour of Europe. The Eiffel Tower and all that nonsense. We're fixin' to see the world together!"

Seeing the glazed look in the old woman's eyes, Annie says, "I'm sorry. Of course, Miss Fenton."

Up until this point, Byrdie, despite her age, had always maintained mental acuity. How could she have forgotten commissioning the mural? Annie casts a disparaging look at the jug on the nightstand. Is Miss Fenton drunk? Annie's disappointment shifts to anger as she thinks about how much this project meant to her, the time she put into it, all washed away by moonshine. She envisions herself shaking the foolish woman to jog her memory. Would the brittle bones in Byrdie's neck withstand the force? *Bones snap, a sick thud, screams.*

Eyelids drooping, Byrdie interrupts Annie's thoughts. "Love, I am so tired. My eyes are gettin' fuzzy. Don't have the energy to stay up all hours jabbering with folk these days." She pats Annie's hand. "You're a dear to call on me. Been sick as a dog. Right before our travels too." She tries unsuccessfully to stifle a yawn. "Drop your pictures on the table over there. Run along, now. Claire or I will telephone you, but I wouldn't get my hopes up."

F or you." Anh shyly handed Mẹ a sheet of white paper folded in half. She was sure folding made it fancier, like the wall of greeting cards she'd admired at the pharmacy.

For the past few weeks her mother had been short-tempered, sending Anh to her room for the smallest infraction. In bed, Anh would soothe herself by stroking the chocolate-brown-and-black rabbit's foot that, by now, had begun to lose some of its fur. Earlier this morning, she spied her mom at the kitchen table, silently sobbing over a pile of bills, then suddenly hurling the maroon vinyl checkbook against the wall.

Lately, she was always tired, always telling Anh not to be trouble—*maybe it is your fault*. She tried to make her mother happy, but something bad always happened.

Anh had slunk back to her room. Sitting cross-legged under her blanket, which formed a makeshift tent, she'd mulled the problem over. Then she'd started drawing.

Anh had been certain this would cheer her mom up. But now, as she stood vulnerable and exposed, Anh's stomach hurt. *It's not good enough. You should've colored in the front.*

Instinctively, the little girl's head dropped, and her shoulders tensed. When Mẹ approved of something, she showered Anh with praise. If something didn't meet her standards, she'd criticize Anh with abandon. She was preparing herself for rejection. As her mother opened the card, Anh held her breath.

"How, Anh? How?" Mẹ gasped in disbelief.

Inside, Anh had drawn her older brother Bảo—not stiff and formal like in the black-and-white photograph her mom kept sandwiched between the pages of her treasured Gaston Lenôtre cookbook. Instead, Anh had brought the boy to life—animating his features with each stroke of colored pencil, giving his eyes the playful glint Mẹ spoke of with such tenderness.

So why was her mom crying? Surely, it wasn't because Anh had omitted her father from the drawing. In fact, the black-and-white photo, taken in Vietnam before Anh had been born, was permanently creased and folded to only display mother and son.

On the rare occasions Mẹ mentioned Anh's father, it was to say he cheated on her and stole from her family. Once, in a fit of bitterness, she'd even said he got what he deserved. *Got what he deserved.* That sounded ominous, but Anh dared not ask what it meant.

"You don't like it?" Anh asked, a lump forming in her throat. "I can fix it. Make a better one." Ashamed, she tried to snatch back the drawing, but her mother held it just out of reach.

Mẹ didn't say anything, but a broad smile broke out across her face. "You do this for me. All this work. You make me so happy!"

Unlike those of the teachers at school, Mẹ's appraisals were rarely about the quality of Anh's art or the nine-year-old's astounding talent. From her mother's words, Anh gleaned that the show of loyalty, the devotion was the most important thing.

Mẹ lifted the scrawny girl onto her lap and hugged her close. Anh, suddenly relaxed, rested her cheek on her mother's shoulder and breathed in the lovely scent of her rose shampoo. She squeezed her eyes shut, willing time to freeze on this moment. Just the two of them. Safe and contained in their own world. All the bad things were on the outside—weren't they?

CHAPTER 24

The lie slid off her tongue so easily. "Byrdie loved the sketches. She asked me how—how I brought her memories to life." Annie hadn't planned the deception beforehand. She just couldn't bring herself to tell Duncan the truth last night.

He came home from work late, his back rigid with tension. His boss wouldn't let the Syria assignment drop. He'd hectored Duncan to "keep an open mind." Site views were down, and they desperately needed a big, splashy series. "Award bait," Jonah called it. The alternative: more layoffs. This time, to Annie's dismay, Duncan didn't refuse the assignment outright, saying he'd think about it. "The team needs me, Annie. It's hard to turn my back on that."

With Duncan in such high demand professionally, she couldn't admit to being rejected or, at best, put off. There was also the matter of Dr. Patel. Duncan had stopped pressuring Annie to make an appointment when he saw how productive she'd been, getting out of the house to sketch and driving herself, even if in a limited capacity.

And after the heart-to-heart with her dad, Tabby attempted to soften the blow of her harsh comments. "I should have told you guys about the party at the Parks' house. I know you're trying, Mom." Her daughter's words struck a nerve, driving Annie to work harder, to be better. How could she admit to being a failure now?

Annie knew she'd need to tell them the truth eventually— maybe next week, after she had a chance to calm down. In the meantime, she would need to act as if everything were normal. So, early this morning, she had packed up her sketching supplies and driven to Lake Gaither. She made sure Tabby and Duncan saw her leave before they themselves headed out for school and work.

It's only nine o'clock but the air is heavy with humidity and thick with gnats. June in Virginia. Annie's light cotton shirt clings to her back. She's already walked the lakeside trail twice because she can't bring herself to sketch. The lake that she found so inspirational last week reminds her of her rejection.

Drowning in self-loathing, she crouches by the shore, where creeping Charlie vine has choked out beneficial native sedges. Her face grows hot as she recalls Byrdie's blatant condescension. Annie snatches the vine and yanks it up from the ground node by node, setting off a series of mini dirt explosions. They sting her eyes, but she doesn't stop.

Unsettled by the manic weeding, a six-inch praying mantis hops toward her. It tilts its flat, triangular head, scrutinizing Annie through bulging eyes. Gauging by the size and wing type, she recognizes it as one of the harmful, invasive species, notorious for the female's propensity toward sexual cannibalization. She's seen clips of giant mantids stalking hummingbird feeders. They stab the pretty birds with spiky, razor-sharp forearms, then devour the blood, organs, and brains, discarding the rest of the impaled body with a casual shake.

Suddenly and swiftly, Annie strikes the mantis with the back of her hand. Then she pauses, raises her arm, and smashes down again. Each blow harder than the last until nothing is left but pulverized, neon-green bits. When her vision clears and her pulse calms, she notices her hand is a mess. She glances at the lake but wipes off her hand with a sycamore leaf instead.

Despite sketching the lake, day after day, she never so much as dipped a toe in the water. There had been local news reports of flesh-eating bacteria, especially in brackish waters. The sensational images of rotting skin disgusted Annie, yet they also compelled her to delve deeper online. She read that flesh-eating bacteria could invade the tiniest cut, scrape, even a mosquito bite. Rapidly, it consumed and killed healthy tissue—up to an inch an hour.

The thought of being forced to see that degradation on her body disturbed Annie more than the thought of amputation or death. OCD swallowed up logic and reason, creating a void. In that void, the condition established its own world governed by exacting sets of rules. Following those rules and rituals gave her peace of mind. But with each day, the rituals—like her mother—demanded more and more of Annie.

Now, the longer she beholds the dark, still surface of the water, the more she suspects the lake will suck her in. Dizziness overtakes her, her fear of losing control heightened—as an acrophobe on a ledge feels the pull of gravity amplified a thousand times over.

Black water seems to swirl in front of her eyes, her face only inches away. Closer still—she can taste the sulfurous rot. *Let yourself go. Give in.*

◆

The next morning Annie continues her charade of working. She sequesters herself in the studio rather than facing the lake again with everything it now holds—darkness, decay, a reminder of her own failure.

However, when she puts pencil to paper, nothing comes. She stares at her fingers, willing them to create. Though she washed her hands countless times, thin crescents of dirt remain embedded beneath her nails. What had she done to get the soil jammed in so deeply? She closes her eyes and thinks but is unable to construct a satisfying story from the images that flash into her mind. She sees herself stumbling, stopping to rest by the lake with her head between her knees. Nauseated, sweaty, dizzy. Choking on clouds of gnats . . . why were there so many flies suddenly? Losing track of time. Blacking out or simply falling asleep? When she sleeps, the nightmares come.

Frustrated, Annie presses down hard, too hard, with her pencil. The tip shatters, sending lead fragments skidding across the page. She hurls her sketchbook across the studio in frustration. If only she hadn't pinned her hopes on the Pinewood mural and foolishly cleared her entire calendar for the summer. She'd been so stupid.

"Stupid as a dog. Playing around instead of taking care of your husband."

Mẹ referred to Annie's professional painting career as "playing around." Annie rarely discussed her work in front of her mother and certainly knew better than to introduce her to her primary benefactor. But over the years, Mẹ picked up on household chatter and overheard snippets of conversations that Annie had on the phone with Byrdie. She even riffled through Annie's mail and packages, threatened by holiday cards and birthday gifts that her paranoid mind assumed were from Byrdie. *"The old lesbian is not your mother. I am your mother. Whose side are you on?"* Irrationally, Mẹ eventually connected all of Annie's artwork with Byrdie and by association hated it even more.

Elbows propped on the drafting table, Annie clutches her head and covers her ears, as if that will stifle her mother's incessant criticisms. Not only has she not told Duncan and Tabby about the aborted commission, she's been too embarrassed to share the news with Ike. Was it possible she'd projected her own enthusiasm for the project onto Byrdie, who, perhaps, was never really interested in the mural? Miss Fenton's confusion as she reviewed the sketches had seemed so genuine.

Annie picks up the stub-tipped pencil and casts about for her Høvel plane sharpener but can't find it. Her eyes land on the dao bào knife instead. It's the only thing salvaged from her mother's mountains of junk. Unable to throw out the only remnant of her mother's escape from Vietnam, Annie had polished and sharpened the carbon-steel blade and used it to cut canvas. The dual blades now come in handy, sharpening the pencil to a fine tip. Pressing the pad of her finger against the sharp point, she smiles weakly, thinking how, in this small way, she finally got her mother to support her career.

Annie slides off the stool and retrieves her sketchbook, but when she returns to the drafting table she sways slightly, suddenly light-headed. There's a strange taste in her mouth; a faint aroma floats across her nostrils. Familiar yet out of place. Somehow wrong. Could it be—charred ginger and star anise?

She feels her whole body trembling, shaking, but quickly realizes it's the phone, vibrating on the edge of the drafting table. Jarred to her senses, she remembers how Mẹ imagined odors all the time—chemicals, bleach, or sewer smells, that her paranoid mind theorized were being used to make her sick.

"Get it together. You're really losing it now," Annie mutters, leaning over to crack the window. She raises the phone to her ear. "Hello?"

"Annie, it's Ike. I'm outside your house. I rang before, but nobody answered."

"I'm out back. What . . ." His pronouncement that he's in the driveway confuses Annie. At this hour on weekdays, and many weekends, he works at his family's convenience store. Something has to be wrong. ". . . I'll be right there."

She spots Ike's mud-spattered red truck, a relic inherited from his dad, parked outside the house. She sprints the last twenty yards. He's slumped in the driver's seat, so she can only see the top of his head. When he lifts his chin to look at her, Annie freezes. Ike's left eye is swollen shut, his lip split, his cream-colored polo shirt streaked with rusty-red stains.

He doesn't move, so she opens the passenger-side door and climbs in.

"What happened?" She's afraid to hear the answer.

"Byrdie's gone. I'm so sorry," he says in a hoarse whisper.

Annie can't look at Ike's battered features. She turns her head, catching a glimpse of her own shocked face in the side-view mirror. "What have you done?"

PART 2

have information to report about a—a missing person. Miss Byr-die Fenton," Annie says, hearing the tremor in her own voice. The desk officer, peering over the rims of her drugstore readers, takes in Annie's unkempt hair, puffy eyes, and saggy sweatpants. Not hiding her disapproval, the woman grunts something unintelligible, then resumes tapping letters lazily into the computer. Annie doesn't move.

"I said, it'll take a minute for someone to help you. You can cool your jets over there," she says, gesturing toward the waiting area. Annie glances doubtfully at the row of institutional, gray metal chairs. They are upholstered in a wavy blue-and-red-print fabric, embellished with dark grease stains and vague crusty spots. She decides to stand.

Arms folded, she glares across the room at the grumpy desk clerk, turning away when it's clear the woman is oblivious to her sharp looks. Annie might as well be invisible.

She'd change her tune if you were with Duncan. When they first started dating, Annie devised a term she dared not share with anybody, save Ike. *Carte blanche.* The freedom to do whatever you wish. When she was with rich, white Duncan, she had carte blanche. For better or for worse, it became a crutch in hostile situations, a shield against unsmiling faces.

As she waits, Annie stares at the cover of an outdated celebrity magazine but doesn't touch the pages or pick it up. She thinks about her white-knuckled drive to the police station. The road blurred by her tears, a string of clear snot bobbing up and down from her nose like a bungee cord. She was too petrified to take her hands off the steering wheel to wipe it away. Every time she thought of pulling over or turning back, she remembered Ike. She had to help him.

◆

The two friends had huddled in the air-conditioned truck while Ike, still in shock, told her what happened.

"I had an early meeting scheduled with Miss Fenton to discuss the foyer. She'd called me to say she wanted a new coat of paint instead of the mural you'd proposed. I usually ring the bell outside the gate but was surprised to find it ajar, a stone wedged between."

Annie raised her eyebrows. "I've never seen it left like that. Lydia locks it each night."

"I figured Miss Fenton had left it that way because I was coming very early before Lydia's shift. I drove in, but when I knocked nobody answered. I tried calling, no response. I was annoyed—I'd specifically arranged the early appointment so I could be back in time for the eight o'clock shift at the convenience store.

"So I walked around to the side of the house and looked through the big sliding door. When I saw the latch was raised, I got worried. Had someone broken in? I entered, cautiously. Just as I reached the foyer, Lydia arrived."

"She must have recognized you?" Annie asked, flabbergasted.

"Well, apparently not. She screamed and called 911 to report 'a Black man' in her house. Either we all look alike to her, or she was just startled, not expecting to see anyone there at that time besides Miss Fenton."

"Maybe a little of both. She also has progressive cataracts," Annie said. "But how did you get hurt?"

"I approached her like this." He raised his hands palms out to demonstrate. "She picked up that lead crystal decanter—the one that always has lilies in it—and threw it at my face! It bashed my lip. The blood was gushing everywhere!"

"When did she realize it was you?"

"Just before the police arrived. She'd started to calm down a little by then, after she realized I wasn't going to hurt her. She tried to tell them—but her English goes when she's upset.

"Two officers stormed in, saw blood on the white marble floor, broken glass, my dark skin, and well . . ." He couldn't stop shaking his head back and forth as though the *no* gesture would erase history. "Things went from bad to worse when we couldn't find Byrdie."

"Did you explain it to them? Why you were there?"

"Of course. They didn't believe me until I had them feel the hood of my truck, still warm, and told them they could check my E-ZPass. It would show me exiting the toll road from D.C. with no time to spare, proving I'd arrived shortly before Lydia. Even then, they only let me go once Lydia vouched for me. To her credit, she did that even though Byrdie forgot to write the meeting down in her planner."

"I'm sorry, Ike."

"I have to clean myself up before my mother sees me. She will worry. Your home was so close. I thought maybe I could borrow a shirt and leave."

"You need to come in and let me clean those cuts too." Annie said. Then, seeing the hesitation on her friend's face, she added, "I insist."

In Duncan and Tabby's bathroom, Annie bathed Ike's wounds and dabbed on antiseptic. Delicately applying gauze and tape, she breathed in his lime-and-mandarin cologne, comforted by its familiarity. As if the unisex scent he'd worn since college confirmed that, yes, this was still the same Ike—despite his badly swollen face. Then she lent him one of Duncan's checked button-downs—far too large for his slender frame but better than the bloodstained polo. Before Ike left, she'd asked, "Do they still suspect you of anything?"

"I don't think so, but who knows. I wasn't about to stick around to ask. You see what they did to me." He gestured at his bandaged and bruised face.

As soon as Ike's truck pulled away, Annie called Duncan. Straight to voicemail. She couldn't bring herself to call Danielle. They hadn't spoken since Annie's jealous outburst the night of Tabby's birthday buffet. So Annie grabbed her keys and left.

"Miss Shaw? Annie Shaw?"

She swings around, her eyes landing on a young, ruddy-faced police officer with a clipboard. "Yes, that's me," she calls out, raising her hand in a half wave.

He approaches her and sits down on one of the metal chairs, gesturing to the empty seat beside him. Reluctantly, Annie sits down. Nobody else is in the waiting room, but she's surprised they're talking in such a public place.

"My name is Officer Tyler Williams." He absent-mindedly wipes his nose on his sleeve before extending his hand. Annie pretends she doesn't see his outstretched palm, and he lets it drop. "Ah, can I get you some water?"

Her throat is parched. *Drink it and you'll need the toilet, the same filthy stall used by perverts and deranged criminals. What if he fills the glass in the restroom?* "No, thank you. I'm fine."

The officer cocks his head toward the front desk attendant. "You told Judy you have some information about Miss Byrdie Fenton?"

"Yes. My friend Ike Oteh was at Pinewood Manor earlier. There was a . . . misunderstanding."

Officer Williams nods warily but says nothing.

"Miss Fenton was also a client of mine. I thought you should know she's been acting strangely. Drinking again and even talking about her dead friend Claire as though she's still alive."

"Ah, yes. Mrs. Ivanova, the housekeeper, explained that her boss has not been feeling well."

Annie babbles, "You see. I know Ike couldn't have done anything. Byrdie's been imagining things. She hasn't been right in the head."

The officer nods, but sensing Annie has no information of value to offer, he moves to end the meeting. "Yes, well, thank you, ma'am. I'll make a note of that. Was there anything else you wanted to add?"

"No. I guess not. That's all."

After the emotion of seeing Ike and the adrenaline of driving to the police station, Annie deflates. Officer Williams mistakes her downcast expression for concern. He clears his throat. "I wouldn't worry about your friend. She hasn't been missing long. Since she has no direct next of kin, we've issued a Silver Alert just to be cautious. More often than not, in cases involving senior citizens, the person has lost their way on the bus or gotten turned around in a supermarket or shopping mall. In my experience, they almost always wander back. If not, we find 'em. Nothing too exciting."

She nods, unconvinced. Most likely, he's right, and they'll discover an innocent explanation for Byrdie's sudden disappearance. But the thought of Miss Fenton doing her own grocery shopping is laughable. In her bones, Annie just knows there's more to it.

Outside the station, the sun beats down on her head, the air thick with humidity and gutter stench. She thought she'd feel better after telling the police what she knows, but maybe coming here was a mistake. Her involvement hasn't really done anything to help Ike.

Annie's head throbs and her eyes are dry. She blinks hard as she steps off the curb, narrowly missing a collision with a cyclist.

"Watch it, lady!" he shouts.

Annie stumbles toward the lot but realizes she has no idea where she's parked. She pauses, shielding her eyes against the glare of row after row of windshields. The asphalt scorches through the flimsy soles of her ballet flats. She winces, lifting one foot, then the other, and almost loses her balance. Beads of sweat pour down her face, and she runs her tongue over parched lips trying to catch them. As heat bounces off the pavement, she regrets refusing Officer Williams's glass of water.

She wanders up the aisles searching for her old sedan. The colors of the cars blur; their contours warp. She's dizzy, can't think straight. *"Too dumb to find your car. Too dumb to drive."* She can barely make out her mother's voice over the intense, pounding headache. She stops at a blue Corolla and tries the door, but it doesn't open. Not hers. A young woman passing by regards her with suspicion.

Just then, Annie spots a figure in the distance. There's something uncanny about the way it's moving. First, far away, then suddenly closer, closer each time. Jump cuts. The features are distorted—blurred yet familiar. Annie gasps, "Mẹ?" The woman is her mother. But she is the same age as Annie. They stand face-to-face like a mirror image.

"We are the same, Anh. You did this for me. The old lesbian is gone."

Speechless, Annie falls into her mother's embrace—arms wrapped around her tightly, so tightly it feels as though her chest might cave in.

CHAPTER 26

The bedroom light fixture makes a strange tapping sound. Trapped inside its milky glass globe, a damselfly careens about. It crashes into the walls of its prison, injuring itself and growing weaker with each frantic movement.

Annie props herself up by the elbows. But as soon as she sits up, she falls back down, struck by the sudden recollection of Ike's face, Byrdie's disappearance, the police station, and the woman who looked so like her mother. Her stomach heaves. She rolls onto her side and realizes she's not alone.

In an unlit corner of the room, Duncan waits with his large, soft hands folded in his lap. He doesn't smile. His eye twitches as he prompts her. "Well?"

"How did I get here?" Annie groans and rubs her eyes. "My car—"

"The police station called me at my office—I was in the middle of an editorial meeting. You passed out in the parking lot. The desk clerk asked me to 'promptly remove my inebriated wife,'" he says, his tone heavy with disappointment. "They looked through your wallet and found my number. You barely drink, much less *day drink*, so what happened?"

"Of course, I wasn't drunk . . . maybe just dehydrated or sunstroke. Byrdie's gone missing."

"I gathered that in speaking with that woman at the front desk," he says. "But I don't see why you had to get involved. Do you have any reason to believe Byrdie won't turn up perfectly fine?"

When Annie doesn't answer, Duncan nervously pushes his glasses up at the bridge. He struggles with his next words.

"I'm pretty sure Byrdie will be just fine. The thing is, you're obviously not fine . . . and *I'm* not fine anymore. I'm completely exhausted at this point. It's always some drama you're experiencing, and I can't do it now. I've been coming to the rescue for the past twenty years through thick and thin. My career has taken a back seat. That editorial meeting was important. The publisher was attending, for god's sakes. Having to leave was humiliating. Those writers need to look up to me, revere me. Dammit! Clout is everything in the newsroom."

"Oh, Duncan. This one isn't my fault. Can't you see that?" She doesn't wait for his response. "I saw my *mother*, Duncan. In the parking lot today."

"*What?* That's impossible. You *have* to know that."

Is it impossible? The question slices through the fog in Annie's brain. When she found her mother's body lying in the carriage house, she stumbled out without taking a pulse. She telephoned Duncan. He was the one who lifted the body out of the mess, called the paramedics, and arranged the cremation. How could she be certain the ashes she spread were, indeed, her mother's?

After her encounter in the parking lot, she desperately needs reassurance. She wants to ask Duncan if he's certain Mẹ is dead. Did he actually watch the cremation himself? But she knows irrational questions will only feed her husband's concern. She holds back, breaking into messy, heaving sobs instead.

The furrow in Duncan's brow deepens. "Listen, I'm really worried about you. Your mother may be gone, but the more irrationally you behave, the more I see *her* in *you*. You don't have to carry on her illness. I hoped you'd seek help on your own eventually, but given the circumstances, I've gone ahead and called Lily Patel. She's willing to make a house call.

"Maybe she can help you process your feelings about your

mother, and you can start dealing with your grief instead of stuffing it all down until you have a breakdown like this."

He hesitates, the unspoken ultimatum looming like a hammer about to drop. "You don't have a choice right now, Annie. Either you get professional help, or I'm going to look into—be *forced* to look into—other options."

Her chest tightens. She knows he's referring to a psych hold or involuntary commitment. The topic came up years ago when they brought Tabby home from the hospital. Annie was paralyzed by doubt, finding it nearly impossible to even bathe the premature newborn. *What if you accidentally scald that tissue-paper-thin skin? What if you mistakenly grab the bleach instead of the baby shampoo?* Tabby was so tiny, Annie envisioned her slipping down the drain. She imagined her husband's rage when he returned from the store and discovered she'd lost their daughter.

Now that he's dropped his bombshell, the anger drains from Duncan's face, leaving exhausted lines around his eyes and mouth like ripples in sand. He studies her face. His pale blue eyes soften but he remains immobile, coming no closer to her. This time, he must be resolute. There will be no conciliatory hugs. He forces himself to harden his expression again.

"I told Jonah I'm taking the assignment in Syria."

Annie closes her wet, swollen eyes in disbelief. She feels like a hole has opened in the mattress, in her stomach, and she's in free fall, caving into the world, into herself.

"You—you're leaving us? How can you even think of abandoning us at a time like this?"

Duncan looks away, but not before she sees his chin quiver and his eyes well up. Above all, this is a man who loves his family. "You think this is easy for me? I'll be gone a month or two at most. Tabitha will be at away at camp most of the summer. I should be back by the time school starts up. If not, she's bigger now. She doesn't need me as much." Saying this aloud for the first time breaks something in him. In the silence of the room, she can almost hear it shatter deep within his chest.

"And we both know I'm enabling your OCD. Your symptoms aren't getting better. Maybe if I'm gone, you'll pull yourself together." Then he lets out a bitter laugh, sounding more like a stifled sob than anything. "The time apart will be good for both of us. Either you haven't noticed or don't care, but you aren't the only one who's struggling."

Tired of fighting, neither of them has anything to add. Annie watches as the damselfly succumbs to its prison.

CHAPTER 27

From the sitting room window, Annie stares at the driveway in disbelief. Duncan heaves his large duffel bag into the trunk of a waiting car. For more than a week his trip to Syria remained a vague hypothetical. Even after he reserved tickets, she refused to believe he'd actually go through with it.

So as the calendar hurtled toward his departure, Annie continued to ignore her marital problems. It was easier to fixate on Byrdie's disappearance instead. The police had done little, as far as she could see, aside from issuing the initial Silver Alert. As a courtesy, Officer Williams had given Annie his card. Three times she called. Three times it went to voicemail. When she finally did reach him, the young officer sounded harried, insisting there was nothing to be done at the moment.

"No sign of forced entry—aside from the door your friend opened, the gate and the locks were completely intact. No theft, threats, or demands for money." In addition, he explained that while Miss Fenton may have been more forgetful than usual, nothing indicated her behavior had crossed the line into serious cognitive impairment. "We canvassed the neighbors. The closest one is out of the country traveling, and the other immediate families noticed nothing out of the ordinary. Basically, there's no reason to believe your friend is in danger or that she's a danger to herself. She probably decided to take a trip, doesn't want to be bothered."

Ike's initial statement to the police lent credence to the trip theory. He said Byrdie had talked about traveling to Europe soon, "to see the sights. The Eiffel Tower. Buckingham Palace, the Coliseum."

"She was talking about taking a trip—with her friend who died years ago!" Annie said, sarcastically. "If she were going to travel, she would have told Lydia, her housekeeper."

The officer sighed. "Ma'am, I'm not going to rehash the investigation with you right now. That wouldn't be appropriate, not to mention I have a stack of paperwork and actual cases I need to deal with. At the end of the day, Miss Fenton is an adult. We have to respect that."

Annie spent hours delving into online crime discussion forums, reading up on missing-person cases. The ones that involved the elderly usually came down to mild dementia, Alzheimer's, or some other medical condition. However, Annie discarded these explanations, fixating instead on disturbing accounts of the ones who were never found. The ones who vanished abruptly, without a trace—or worse, the times when there *were* artifacts of violence. A blood-soaked canvas sneaker kicked off in the woods. Grainy security-cam footage of a shadowy figure stalking. A station wagon inexplicably abandoned on a remote desert road.

Such salacious details compelled Annie to decontaminate her body and her brain. Increasingly hot sprays of water, clouds of steam, caustic soap stripped everything away as she plummeted deeper into her compulsive rituals.

Outside, a car trunk slams shut, pulling her into the here and now, into the reality where her husband actually *moved up* his flight to the Middle East. Duncan was really going to leave today, just one day after Tabby had departed for equestrian camp.

At the bus depot, the teenager bade her good-byes with a bear hug for her father and a careful wave to her mother, which just made Annie feel worse. Her own daughter acted as if she were too fragile for affection. On the drive home, Annie questioned the timing—one leaving directly after the other. Had Duncan and Tabby coordinated their trips, so she'd be left alone?

Now, as she lies curled up alone on the sofa, an irrational fear surges through Annie. The familiar feeling of powerlessness returns. After she outgrew stowing away in the back rooms of nail salons, Annie stayed home by herself while her mom worked long hours. Mẹ wasn't physically present, but her paranoia still controlled every second of Annie's experience. Before leaving, Mẹ methodically blockaded the doors with chairs, booby-trapped the windows with glass jars, closed all the curtains, and double- and triple-checked the stove. The ritual alleviated her mother's anxieties but inflamed Annie's. Everything she touched, everything she did while home alone carried one of her mother's warnings. *"Don't go outside; you could get kidnapped. Don't turn on the stove; you could start a fire. Don't shower; you risk slipping and cracking your head. Don't turn on the lights; they might see you."*

A draft ruffles her hair as the front door opens. In the entryway, Duncan awkwardly shifts his weight from leg to leg. For a hopeful moment, Annie interprets his fidgeting as a sign of indecision— maybe he won't leave her. But before he says a word, she spots the determination in his eyes, the set of his jaw, and her chest tightens.

He clears his throat. "All packed up. Gotta run to make my flight."

The dark specter of recent arguments, too many to count, looms over them. Annie stares down at her hands. They're clasped together, her knuckles white, her skin red and cracking. Even her nails are peeling from too much washing, too much cleaning.

"You better go, then," she says, fighting back the inevitable tears.

"Lily, Dr. Patel, will call you in the next few days to set up the appointment. I asked her as a personal favor to make the time to see you. *Please* try, Annie. You've beat this thing before. I'll be back before you know it. I-I love you."

"I'm trying—I'll try. Good-bye, Duncan." There's a note of finality in her tone. She has the sinking feeling she may never see her husband again. As if an unseen hand were pulling out each thread of Annie's existence one by one—her mother, Deja, Byrdie, and now Duncan.

A nh pulled the blanket tighter over her head and buried her nose in the matted fur of her stuffed bear. His lower half could be turned inside out into a plush red stocking. Now that she was twelve, she never played with him that silly way anymore. However, there was a telltale stain on the bear's fur where Anh still sometimes "fed" him by pressing morsels of food against his mouth in case he was hungry.

Her mother had given her the bear last year. At the time, Anh was having difficulty adjusting to the intense loneliness of staying home all the time. Increasingly paranoid about losing her daughter to the influences of a foreign land, Mẹ had pulled her out of school and called it "homeschooling." They didn't bother to check back then in Ohio. Her mother controlled every aspect of Anh's life, save a tiny portion of Anh's brain where her imagination conjured up stories and painted secret pictures. Everything else passed through the mental filter of her mother's approval. It wasn't homeschooling—it was a cult of two, and there was no doubt Mẹ was the leader.

As she often did when her mother worked late, Anh lay in bed daydreaming. She'd insert herself into whatever tattered library book she was reading at the time. Lately, she loved murder mysteries. If she was lucky, she'd fall asleep, and the fantasy would come to life in the "reality" of her dreams. Anh spent so much time at home—bored and alone—that her dreamworld seemed more alive to her than her waking hours.

She had started drifting off when the doorbell rang. Broken for years, it emitted a strangled ding. The muffled sound was enough to make Anh sit straight up. Nobody visited them anymore, and Mẹ wouldn't try to use the broken bell. Whoever it was quickly gave up on the weak bell and knocked.

"*Hello!* Is anyone there? If you're home, open the door."

Afraid to move a muscle, Anh listened but didn't recognize the male voice with its southern Ohio twang. The stranger, apparently frustrated with knocking, hammered at the door with a closed fist. He struck the flimsy pinewood barrier with such force the house seemed to tremble. Anh slithered out from under her blanket, tucked the bear into safety, then crept to the living room window. Here, concealed behind the musty boxes of used library books her mother hauled home with increasing regularity, Ahn would be able to see the front doorstep without being detected.

She hadn't yet mustered the courage to peek out when the doorknob rattled. He was trying to get in. What could she do? Her eyes fell on the beige plastic telephone across the room, but her heart sank as she remembered the service had been shut off last month. Could she get to a neighbor's house? No, if she escaped out the back door, he'd be able to see her and outrun her. Her shoes were in the garage and her socked feet wouldn't get her far in the ice and snow.

Anh's panic-stricken mind raced, leaping from the more practical survival solutions to placing blame. *How could Mẹ leave me like this?* Not knowing what to do without her mother, she suddenly felt much younger than her age. Then she wondered if her mom could do anything to protect her even if she were home—and this realization disturbed Anh almost as much as the stranger outside.

Again, she forced herself to steal a glance. The man was dressed in a canvas utility jacket, jeans, and a gray knit cap pulled low enough to nearly obscure his small, sunken eyes.

"I know you're in there." This accusation was followed by swearing, ugly words that terrified Anh.

Had he been spying on the house? Did he know she was alone? Had she somehow brought this evil to their home—her fear reeling him closer? The pounding in her ears was deafening. She had to protect herself. Crawling between piles of old newspapers, she made her way to the kitchen and grabbed her mother's dao bào knife. She crouched in the hallway. Her hands trembled as she clutched the weapon and imagined herself lunging forward, jamming it into the man's exposed throat. *Could you do it? Yes, you can kill.*

"Y'all can't hide from us," he yelled. After a while—what felt like hours—the cursing and thumping stopped. Tires screeched out of the driveway and up the dead-end street.

Anh waited to make sure it wasn't a trap before standing up, her knees wobbly and her legs numb from crouching. She peeked out the front window. The man's boot marks were already beginning to fill with fresh snow. Seeing no one, she opened the door a crack. Paper rustled. It was taped to the door.

NOTICE OF EVICTION

Anh shut the door. She jammed a chair underneath the knob before getting back into bed. She snuggled the bear against her chest and inhaled deeply until, gradually, her pulse stopped racing.

Anger took the place of fear, as she could no longer reconcile her experience with her mother's. In Mẹ's world, everyone was either a Communist agent, a thief, a rapist, or a pedophile. In reality, the threats were more pedestrian; the bogeyman was a bill collector.

CHAPTER 28

In the cool darkness of her bedroom, Annie fumbles for her phone. She powers it on, rubbing the sand from her eyes as she waits for the time and date to appear. Nine o'clock at night, two days after Duncan left the country. After months of interrupted sleep, her body finally gave out, and she descended into a dark, dreamless sleep. Sweat-soaked sheets that cocooned her for the past forty-eight hours cling like an ill-fitting second skin. She wriggles free and swings her legs over the edge of the bed.

In her hand, the screen flashes with unread messages, unheard voicemails. She curls her knees to her chest, bracing herself to re-enter the waking world, and presses play.

> **TABBY:** *"Hi. They make us call a parent once a week to say we aren't dead. I'm alive more or less, so uh . . . I guess that's it. I cannot believe they lock up our cell phones and make us use a freakin' landline. It's like that farm Dad dragged us to in Colonial Williamsburg. Bye-ee!"*

The purpose of the camp was twofold: to polish equestrian skills and to foster community building and independence—which meant not texting Mommy and Daddy or your besties every two minutes. Despite the flippant tone, Tabby's voice makes Annie smile. She archives the message.

DUNCAN: *"Annie. Can't really talk. I just landed in
Damascus. I'm safe, but I probably won't be able to call again
for a while."*

The line crackles, and in the background there's a constant
murmur of a language she doesn't understand, and then the call
cuts off. There's a second message, though her husband's voice is
faint, nearly inaudible above the static.

*". . . was saying you and Tabby mean everything to me.
You've gotta know that. I love you. Let's talk when I get
back."*

Annie deletes his voicemails as though the action will erase
their marital troubles.

The final message sends a shot of electricity through her.

GABE: *"Hey, it's Gabe returning your voicemail. Yeah, let's
get together. Are you free Saturday by any chance? Uh . . .
well, I'd really like to add something witty now to impress
you, but I can't think of anything. I'm just happy you called.
How about that? Gonna say bye before I make a fool of
myself. Talk soon.*

Annie gasps. As the weeks passed without hearing from Gabe
again, she stopped being suspicious of him—if Gabriel was a scam
artist or a stalker, he was a lazy one. But she doesn't remember
calling him. Her mind strains to summon up a hazy milieu of
dreams and inconsequential memories from the past two days:
stumbling to the bathroom, eating saltines, guzzling water from
the tap. Glancing over at the nightstand, she sees the empty sleeve
of crackers surrounded by crumbs and salt specks. *Well, that's real.
You must have called him.*

When she's thinking more clearly, she'll return Gabe's call—it would be rude not to do so. After thanking him for helping her at the festival, she'll apologize for any misunderstanding and explain that she's married. Annie may be intensely lonely, but at least her life is safe and contained right now. She considers calling Danielle for advice, but the sinking feeling in her belly reminds Annie how cruelly she dismissed her friend the last time they spoke. Her mother's familiar refrain consoles her. *"You don't need anyone else. We don't need outsiders."*

Seeking the undemanding companionship of Netflix, Annie powers on her tablet. But all the "Top Picks for ANNIE" are true crime shows: *Mom Was a Real-Life Dexter, Nightstalker Nurses, Profiles in Carnage.* The watch history is full of stuff she doesn't recognize. Tabby must have borrowed her tablet. The thumbnails feature menacing portraits shot in photo negative, a lone red stiletto tossed in the dirt outside a remote cabin, a child's bike abandoned on a railroad track. There's an entire subcategory dedicated to eerie, unsolved missing-person cases. She thinks of Byrdie and feels sick.

As a mental cleanser, she taps on a mindless action movie, pops in her earbuds, and cranks the volume up. Despite her drowsiness, she's sucked into the boilerplate plot. A retired hit man (aka aging action star) must rescue his teenage daughter from kidnappers hell-bent on recruiting her into high-end prostitution. Annie is alone in the house, and her nerves are raw. The movie's ever-increasing tension rubs her like sandpaper on a canker sore.

A yacht explodes on-screen with a boom loud enough to make her ears bleed. She lowers the volume on her earbuds. *Scritch. Scritch.* The sound has nothing to do with the on-screen action, which involves a scantily clad teenager racing toward the camera to safety. Lowering the volume even more, she detects strange, soft utterances in the cadence of human speech: *scritch, scritch, scritch.*

As Annie switches the tablet off, she recalls a story she saw on the news years ago. A homeless woman hid in a man's closet for over a year—pilfering food, showering, watching television when he went to work. Annie fixated on the idea of someone using her toilet, touching her remote controls, rifling through her underwear without her knowing. It could happen. *It had happened.*

The noises seem to be coming from downstairs or outside on the porch. Suddenly, she feels exposed in the brightly lit room with the curtains open to the expansive night. She slithers across the floor on her belly, switches off the overhead lights, and is plunged into darkness.

The Colonial Revival home has no walk-in closets in which to hide, so she crouches beside a large dresser and listens intently. She's frozen like this, afraid to breathe, for several minutes, which pass like hours.

A sudden flash of blue-white light cuts through the darkness. It's followed by a vibration that rattles her body. She exhales as she realizes it's just her phone. Without pausing to see who it is, she takes the phone out of her pocket and swipes to answer. She pushes herself farther back against the wall to avoid being seen.

"Hi, Annie. It's Lily Patel. Sorry to call so late. I just finished a rotation in the clinic and thought of you on the way home. Are you there? Annie?"

"Yes," she whispers.

"Are you okay? I think the connection is poor. I can barely hear you."

In fact, the reception is crystal clear. Annie can hear the soft purr of a cat in the background and the ding of an oven timer. *If you tell her about the weird sounds, she'll think you're nuts. And whoever got into the house might hear you talking.* Annie says nothing, but she turns the brightness on her screen way down.

Dr. Patel fills in the awkward pause. "Well, I'm glad I caught you. My assistant Regina has left messages but hasn't been able to reach you. Listen, I have an unexpected break in my schedule tomorrow afternoon. If you're available, I could swing by around four-ish—"

She's trying to have you committed like Duncan wants.

Despite her misgivings about the psychiatrist, she's desperate not to be alone in the empty house. She hears herself whispering, "Yes."

Dr. Patel seizes on Annie's agreement. "Lovely, lovely. I am so happy we'll be able to talk face-to-face. We can have a casual chat. Looking forward to catching up. You have a good night!" She hangs up abruptly before Annie can change her mind.

The strange sounds have stopped. She waits a few minutes, then scoots over to the window on her bottom and peeks outside. The moon has risen, allowing her to see the absence of anyone lurking, watching her from the porch, driveway, or front yard.

Annie steals out to the hallway to check the second-floor Guardian Angel Sentry system box. She presses a button, and the little screen comes to life: *STATUS: ALL IS WELL.*

Relieved but also not taking any chances, she locks herself inside her room and collapses wearily onto the bed. All the sleep she's gotten over the past two days seems to have made her *more* tired. As she drifts off, a mishmash of disconnected thoughts float through her mind, from the silly plot holes in the movie that led to the painfully loud yacht explosion to wondering what Dr. Patel had been cooking for dinner that set off the oven timer. The purring cat—Lily fostered them and always seemed to have a few around. She laughs to herself about how the doctor had blamed the awkward silences on a "poor connection." Like Duncan, Lily came from a well-to-do family and was accustomed to polite subterfuge.

But something nags at Annie, preventing her from escaping into the deep, blissful oblivion she so desperately seeks. She tosses herself onto her side and feels the lump of the earbud still in her ear. She pulls them out and tosses them onto the nightstand. Night sounds flood the room—the throaty call of a toad, the trilling of crickets, the soft pattering of rain that will soon relieve the humidity.

She didn't hear the nocturnal chorus earlier because her earbuds were set to block all background noise. The noise-canceling function worked so well that she could hear what was going on in Dr. Patel's apartment. Then how had she heard the soft scratches and noises coming from downstairs?

Annie sits up straight, struck by a realization more alarming than any intruder. She must have imagined the noises, hatched them from her fears and anxieties. But did this make the sounds any less real?

GRACE FALLS, 1994

The forecast called for subzero temperatures. The house had no heat—yet her mother had left Anh alone at home. The teenager's belly roiled with hunger. To distract herself, she picked up a dried pine needle that she kept hidden in a tissue under her pillow. Stabbing at the pads of her fingers with the pointy end, she marveled at how she felt nothing. Her digits had gone numb from the cold, unheated house. She poked at the skin again and again until a tiny bead of blood formed, then stopped and sucked it until the bleeding stopped. This left no mark, but the skin on her fingertips had gradually gotten thicker and rougher. Anh folded the pine needle back into the tissue and restored it to its hiding place.

Now that she was fifteen years old, she'd taken a part-time job at the public library. Her mom only allowed it because they needed the money. Mẹ staved off eviction by working nights at a processing plant that produced frozen TV dinners. They'd managed to get by so far, but each late-payment notice ate away at her mother's sanity. With the extra cash from Anh's job, they could just keep up with the bills.

But early this morning, Mẹ had driven away in the beat-up hatchback with twenty dollars in her purse. She was headed to a big flea market more than an hour away. "Don't go outside. Be good, Anh. Looks like they have good stuff!" she said, tapping the newspaper listing with a chipped nail.

Anh had angrily buried her head in a book. She felt betrayed.

That money could've been used for food, or to go toward getting the electricity turned back on. Instead, her mom was "investing" it in more junk, which they already had *plenty* of—not to mention the gas money wasted driving farther into the boondocks.

"People are simple in the countryside. They don't know how valuable this stuff is," she'd said. "They don't know what they have. I do." It was a constant refrain Mẹ used to justify her hoarding, but the words had done nothing to satisfy Anh's growling belly.

She'd been allowed to return to the public school last year when her mom came to terms with how important it was for getting a job. However, Anh wasn't allowed to participate in any extracurricular activities and went nowhere other than school, where she had no friends, and the library. Her mother kept her as isolated as possible. *One way or another you'll get out. She can't keep you here forever.*

Anh's head pounded with dehydration. No electric meant no heat *and* no well water pump. Mẹ collected buckets of water from the elderly couple next door. This was something Anh was too ashamed to do herself. There was only enough now to flush the toilet once and boil a kettleful to drink.

But boiling water or cooking on the stove required her to use a propane lighter to ignite the gas flame. The process scared Anh. She was hungry, though, so she made her way to the kitchen, carefully navigating through stacks of books and boxes of junk.

They stored food inside the oven. It was one of only a few places safe from the rats that roamed freely about the house. Not wanting to touch anything, Anh used the edge of her sleeve to open the oven door. Inside, she found a couple cans of clam chowder, a few ends of moldy Wonder bread, and a jar of peanut butter. She tore off the green bits from a slice of bread and covered it in a generous dollop of peanut butter. No need to ration, since this would be both breakfast and lunch and who knows when her mom would be back.

Behind Anh, an empty cider gallon clattered to the ground,

seemingly of its own accord. Terrified, she spun around. Two of the biggest rats she'd ever seen were fighting. They launched themselves into the air, propelling their bodies into one another, teeth gnashing, flesh tearing. She stood transfixed for a moment by the horror of what she saw.

Then she raced back to her mattress and pulled the blanket over her head. She wasn't hungry anymore—she was disgusted. But Mẹ would be furious if Anh wasted food. So she forced herself to chew the bread, the peanut butter sticking in her throat. With each bite, her resentment grew; she hated her mother for making them live like this.

CHAPTER 29

D r. Lily Patel bites into a blueberry scone with unbridled relish. "So yummy! Did you bake these, Annie?"

"Er . . . I had them delivered from Whole Foods and popped them in the toaster oven. Does that count?" To avoid the extensive cleanup involved *after* a visitor came inside the house, she'd set up refreshments on the porch.

"In my book, yes. Good enough." Dr. Patel chuckles. Other than a slight yellowing of the teeth, she hasn't aged since Annie last saw her a decade ago. But the long black hair of the doctor's twenties and thirties is now barely shoulder length. "Less fussy," she said when Annie complimented it.

Dr. Patel had never bothered to marry. Instead, she devoted her time to her clinical trials and her ever-growing number of cats. Preferring the quiet solitude of the lab, she'd abandoned private practice decades ago but agreed to resume seeing Annie based on their past success, as well as her long-standing acquaintance with Duncan.

Dr. Patel sets her scone down on a plate, licking a stray crumb from the corner of her mouth with a feline flick of the tongue. Stretched out on a wicker bench with her back leaning against the armrest, she seems more like a patient than a doctor.

"*Ahhh!* It's absolutely lovely here! I have to tear myself away from the clinic more often." She folds her hands on her lap and closes her black, beadlike eyes. For a moment, Annie wonders if she's fallen asleep.

"Dr. Patel?"

"Yes, dear."

"Thank you for coming out to the house to see me. I suppose I haven't been . . . myself."

"Yes, yes. Duncan told me you have been turning to your rituals again," she says, now sitting at attention with her feet on the deck. Unlike some therapists, she never uses a notebook. This is partially due to her steel-trap memory, and partially due to her opinion that note-taking made patients feel like lab rats under observation. "I'd like to hear about it from you in your own words, not Duncan's. When did the OCD symptoms start interfering with your life again?"

"Well . . . I don't know exactly. I've been under a lot of stress lately. On Mother's Day my dog died in a terrible accident."

Hearing the quiver in Annie's voice, Dr. Patel shakes her head in genuine sympathy. "I'm so sorry to hear about that. The loss of a beloved pet is—"

But Annie interrupts. Having not spoken to anyone in days, she finds herself unable to hold back. "Earlier this month my biggest client, an elderly woman, went missing."

Dr. Patel draws her breath in sharply. "My goodness. I do hope she is found safe. How has this affected you?"

"It's frustrating. I'm not sure how much the police are doing to investigate her disappearance. They seem to think she went on a trip."

"Is that a possibility? Sometimes the truth is mundane."

"Well, yes. But no. It's strange. She was confused, disoriented before that. I've been doing a lot of research online about strange missing-person cases." For several minutes, Annie spills general armchair-detective theories and lurid specifics about various cases she's spent far too much time researching. Her words tumble over one another, her eyes wild.

"I see," Dr. Patel interjects, finally, her forehead wrinkled with concern. "It can be terrible to feel powerless in situations like these. But more information isn't necessarily better. Given your history of fixation, we should focus on your own well-being right now. Trust the police to do their jobs." The doctor pauses and eyes Annie intently before continuing. "And if I'm not mistaken, Duncan said you lost your mother a couple months ago?"

"Yes, of course. I must have mentioned that . . ." Annie falters. Her cheeks flush at the glaring omission. She had not told the doctor about her mother's passing, because in many ways it felt as if Mẹ never left. "She was in her eighties."

"Even when the death of a parent is expected it doesn't necessarily make it any less painful. Arranging practical matters of funeral and estate can also be incredibly stressful." Again, Dr. Patel waits for Annie to pick up the conversation, but there's an uncomfortable silence. The doctor clears her throat and continues.

"When we met years ago, you told me your mother also displayed obsessive-compulsive behaviors such as hoarding. Indeed, there is strong evidence of a genetic component to OCD. It has also been documented that the incidence of mental illness—not just OCD, you understand, but depression, schizophrenia, stress disorders—is higher in refugee women. Not to get into too many confidential specifics, but I'm involved in a research study on generational trauma in immigrant families."

"You understand, then. My mother struggled to feed us and keep a roof over our heads. The stress of being alone in a foreign country, the pressure of being responsible for me while barely able to take care of herself . . . it drove her mad." Excited that the doctor understands in a way her own husband never could, Annie continues. "My mom perceives everything and *everyone* as a threat."

"Hypervigilance is common in PTSD patients. The trauma of bombs raining down on your head, dodging bullets—these unseen wounds aren't limited to soldiers."

Talking about her mother's mental illness to an outsider feels like a betrayal. Annie, suddenly reticent again, inspects the fine hairs on the back of her hands.

"Hmm. If it's okay," Dr. Patel says, "I'd like to return to something you shared earlier. You said your mother 'perceives' everything as a threat. You referred to her in the present tense as though she is still with us."

"I-I don't think I said that," Annie sputters, panic washing over her.

You shouldn't have said anything. This American doctor will use your words to trap you. Duncan will get his way. They will take your daughter from you.

"Have you given yourself a chance to accept her death and to grieve?" Dr. Patel asks.

Not wanting to sound outwardly defensive, Annie pivots. "I mean, we all carry a piece of the departed with us, inside us. That's normal, isn't it?"

"Yes, it's perfectly healthy to cherish happy memories," Dr. Patel responds. "Reflect on the good things about your relationship with your mother and the time you had together, rather than the loss."

Good times were few and far between, but one memory flashes vividly into Annie's mind. "My mom cooked phở for us on Saturdays sometimes. Toasting the star anise, charring the ginger and onion for the broth—the familiar smells lifted her spirits. Even when she was dead tired, it was like the ritual brought her back to life."

The doctor smiles, appearing genuinely touched. "You keep those bits of the past close to your heart. Treasure them." She pauses, considering her words, before continuing. "What you want to watch out for is allowing thoughts of the deceased to take over your life *today*. Your mother's voice, her opinions, do they dominate your thoughts? Or can you control them?"

"I'm not sure what you mean by that."

You can't control them. Our thoughts are the same. We are the same.

"The mother-daughter bond is one of the strongest in nature.

When you're young, it keeps you tethered, protected. Later the same ties can hold you back, strangle you," Dr. Patel says, deep in thought.

Annie's throat tightens. Her hand flies to her neck. She recovers quickly by reaching for the plate of pastries. "More scones, Doctor?"

"Oh, I mustn't," says Dr. Patel, with a nervous glance at her wristwatch. "Time has certainly flown by, and I have a long drive back to the city. We should wrap up. Is there a time we can resume our conversation, Annie? I could drive out after work. I'm away at a conference the first half of the week, but how about next Thursday?"

Just get rid of her. "Yes, that's great. I can make the appointment with Regina," Annie says, with no intention of doing so.

"That's fine. I will update my calendar myself. I don't like to trouble Regina with after-hours appointments. And before it slips my mind, how are you doing with your medication?"

"Well, actually, I haven't found it to be as effective lately. It worked so well for over a decade, though."

"Hmm. Since you responded so well to the sertraline and, as I recall, experienced no side effects, let's stick with it and play with the dosage," Dr. Patel says with a quick nod and self-satisfied smile. "I'll call in the order and have it shipped directly to your house, if that helps."

"That would be wonderful," Annie says, relieved not to have to visit a pharmacy.

"No worries. I'm so glad we had a chance to speak today."

As Annie walks the psychiatrist to her car, a suspicion clouds her thoughts. "Will you—will you be sharing our conversation with Duncan?"

"Of course not! That would be entirely unethical. The content of our sessions remains confidential."

As Annie stands in the driveway, waving good-bye to Dr. Patel, she wonders how long it will take the therapist to break that promise.

CHAPTER 30

Not only does Annie sleep through the night again, but she also wakes up late. Her body is still compensating for weeks of sleep deprivation; her brain, overloaded after the psychiatric consultation, completely shut down last night.

Set on restoring a sense of normalcy, she showers, slips into a fresh T-shirt and jeans, and heads downstairs for a cup of coffee. In the pantry, there's a bare spot where her ground coffee should be. She studies Duncan's exotic coffee tins—Esmeralda Geisha, Ospina, Fazenda Santa Ines—not to mention the whole-bean grinder she never bothered to figure out. She backs out of the pantry before slamming the door shut with surprising ferocity.

Almost instantly, her frustration morphs into guilt. *You took your husband for granted. You drove him away. You deserve to be alone now.* Forging ahead, she drops a stale tea bag into her mug and switches on the electric kettle. But upon checking the wire fruit basket, she nearly breaks down in tears. A moldy navel orange and two black, leathery bananas stare back at her from inside their steel cage.

"Stop feeling sorry for yourself," she mumbles. She takes a magnetic notepad, the one the family uses for grocery lists, off the refrigerator and begins to jot down a to-do list: *1. Buy fruit. 2. Reschedule Tabby's dentist. 3. Reorder Deja's heartworm pills.* The dog's death hits her afresh, a sucker punch to the stomach. Simultaneously, the pen runs dry. *Everything is conspiring against you.*

"Stop feeling sorry for yourself," she mumbles, dismissing the paranoid thought and determined to get back on track. She rummages around in a junk drawer, finds a pencil, then settles down again with the list. But her fragile concentration has been broken, and she doodles mindlessly. She uses the dullness of the pencil tip to softly shade and create dimension, rather than outlining. The effect is shockingly realistic. Inadvertently, she has re-created the face of the young woman in the parking lot at the police station—her mother.

When she reaches the jawline, letters appear. *S-U-N-S-*. The previous list maker must have pressed down on the pad hard enough to create an imprint on the page beneath. As Annie continues her drawing, the pencil strokes reveal the word: *S-U-N-S-C-R-E-E-N*. Duncan's fair skin burns easily. After years of desk duty, the sun of the Syrian desert would be brutal. She wonders if he remembered to pack his hat, only to have her question answered immediately as she continues shading in the slender neck. *C-A-P*.

Below on the list, the letters *C-O-N-* appear. To expose the remainder, she must use wider strokes that far exceed the sketched contours of the woman's neck and shoulders. The resulting figure is ugly, distorted. It also reveals the word in its entirety: *C-O-N-D-O-M-S*.

The paper spins in front of her eyes, transforming the drawing of her mother into a monstrous whirl of judgmental eyes.

Blind and dumb. Your father cheated on me. Did you think you were special?

As farfetched as some of Annie's suspicions had been—like Duncan and Tabby coordinating their trips to precipitate her mental breakdown—her paranoid theories hadn't ventured to adultery or condoms. Duncan never seemed interested in other women.

You haven't been having sex. What did you expect?

Guilt washes over Annie as she recalls refusing the romantic cabin getaway and the look of disappointment on her husband's face.

You are not a good wife.

And all those late nights at the office—was Duncan really working then? Was he even on assignment now? Impulsively, she rings the newsroom and asks to speak to Duncan's boss Jonah.

"Annie! What a pleasant surprise. What can I do for you?"

"Um . . . I was calling . . . calling about an internship for one of Tabby's friends. Do you have any openings?"

"Ah, our summer intern slots are full, I'm afraid. But fall/winter—"

As Jonah prattles on with a self-important discourse on the importance of hands-on experience in journalism, Annie's mind races. She's not sure how to ask him about Duncan, but she doesn't have to.

"—and that is why on-the-ground reporting is more important than ever. That is why this matters, Annie. Boots on the ground. I can't thank you enough for your family's sacrifice—the long hours Duncan has been putting in at the office and now the assignment in Syria . . ."

Embarrassed now that her question has been answered, Annie quickly thanks Jonah and hangs up. She rests her forehead in the palms of her hands. *You barely avoided making a fool of yourself.* None of it made sense. Duncan had never actually cheated on her in the past. There was a single incident years ago, before they were married, but he hadn't been able to go through with it. For fifteen years, he's been absolutely devoted to Annie.

But the word on the notepad stares back at her. Has she finally driven him away? Bent on finding evidence to either prove or disprove her suspicion, she marches into Duncan's study. She rarely ventures inside, so she lingers for a moment in the entryway. On the lone wall not lined with bookshelves, her husband has proudly displayed a framed copy of his Pulitzer-winning piece. Beside it, in uncomfortable proximity, hangs a printout of Annie's *SouthernHer* magazine article, appearing even more absurd by contrast.

She forges ahead, scoping out the antique pedestal desk. The green leather top is completely bare, so she opens the drawers. Each, in succession, reveals tidy and completely innocuous contents—

pens, a stapler, paper clips. She wonders why he bothers with collation materials as he doesn't seem to keep papers. But Annie won't give up. She needs to know, or the uncertainty will torment her.

Her eyes fall on his old-fashioned landline telephone. It's one from the newsroom, the kind with flashing buttons that light up. Duncan prefers it for conducting interviews and for conference calls when he works from home. Annie presses through the menu, searching around until she locates the call history. At first, there's not much. Mostly Jonah and a number she recognizes as the newsroom's international conference line. But as she hits the down arrow, another number appears with astonishing regularity in a cluster. She punches the digits into her own cell phone but doesn't need to hit the call button. The phone recognizes the number as part of her contacts list and displays the corresponding name. The name is Millie Rae.

Bewildered, Annie drops her cell phone. It lands with a dull thud, face-up on Duncan's green leather desk pad. What possible reason could Duncan have for speaking to the college intern? For a moment, she stares at the black cell phone screen, as if looking at it hard enough will reveal the answer to her question.

Just then, the screen lights up. Her heart skips a beat. Perhaps she pressed Millie Rae's number accidentally. But no, the young reporter's name doesn't flash onto the screen.

Annie hurries out of Duncan's study before she answers the call, as though the person on the other end of the line will somehow see she's nosing around.

"H-hello?"

"Good afternoon, Mrs. Shaw. This is Officer Williams from the MPPD."

Nearly two weeks have passed since Byrdie went missing. Had they found her? Holding her breath, Annie listens as Officer Williams continues.

"I'm calling about the Fenton investigation—"

"Do you have news?"

"I think it's best if we spoke in person, Mrs. Shaw. You might be able to assist with our investigation. Could you come to the station first thing in the morning?"

Though it's phrased as a question, it's clear to Annie this is not a request. *How much do they know?*

◆

Unable to sleep that night, Annie lies on her back, her muscles tense and stiff, her mind roiling with worst-case scenarios. Have the police located Byrdie or have they discovered her dead body? Why do they want to talk to Annie? Is she a suspect?

After hanging up with Officer Williams, she texted Ike to find out if he'd been invited to the station as well. His response came almost immediately:

No, nobody's contacted me.

Followed by another message seconds later,

Don't talk to the police alone. Call a lawyer.

Though Ike's advice confused Annie initially—did he think she was guilty of something?—she quickly realized it made sense for him to possess an elevated distrust of the police, especially given the brutality of his recent encounter with them.

Regardless, an attorney was not a bad idea. She'd read enough books where the main character makes the critical mistake of re-fusing legal representation so as not to "appear guilty." So she called the firm Duncan had hired to oversee his trust and the family estate. An attorney named Ed Perez would accompany her to the police station in the morning. He'd been acquainted with Duncan for years; their fathers had gone to law school together.

Now, exhausted by her circular thoughts, she reaches over to the nightstand and extracts a melatonin bottle from inside a drawer. She pops a strawberry-flavored tablet under her tongue, lies down, and squeezes her eyes shut. She breathes in and out, slowly and rhythmically, as the tablet dissolves, but nothing happens. After what seems like an eternity, she gives up, tosses off the covers, and fetches her laptop. *Blue light be damned.* She searches for articles about Byrdie but discovers there have been no new developments. Then a different worry moves in to occupy her brain. Duncan's infidelity.

She spends the next two hours scrolling through images of Millie Rae. Millie Rae, sorority president, surrounded by her "sisters" who are near carbon copies of herself; Millie Rae front and center in a group shot of college newspaper staff; Millie Rae in a crowd of bikini-clad students spring-breaking in Cancun; Millie Rae, bookended by beaming parents, brandishing a certificate. Annie zooms in on the paper, her blurry eyes making out the words *Dean's List.* Hundreds of images readily available online of the pretty, popular girl. Hundreds of daggers Annie could use to torture herself.

In each shot, Millie Rae looks improbably perfect—almost as though she'd been Photoshopped in among the mere mortals. Glossy, golden hair, gleaming white teeth framed by full, pink lips. Always dressed to accentuate her petite yet curvaceous figure. Closing her eyes, Annie slams the laptop shut. "Enough!"

Outside, the birds have begun their dawn chorus. In a few hours, Annie must face the police.

HOTEL

His facial features are distorted, swollen beyond recognition. Red pin-pricks punctuate the flesh on his neck and torso. The skin around each puncture wound, swollen with fluid, forms an irregular pattern of pustules.

Annie can't tear her eyes away. Her gaze tracks down his body and halts at his penis. It's frozen in an erection.

Last night, alone in the elevator, he grabbed the back of her thigh and ran his palm up, lifting the hem of her dress. She slapped his hand away. "Not yet. Did you do this with the other girls you brought here? Not until I say."

The delicious possibility of the elevator stopping and the doors opening at any moment was exhilarating. She pushed him against the wall of the elevator, pressing her body into his, salivating at the aroma of his sweat mingled with his expensive fragrance. Wordlessly, she unzipped his pants and slipped her hand inside. Tracing lightly over the cloth of his boxers, she leaned in close to his ear and whispered, "I like to know what's waiting for me."

But what excited her hours ago now fills her with unbearable disgust. She recoils. Adjusting her focus, she recognizes the source of the movement: dozens of dun-colored spiders. Each about the size of a dime, they crawl over his bare flesh. No longer sealed in by the tightly woven sheet, they scatter in every direction. They'll be on top of her in *seconds. Horrified, Annie scoots away on her backside, stumbles off the bed.*

All those disgusting images cycling through your brain. You know what you did.

◆

CHAPTER 31

Yellowy-beige walls, a chipped wood veneer table, the smell of lavender potpourri. More like a teachers' lounge than the gritty interrogation rooms Annie's seen on television. There's no one-way mirrored wall or metal table bolted to the floor, but there is an attorney.

Ed Perez barely looks at Annie, his head of wavy black hair bent over a yellow legal pad. She swallows nervously, watching as he prints her name and the date and time on the top of the page. His pencil strokes are measured and efficient, like his words and mannerisms. He seems to approach life as a series of swim strokes to be optimized for speed and distance. Occasionally, he glances at his phone, which he's silenced and placed parallel to his notepad, but he doesn't engage her in conversation. As they wait, Annie grows increasingly anxious.

Are they listening? Maybe that's why Ed isn't speaking. She casts a suspicious eye over the electronics in the room, from the conference phone to the antiquated A/V setup on a wheeled cart in the corner. *Do the police have to tell you if they're recording you?* In any event, there is nothing else to say to the attorney. She's already shared the little she knows with Ed on the phone and in the car ride over.

A cursory knock at the door, like the warning the doctor gives you before entering an examination room, rouses Annie from her thoughts. A lanky man in an inexpensive but crisply starched navy suit strides in. His skin is a shade of warm fawn and his brown hair streaked with silver. Pinched between his index finger and thumb, a slim manila folder.

"Detective Eric Harper," he says, extending his hand first to Ed, then Annie. She notices the wedding band settled so comfortably on his ring finger that it appears to be melded into the skin.

"Thank you both for coming in today." Before his bottom hits the chair, Harper has the file open. He scans the contents with clear, amber eyes that are troubled but not unkind.

"Officer Williams has noted how helpful you've been in our investigation. It says here you've called . . . a half-dozen times. And you visited the station in person the day Miss Fenton's disappearance was reported."

Unaware of these encounters with the police, Ed casts a sharp glance at his client. However, she's too focused on the detective to notice.

Annie blushes. "It was nothing. I just wanted to help. Have you found her?"

Harper doesn't answer her question. "We appreciate your interest in the investigation, Mrs. Shaw. We're hoping you can clarify a few details for us." He pauses, looking to Annie for agreement. Only once she nods does he continue. "When was the last time you saw Miss Fenton?"

Annie flounders. Her head is muddled. "I-I'm not really good with dates. Late May. Um . . . maybe the third week? I think I told Officer Williams the last time I was here. It must be in his notes."

"Yes, let me see. In your initial statement, you mentioned leaving your portfolio at Pinewood on June 10," Harper says, peering at her over the top of the file folder.

Annie wrinkles her brow in confusion. The conversation with Officer Williams in the waiting room was so casual, she wasn't aware she'd been giving a statement. "Sure, if that's what I said then . . ."

"Can you tell me about your encounter with Miss Fenton that

day?" Harper asks, his amber eyes cooling from warm syrup to sharp glass.

"'Encounter'?" Annie hesitates, her eyes fixed on a wad of gum, still slimy with saliva, stuck to the side of the fiberboard table. "Byrdie . . . Miss Fenton wasn't feeling well, so she was in bed."

"I see. And what was her reaction to your work? Was she impressed?"

"Not exactly. I mean, she was confused. Not herself that day. She asked me to leave the portfolio with her. She said they—she—would call me later."

Harper's expression softens, his tone now reassuring. "I understand Miss Fenton has been a big financial backer of yours over the years. This must have been disappointing for you, no?"

"It gutted me. We'd discussed the project in detail. It was this complicated mural. I never would have spent so much time on the preparatory drawings if Byrdie hadn't been so certain of what she wanted. To be honest, I was shocked by her response to the sketches. It was as if she never commissioned it at all." Annie blurts out the response almost without pausing, before realizing she's raised her voice.

Ed clears his throat loudly. He opens his mouth to speak, but the detective jumps in first.

"Of course, of course. I understand. Since that's the last time you saw her, your portfolio would still be at Miss Fenton's home," says Harper. "I could have one of my people retrieve it for you."

"Yes. Oh . . . no, that won't be necessary. I think it's back at my house now." Annie vaguely remembers seeing the leather folder on the credenza this morning, near the front door. Yes, she definitely saw the portfolio there because she had needed to move it to find her watch.

"You *think* it's at your house?"

"I have it. I remember now . . . I stopped by Pinewood to retrieve my portfolio. The more I thought about it, the more painfully obvious it was that Byrdie had no interest in continuing with the project. I couldn't stand the idea of her showing my sketches to people, laughing and telling them how foolish I'd been. I wanted the draw- ings back." Annie looks down at her hands, which are now balled into tight fists.

"Thank you. Very helpful," Harper says, scanning an itemized list in front of him and performatively jotting down a note. "This explains why we found no portfolio among Miss Fenton's posses- sions." When he looks up, his eyes are no longer friendly or reas- suring. "I assume that you picked it up, but did not see Miss Fenton that day?"

"Well, as a matter of fact, I did. It was such a quick visit. I forgot until now. It was raining, getting dark. I'd been at the lake all day . . . sketching. I don't like to drive after dark, so I just ran in and rang the bell. I guess Lydia had left for the day, so Byrdie—Miss Fenton—gave it back to me. Then I left."

"That's it? Did you have a conversation with her?" he asks.

"Oh, actually, she offered me a drink. She was finishing off the last of the family moonshine. I got the sense she didn't want to be alone."

"And so you went inside and had a drink with her?"

"No, no. I was too humiliated. What was there to toast? The fact that she was rejecting my art? Besides, I wouldn't drink before driving. It was getting darker by the minute, the rain was picking up, and I was distracted. I remember now, my shoes got muddy walking back to the car and I worried the soles would slip on the accelerator."

She squeezes her eyes shut trying to force clarity. Messy details come back to her—ones she isn't willing to share out loud. She re- calls opening the trash can in the garage at home and throwing out her mud-splattered clothes. Who knew what was in the mud or *if* it was just mud. There could be traces of urine, fecal matter, se- men, even blood.

Inside the house, she found Tabby in tears over some teenage melodrama. When she tried to comfort her, Tabby pushed her away. "Look at you! Your hair is soaking wet, and you're in your underwear. You're a mess! And *you* think you can help *me*?" Afterward, Annie took a hot shower and stole the bottle of Ambien that Duncan kept stashed away in his Dopp kit for international flights. Upset and unable to make out the tiny print of the dosage, she took several of the pink pills and blacked out. She'd wanted to forget the whole evening. It worked.

But Annie couldn't confess to taking the pills now. She'd heard of Ambien "zombies" who not only walked in their sleep but also unwittingly shopped online, took baths fully dressed, plucked their eyebrows off, even drove. *Who knows what you might have done?*

"Mrs. Shaw? Do you recall exactly what night you retrieved your portfolio?"

"N-no. I'm sorry, I don't." She looks desperately at Ed, who stares down at his legal pad. "It's been a couple of weeks."

"Our investigation may have shed some light on the matter. We interviewed a neighbor who recently returned from a trip abroad. He recalled passing Pinewood on his way to Dulles and noticing a light blue Corolla parked—quite badly—outside the gate."

Harper pauses to let it sink in. "Cross-referencing the neighbor's date of departure with Miss Fenton's phone records—it would appear this is the very night Miss Fenton went missing. She made a few phone calls earlier in the evening, but nobody saw or heard from her after seven o'clock."

"I didn't realize." Blood rushes to Annie's face.

Seeing her distress, Ed intervenes: "Do you need a minute, Annie?" He places his hand on top of hers in a gesture of compassion that seems out of character.

She fixates on his torn cuticle, a sliver of blood dried in the nail bed. His palm feels clammy on top of her hand. She pulls her hand away.

In the moment of ensuing awkwardness, a scene flashes into her mind. Byrdie's hand felt clammy that night. She looked up at Annie, watery eyes full of pity, and pressed her damp claw against

Annie's cheek. When she tried to stroke her hair, Annie recoiled. "I'm not a dog! How would you like it if I petted your hair like this?" Had she actually said that out loud at the time or just thought it? Had she actually grabbed the old woman's hair? She's not sure, but she has an image fixed in her mind of Byrdie's shocked face, pale and stricken.

"By all means, we can take a break if you need it, Mrs. Shaw." But Harper doesn't wait for a response before charging ahead. "Can you tell us what state Miss Fenton was in when you left her house that night? Did anything strike you as unusual?"

Realizing she's divulged too much, Annie's response is curt. "No. I don't think so. She just handed me the portfolio. I didn't even go inside. I told her I had to drive home."

"Approximately what time did you leave?"

"I don't remember. It was getting dark like I said."

"So eight P.M.? Or maybe eight thirty P.M. then?"

"I really don't know. I was . . . flustered."

"And why was that? Did you and Miss Fenton argue?"

"Not that I . . . no." Annie realizes too late that she doesn't sound in the least convincing.

Ed goes on the offense. "Let's cut to the chase, Detective Harper. My client may not recall every detail of what was most likely, to her, an inconsequential evening weeks ago, but that does not indicate her involvement in Miss Fenton's disappearance.

"We've been one hundred percent cooperative. In return, we ask for *transparency*. Can you tell us why you seem so focused on Mrs. Shaw?"

"Of course. There's been a breaking development." Harper's eyes lock on Annie's, his words tight as a vise. "At seven twenty-two yesterday morning, county police responded to a report from a recreational fisherman. They located Miss Fenton. Her body was found floating in Lake Gaither."

CHAPTER 32

Without dropping his gaze, the detective pulls a printout from the manila file folder. He slides the paper across the table. "I offer this to you in the interest of *transparency*," he says, with more than a hint of sarcasm.

The black-and-white image of Byrdie's bloated, bruised corpse stares up at them. Annie's stomach plummets like she's on a hellish drop tower ride. She pushes hard against the edge of the table, trying to distance herself from the disgusting image. Her chair slides back sharply, teetering on two back legs. Reflexively, Ed catches her and steadies the chair.

Harper, who has been silently observing her, speaks. "It's a tragedy. As you can see, her body shows signs of trauma." He tosses out another photo, this one close-up. "Note the clumps of hair ripped from her scalp. It's possible her hair caught on a root at the bottom of the lake, and the warm spell sped up bacterial decomposition—"

"B-bacteria ate away at her corpse?" Annie interrupts, not realizing at first she's spoken out loud.

Harper nods. "Bacterial decomposition results in the buildup of internal gases in the corpse. Eventually, when she became buoyant enough, the chunk of hair and scalp . . . separated. Her body then floated to the surface."

The detective evaluates Annie's reaction to each gory detail. Her mouth hangs open as she silently stares past him, gazing out the window and shaking her head in denial. But she doesn't see beyond the conference room glass to where the sky has darkened with an impending summer storm. She sees her reflection, hears her mother: *You get what you deserve, Anh. You know what you did.*

"Mrs. Shaw? Are you listening to me? The lake, which is surrounded by woods, abuts the Pinewood estate, about three miles due east of the manor. That is quite a distance for a sickly eighty-six-year-old woman to have trekked. Do you have any idea how your benefactor ended up in the lake?"

Before Ed can caution her, Annie shouts, "No! I don't know . . . how could I?"

Harper glances at his notes before firing off another question. "You mentioned being 'at the lake' on the day in question. Would that be Lake Gaither?"

"Yes. It was Miss Fenton's idea, not mine. It was supposed to be the focal point of the mural."

"Ah, yes, so this *is* your work. I thought I recognized your style."

He places a clear PVC envelope on the table. It contains a crumpled drawing of the lake. Delicate pencil strokes expertly give form to a serene vista of trees, shoreline, and water—the controlled lines marred by rusty splatters of mud and dried blood.

◆

Detective Harper didn't hide his skepticism when Annie pleaded ignorance. However, given the circumstantial nature of the evidence against her and no definitive proof of a crime—after all, Byrdie could have slipped and fallen into the lake—the police released her under a no-travel provision.

Ed drives Annie home from the station. Her mind is reeling. She must have dropped the sketch during one of her many sessions at the lake. As for the blood splatters, she'd have no way of knowing what happened to the sketch after she lost it.

Ed reassures her: "The police cast a wide net. They're just seeing what they can shake loose and from whom."

When they reach the house, it's still raining, the tail end of the storm lingering. Ed gallantly insists on walking Annie to the front door, under cover of his tiny travel umbrella. The heat feels oppressive after the Mercedes's climate-controlled interior, and, without thinking, she undoes the second button on her blouse. Ed's eyes wander down to the newly visible sliver of pink lace bra, his robotic efficiency momentarily suspended. Annie, sandwiched between the attorney and a glass storm door, is suddenly aware of his proximity. Despite the covered porch, he continues holding the umbrella over her, standing so close she can discern the clean, grapefruit notes of his aftershave.

"Are you sure you don't need anything? I know Duncan is out of town." He glances over her shoulder. "This is a lot to process." A nervous look plays across his face.

The mention of Duncan's name recalls his absence and his betrayal. Annie notices that a lock of Ed's neatly combed hair has fallen onto his forehead, slicked down by rain. She resists the urge to push it back. "No, I'll be okay. I just need to take a hot shower and get into bed." After an awkward pause where neither of them speaks, she adds, "Thank you for coming out here on such short notice. You probably need to get back home to your family . . ."

Annie isn't sure what she wants him to say, but she's relieved when Ed says good-bye. She darts inside the house, even before he's started the engine.

CHAPTER 33

On Thursday, the doorbell takes Annie by surprise. She isn't expecting any deliveries or visitors. The second ring is followed by a series of gentle but persistent knocks. Annie slips into her bedroom and peeks out the window but can only make out the rear fender of a dark-colored sedan. Her heart skips a beat . . . the police? Ed assured her he'd be in touch with any developments.

Throwing a slouchy cardigan over her tank top and lounge pants, she tiptoes downstairs. Through the distortion of the peephole, she doesn't recognize the face. Not at first. Then it hits her—Dr. Patel. Annie completely forgot to cancel the appointment. She could pretend she's not home, but her car is clearly parked outside, and the house lights are all on. She opens the door a few inches, just enough to talk.

"Hello!" They say it simultaneously, adding to the awkwardness.

"I'm so sorry, Dr. Patel. I actually forgot about our appointment. So much has happened since our last session . . ."

"Well, that sounds like this is perfect timing, then!" the doctor says, beaming with characteristic optimism.

"It's a little messy in here. Let me come out onto the porch. Can I get you some water?"

"That would be lovely. It's very warm out here." Annie still only has the door open a crack. Always curious, Dr. Patel tries to peek inside, but Annie closes the door. In a minute she emerges with two glasses of water in her trembling hands.

"I can't believe this appointment slipped my mind, and you've driven all this way." Annie could kick herself for not calling Regina to cancel. She's been distracted, her mind fluctuating between the confrontation with Detective Harper at the station on Friday and Duncan's affair.

"No worries. It is a lovely, lovely drive and a refreshing change of pace from the five-hour clinic meeting I had today," the doctor says, frowning. This must be why she's dressed up more than usual, wearing brown linen trousers and a short-sleeve button-up blouse, both covered in cat hair.

Annie spots shadowy sweat stains spreading under the armpits of Dr. Patel's blouse. It's steamy on the porch, but Annie can't bear to have someone in the house right now. She can't deal with the intrusive thoughts, the nagging questions, and the cleanup afterward. Despite the heat, Annie pulls her cardigan tight around her body like a suit of armor.

"And, before I forget, you should have received your medication by now. How are you doing with it?"

"Ah, yes. It arrived. Thank you." Annie elaborates, glad to have a relatively easy question to answer. "I've been taking the higher dosage for about a week now. It nauseated me at first, but that's gone away."

"Well, keep at it. Remember it's a cumulative effect. It could take another week or more to see results. Still, I have high hopes it will help given your history." Dr. Patel keeps her beady eyes trained on Annie. "So you also mentioned that a lot has transpired since our last visit. Tell me about that."

Annie hesitates. Her visit to the police station left her feeling dirty. Not wanting to relive the experience, she hasn't talked to anyone about it outside of Ed and a hurried text to Ike telling him everything's fine. But the fact that Dr. Patel has driven out to Mount Pleasant to help her compels Annie to be frank.

"The police investigation into my benefactor's disappearance has taken a turn. You may have seen the story on the news—they found her drowned in Lake Gaither."

Dr. Patel inhales. "No, I don't follow the news. It disturbs me and, in turn, upsets my cats. They're very intuitive." But the doctor's curiosity has been piqued, and she whispers, "Do the police suspect *foul play*, as they say?"

The Lake Gaither crime scene photo flashes in Annie's head. Each time she envisions it, her brain embellishes the images. Byrdie's round cheek pitted with black spots, ulcers—more disgusting than any lotus pod. A torn pant leg revealing discolored flesh, eaten away as if by bacteria or scavenging organisms. Red, broken blood vessels spidering through unseeing eyes. Visceral details that seemed far too real to be imagined. Had she dreamed them? *Were you there?*

"The police questioned me about the last time I saw Byrdie. They seem to think I'm involved in her death somehow. But there's been no official statement. I mean, for all we know, Miss Fenton might have gotten disoriented, wandered to the lake, and fell in the water."

"That must be stressful. I can't imagine. But I'm sure the police are just doing their jobs. Though it might feel like they're pointing a finger at you, I suspect they are questioning others, investigating every avenue. Clearly, they don't have any real conviction you're guilty, or you and I would not be sitting on your lovely porch chatting."

"Then why does it feel like everyone is talking about me behind my back? I walked downtown to the coffee shop the other day and overheard two women gossiping about the case. I'm not sure, but I-I think they said my name." She recalls fleeing the shop empty-handed with no plans to return until the investigation ended.

"Have you told anyone that you've been interviewed? Is that public information?" Dr. Patel asks.

"Well, no. Only my lawyer and my friend Ike. He doesn't exactly hang out in suburban mom circles, though."

"In that case, I would posit that while it might seem like there are whispers, most people are too wrapped up in their own lives. Even the most avid gossip hounds lose interest quickly and move on to the next rumor." Dr. Patel smiles reassuringly. "Annie, you're not guilty—you don't have to live your life like you are. The best thing to do right now is to go about your business as usual."

Annie nods. She takes a deep breath, inhaling the warm, earthy smell radiating off the sunbaked wood planks. Momentarily aware of her surroundings and outside her head, she loosens the protective grip on her cardigan.

"Now, I'd like to pick up where we left off last time. We were discussing the extent to which thoughts of your mother still exert control over you."

"What? Did I— I don't think I said that exactly," Annie says, genuinely confused.

"You've told me she perceived threats everywhere, real or imagined. Hoarding things, clinging to *you*, made her feel protected. How did this behavior affect you?"

"I wasn't like her. I didn't think everyone was out to get me. I wasn't paran—" Annie stops abruptly, hit by the realization that she's just spent ten minutes accusing perfect strangers of whispering behind her back.

"I agree that your OCD manifested itself differently. Contamination, disgust. Your mother was anxious for her life. But you— what things disturbed you the most as a child?"

Annie reflects a moment, her mind landing on an oddly specific memory, something she hasn't thought about in years. "Once, when I was maybe eight or nine, my mom caught me looking at the cover of *Rolling Stone* in the library. The band on the front was naked. She said it was perverted, asked me why I had a filthy mind. I'll never forget how she looked at me, disgusted."

"Why do you think that incident stuck with you all these years?"

"I felt humiliated, dirty. My mother was all I had. I suppose she made sure of that. The thought of her rejecting me was terrifying. I walked on eggshells to avoid her disapproval."

"Did you ever try to rebel against her control?"

In response to Dr. Patel's question, the audio memory replays in Annie's head.

Bones snap. Steel crunches. The sick thud of a skull slamming against the dashboard. Screams. A child cries.

She can never tell anyone about the day she watched the life drain out of another human being's face. So she lies.

"Not really. I wasn't a rebellious teenager."

"Well, I'm curious about something. Have you ever reflected on how your relationship with your mother may influence your interactions with your daughter today? Tabitha must be what . . . fifteen?"

"What?" The question catches Annie off guard. "I've always kept Tabby away from my mother's illness. I don't involve her in my own either." She shakes her head vigorously. "And with Duncan as a father, she has everything she could ever want."

Dr. Patel counters Annie's defensiveness with a gentle tone. "In my experience, kids notice a lot more than we give them credit for. We must try to maintain an open line of communication."

Don't let this woman frame you as a bad mother. Get rid of her.

Faced with Annie's stony silence, Dr. Patel forges on. "When it comes to your OCD—and your mother's—try to remember it isn't your fault.

"Research indicates OCD patients have a disconnect between the brain system that recognizes wrongs and the system that allows them to properly address those wrongs. Think of it like this: You're driving. You see a pedestrian collapsed in the road. You know you need to stop, so you slam your foot on the brake, but the brake isn't physically attached to any part that can stop the wheels."

Tears well up in Annie's eyes. Dr. Patel's description captures the powerlessness she feels with OCD. The endless cycle of distress, doubt, and compulsion—not being able to stop yourself even when you recognize what you're doing isn't working.

"I can see my metaphor hit home. It's scary to feel as if you have no control." Dr. Patel pauses a moment before continuing. "Presently, beyond the police inquiry and the loss of your mother, are there other sources of stress that might be affecting your mental health?"

"I've had doubts about my marriage, even questioned if my husband has been faithful." Immediately, Annie regrets her carelessness. Dr. Patel's past acquaintance with Duncan slipped her mind. It wouldn't be right to accuse him of infidelity without hard evidence—evidence that she'd been too cowardly thus far to acquire by confronting Millie Rae. Annie backtracks. "It's nothing. Please forget I said anything."

But it's too late; Dr. Patel's dark eyes have taken on a new intensity. With a raptorlike focus, they pierce her patient's flesh. "What prompted these doubts? I'm sure Duncan is devoted to you and Tabby."

Annie obfuscates. "I-I don't know. It's hard when I'm alone. Too much time to worry, I guess. All the thinking in circles makes my head fuzzy."

Dr. Patel relaxes, accepting the explanation. "It's a difficult time, no doubt. I think you're doing splendidly. Keep on with the medication and, like I said, try to remember the good memories too—the, what was it, star anise?" The doctor giggles, a youthful affectation incongruous with her coffee-stained teeth.

Dr. Patel glances at her watch. "Oh dear, I need to get home. Dirk expects me to make dinner—busy day or no."

Reading the quizzical look on Annie's face, she adds, "Dirk is diabetic. It's very rare in cats, but I don't suppose we get to choose our ailments, do we?"

Six months ago, Annie could count the number of times she'd flown on one hand. Now, she and Duncan had visited dozens of countries on what he'd dubbed the "Annie Meet World Tour."

She'd had misgivings about such a long trip, but he had an answer for everything. The cost—he'd pay all expenses from his trust fund. Her job—gallery assistant jobs were a dime a dozen and she'd easily find another. His career—he was fresh off his stint in Kabul and due for a vacation. The Morningside Heights studio they'd shared since she graduated from RISD and he from Columbia's journalism graduate program—it was too small and cramped anyway. And most concerning to her, her mom—they'd arranged to have money wired back to her each month. And besides, she'd been doing better lately, working part-time again.

Annie had felt lost during the fourteen months Duncan was embedded in Afghanistan. Together, they had explored New York, dined out, and swum in his social circles. Alone, she ventured no farther than the 1 train to her job at the gallery and back. She had no incentive to propel her outside, no friends of her own. Having showered after work, the idea of stepping outside onto the urine-soaked streets disgusted her. When he returned, Duncan was shocked to find her looking wan, depressed, and nearly unrecognizable. Her hands were covered in tiny blisters from overwashing.

He'd always run somewhat dispassionate. This Annie attributed to his staid upbringing. But Kabul exacerbated this trait to the extent that he seemed callous at times. His approach to Annie's condition was entirely pragmatic—a problem to be solved. The "Annie Meet World Tour" was his solution. It was also his way of trying to shake off the violent memories that followed him from Kabul.

At times, she was alarmed by the intensity of his planning wherein he detailed out their agenda in fifteen-minute increments. However, she convinced herself the trip would be good for them as their relationship had been suffering. Upon his return, there had been no grand romantic reunion. They'd had sex once, an impersonal fumble that lasted less than two minutes. Duncan was checked out.

Annie blamed herself for the lack of intimacy—her depression and anxiety. Traveling outside her comfort zone was the least she could do. So, despite her reservations, she went along with her boyfriend's tightly orchestrated schedule. She quit her job, got a passport, and packed her only piece of luggage, a dingy nylon duffel bag.

The trip was, indeed, good for her. She drank in the splendor of the Louvre, wiggled her toes in the pristine sand of hidden Mediterranean beaches, and took in the majesty of the Alps by rail and all the myriad wonders she'd only seen flattened in the pages of library books. Like a tonic, it injected her with renewed vibrancy and served as a much-needed distraction from her anxieties.

Though they traveled together, Duncan remained emotionally distant. By day, they'd sightsee. Conversation was superficial. He made it clear he wasn't ready to discuss his time in Kabul, and Annie wasn't the sort to push him into anything. At night, she would retire to their rented accommodations, exhausted from the excitement of the day's sights. Often restless and unable to sleep, Duncan would take long walks. Once, on the Dalmatian coast, she awakened during the night and from their balcony spied him huddled on the beach, staring blankly at the black waves of the Adriatic.

By the time they reached Istanbul, he seemed more responsive.

Upon returning from his nocturnal wandering, he took to waking her up. He'd say nothing and without warning, he'd take her with his mouth until she howled. It was sudden, explosive, and afterward, he'd retreat inward again. Still, she saw it as an improvement over his passionless state.

After Istanbul they journeyed to Cairo, then Mumbai, Bangkok, and now Hong Kong. They skipped Vietnam entirely, in part because somehow it seemed disloyal to return without her mother. She'd save that homecoming for another day when her mom could join.

The toll of traveling in Asia was beginning to wear on her. She was tired of being mistaken for a native of whatever country they happened to be in and scolded for not speaking the language—an old street vendor asked Duncan, who knew functional Cantonese, if Annie was mute or brain-damaged. On top of this, she was laid up for several days in Hong Kong with food poisoning.

To make Annie's recovery easier, they had splurged on a luxury hotel suite overlooking Victoria Harbour. "You should still go on the hike to the Dragon's Back today, Duncan. I'm fine here," she insisted, sprawled out on the crisp linen sheets in the hotel's Frette robe.

"I've been to Hong Kong a few times. It's okay. I shouldn't leave you when you're sick," he said.

"But you've never trekked along that trail. You've said a bunch of times how much you've been looking forward to it. Plus, I'd feel better if you weren't right outside the door when I'm rushing in and out of the bathroom," she said, fanning her hand over her nose. "Besides, there's room service here if I need anything. It's practically paradise!" She gestured across the sizable suite, which featured an entire wall comprising a floor-to-ceiling window.

It was enough to convince him, and he set off with a giant rucksack. Annie curled up in bed with a paperback thriller she'd picked up in a glassy Causeway Bay bookstore. By late afternoon she'd finished it. She began to get restless and passed the time looking down at the streets teeming with busy commuters, shoppers, tourists, and touts. She thought of venturing out but knew she wasn't up to facing the oppressive subtropic humidity and the rank sewage smells of the city.

She regarded an old woman, balding and stooped, guiding a small backpacked child across the busy intersection. If it weren't for the war, Mẹ would have stayed in Vietnam. Annie could have had a grandmother to help take care of her—of them. She thought about the father and brother she never met. They could've been a normal family.

With a pang of resentment, Annie turned her attention away from the bustling street. Boats skimmed across the glistening water of the bay. On the Kowloon side, neon signs towered high above the streets, unlit like dead giants.

Something in the window of the by-the-hour motel directly across the street caught her eye. A flash of skin—a couple having sex. She watched, transfixed, though the man was distinctly unattractive, a doughy, gray-skinned businessman. The woman was Asian, no more than twenty-five. They shifted positions and the woman's palms were pressed against the glass. Her lips moved, making sounds, but she was clearly bored. A minute later, they got dressed, and Annie wasn't surprised to see the man pass the young woman a few bills.

The woman stepped over to the light of the window to check the bills, making no effort to hide the activity or her naked body. As she stuffed the money into her purse, she glanced up and her eyes met Annie's. The woman held her gaze, defiant, before stalking away from the window.

Guilty, Annie looked down. A neon-yellow cleaning cart, parked in the hallway a half-dozen floors below, caught her eye for a split second. But it was the movement in an adjacent room that stopped her. A hand jerked the cheap motel shade too hard, so its recoil knocked down the tension rod.

She observed a man bending over to pick it up. The perspective was stilted. She had to peer down at a steep angle, yet there was something familiar about him. As he stretched up to restore the rod, his undershirt lifted, exposing his stomach. She recognized the pattern of hair—sandy blond tinged with red crawling down sinewy muscle. Even from that distance, that angle, she knew who it was.

CHAPTER 34

Annie watches Dr. Patel's hunter-green Audi speed out of the driveway. Baring herself to the psychiatrist left Annie feeling soiled and spent. She undresses and steps into the shower, unable to fathom how she almost let slip the details of Duncan's potential affair with Millie Rae. Dr. Patel had drawn Annie out, gotten her to talk about her childhood and Me. This left her disoriented, vulnerable. Was the doctor intentionally manipulating Annie?

Alone in the house, naked in the shower, Annie lets out something between a growl and a roar. Guttural and dripping with frustration. She knows her thoughts sound paranoid, but she can't help going over them again and again in her head.

Bowed by the weight of her suspicions, she crouches down, hugging her knees, as the shower spits down on her. She can't bring herself to accept that Duncan would cheat on her with Millie Rae. Extroverted and charismatic, the young, blond sorority sister was so unlike Annie. Not his type—but, given societal norms, maybe "young, blond" was every man's type these days. She strained to remember any particular faces from Duncan's past, the time before they'd dated in college. He'd mentioned "friends" and "hanging out" with various girls but nothing serious, and it was so long ago.

Annie dresses hastily and climbs into bed with her laptop. She types Byrdie's name into the search bar in what has become a nightly ritual. When her eyes land on the headline, she gasps. HEIR-

0

ESS DEATH RULED HOMICIDE. The article includes a brief summary of the coroner's report, stating that Byrdie Fenton's death was neither an accident nor suicide. There's also a quote from Detective Harper: *"We urge the public to come forward with any pertinent information. If you know anything that can help with the investigation into Miss Fenton's death, please call our anonymous tip line at . . ."*

She doesn't finish reading, already tapping out Ed's personal number, which he'd given her "for emergencies."

"Annie, I was just about to call you," he says.

"So you saw the news article?"

"No—uh—not yet, but I know of it. The police have reached out to me to schedule another interview with you."

"What? Why—"

"They're grasping at straws," he says. "It's in your best interest to continue to cooperate fully at this point. You have nothing to hide." He pauses, as if waiting for Annie to concur, but she says nothing.

The next morning, Annie waits in front of the police station. Eyes downcast, she clutches her purse against her chest like a shield. When a hand lands on the small of her back, she jumps and spins around. But before she's even seen his face, she knows it's Ed with his subtle aftershave and reassuring presence. He looks handsome in a tailored navy suit and red silk tie knotted in a perfect double Windsor.

"Good morning, Annie. You're early. Detective Harper should be ready for us soon." He ushers her through the double doors. "Have you been looking after yourself? I've been worried."

"What's this about? Do they know something?" Annie asks, unable to contain her anxiety for another second.

Ed gives her an odd look. Just then, a door opens at the end of the hall. To Annie's surprise, Ike emerges from it. He's staring at his shoes, clearly lost in thought. His lip has healed, bruises faded, but the light is missing from his eyes—the spark that was as distinctive as a birthmark or scar on anyone else.

"Ike!" she calls out, rushing toward him. His head snaps up, but he turns away to avoid eye contact.

"What are you doing here?" Annie asks.

Ike cuts her off with a sidelong hug, a ruse to whisper in her ear. "Careful. They know about the key."

His words don't register. *What key?* She pulls away to look him squarely in the face, but the desk officer interrupts before she can utter another word. "Mr. Perez. They're ready for you, sir."

Annie's head spins as Ike leaves and Ed escorts her into the interview room; his hand, again, presses against her lower back. He pulls out a chair for her, sizing up the way she drapes her shawl across the seat before balancing herself on the edge.

Detective Harper greets them with a staccato "Mr. Perez. Mrs. Shaw. Morning." His demeanor impenetrable, he might be filing murder charges against her this morning or merely giving her a ticket for double-parking. "Thank you for your continuing cooperation. We've asked you here to share some new developments in the investigation of Miss Fenton's death."

"I-I saw the news last night," Annie says. "Homicide? It wasn't an accident?"

"Yes. But before we get too deep into the details, I wanted to give you an opportunity to share anything that might have occurred to you since we last spoke. Now would be the time to tell me." He pauses and stares long and hard at Annie.

She feels her face flush red. Doubt has seeped into every crevice of her being. The same way she can't be certain she didn't run over the ginger cat or that she was not sitting on the "dirty" side of the shawl—the side that touched the rideshare seat—she cannot be sure her hands are clean when it comes to Byrdie. The stress of questioning herself constantly, not knowing her own mind, has been wearing on her more and more lately. It was as if some part of her floated out of her body and did things she couldn't be certain of. Annie still has no recollection of calling Gabe, but clearly, she had. This morning she found a jar of dark cherry jam sitting on the counter with the lid off, buzzing with fruit flies—she didn't remember having any. If this seasoned detective is so certain she was involved, maybe she was. She's desperate to cling to any kind of certainty even if it points to her own guilt.

Fortunately, Ed interjects. "My client is not here to answer open-ended questions, Detective. If we had any additional information, I assure you that we would have notified you posthaste."

"Of course," Harper says, smiling in mock defeat. "We were hoping your client could help us clarify some specific details, a few lingering points of confusion." He turns to Annie. "Did Miss Fenton have any health issues that you were aware of?"

"Not that I know of . . . I mean, she was old," Annie says.

"So when you last saw her, the evening you picked up your portfolio, she seemed fine?"

"Yes. I mean no. She was disoriented. As I said, she'd been talking about her late friend Claire as though she were alive."

"What are you getting at, Detective?" Ed asks.

"Well, Miss Fenton's autopsy has given rise to more questions than answers. Six months ago her physician gave her, more or less, a clean bill of health. Yet the postmortem indicated kidney failure and ketoacidosis. She has no family or personal history of kidney disease or diabetes."

"You must be kidding. The woman was in her late eighties, Detective. It's a miracle you didn't find *more* undetected health issues," Ed says.

Ignoring the interruption, Harper continues, "Furthermore, Miss Fenton's longtime housekeeper, Lydia Ivanova, observed a marked deterioration in her employer's mental and physical condition over the final weeks of her life. You started seeing her more regularly around that time, Mrs. Shaw. Is that correct?"

"Y-yes. For the mezzo fresco. I told—"

Harper cuts her off. "After reading the autopsy results, my team worked with Mrs. Ivanova to collect samples of any remaining items she consumed with any regularity prior to her death. We had them tested for contamination." The detective rests his elbows on the table, fingertips touching in a pyramid. "The results came back. It seems Miss Fenton was gradually poisoned. Hence, the coroner's classification of homicide."

Annie's hand flies to her mouth. Instantly wary, Ed narrows his eyes. It's the first time he's hearing about this development.

Harper continues. "Our investigation has pinpointed the source of the poisoning: a bottle of home-brewed alcohol."

"The moonshine?" Annie whispers.

"Would there be any reason for your fingerprints to be on that bottle, Mrs. Shaw?" Harper asks.

"I don't remember touching it . . . I can't be sure."

Ed intervenes before Annie can make another mistake. "Your case is hanging by a thread if you're swearing to the purity of old Southern moonshine. Bootleggers were notorious for using all kinds of substances to boost the alcohol content of their brew. There's no way of knowing when or how any toxic substance got into Miss Fenton's drink."

"Quite correct, Mr. Perez." Harper angles his body, facing Annie dead-on. "But Byrdie Fenton isn't the first elderly woman in your life to die suddenly in the last few months. Isn't that right, Mrs. Shaw? My condolences—but if I'm not mistaken, your mother passed away recently."

Unable to speak, Annie stares at him aghast.

"It seems the cremation happened almost immediately, too soon for an autopsy—"

Red-faced, Ed interrupts. "How dare you? My client has been completely cooperative. She is here of her own free will and has nothing to hide. If you have evidence, make an arrest. We're getting tired of these games."

"Of course," Harper says, smiling in mock defeat. "Thank you both for your patience. One final point of inquiry. Our investigation found that the wrought-iron gates at Pinewood Manor date back to the Civil War. They've been kept in pristine condition and require a unique hand-forged key. Aside from Miss Fenton and her housekeeper, do you know of anyone who has such a key?"

Suddenly light-headed, Annie feels as if the oxygen has been sucked out of the room. Years ago, Byrdie bestowed a tarnished key upon Annie. She needed a cat-sitter for Shug, and Lydia was on her annual pilgrimage home to Bulgaria. "My Siamese doesn't take to everyone, dear, but she just loves you—you both being from the Orient and all," Byrdie insisted, stroking Annie's silky black hair in much the same way she petted the cat. Afterward, the old woman rebuffed her repeated attempts to return the key, concocting tasks she needed Annie to do that her gardening service or housekeeper "couldn't be trusted with."

"I have a key," Annie whispers. She realizes how guilty she sounds. "But I didn't . . . I couldn't have . . ."

Harper cuts off her denial. "As you know, the gate was unlocked the morning Mr. Oteh arrived to find Miss Fenton missing. One might argue the lock could be picked, but that would likely result in signs of stress, scratches to the antique metal. In many ways, old 'technology' can be so much more helpful in an investigation than modern security systems. We'll have to investigate this further, but I wanted to give you a chance to tell your side of the story."

"I think we're done here, Detective," Ed says. He casts a glance at Annie, concern now blooming on his face.

Harper stands up to shake hands, but his arm falls back down to his side when it's clear nobody is going to reciprocate.

CHAPTER 35

Perched on the edge of a park bench in Falls Church, Virginia, Annie scans the crowd looking for Ike. He wanted to meet in person but hadn't been able to get away from his family's convenience store for an extended period. Knowing Annie's discomfort driving, Falls Church was their compromise: a short trip over the river for Ike and a location Annie knew, having driven her mother to the big Vietnamese markets here twice a month.

In the distance, she spots him. His face stark amid the throngs of Asian schoolkids and midday shoppers. To any passersby they would be a mismatched twosome, but the bonds they share as refugees are strong.

The plane that brought her to Providence's T. F. Green International Airport was the first she'd ever stepped foot on. In college, Annie found herself suddenly having to master things others took for granted, like eating with a knife and fork. At home she and her mom used chopsticks or a mismatched fork or spoon. Annie—who created her RISD admissions portfolio with dollar-store watercolor paper, a Prang paint set, and the anemic brush that came with it—was mystified by the freshman supply list packed with foreign and expensive items like gouache and gesso.

Both Ike and Annie were quiet and observant, traits that worked in their favor. Leaving a gap allowed others to fill in the space with their own stories. Affluent classmates interpreted Annie's skin-and-bones frame as heroin chic rather than malnutrition. They assumed her ragged clothes were thrift-store finds rather than hand-me-downs from a Catholic charity.

The two friends played the part of carefree, cosmopolitan art students, copying the rich kids' cadence and disaffected mannerisms. It became an inside gag. When offered party drugs, they'd turn up their noses and exchange knowing smirks. Invariably, the other kids would assume their drugs weren't a pure enough grade or on trend. It never occurred to them that the two first-generation immigrants had never even sampled drugs or that both needed to get up early for their food-service jobs slinging tempeh and vegan sloppy joes.

As long as they remained cloistered on campus, they were protected by this perceived privilege. Even venturing a few miles out beyond the Providence city limits changed everything. They were no longer contained and safe. Especially not Ike. The eye of the beholder would shift suddenly, transforming him from a soft-spoken, international art school prodigy into a menacing Black man.

The image of Ike's bloody, bruised face in her driveway flashes in front of Annie's eyes, only to be usurped by the real Ike, whose superficial wounds have healed. He sits down beside her. His tone is serious.

"Annie, I wanted to explain face-to-face. The police were pressuring me. They said they could charge me with breaking and entering for letting myself into Pinewood Manor to look for Byrdie. They asked how I got through the gate that morning without breaking the lock. They questioned my statement that it was ajar when I arrived—and then they asked about a key."

"I didn't even think to mention the key before," Annie says. *He won't look you in the eye.* A thought pierces Annie like an arrow through the heart. "You don't think I had anything to do with Byrdie's death, do you?"

"If I did, I would not have tried to warn you." He regards her sternly. "What I do believe is the police can jump to conclusions at the slightest provocation. I have firsthand experience." As he says this, he traces over the subtle raised scar that's formed above his eye.

Feeling deeply for her dear friend, Annie reaches over and caresses his cheek. A nosy Vietnamese granny pushing a baby stroller gawks openly at them. Gently, Ike removes Annie's hand and places it onto her lap. Neither feels the need to speak.

Despite Byrdie's assumptions, Ike has dated men and women for as long as Annie has known him. The timing had never been right for them, but Annie sometimes wonders what would have happened if she hadn't met Duncan when she did.

At the time, she was a twenty-one-year-old virgin. Annie, a reluctant third wheel, trailed behind Ike and his then-boyfriend Geoff. They were headed up the hill for a free concert at Brown. As the couple held hands and laughed, jealousy welled up inside Annie. Ike was the only real friend she'd ever had, the only person she'd been close to besides her mother. And they'd shared that drunken kiss—her first—freshman year.

She found herself picking at Geoff with an internal monologue of catty criticisms. *He isn't nearly good enough for Ike. Khaki cargo shorts—no real art student would be caught dead in those. What he lacks in charisma and talent, he compensates for in body odor.* Once, on a whim, she'd tried to draw Geoff's face from memory; the result was a featureless blob.

A few weeks before, Annie had found herself alone in Ike's apartment. She'd let herself in, as usual, for their Thursday movie rental night. It was his turn to pick the video. While waiting, she'd poured herself a shot of fruity sake. Ike detested the sweet stuff but kept a bottle on the shelf just for her. She was surprised he wasn't home until she glanced at his semi-ironic *Firefighters of Providence* calendar. He'd drawn a heart around the date. At once, she remembered it was Ike's six-month anniversary with Geoff.

Geoff. It irked Annie that this hack was in her fine arts painting program. Of course, his mother was director of the Museum of

Fine Arts in Houston and a RISD alumna. As she cast a possessive gaze around Ike's apartment, her eyes landed upon a canvas. A painting of Ike. The work was lackluster and uninspired. The very conventionality of it irritated Annie. However, she could never share her true feelings with Ike. Part of her didn't want to risk hurting her friend, and an even larger part didn't want to risk losing him. Lonely and feeling sorry for herself, Annie helped herself to a couple more shots of sake before leaving.

By the time they passed through the Van Wickle Gates, delicate wrought iron wedged between two clunky brick pillars, Annie felt acutely aware of her status as a hanger-on. Ike and Geoff immediately joined the throng of dancing kids on the College Green, while Annie swayed awkwardly to the music a few feet away. Because her mother kept her close at home, she'd come to college having never attended a sleepover, camp, or school dance. After a few minutes of lonely shimmying, she sought refuge in a quiet corner, sitting down on the steps of a lecture hall overlooking the Green. That was when she heard it, felt it. A gagging sound immediately followed by a heavy wet plop.

"Dude, watch where you're going . . . sitting . . . heh," said a smirking boy in a Phi Kappa Psi cap. As he stumbled over her, she realized he'd thrown up on her skirt. Rather than lashing out at him, she instantly felt ashamed and embarrassed. Her face grew hot, and she imagined that every single set of eyes on the Green were staring at her. She was no longer invisible, no longer safe.

"Are you okay?"

She nodded and looked up to see that the soft, concerned voice had come from an enormous, sandy-haired guy. Before she could react further, he flew down the steps two at time. She gawked as he grabbed the frat boy by the shoulder, spun him around, and demanded he apologize. Not waiting for a response, the gentle giant dragged the drunk up the steps like a doll and propped him in front of her.

"Say sorry, jackoff. NOW!"

No longer smirking, the frat boy dutifully muttered an apology before slithering off.

For the first time, Annie and her mysterious savior actually looked at each other. He wore a maroon rugby shirt that looked like it belonged on his athletic frame. He could very well have been an actual rugby player. Both his jeans and leather loafers were expensive but well-worn, indicative of someone accustomed to wealth with no desire to flaunt it.

Duncan's soft blue eyes appeared as safe and expansive as the College Green below. They drew her in, and she allowed herself to fall, drifting deeper and deeper toward him. Once again, she felt protected and invisible.

The afternoon dismissal bell sounds at the nearby elementary school, bringing Annie back to the present. "That is my cue," Ike says, rising from the bench and stretching his lanky frame. "I have to be back at the store by four. I'm glad we spoke in person, Annie."

Then he opens his arms wide, and she slips into his friendly embrace.

"Thanks. I miss you so much, Ike." She pulls back, clasping his hands in hers. "Let's get together after this nightmare is over. The whole thing is insanity—how can they think I killed Byrdie! I'm not some maniac . . ."

For the first time in a long while, Ike's impish grin returns. "We-ell, I think my old friend Geoff would disagree. I never told you we knew about what happened to his senior project."

"What do you mean?" Annie asks, bewildered. Alone in Ike's apartment staring at the mundane portrait, she picked up a dry paintbrush and imagined how she'd improve it. The bristles grazed the canvas as she tenderly traced over the curves of Ike's face. After a few minutes, she put the brush down and left, locking the door behind herself.

The incident was sad and maybe a little pathetic, but what could Ike be referring to? "What happened to Geoff's senior project? I don't know what you're talking about."

Ike takes a step back, seeming to read the distress on Annie's face. "It was nothing. We came back that night and saw the slash in the painting Geoff did of me. You were the only one I gave spare keys to besides him. I helped him patch and gesso the back. It was fine." Ike stares at Annie as if seeing her for the first time. "I knew it must've been an accident, but he had some preposterous theory that you stabbed the painting out of jealousy. 'A fit of rage' was the phrase he used."

◆

Slumped on the sofa, Annie flicks mindlessly through television channels. She'd denied damaging the painting intentionally but spent the next six hours racking her brain, trying to make sense of it all. For the umpteenth time, she reconstructs the scene in her mind, straining to recover long-forgotten details. She'd held a dry paintbrush against the canvas. How could the piece have gotten damaged that way? Perhaps a minor scratch to Geoff's clumsily applied acrylic—nothing more. But Ike had used the word *slash*.

Slash. The word triggers a mental image. A palette knife resting on the easel ledge. Cadmium blue paint on the blade and handle. Scrubbing her hands as the dorm's white porcelain sink fills with blue water. *Could she have mistakenly picked up the knife instead of the brush?*

Annie clutches her head, unable to remember with any certainty. One night, twenty years ago. A lifetime—death—in between.

Her phone buzzes, making her jump. A text from an unknown number. She clicks it and gapes at the screen. A grainy photo of her and Ike, taken today. Seated hip-to-hip on the park bench. Her hand caressing his cheek as she gazes into his eyes. The message reads:

Does Duncan know?

HONG KONG, 2002

Had he seen her? It wasn't likely, but she couldn't be sure. Annie immediately sank out of view and made her way to the bed, knowing her knees were in danger of buckling.

Her initial confusion quickly gave way to a sense of betrayal. Instead of hiking, Duncan had spent the day—or at least the hour—in a seedy hot-sheet motel. She fought back a wave of nausea. Their relationship had been on the rocks, but it was getting better lately. Her mind struggled to devise an explanation for what she'd just seen, anything other than Duncan cheating on her. Unable to avoid the truth, Annie felt not only hurt, but incredibly gullible as well.

All of a sudden, it occurred to her how vulnerable she was—in a foreign land, no money of her own, and still very little travel sense. She'd have to ask *him* for help getting home. She'd foolishly put herself in the position of trusting her boyfriend with every-thing.

Duncan came back to the room about an hour later, tired and drenched with sweat. "The heat is brutal out there. It's a sauna," he said as he plopped his backpack down on the floor. He hadn't made eye contact with her yet. When she didn't respond, he looked over at the bed and inquired, "Are you feeling any better?"

"No, definitely not."

"Do you need to go to the clinic? There should be a walk-in place near the YMCA." His crystal-blue eyes were clouded with what seemed like concern—or was it annoyance? However, he didn't join her on the bed, explaining that he stank from hiking.

She couldn't hold it in any longer. "Stop it, Duncan. Stop lying to me! I trusted you."

All the color drained from his face. His expression was one of a cornered animal. "What do you mean?"

"I saw you! You were in that motel across the street. Was she a hooker? Do I need to get tested? What the fuck, Duncan. I trusted you." She broke down into angry tears.

"Is that what you think? I could never . . ." He exhaled loudly and paced to the picture window, for a moment staring at the sky-scrapers outlined against a red, red sky. When he turned back to face Annie, he looked much older than a man in his twenties, and he sounded defeated. "I tried, but I couldn't go through with it."

She grabbed a tissue from the silvery holder on the nightstand, listening but giving no response.

"You haven't been well and I . . ." His voice broke. "I haven't been either." Real tears spilled down his face. She'd never seen him cry and was shocked by the sight. Despite her disgust—he was probably filthy from the motel—she got up and put her arm around him.

His body was racked by sobs. "I haven't been myself since Kabul. That fucking assignment. I saw things . . ." He straightened himself up and looked into her eyes. "I haven't been able to get an erection, Annie, not really. I wanted to fix myself by hiring a pro-fessional, but it didn't work. I don't know what I was thinking. But you forgive me?"

Annie pulled herself free and backed away, overcome with dis-gust. "I love you, and I want to understand. But I don't— I mean, a prostitute? I just don't know."

His eyes narrowed. "I never ask you for *anything*. I take care of everything. Of *you*, as if you were a child! Why can't you give me a break? I've never, *ever* cheated on you." There was a loud thump on the wall from the next room—too much noise.

In an instant, Duncan's posture deflated. He reached toward Annie. "Can we lie down? I need to hold you."

Annie, thoroughly unsettled by her boyfriend's quick shifts in mood, backed away. The thought of his touch on her skin repulsed her. Suddenly, the suite seemed to shrink until it was too small for the both of them. His face, the smell of his sweat, even the pitch of his voice disgusted her.

"I need some air . . . space to think. Take a shower, lie down, okay? I'll be back later." But even as she said it, she knew it was a lie.

CHAPTER 36

As Dr. Patel predicted, the new sertraline dosage was already proving effective. Annie's results were gradual but noticeable, the intrusive thoughts slightly less frequent and slightly easier to dismiss. Just as her irrational concerns have begun to diminish, her all-too-real problems have flourished.

Is Duncan cheating on her? What happened to Byrdie? Who sent the photo of her and Ike?

Annie considered calling Millie Rae directly about the affair. But it was unlikely she'd get a straight answer and didn't want to risk humiliating herself in front of the sorority sister, who, judging by her online profile, was queen of the world. Besides, even if Millie Rae did confess, Annie wouldn't be able to confront her husband for weeks. With Duncan still unreachable on assignment, she'd be left in an even worse purgatory. At least by doing nothing she could preserve the possibility in her mind that he hadn't cheated.

Try as she might, Annie could not explain Byrdie's death. She knew of nobody who would want to hurt the dowager. Perhaps, as Ed suggested, the Fenton family moonshine had been tainted decades ago. That would explain the poisoning but not how the old woman ended up at the bottom of Lake Gaither. A random act of violence would explain the latter but not the former. Whenever Annie considered these theories, Detective Harper's leathery face loomed in her mind's eye, his expression accusing her over and over.

She spent hours ruminating over the third question. Who sent the black-and-white photo, along with the insinuating message: *Does Duncan know?* She'd called Ike immediately after receiving it. He was confused and mildly alarmed but soon fell into a giggling fit at the "ridiculous" idea of him and Annie being linked romantically. His reaction stung, but she hid her embarrassment by joining in the laughter.

Her suspicions quickly fell on Millie Rae. She was a journalism student, after all, who potentially had a vested interested in splitting up Annie and Duncan. An unknown blackmailer was another possibility that sprang to mind. However, when days passed with no demands, Annie surmised the photograph might have come from one of the local journalists covering Byrdie's murder. Rumors swirled in the small town but without enough evidence to point the finger at her in print, maybe they'd had her followed. She also considered Ray Park and his grudge against her, but he and Danielle, seemingly more lovey-dovey than ever, were off on a Mediterranean cruise.

Annie felt vulnerable knowing that any one of these people—or even a stranger—might have it out for her. She called the Guardian Angel Sentry security company and had them add a secondary verification code. Access to the Shaw home now required both the new PIN code and biometric verification.

Now, alone in the house, she mulls over each theory in turn. Repeating the cycle of thoughts again and again yields no answers. In fact, she feels more uncertain than ever. Her stomach growls— lunchtime and she hasn't thought to eat. "At least there's one problem I can solve," she says, addressing her midsection. She slides Duncan's Santoku knife out of the wooden block and slices two pears and a wedge of brie.

She scarfs down the food then washes the knife, taking a moment to appreciate how much the new dosage has helped already. She had no thoughts of losing control, cutting herself, and had eaten the cheese without thinking about who had touched it.

Lost in thought and with the faucet running, Annie doesn't hear her phone buzzing. When she retrieves it from the counter a few minutes later, a missed-call notice pops up. Gabriel. She'd completely forgotten to return his message. So much happened since the spring festival, so many strange events crowding out her memory of the handsome stranger. He almost doesn't seem real.

She should call back now and tell him she's married—but that would be awkward. If she ignored his calls, he would soon stop trying. Gabe is a good-looking guy. Annie's certain he has no trouble dating. Catching a glimpse of herself reflected in the French doors—unkempt hair, baggy sweats, plastic slippers—she closes her eyes and allows herself to feel flattered again. In her mind, she replays their brief encounter, enjoying the rush from how he looked at her and the lightness of their conversation.

Just then, the phone comes to life again. When she sees his name on the caller ID, her stomach somersaults. She answers before second thoughts can intrude.

"Hello? This is Annie."

"He-ey! Thought I'd try one last time. Hope you don't think I'm a stalker or anything." He laughs awkwardly, then continues. "Just glad I reached you."

Annie savors the rich glide of his baritone. "Sorry, I meant to call back sooner . . ." She knows what she's supposed to say—thank him for helping her at the spring festival, apologize for any confusion, and tell him she's married. But she says none of these things.

"So about that drink . . . I was thinking tomorrow night after work? I know a great whiskey bar in Arlington, or we could grab a bite to eat."

"No . . ." She starts to refuse, then stops herself. It would be a taste of freedom—from this house, from her worries, and from the person she's become. ". . . I mean no, I don't need food. Whiskey sounds good." Slightly dizzy with nerves, she realizes too late that she sounds like a lush.

"Done. I'll text you the details. It'll be fun."

"Hey, there's something I wanted to ask you. How did you get my number?" she asks.

"Uh—you gave it to me at the fair? Sorry, I have to grab this other call. A client. See you Thursday!"

After she hangs up, Annie scrubs the kitchen from top to bottom in a form of misguided atonement. She tries to convince herself it's just a drink—nothing more. Who knows what Duncan might have done with Millie Rae? Perhaps they'd only talked on the phone, but why hadn't he mentioned it to her? And if it hadn't ended there—if they'd met in person—then what? At least Gabe was approximately Annie's age and not a college student.

When her rationalizations do nothing to absolve her, Annie decides to clean Tabby's room. Upon entering, she crinkles her nose at the unmistakably teenage combination of stinky socks, sweaty athletic gear, and too-strong perfume. Wistfully, she recalls how wonderful her daughter smelled as a baby.

Then, for the second time that afternoon, Annie's phone rings. She sets down an armful of dirty laundry. "Hello?"

"Hi, Mom. Uh . . . so this is my mandatory weekly call."

"Wow, I was just thinking about you. Are you okay? Are you eating?"

"Yes, and yes. Can I go now, Mom?"

Annie misses her daughter and tries to keep her on the line. "Funny you called when you did. I'm picking up your room."

"What the fuck, Mom? Can you *please* stay out of my room? Don't you have anything better to do?"

Silence stretches across the line. Tabby, to her credit, tries to close the wound. "I-I'm looking forward to coming home. Can't sleep here. One of the girls in my cabin snores."

Annie knows her daughter could sleep through a marching band. Sensing something is wrong, she plays along, teasing out information without appearing too obvious. "That *is* annoying. But your roommates are all nice? You like them?"

"Some are my friends. Some are super bitchy. There's this megayacht-rich girl from Florida who told everyone she saw me making out with a horse. She said I have bad breath because of it."

"*What?* That's just silly. Nobody will believe that! And you don't have bad breath."

"A bunch of them laughed, and the worst part was, she knew I could hear when she said it—that I wasn't asleep yet. I'd just been sitting up in my bunk a minute before. It was humiliating. This girl doesn't even know me!"

Careful to contain the anger welling up inside her on her daughter's behalf, Annie speaks calmly. "It's not about you—she's just trying to be queen bee. She probably sees that you're the best rider there, that you're confident and strong. Wants to knock you down a peg. My guess is if you stick with your friends and keep doing what you do, she'll lose interest."

The line is quiet, and Annie holds her breath wondering if she's somehow messed this up too. "I actually think you're right. Thanks, Mom."

Gratitude wells up in Annie's chest. She savors the rare moment of closeness. She doesn't even mind when a moment later, Tabby falls back on her trademark irreverence. "Whatever. Gotta run. And for the love of god, stay out of my room!"

After her daughter hangs up, Annie keeps the phone by her ear a moment too long, clinging to the glorious moment of clarity. The words came easily when she needed to address her daughter's bully. When it comes to her own demons, Annie remains mute, her silence complicit.

Before she leaves, she bends down to retrieve a rumpled sweatshirt that's sticking out from under the bed. When she gathers it into her arms along with the rest of the laundry, something shiny falls out, catching her eye. A strip of red foil packets. Condoms.

HONG KONG, 2002

She sized him up from behind as he stretched for the bottle of triple sec, stared as the individual muscles of his forearm flexed and contracted when he agitated the cocktail shaker.

"You've never seen the show?" the bartender asked incredulously. Even though it was busy at the hotel bar, he made time to talk to Annie.

"Not once," she said, her delicate frame already buzzed from her first cosmo and eager for a second.

"Ah, well, that's a point in your favor, I guess," he said, grinning. "Let's just say they live in New York City, go to brunch a lot, and usually they keep their bras on during sex."

"And you object to that?" Annie asked. She felt reckless, not caring that she was treading on dangerous ground. Duncan's betrayal had left her feeling ugly and stupid.

Even though they'd just met, this stranger, Winston, made her feel like the only person in the room. In response to her playful question, his onyx eyes danced from her face down to her blouse. "No, I probably would not object."

With a flourish he placed another bright cranberry concoction in front of her. "And would you like to charge that to a room?"

"No, I'll give you a card," Annie said. She slid her Visa across the table, praying that it worked. The sooner she cut herself off from Duncan the better. Since storming out of their suite, she'd spent the past hour flirting with Winston and racking her brain trying to think of the best way out of her relationship.

Annie had come to the conclusion that her boyfriend was not who she thought he was—he'd met with a prostitute, he was dirty, depraved. The more she thought about all the ways she was dependent on Duncan in this unfamiliar place, the more resentful she became.

"So you're not staying at the hotel?" he asked.

"I am. It's my b-boyfriend's suite." She faltered, then fended off tears by taking another sip. "But I'm done with him."

"Oh no! Sorry to hear that." He then had to excuse himself to tend to a trio of Australian businesswomen who already seemed tipsy though they'd just arrived at the bar. It wasn't long before he was drawn back to Annie.

"They seemed to like you," she said with a nod toward the pretty thirty-somethings who'd left in search of a table.

"Eh—being extroverted is part of the job. The accent doesn't hurt either. Tourists don't expect a Malaysian guy to sound like James Bond. You have to chat them up to get decent tips."

"Is that why you're spending so much time talking to me?"

"Hmmm . . . Maybe I'd just like to see if you keep your bra on."

CHAPTER 37

It's been years since Annie's done this, whatever *this* is. She refuses to call the drinks with Gabe a "date," because that would make seeing him much worse than it actually is. Though she'd used Duncan's affair to justify her actions, she now knows that her daughter could very well have been the one to jot down the word *condoms*. Still, it didn't explain the calls from Duncan's phone to Millie Rae.

Besides, was having a drink with Gabe so different from having a drink with Danielle? In answer, the silky strap of Annie's black lace bra, purchased just this morning, slips down from her shoulder. Feeling exposed, she draws the curtains closed even though she doesn't believe anyone is outside. She hasn't received any more surveillance photos of herself. Whoever sent the one of her and Ike has most likely given up by now, considering how infrequently she left the house. Maybe it was a bizarre prank that had little to do with her, a one-off sent by a jealous friend of Ike's.

Annie selects another dress to try on—her fourth in the last hour. She starts to wiggle into the red knit fit and flare but stops at the crunch of tires on the gravel drive. Something clicks in her head. It's Thursday. Thursday means Dr. Patel. Today's appointment slipped her mind entirely. Tossing the dress aside, Annie snatches a yellow tank top and denim skirt from a pile of lightly worn clothes and throws them on. She races downstairs, flings the door open, and steps outside, rather than inviting the doctor in.

"Hello!" Annie, out of breath, again makes excuses for the porch visit. "It's a beautiful day. Shall we meet out here?"

"Indeed, it's lovely." Dr. Patel turns to take in the Shaws' view of the gardens and the forest. Sighing with appreciation, she comments, "If I didn't need to be in the city for work, I'd want a house in the country. One just like yours."

Then, selecting a comfy wicker papasan chair, she kicks off her shoes and nestles with her feet curled under like a cat. "How have you been holding up? Have you tried to go about your normal routines as we discussed? Living your life until the investigation is over—or has it been *solved*?" Dr. Patel leans forward, evidently enthralled by the case, and in a stage whisper says, "It was the housekeeper, wasn't it? It's often the butler or the maid."

"Huh? Lydia? Absolutely not. She felt awful about not recognizing Ike, and she called him to explain that she was exhausted, having driven straight from her son and daughter-in-law's home in Pennsylvania early that morning. They have a new baby. Lydia has worked for Miss Fenton for decades and given her age, she's afraid she won't find another job. The woman is absolutely distraught."

"Fascinating. And how have you been coping day-to-day given the lack of resolution?"

Annie doesn't hear Dr. Patel's question. She's looking at her watch. She has less than an hour now to change clothes, put on makeup, and order an Uber to downtown Arlington. The rush-hour traffic can be brutal, and getting a car service to come all the way out to Mount Pleasant at that time of day won't be easy.

"Annie? I was asking how you've been coping. Are you relying on your rituals for comfort?"

"The prescription adjustment is already making a difference. The doubts, the intrusive thoughts—they're not gone but they're becoming easier to ignore. I've had a lot of distractions too."

"That's wonderful! I'm so happy to hear that." Dr. Patel nods vigorously. "And, accordingly, are you getting out more?"

This time, Annie catches herself before mentioning Gabe.

"With the medication, it's getting a bit easier to do things. I'm driving again, local roads only, but still . . ."

"Your response to this police business has been outstanding, Annie. I commend you. Controlling your own actions is all you can do when circumstances spin out."

Annie's brief moment of pride is burst by Dr. Patel's next sentence.

"Now picking up where we left off, you were having doubts about your marriage."

The skeptical look on Dr. Patel's face vexes Annie. She wants to offer some justification for her comments last session. "I don't know if Duncan is cheating on me. But without the day-to-day distraction of taking care of my mom, I'm seeing everything more clearly now." Noting the doctor's pursed lips, Annie says, "I'd talk directly with Duncan about it, but he isn't here, is he?"

Dr. Patel's beady eyes widen. "By no means was I inferring any lack of commitment on your part, Annie. I thought Duncan was back—that he'd be back by now."

"No, when he's covering a combat assignment like this there's no way to reach him. He lets me know right before he flies back."

"And do you anticipate any communication challenges when he returns?"

"Frankly, yes. We argued before he left. It's been difficult. And if I'm being honest, I'm probably the one at fault. I haven't felt like myself for a while, not since my mother died."

"Are the nightmares back, Annie?"

"Yes. I mean they were. I've been able to sleep for a few weeks now." In fact, the nightmares stopped interrupting her sleep just as her waking nightmare began. Annie tells the doctor about her disgusting visions of the lotus pods, flesh-eating bacteria, and Byrdie's similarly putrefied body.

Dr. Patel answers slowly. "An intelligent mind draws connections between disparate events. The connection, the relationship, isn't necessarily causal, though. You recognize that, don't you?"

Registering the concern on the doctor's face, Annie replies. "Of course, I do. I wasn't suggesting . . ." *Less than thirty minutes to be dressed and in downtown Arlington.*

"I'm sorry," Annie says, trying to put an end to the meeting. "To be honest, I forgot about our appointment again and arranged to meet a friend in Arlington"—she checks her watch again before continuing—"in twenty-five minutes. Maybe I should just cancel at this point."

"My dear, it's splendid that you're enjoying public places again! Don't worry about the time. I drive right by Arlington on my way home. I'll drop you off!"

It's probably not a good idea to bring the doctor so dangerously close to her liaison with Gabe. But if she doesn't go through with it tonight, she's likely to lose her nerve. Gabe will remain a question mark; Annie can't stand uncertainty. She studies Dr. Patel's beaming face for a moment and decides to risk it.

CHAPTER 38

In the car, Dr. Patel switches on the classical music station. She played violin until college, even earning a spot in the American Youth Philharmonic Orchestra. The doctor hums along with the radio as the bucolic views of Mount Pleasant change into suburban strip-mall sprawl. Dr. Patel clearly relishes driving fast, and soon they're on the highway.

Annie is surprised to see the mild-mannered doctor's aggressive driving. She weaves the sleek green Audi in and out of traffic, tailgating and honking with glee. "You've got your seat belt on, right, Annie?"

Annie double-checks her seat belt for peace of mind. She didn't have time to change with Dr. Patel waiting in the car downstairs, so she's still wearing yesterday's pale yellow tank top and denim skirt. *At least it's clean. At least you had a chance to do a couple swipes of concealer, mascara, and lipstick.* Annie catches a glimpse of herself in the side-view mirror. She reassures herself with the thought that it's better to look like you aren't trying too hard.

Dr. Patel shouts over the concerto, "I simply love driving. I didn't really learn until Providence. My parents felt it was safer to have a driver, not to mention it was easier for them to keep tabs on me!"

Annie inhales sharply as the doctor darts in front of a truck carrying gravel. "I learned as an adult also," she replies, not pointing out that her family's circumstances were decidedly different.

"I loved racing down College Hill in that beat-up VW van."

"Duncan had a VW van too!"

"One and the same!"

Annie knew that Dr. Patel and Duncan were friendly acquaintances at Brown, but she didn't realize they had been on car-sharing terms.

"That's how I learned to drive, and stick shift at that. Your husband taught me the year we were housemates."

"You and Duncan *lived* together?"

"Yes! Four of us rented an entire floor of an old Victorian off Wickenden Street junior year. Has he really not mentioned this?"

"I certainly would have remembered if he had—I didn't know the two of you were that close."

"Oh no! We weren't that close. Don't get the wrong idea," Dr. Patel says, distracted, as she capitalizes on a small gap created by a truck changing lanes. "We only dated a short time. Nothing serious. Then decided it would be better to be friends. Honestly, I have no idea why he was interested in me. I was a mess back then and truly more interested in lab hours than socializing."

Has Duncan slept with her therapist? Annie hadn't yet met Duncan then, but the revelation is more shocking to her than the possibility of his affair with Millie Rae. She had no idea her husband and therapist were anything more than pleasant acquaintances in college—two smart people who recognized and appreciated intelligence in the other but who were never especially close. Now she's learned they lived together and *dated*. The fact that it was brief matters little. *Have they seen each other naked?* She takes a deep breath, making a conscious effort to compose herself.

"And we have arrived!" Dr. Patel announces triumphantly as she parallel parks in front of Whiskey Haus, on a tree-lined street in downtown Arlington. "Five minutes faster than the navigation system said. Dirk will be pleased."

There's a lull, in which Annie starts to panic. What if Dr. Patel needs the restroom or wants to look around inside? Gabe is probably there already. She'd have to introduce them to each other.

Then as if reading her mind, Dr Patel clears her throat. "Annie?"

Annie clenches her jaw. "Yes, Dr. Patel?"

"I'd rather not pay for parking."

"Oh! Of course not." Annie is halfway out of the car before she has the presence of mind to add, "Thank you for the ride."

Dr. Patel zooms off, shouting, "See you next Thursday, same time, same place!"

Annie watches the car speed off into traffic. Relief, confusion, shock—a tangle of emotions envelops her. Duncan . . . and Dr. Patel? Any qualms Annie had about drinks with Gabe are gone—smashed to smithereens in the car ride here.

CHAPTER 39

Despite Gabe's reassuring presence, Annie's insecurity surges once they sit down at the bar. Glittering bottles line the exposed brick wall, their contents entirely foreign to her. "I haven't a clue what to order. I'm not really a big drinker."

Gabe licks his lips nervously, "Sorry. I probably should've picked a less boozy place. We could go somewhere else?"

"Oh no! I like it here," she says, looking at the pendant light fixtures and vintage advertising prints lining deep red walls. "I'll leave it to you to order. Fair warning: I have zero tolerance." She immediately regrets her words—this guy is a virtual stranger—but his quiet confidence quickly puts her at ease.

"In that case, let's just start you with a glass of wine and an appetizer. The empadinhas are excellent and the fried cassava will make you weep."

After they place their order with the young, raven-haired waitress, there's an awkward moment of silence. Then they both start talking at once. She pauses to let him go first.

"The Brazilian food's great, but I thought you'd like this place because there's a gallery attached." Distracted, he traces wet circles on the bar top with his glass.

"Really? That's so cool! Let's take a look after . . ." Her voice trails off as she realizes this means he's looked her up and knows she's a painter. She doesn't have her own website, so he must have seen the *SouthernHer* feature. What else does he know about her?

A boisterous group of finance bros sits down at the other end of the bar. Annie counts four of them, all in expensive tailored suits that were probably worth more than the Blue Book value of her Corolla. They overcompensate for their mind-numbingly dull jobs by telling loud, raunchy stories.

Giving them a sidelong glance, Gabe says, "Hey, let's grab that booth by the window. It'll be quieter."

They carry their drinks over to the plush velvet seating. Annie isn't sure she wants her bare skin to touch the fabric, but she has no choice but to slide into the booth. Gabe sits down across from her so there's space between them.

He clears his throat. "Yeah, so, I looked you up. Your work is amazing. My job is boring by comparison. But why did you let me think you were a teacher?"

Annie studies his profile, the way his slightly shaggy, dark hair flips out above his ear. A shot of adrenaline zips through her body, and she's overcome with the reckless desire to be honest with him—about that anyway.

"I suppose I just wanted to be someone else. Maybe try on a new life for a while."

He glances at her, looking a little concerned. "Eh? Is yours so bad?"

"I-I don't know. I guess not." She certainly isn't going to tell this handsome stranger that she's involved in an open murder investigation.

Gabe pauses, waiting for her to elaborate. But her bravery disappears, consumed by the suspicion that he's judging her. And she knows he'd be right to do so—she hasn't been up front with him about being married.

Part of her rationalizes that men do this sort of thing all the time without a second thought. Besides, there was a deep truth to what she told him. She wants to be someone other than Annie Shaw, bad daughter, bad wife, bad mother. Tonight, seeing herself through Gabe's eyes, she feels amazing—carefree, gorgeous, artistic, and accomplished.

One of the guys sitting at the bar whoops at something he's looking at on his phone, but the sound is contorted as he belches simultaneously. His friends roar with laughter. Annie can't help but giggle, and Gabe rolls his eyes, his lips curling up in a half grin. Any awkwardness has evaporated.

A handsome waiter with black-rimmed glasses arrives carrying a dish of crisp, golden pastéis.

"Ah, let's dig in!" Gabe says, rubbing his palms together. "If you like these, you'd love my mother's recipe." He places a small, savory turnover on her plate and watches as she blows on it before taking a tentative nibble.

"Mmm, this *is* amazing!" she says, suddenly ravenous after weeks of no appetite. As they eat, she observes all the ways in which he differs from her husband. Unlike Duncan, who was raised by a nanny and faceless cooks and cleaners, she imagines young Gabe playing underfoot as his mom prepared home-cooked meals. Maybe he even lay on the floor coloring and listening to his mother sing as Annie had in her happiest days.

They talk effortlessly about his work and her painting, moving closer together as if drawn together magnetically. Gabe observes her glass, the wine long gone. "Let me get you a real drink," he says. "And I'm ready for another too." He extricates himself from the low booth, stretches, and heads over to the bar.

The loud crowd of businessmen is soused now and discuss their plans to hit a lounge. "I gotta take a piss first. You guys settle up," one of them says. He's South Asian, tall, and solidly built with black, wavy hair. He passes the booth on his way to the restroom, stops, and glances over his shoulder at Annie before continuing. *Creepy, but is there something vaguely familiar about him?*

Less than a minute later, he exits the restroom and ambles past their table. As he does so, she's shocked to hear him say, "Hey,

Annie. Hope you're enjoying your evening." He keeps on walking, joining his friends who have paid their bill and stand on the sidewalk smoking.

Annie's rattled and she still can't place his face. *Maybe someone from an art fair? Or Tabby's school?* But he didn't look the type to attend suburban art fairs or PTA events. She pushes aside the thought as Gabe returns to the booth, placing two identical glasses of scotch, neat, on the table.

"Tonight, you'll forget your troubles. This magic elixir will transport us to a smoky glen deep in the Scottish highlands," he says as he slides into the booth next to her, thighs touching.

"No loch monsters, I hope?" she asks. She feels his eyes on her, but having exposed herself so much already, she retreats. She stares down at her glass, too timid to meet his gaze. She takes a sip. It burns her throat, but she likes the aroma. "Wow!" She inhales deeply and takes a longer sip.

"Good, right?" Impulsively, he says, "You smell fantastic. I don't mean that in a gross way. I was just leaning over and I, uh, noticed your hair." He cleared his throat, a self-conscious *hem-hem.* "I should stop while I'm ahead, huh?"

She laughs. "You too, you know. You smell phenomenal." The alcohol is going to her head, and she stumbles over the last word. "This is strong stuff!" she says. Emboldened by the spirits, she rests her head on his shoulder. He stretches his arm around her, resting it on top of the booth's cushion. "I could fall asleep here. It's so comfortable," she murmurs.

For a while they sit like that. His necktie is loosened, and the sleeves of his dress shirt are rolled up. She strokes the thick, sinewy muscle of his forearm, reveling in the texture of the dark, coarse hair that is so unlike her husband's.

"How come nobody's snapped you up?" It's not a question she would ask if sober. "I can't figure out what's wrong with you, Gabriel Correa."

He tilts her chin up to face him as if confronting her. But looking into her eyes, he melts. He leans down, brushing his lips against hers, not quite a kiss. His hand slips under the hem of her skirt, sliding a few inches up her inner thigh before retreating. "I'd tell you but then I'd have to kill—" She smothers his mouth in a kiss before he can finish.

◆

Without traffic, the ride home is short. Annie stares out the window as the suburban nightscape whizzes past, but she sees Gabe's face in her mind's eye. She wants to savor the thought of him, the memory of his smell and touch. But it seems wrong to relive the experience within the stale air of the rideshare car, as if the grossness of the cloth seats will taint her connection to him.

She tries to think about tomorrow's chores—groceries, recycling, that pediatrician appointment she has to set up for Tabby—but her mind takes her back to the bar. Right now, she prefers that version of herself. As the scenes replay in her head, she hums softly to herself. All of a sudden, she stops and sits up straight in her seat, struck by a sudden, damning realization. The man who greeted her by name on his way to the restroom—she's met him several times. Each occasion was brief, and she'd always been with Duncan. His name is Dev. Dev works for Ray Park.

HONG KONG, 2002

Annie sat in a dumpling shop waiting for a hotel bartender to do her the favor of blowing up her life.

"Shift's over at nine," he said, winking at her over the bar. "I'll introduce you to the *real* Hong Kong, starting with this kick-ass, hole-in-the-wall dumpling shop I know."

The restaurant was easy to find, in a Tsim Sha Tsui alleyway, steps from the hotel. On the way, she'd left Duncan a message on the room phone. "Don't worry. I just need to breathe. I'll find someplace else to stay tonight. Please don't look for me."

The shopkeeper sets a steaming bowl of soup in front of her. After shooing him away several times, she'd finally had to order. She glances at her watch for the umpteenth time, self-doubt prickling her.

Was it all a game to him? Flirting with pathetic tourists for tips. Five more minutes passed, ten, twenty, thirty—she waited in the restaurant for a man who might never show, her face burning with shame.

The shop's stark, white fluorescent lights exposed her every pore. Seated by the window, Annie pictured the bartender and his friends standing outside, invisible on the dark sidewalk, pointing and laughing at her. She felt the kind of hot rage that can only be kindled by betrayal. Then, sick to her stomach, she became acutely aware of the intense heat and the fishy stench that drifted from the kitchen and permeated her skin.

◆

Annie didn't remember passing out. When she opened her eyes, she found herself lying on a cot in a strange clinic. With confusion and rising panic, she listened to the voices around her, not understanding a single word of the Cantonese. An attractive woman in a nurse's uniform was holding Annie's arm, checking her blood pressure. Groggy, Annie spied rust-colored stains on her own sleeve. Registering her confusion, the nurse offered an explanation, "Your arm. Maybe you cut yourself when you passed out."

At the sound of a gentle cough by the foot of her bed, Annie lifted her head. Had the bartender found her after all? A mix of emotions washed over Annie when she saw Duncan watching over her anxiously. His face full of love and concern.

Just then, the doctor arrived, returning on the tail end of his rounds. "Mrs. Shaw. We're going to do a few more tests. Your husband said you haven't been feeling well—"

"We're not married," Annie said. The nurse raised her eyebrow at the interruption.

It wasn't worth explaining to these strangers that she and Duncan were not, nor would they ever be, joined in holy matrimony. A sudden wave of fatigue hit Annie. She fell back onto the pillow and closed her eyes again.

She awoke to the sound of Duncan's voice. He was engaged in an animated conversation with the nurse. Annie pretended to be asleep until she left.

"So, do you want to sleep with her too? The nurse?" Annie asked. The fact that she'd tried to sleep with someone else hours ago didn't make Duncan's betrayal hurt any less.

He inhaled sharply. "Of course not. You can trust me, Annie. I was confused. I messed up once, but I love you more than anything. Nurse Lieu was just congratulating me—"

Annie looked up questioningly. "On what?"

"You're—we're pregnant, Annie!"

The next forty-eight hours passed in a blur. The following evening, Duncan proposed over an expensive dinner in Macau, a dinner Annie was too nauseated to touch. All she could think about was how it must've been a mistake—he wore a condom during the one occasion they'd had sex after his return from Afghanistan.

"Let me take care of you and our baby. Forever. Marry me, Annie."

She barely heard him, though, not over the voice of her mother.

"Don't throw him away. You don't know what you have. I do."

CHAPTER 40

By the time the rideshare drops Annie in front of her house, it's very late. Too late to text Danielle—but Annie does it anyway. The whisky is still coursing through her veins, and she's desperate to find out more about Dev. Besides, she's been meaning to apologize to her friend for weeks and saw on social media that Danielle and Ray only just returned from their cruise.

Hey, can we talk? I'm sorry. I miss you.

She hits send, hoping Danielle replies in the morning. She's surprised when seconds later, her phone dings.

Hiya. Not pissed anymore. Can't sleep? You have to see my tan. Luv ya. -D

Annie smiles. Danielle's secret to happiness is her short emotional memory. She never holds a grudge.

Awake and bored with jet lag, Danielle calls Annie to catch up on the investigation into Byrdie's death. When the headlines broke, she was baking on a yacht in Croatia. After Annie delivers a slurred version of recent events, Danielle sums up her feelings about the case: "It's ridiculous. First Ike and now you. The police have their heads up their asses."

Without pausing to hear Annie's response, she continues her rant. "I mean, how could they even *think* you're hiding anything?"

But Annie knows she *is* keeping secrets. For one thing, she still hasn't told Danielle about seeing Ray and Nina together. But how could she explain not saying anything on the day it happened?

This time, Danielle picks up on her silence. "Well, have you told the cops everything you know? Talk to me, Annie."

"I-I dunno. Hate to admit it, but things unraveled after my mother died. I was fuzzy on the dates when the policeman questioned me." Drunk Annie sounds fuzzier than ever.

"Fuzzy dates isn't a felony. They have no right to treat you like a criminal!"

Annie itches to change the subject to Dev but doesn't trust herself not to blab in her current state. She's not sure how much she wants to share about Gabe. Deciding it would be best to meet in the morning after the whiskey's worn off, Annie makes Danielle an offer she can't refuse. Exercise.

◆

"Hello, hello, love!" Danielle says, greeting Annie with an air kiss. It's seven in the morning. "Ready for the mother of all power walks?" She smiles broadly, her skin so unnaturally tan that her teeth glow by comparison.

Annie wants to turn around and crawl back into bed. Just a few short hours ago, she collapsed directly onto the sofa in an alcohol-induced haze. It occurred to her that she should shower away any traces of the bar and rideshare, but she was able to dismiss the thoughts enough to fall asleep—a strong testament to the medication. When her alarm went off, she caught her reflection in the flat-screen TV: disheveled hair, wrinkled yellow tank top, denim skirt twisted sideways. Charming, she thought, fumbling around for her phone—anything to stop the alarm stabbing her hungover eardrums. She hit snooze, then fell asleep again, waking with just enough time to stagger into a pair of track pants and a sweatshirt.

In response to Danielle's chipper greeting, Annie's mouth stretches into a wide, uncontrollable yawn. The yawn transforms into a startled shriek when Danielle grabs her by the shoulders and spins her around. Danielle grins mischievously, appraising Annie at arm's length.

"Hmm. Something's different about you, girlfriend. Your aura has changed. Red, yellow . . . I haven't seen it this vibrant *ever*."

Annie blushes, wondering if her friend is psychic. Against her better judgment, she's dying to tell Danielle about last night's semi-illicit evening. She needs to find out about Dev anyway.

By the time they reach the bottom of the hill, Annie has finished her story.

Danielle's jaw hangs open. "Excuse me? I can't believe you actually went out with Mr. Hot-for-Teacher. I'm kind of shocked. And—uh—I didn't realize things were quite so rocky between you and Duncan."

"It was just a drink. Things with me and Duncan are . . . delicate. I discovered he's been making calls to the pretty college student who interviewed me for the magazine. Her name's Millie Rae."

"There must be some explanation," Danielle says. "Duncan would never . . ."

Danielle's skepticism irritates Annie, but she doesn't want to ruffle any more feathers by arguing with her friend. "Maybe you're right, and it was harmless. But there's something else I really need your advice on." As Danielle stretches her calves on the edge of the curb, Annie describes how Ray's employee approached her last night.

Danielle's face flashes concern, but she masks it quickly with a smile. "Dev is harmless. Drinks like a fish. If it was Thursday, he probably blacked out later that night and forgot he even saw you."

"So you don't think he'll tell Ray?" Annie asks. She considers mentioning the photo of her and Ike to Danielle but decides against it.

"Well, if he does, I'll know right away. My husband is the worst gossip. He's worse than any girls I've ever met. And if he finds out, I'll deal with it." She speaks with a comforting firmness.

Leaning against a tree, Danielle clears her throat and steeples her fingers in expectation. "So, did you get to second base?"

"I don't even know what that is!" Annie laughs, then looks around nervously at a passing jogger. "Let's head back." After they walk several yards, Annie lowers her voice, though nobody is within earshot. "I've only ever been with Duncan. We got married so young and had Tabby so early. There's this whole other world I've never explored. I know that sounds selfish." Her voice falters, and she looks down at the pink flashes of her Adidas.

"We're moms and wives and daughters, but we're also human," Danielle says. "Think of all the dudes who have midlife crises and it's lust at first sight with the babysitter! Because we're middle-aged women we're judged by a different standard. Not exactly fair."

Sweat drips down Danielle's hairline, but it just seems to make her glow brighter. Her expression is serene, unlike her usual hyper-extroverted self.

"When I was younger, I was a real party girl, if you can believe it," Danielle says with a wink. "I did a lot of shit I wasn't proud of, like waking up in strangers' beds. Drugs . . . you name it, I tried it. I've never told anyone this, but the first couple years Ray and I dated, that lifestyle didn't completely stop. Poor guy was head-over-heels for me—then, at least!—and wouldn't dream of cheating. He did right by me, saw to my rehab, supported me through it all.

"When I got better, we got married and I turned around and slept with his best friend. I don't know why I did it other than slipping into old habits. It crushed him. Maybe that's why I'm more forgiving of his ways now. I know what people say about him but he's trying, and he loves me. He has an addiction of his own—slips up sometimes. The thing is, we don't stop being human or having needs when we get married or have children."

Annie remembers the scene she witnessed in the art room at

the spring festival. She has no doubt now that Danielle knows about Ray's dalliances and has chosen to forgive them. Telling her about Nina wouldn't change that, but it could make things more uncomfortable between Annie and Danielle.

"Ray and Aimee and me . . . we're all lucky to have you in our lives, Danielle," Annie says with conviction. "I've decided to end things with Gabe. I don't want to be responsible for anyone getting hurt. I couldn't live with myself."

"That's the thing. I don't think you can really live, much less fall in love, without the potential of hurting someone. You have to accept that risk. Relationships are living beings that grow and change. We can control them about as much as we can control our teenagers."

Annie wants to accept this open-minded perspective, which has clearly brought peace and resiliency to her friend, but she can't. The compulsions to control and contain are embedded in her, passed down genetically and behaviorally from mother to daughter. To truly live, Annie has to be strong enough to break free of them.

Danielle takes Annie's hands in hers when they're ready to say their good-byes. "I didn't want to bring it up again, but I'm sorry you have to deal with this bogus investigation alone. Why don't you stay with us until Duncan's back? I've already run it by Ray. It's fine."

"No!" Annie tries to hide her distress at the mention of Ray's name. "I gave the police, my attorney, my home address. I really shouldn't leave. It wouldn't look right."

"Your call," Danielle says, throwing up her hands and backing away slightly. "But anything you need, I'm here. We know you're not guilty."

Annie reaches out and hugs Danielle, not wanting the uncertainty on her own face to betray her.

CHAPTER 41

I'm really proud of you, Annie," Duncan says, giving her shoulders a squeeze. An hour ago, the house had been filled with a dozen runny-nosed, sticky-fingered toddlers and their harried parents. They just finished throwing out the remains of the party and tucking the exhausted birthday girl into bed. Now, they're collapsed on the sofa with the dog snoring at their feet.

"I can't believe I did it myself," Annie says. Last year, before she first started seeing Dr. Patel, she'd never have been able to host a party in her house. The group stayed cramped into two rooms on the first floor, but it had been a party, nonetheless. "I did it for Tabby. She needs to have a normal childhood. She shouldn't suffer because of my disordered brain."

"Tabby was ecstatic. It was superb, Annie. You didn't even flinch—well, not that much—when that boy's mom asked you where to put his loaded diaper."

"I was just surprised! I thought a three-year-old would be potty trained!"

"Hey, I wasn't completely until I was four. Boys just learn later."

"Where did you put it, by the way?"

"The diaper? Straight in the trash in the garage. Don't worry, I pulled the can out to the curb."

"Thanks. Did you wash your hands after?"

"Of course. You aren't really supposed to ask me those things, Annie. Remember what Dr. Patel said." Stretching his arms high and yawning, he says, "I'm just about done for today. Mind if I re-tire to the booo-doir?"

"Not at all," Annie says, too tired to acknowledge her husband's corny attempt at levity. "You go ahead. I'm gonna bring my mom a piece of cake."

"To the carriage house? What about the mice, Annie?"

"Tabby didn't want her at the party. So it's the least we can do."

When she approaches the carriage house, she immediately senses something is not right—or at least, something is more wrong than usual. The front door is ajar, but her mom sometimes leaves it that way, thinking poisonous vapors were pumped through her pipes and out the drains.

In the moonlight, Annie sees a dark, syrupy substance oozing out from beneath the door. The sound of scurrying, scratching, and slurping—the rats are drinking the liquid. A gray-faced rat turns to ogle this new intruder, then lunges at her. The fur around its mouth is drenched in blood. Annie screams and covers her head with her hands, realizing the animals are drinking blood.

You need to check on your mother. She kicks the door open the rest of the way with her foot, causing the rats to scatter. Inside, there are more rodents piled up on her mother's furry blankets.

"Mẹ! Mẹ! Are you here? Where are you?"

"Help me, Anh! How could you let this happen? It's your fault!" She hears her mom's voice but can't see her.

The pile of rats rises up, suddenly animated. It comes toward Annie, close enough for her to see flashes of torn flesh between the writhing creatures. Annie backs away, turns, and runs.

"How can you leave me, Anh? The sickness will eat me alive. You leave me to die?!"

Annie races past beds of pasture roses, the thorns cutting up her ankles. *Almost home. Almost home. Keep going.*

Rising above the sound of her panting, a horsey laugh. It's jar-ring, eerie, and she has no idea where it's coming from.

She slams the front door behind her and bolts it. She thinks of calling Duncan but doesn't want to wake Tabby. Instead, she races from window to window fastening the locks. There are so many more windows than she remembered. Hundreds of windows.

As she reaches the last window, a face pops up. Dr. Patel. She pauses her maniacal cackling and opens her mouth wide, mocking Annie's shocked expression. Blackish red blood rings her lips, giving her the appearance of a murderous clown. The doctor presses her face against the glass pane, distorting her features.

She presses so hard the glass cracks, triggering peals of earsplitting laughter. Annie stands paralyzed, unable to speak. Dr. Patel could enter through the broken window, but she doesn't. She slides her thumb along a broken shard, drawing more blood. She uses this to write a message to Annie on the glass:

YOU KNOW WHAT YOU DID.

◆

Annie wakes up in a clammy sweat. The synthetic fibers of her workout clothes cling to her skin. After the morning walk with Danielle, she collapsed on the sofa, intending only to nap. But glancing at her phone, she discovers she's been out for nearly an hour.

Her voicemail alert dings. The incoming call must have woken her up from the nightmare. Before she presses play, she rubs her eyes in an attempt to erase the images from her head.

"Annie, it's Dr. Patel! I hope your night out at the bar was enjoyable. I had fun just driving you there. I had no idea downtown Arlington was such a lively scene. I've got to take a stroll down there sometime with my cats. I'm trying out some new harnesses with them. They don't drink, though," she chuckles. "Anyhow, I'm calling because in all the excitement we forgot to set a time for our next session. I have a window between six and seven, next Thursday. If that works for you, do ring me directly at this number. No need to bother Regina in the office. Hope you're doing well! Ta!"

Annie groans, rolls over, and puts the pillow on top of her pounding head. Just as she's about to fall asleep again, a loud honking from the driveway startles her so that she almost bites her tongue. She crawls out of bed and scuttles over to the window. Her eyes fall on a very recognizable, matte-black Land Rover with monster tires. He won't stop honking. She has no choice but to rush downstairs and open the door.

"Hi, Ray. What's going on? Danielle's not here."

Leaning his head out the window, he says, "Uh-duh. I know that." Then he climbs down from the car. Clad in basketball shorts, black crocodile loafers with no socks, and a plain white T-shirt that looks like Hanes but probably cost hundreds of dollars, Ray eyeballs Annie. "Sleep late, Shaw? You look like shit."

"I-I had a headache. What do you want?"

"What's this crap about you staying with us? I assume you got the photo my guy sent. The one of you and your chocolate boy toy? Consider that photo your first and only warning."

Annie nods, taken aback by the sudden meanness in Ray's eyes.

"For whatever reason, Danny listens to you. For her sake and yours, shut the fuck up and stop worming your way into our marriage. Trust, Annie. I can have you followed twenty-four-seven. I won't hesitate to manufacture dirt if I have to—hell, I might even enjoy it." He chuckles, genuinely having fun. "But I've called off the dogs, for now, and as long as you keep quiet about what you saw at the spring festival, you and me—we're all good."

Once he's gone, Annie sinks into the papasan chair and massages her temples. Her head is on fire and her throat bone dry, yet she smiles. Ray threatened her with the photo of her and Ike—

That means he still doesn't know about Gabe.

CHAPTER 42

Annie's car idles outside the bus depot. After Ray left, Annie was surprised to see Tabby's name flashing on her phone.

"Hello? Tabby? Everything okay?"

"Uh . . . is everything okay, Mom? You sound weird."

"Of course I'm okay." Annie realized she sounded defensive. "I can't wait to see you tomorrow."

"Ha-ha. You're not funny. Anyway, the bus is stuck in traffic. You won't be able to pick me up until noonish, so don't go early. I would've texted, but I know you don't always check your messages in real time like any normal person under the age of seventy-five."

"Yes, the twenty-seventh. Of course, that's today." Annie had thought it was tomorrow and had *not* planned accordingly.

"Uh, yeah. It's the twenty-seventh of July, ten forty in the morning, and the temperature is—let me check—seventy-nine degrees. So, uh . . . bye, Mom." *Click.*

She barely had time to change out of her workout clothes.

You are the worst mom ever. She starts to chastise herself before realizing with a touch of relief that her own mother, guilty of child neglect, had been somewhat worse.

Behind her, a white Mini Cooper honks, rousing her from her thoughts, and she pulls forward. Kids stream out of the camp bus. Tabby's chestnut hair glimmers in the sun as she retrieves a large blue duffel bag from the coach's storage compartment and hoists it onto her shoulder. Spotting her mom's aging car, she waves a sun-tanned arm and, despite herself, flashes a white-toothed grin. Her fifteen-year old daughter is so healthy, so perfect. Annie takes it all in as Tabby hugs her new friends good-bye and strides confidently toward the car.

◆

"Why do you keep checking your phone, Mom?" Tabby asks in be-tween mouthfuls of roast chicken and rice noodles. After days of bland camp food, she requested they have lunch at a Vietnamese spot called Nice Búns. Pun-laden names like this irritate Annie since the words don't sound alike if you speak the language.

"Hmmm? Have I been? I didn't realize." She's in the middle of exchanging texts with Gabe. Last night was the escape she needed, but after the encounter with Ray's coworker and her daughter's return, the reality of what Annie had done hit home. She had de-cided to put an end to things before they went any further. When Tabby left to use the restroom, she'd texted Gabe what she hadn't been able to say to him in person.

> The other night was amazing. You can tell how into you I
> am . . . but I haven't been honest. I'm married. Things
> are . . . complicated.

For the past twenty minutes, three dots have been blinking at her in response. Annie turns her screen away from her daughter. She puts down the disposable chopsticks that she's been using to poke at the noodles that smell too pungent in her hungover state and turns her attention to her daughter. "How's your food, honey?"

"You mean how *was* my food?" Tabby swallows the last bite and sits back in her seat, rubbing her belly in exaggerated satisfaction. It's a silly gesture she picked up from Duncan as a kid.

"Do you know how to cook this kind of food, Mom?" Tabby's

cheeks flush slightly as she asks the question. She finds it awkward to talk to her mom about anything related to her Asian heritage. From a young age, she distanced herself from her grandmother with the embarrassing broken English and dirty house. She identified closely with her private-school classmates, a pan-ethnic cohort privileged enough to not see themselves in terms of race or ethnicity.

"Er . . . no. But your grandmother loved to cook. She was really good at it too." Annie points at her soup bowl. "On Saturdays, our house was filled up with the aroma of beef, charred ginger, onions, and anise. It's what goes into this broth."

"Why didn't she teach you how to cook?"

"She worked a lot, and there really wasn't ever enough money." Annie dumps the rest of the too-tiny plastic container of dipping sauce on her noodles.

"Like, not enough money for food?" Tabby asks.

Annie studies her daughter's incredulous face, so innocent and sheltered. *Maybe you have sheltered her from too much.*

"Yeah. It was hard. My mom tried, but the war took its toll on her. She wasn't well mentally. Our stove didn't even work anymore by the end."

"Is that why you're so skinny in that one picture you have from your RISD orientation? I just figured you were anorexic."

"Oh my god, Tabby. The things you say. I weighed eighty-five pounds when I got to Providence, same weight I am now."

"Sorry, Mom." Tabby's eyes cloud over with concern. Displays of empathy for her mother were rare this year. She catches Annie off guard by reaching across the table and squeezing her hand. For a moment they sit like that, and then Tabby cracks a joke to lighten the mood. "Don't worry. We won't go hungry as long as there's Uber Eats."

Annie smiles. The teenager's simple act of reassurance, the fact that she cares, brings tears to Annie's eyes. Her daughter is growing up and probably a lot stronger than Annie ever gave her credit for.

"Listen. I wanted to tell you about something that happened while you were away. A terrible misunderstanding," Annie says.

"You mean the whole thing with Miss Fenton and the police? I had a whole bunch of texts from Aimee waiting for me when I got my phone back. I read them on the bus. I know all about the stupid rumors, Mom."

"I'm so sorry you didn't hear it from me directly." Annie regrets being so focused on Gabe—and on herself—that she hadn't prepared to welcome her daughter home. "Well, how do you feel about it all?"

Tabby rolls her eyes. "Mo-om! It's so lame. Miss Fenton was always a little—" She spins her finger around her temple in a cuckoo gesture. "She probably offed herself. Seriously, who would think *you* could murder someone?"

She knows her daughter is wrong.

You get what you deserve, Anh. You know what you did.

Annie is desperate to change the subject. "Listen, when I was cleaning your room, I found something. Condoms."

The teenager, who has been picking at her mom's bowl, stops chewing and shoots a nervous glance at her mother.

"Yeah?"

"You have a serious boyfriend?" Seeing her daughter's expression harden, Annie lowers her eyes, staring down into her bowl of congealed noodles.

"Yeah, I have a boyfriend. Austin. Five months."

Tabby spits out her words, her tone verging on anger, but Annie detects the underlying vulnerability. She meets her daughter's gaze. "I'm glad you're taking precautions, being safe. That is, if the two of you are actually . . . umm," Annie stammers. Having never been on the receiving end of this conversation, she's parroting television scenes imprinted in her brain.

"Yes. I buy the condoms myself. Why do you look so grossed out?" Tabby asks, clearly jacking up her irritation to hide an underlying embarrassment.

"I'm not saying anything, Tabby. I'm just trying to listen." Annie hears the defensiveness, judgment in her own voice. And for a moment, the two stare at each other, waiting.

Then Annie's phone vibrates with a text. Thx for being upfront before things got any farther. Really like you but gonna have to bow out. Get in touch if your sitch changes . . .

Gabe's message highlights Annie's hypocrisy. She has no right to be judgmental. Jamming her phone into her bag, she replies to Tabby with raw emotion. "I'm sorry I ever made you feel like you couldn't—couldn't talk to me. I'm here. I've been here."

The anger drains from Tabby's eyes, and relief takes its place.

"I know, Mom. It's just that you've had a lot going on with Grandma, Deja, and you and Dad fighting constantly. It didn't exactly seem like you could handle more." Tabby's voice is calm and steady, but there's an argument like a prosecutor laying out a case.

"Everything's happening so fast. You've grown up so quickly. I guess, in some ways, I've just started growing up myself since my mom died."

"Yeah, parents can really fuck you up," Tabby says, chuckling.

Annie's phone vibrates, cutting the moment short. A text notification. She doesn't recognize the number but clicks anyway. Ice shoots through her veins.

Ray looked like he meant it when he said he'd called off the dogs. But someone has just sent Annie photos of her and Gabe. Someone is trying to hurt her. If not Ray, then who?

All of a sudden last night has become more than a flirtatious drink. It has the power to blow up her marriage and upend her family.

CHAPTER 43

After lunch, Tabby disappears into her room and Annie into her private bath. But this time, as the hot water pummels her body, Annie focuses on actual problems and not the irrational thoughts that circulated in her head for months.

She called Ray as soon as they got home before she could lose her nerve. "I told you I'd keep my end of the bargain. Why did you send me those other pictures?"

"Uh, what are you talking about? I haven't sent squat since we talked this morning," he said, sounding genuinely confused and irritated. It sounded like he was eating chips.

"You—you mean you didn't send me more photos?"

"Negative. Heh. What did you do now, Shaw? Something juicy? Something blackmail-worthy? Maybe I shouldn't have stopped having you tailed after all."

He was still chortling with his mouth full when she hung up on him.

Annie believed him. Ray manipulated via cash and connections, not cunning. He was too dim to lie convincingly. *But if it wasn't Ray, who sent the photos?*

In the shower, Annie runs through potential suspects, each more ludicrous than the last. Though Danielle had been rightfully miffed at her previously, she was more than fine when they saw each other this morning. Danielle wouldn't have any reason to hurt her, would she? Then there's Ed Perez and the way he sometimes looks at her. Has she led him on?

As for her family—Tabby was sitting across from Annie when she received the text, and Duncan was embedded in the Syrian desert. Could her husband have hired a private investigator to follow her? But why? Duncan himself couldn't get away from Annie fast enough, moving up his departure date. What's more, a private investigator would show the photos to his client, Duncan, not Annie.

However, Duncan is a wealthy man. Could someone be attempting to get to *his* money by blackmailing her? It occurs to her that Ike has been saving up to go to graduate school for years, while the convenience store has barely kept them afloat. But she hates herself for even thinking it.

Annie ties up her wet hair, throws on a sundress, and considers her next move. She decides to lay low until she finds out who is surveilling her. The hungover part of her wants to nap, but she can't risk disrupting her sleep pattern and returning to endless nights of insomnia. After a glance at Tabby's closed door, she fills her water bottle and heads out to her studio.

By the halfway point, her hair is wetter than when she left, Virginia humidity offsetting the drying effects of late-summer sun. Annie dawdles along a cool, shady stretch where woodland stonecrop edges the paving stones. The succulent provides nectar and pollen for the bee population, dwindling elsewhere but thriving in Annie's native plant gardens. She continues on the trail, admiring the balanced ecosystem. Like her paintings, her gardens are a world she can control—as long as she keeps the harmful invasives at bay.

Near the carriage house, the pasture roses have not recovered. In place of dark green leaves and candy-pink blooms, brittle stems jut out of the soil where she spread her mother's ashes. Since Deja died, Annie has avoided the spot, suspecting an evil, otherworldly presence. She knows it's not rational, but, as she passes, she breaks into a trot.

It's sweltering inside the carriage house. Annie switches on the lights and makes a beeline for the air-conditioning box, grateful the renovation included a complete HVAC overhaul. Her mother never approved of central cooling and slept with the windows open three seasons out of the year and cracked them even in the dead of winter. She refused to linger inside the Shaws' main residence, accusing them of trying to suffocate her and warning, *"Without fresh air, you will die in that house. All of you."*

Annie's sketchpad lies open on the drafting table, the blank sheet enticing her. She straddles the stool, picks up a pencil, and draws. For the first time since the failed mural project, each stroke comes effortlessly. Full lips, strong jaw, thick brows, dark wavy hair—Gabriel Correa smiles back at her. Overcome with want, she lets her fingers caress the paper, blurring the charcoal.

Just as she used to idealize life without the burden of elder care, she now fantasizes about life without the bonds of marriage. *What if Duncan doesn't make it back from Syria?* It's a horrible thought and she knows it. Her mother's words echo in her head: *He is a good, kind man. You don't deserve him, Anh.*

She flings her pencil down, casting a glance around the studio for a distraction. A small stack of moving boxes remain unopened, months after the renovation. She's procrastinated by shoving them into a corner and reasoning she'd know soon enough if anything important was missing. Now, she scans the desk for the dao bào to slice through the glassy packing tape. Its curved blade comes in handy with surprising frequency. But the knife isn't where she usually leaves it, tucked into a mason jar on the drafting table. It only takes her a couple minutes of searching before she spies the old wooden handle sticking out from a low shelf. When she picks it up, she notices the blade is darkened with rust. She'll have to soak it in vinegar and scrub it with steel wool later. The blade is gummy with tape adhesive anyway; a few fine hairs stick to it.

Annie considers the neglected boxes, considering how the final few take as much time to unpack as the first twenty. She picks up the top box but doesn't remember packing this one. It's smaller than the rest and sealed with brown tape instead of clear. She carries the cardboard box over to the drafting table where the light's better. It barely weighs anything. Using the tip of the dao bào, she stabs through the tape, then drags the blade along the seam. She lifts the flaps and peers inside. A cloud of tissue paper crinkles when she sticks her fingers in and spreads out the sheets. In the middle, a chocolate-brown-and-black rabbit's foot, like the one her mother's boyfriend gave her when she was little!

Disoriented, she stares at it. How could an artifact of her childhood end up here? But as she stares at the strange object, the grisly truth dawns on her. It repulses her, but she has to be sure. Slowly, between her thumb and index finger, Annie extracts the object from the box.

"It's black, it's white. It's black, it's white." The lyrics play as her eyes dart from claw to claw, alternately dark and clear. Deja's paw. Annie flings it across the room, the dog's nails skittering on the wooden floorboards just as they used to.

Mumbling incoherently, she staggers backward toward the door, instinctively afraid to turn her back on the thing. Sobbing, gasping with each breath, she feels her windpipe closing up. Someone, something is choking her. Only then does she recognize the aroma of charred ginger and star anise floating in the air.

D isgusting!" Mẹ sneered. Her voice was deeper than usual, weighed down by hatred. Anh cowered behind her. Her mother had discovered a folder of drawings she'd done for school.

The new art teacher, Miss Graham, was young and—her students widely agreed—cool. She wore sack dresses with neon-bright tights and sneakers. Anh adored her and the feeling was mutual. Unlike all the other new or substitute teachers, Miss Graham did not ask Anh the question in front of all her classmates, "Where are you from?" Each time, the other students would snicker, and Anh felt her face grow hot with hatred.

One day in class, Anh drew Miss Graham in colored pencil including all the wonderful details—her asymmetrical blond hair, blue eyeliner, purple stockings, and Converse—and presented it to the teacher.

"Phenomenal! You are an excellent artist, Anh." The next day Miss Graham brought in a thick library book all about fashion illustration. For the next month, Anh practiced re-creating the glamorous drawings of sleek, long-legged models clad in couture. Her teacher heaped praise on her.

Without understanding exactly why, Anh knew she shouldn't show the drawings to her mother. Instead, she'd bring the pages home in a folder stuffed inside her Trapper Keeper, and when her mother was at work, she'd secrete them into a drawer as if they were dirty magazines.

"Monsters. Whores. They are disgusting!" Her mother shouted as she crumpled drawings in her hand. With each crunch of the paper, Anh shook. Her mother ripped pages in half. The sound tore through Anh's chest.

"Red lips. Short skirts. High heels. Why you do this? Why?" she shouted over and over.

Anh cowered, hiccupping with tears, each breath ragged with phlegm. It had always been just the two of them. Her mother's approval was everything, her rejection absolute annihilation.

Miss Graham had called her mother to talk about Anh's wonderful fashion illustrations. She suggested they consider signing her up for supplemental art classes. After the call, Mẹ tore up the house searching for the drawings and had then spent the past twenty minutes raging about what she'd found.

Anh was mad at herself for not hiding the drawings better. She was also mad at Miss Graham for telling her mother about them. *She betrayed you.*

"American school gives you filthy ideas! I will report that woman for poisoning your mind."

Then Mẹ did something she'd never done before: She cuffed Anh across the side of the head. One swift stroke.

It was hard enough to make Anh's ears ring but not hard enough to actually injure her. Instead, it was a message of ownership, an invasion of her personal space. *I control you.*

Anh had spent her entire life devoted to Mẹ—obeying, emulating, and defending her. At times, Anh feared her. This was true. But until that moment, she had never hated her mother. Now she could no longer deny the poisonous seeds of hatred germinating in her belly, sown in that split second of violence.

CHAPTER 44

Two days after the gruesome discovery in the carriage house, Annie still has no appetite. Feigning illness, she instructed Tabby to fix her own dinner tonight. The teenager shrugged, content to make a meal of bagged snacks and microwavables.

Now, buried under the bedcovers, Annie's brain cycles. Again and again, she asks herself who would play such a sick joke on her. She considers Millie Rae. The young reporter would have seen how much the dog meant to Annie. Maybe it was a *Fatal Attraction* scenario. Doubtful, though, given how much the girl doted on Deja during the interview.

Ray Park, on the other hand, was no animal lover. Though she wouldn't put it past him, she's pretty sure the grisly prank required too much detail, too much work for Ray. Danielle's husband never looked twice at Deja and was unlikely to source a paw that so closely resembled the dachshund's.

Then Annie thinks about how jealous Mẹ was of Deja, calling him a stupid waste of time and money. The charred aromatics in the carriage house—had she imagined them *twice* or was her mother somehow clinging to this earth in order to shame and punish Annie? *You get what you deserve, Anh. You know what you did.*

Annie knows it's impossible, but an otherworldly theory jibes with what she experienced right after her mother's death. The nightmares that haunted her. The way her skin prickled as though someone were watching her. The fits of panic that overtook her without warning, so intense they made her vomit. How else could she explain the distinct aroma of ginger and star anise?

Hungry for evidence, for or against a supernatural explanation, she kicks off the covers and props herself in front of her laptop. She skims a few articles, but they're largely unhelpful—except one that mentions DOPS, the Division of Perceptual Studies at the University of Virginia's School of Medicine. She clicks the link to their About page.

> Current mainstream science and philosophy portray mind, personality and consciousness as nothing more than byproducts of brain activity encased within our skulls and vanishing at death. . . . DOPS strives to challenge this entrenched mainstream view by rigorously evaluating empirical evidence suggesting that consciousness survives death and that mind and brain are distinct and separable.

Annie finds the concept compelling, perhaps because it would rule out having to confront a living perpetrator. Just then, she remembers the last time she saw Deja alive, how the drowsy dog had wandered into the mudroom after she returned from burying her mother's ashes, and how she'd scrubbed her nails the next morning until they bled. The painful memory extinguishes Annie's burst of concentration. The type on the screen starts to run together. She copies the department contact list and navigates to her cloud drive to paste the information into a new document. And then she stops.

Blurry, peachy rectangles on her cloud drive. Thumbnails—but they're not hers. Annie doesn't remember snapping any photos since Deja died and the mural project ended. Her skin tingles. Hearing Tabby banging around the kitchen, Annie gets up and closes the door before clicking on a thumbnail. The image fills her with a mixture of fear and disgust. One by one, she opens the rest. They grow and multiply on the screen like virus-laden porn pop-up windows. In fact, the photos aren't just *like* pornography, they are porn—and the subject is Tabby.

There are about a dozen. Annie prints them, deleting the file and emptying the trash after each one. By the time all of the pages print, Annie realizes what must have happened. Periodically, Tabby logs into Annie's account to look at baby pictures of herself and her friends. Sometimes she forgets to log out before taking new photos.

Annie's mind immediately leaps to her own mother. What would Mẹ say about this? *You give that girl everything. She throws it away with dirty pictures. Disgusting! Whore!* Clutching the printouts to her chest, Annie flies into the hall and down the stairs. Annie's rage grows with each footfall, her mother's voice louder. "Tabby!" she shouts, even though she has almost reached the kitchen.

Tabby pokes her head around the corner. In a lavender sweat suit with no makeup, she looks like she could be four years younger. "Whoa—you bellowed? What . . ."

"What are these filthy pictures?" Annie waves the printouts in the air. Shaking with rage, she rips the pages in halves and halves again. "Disgusting!" Then she hurls the pieces at her daughter. Body parts fall to the floor.

Tabby looks terrified, tears already streaming down her cheeks. All she says is, "Shit . . . shit, shit, shit!" Then she drops the butter knife she's been using to spread peanut butter and runs upstairs to her room.

Annie chases her. She pounds on the closed door, screaming, "Tabby, open the door! I'm your mother!" She's hitting the door so hard that when it suddenly flies open, she has to catch herself from falling.

Tabby stands in front of her, her tearstained face now a mask of angry defiance. "What? Want to snoop in my room now?"

"I didn't mean to snoop, Tabby. You were logged into my account when you snapped the photos."

"Yeah? So I sexted Austin. Every single fucking girl at school does it." Tabby rolls her eyes.

"Why did you do this? Why?"

"Austin is the only one who pays me any attention—and then he wasn't as much. He stopped messaging me back right away when I wrote him, sometimes not even until the next day! Then I heard he was hanging around this other girl. I just wanted to keep him." Tabby hiccups, tears spilling anew despite her bravado. With her face inches away from Annie's, she screams, "You should be ashamed of yourself, not me. *You* are the one who is a terrible mother."

They're so close to each other—Annie feels her daughter's breath, her spittle hitting Annie's cheek. Helplessly, she watches as her own hand flies up to strike Tabby's head.

At the last second, Annie stops. Her arm drops, hanging limply by her side. History will not repeat itself. Her daughter will not hate her.

When Annie takes a steps back and looks into Tabby's brown eyes, she does not see hate. She sees fear. She'd wanted nothing more than to give her daughter the sense of security and protection that she herself lacked at that age. But as she regards the trembling girl in front of her, Annie's stomach drops. She reaches out to hold Tabby, but she flinches and sidesteps her mother. Backing slowly down the hallway, the teenager whispers in disbelief, "You almost hit me. You almost hit me." Then she turns and races down the stairs, her voice rising sharply to a shout, "You almost fucking hit me! I-I'm going to stay at Aimee's house."

Leaning her back against the wall, Annie feels herself sliding, sinking. The front door rattles open, then slams shut. She won't chase after Tabby. Right now, her daughter is better off without her.

Fifteen minutes after Tabby storms out, Aimee's white SUV pulls up. Annie watches over them from the attic window, the only spot in the house with a sightline to the mouth of the driveway.

"At least she'll be safe," Annie mutters, disregarding the wrenching in her gut.

Too upset and ashamed to recount the fight via telephone, Annie texts Danielle a brief explanation. She holds her breath as the three dots blink back at her.

> Tabitha is always welcome here. As long as she needs. Call me if you want to talk.

Danielle signs off with a peace emoji.

Danielle's nonjudgmental response touches Annie deeply. Feeling unworthy of her friend's unconditional love, she squeezes her eyelids shut, fighting back an onslaught of tears. When she opens them a moment later, she catches sight of a pastel-blue rabbit tucked into the rafter storage space. The stuffed animal had been Tabby's favorite companion for years. Vanquished to the attic, it stares down at Annie with doleful eyes. She's overtaken by a sudden need to rescue the toy. Just as she's reaching up for the rabbit, her phone rings.

The sound is so loud, it seems to be ringing inside her head. Desperate to stop the painful reverberation, she scrambles to answer. It could be Tabby.

"Hello?"

"Hi, Annie. It's Gabe."

"Gabe? I wasn't expecting to hear from you." After their last text exchange, she had no plans to contact him but can't ignore the warmth rippling through her lonely body.

"About that—I was a little freaked out when you told me you were married. I thought I should step aside or, at the very least, play it cool," Gabe says. "Then I did some thinking the last couple of days, and let's just say I'd rather be happy than cool."

Despite how miserable she's feeling—or perhaps because of it—the corners of Annie's mouth lift in response to Gabe's rich baritone and the frankness of his words. "For the record, I never thought you were cool," she says, descending the narrow staircase from the attic.

"Ouch. Well, maybe you can help me with a problem I'm having."

"What's that?"

"I've got a good life. Made partner at the accounting firm this year, my basketball team won the championship in the Arlington Rec League last month, and I'm like five-eight. Like I said, I've got a good life, so the last thing I need is to get involved with a married woman." He clears his throat. "But I can't stop thinking about you."

"I know I should've told you sooner. I just wanted . . ."

"I have a feeling deep down we want the same thing. Can I see you again?"

Warning bells blare in Annie's head, but she ignores them. The surveillance photos of her and Gabe flash in her mind's eye like a giant stop sign. She knows it's dangerous. She has to stop. She hears herself say "Yes."

CHAPTER 45

Annie's eyelids fly open. There's an insistent thrumming against her cheek like a record player skipping. Her phone vibrating—she must have fallen asleep with it on her pillow. The middle-of-the-night call makes her heart skip. She fumbles to answer: "Tabby? Hello? Hello?"

"Annie? I can barely hear you. It's me."

"Duncan? Are you back in the States?"

Her mind reels. Hopefully, the bad connection is enough to hide the panic in her voice. She's not ready to tell him about how she almost struck their daughter, that Tabby ran away to Aimee's house—anything happening to Tabitha was Duncan's worst nightmare. Guilt grips Annie like a vise as she remembers agreeing to meet Gabe.

"I'm in Damascus. At the airport. Oh fuck, did I wake you? Dammit! My brain's wrecked."

Glancing down at her screen, Annie notes the international phone number. She can feel herself breathe again. Duncan's uncharacteristic profanity reminds her how deeply he immersed himself in the ranks during his previous embed, how he smoked and swore like a soldier for months until the effects of military life were subsumed by suburban dad life. Last time, when he came back from Iraq, he'd also been depressed and fragile.

"It's okay. I'll fall back asleep." She's not sure if he's heard her as he keeps talking.

"I have a long layover in Dubai and a bunch of connections . . . stopping over in London . . . face time at the UK office." His words are garbled, swallowed up by the crackling line. "Annie? Are you there?"

"You're cutting in and out."

"Yeah, the connection's shit. But I can't talk long anyway."

"When will you be home?"

"I touch down at Dulles Wednesday, but I think it's best if I stay in a motel for a couple days to decompress. Between jet lag and cramming to get the piece done, I'm going to be a zombie. But I know we have a lot to discuss . . . I'm sorry about the way I left things. I want to— I want *us* to try. Annie?"

She doesn't know what to say. But she knows she's running out of time.

Without waiting to hear his wife's response, Duncan continues. "Give Tabitha a kiss for me. I miss her so much. See you soon."

"Bye, Duncan." Her words are choked with emotion, with the knowledge that she can't kiss Tabby, that she's destroyed her daughter's sense of security and driven her away.

It's three in the morning but she texts Tabby.

> Sorry about how I reacted. Can we talk? Your father called. He'll be back in a few days.

A pulsating ellipse flashes, so briefly she's not sure if it was a trick of her groggy eyes. She stares at the unresponsive phone for a full minute, then tosses it down on the bed in disgust. Rather than lying awake in bed worrying until daybreak, she dresses and wanders downstairs. The silence is suffocating. She switches on the television but can't focus on the predawn programming. Chirpy voices emanating from the sound bar make the house seem even emptier. She paces around, gazing out into the pitch-black night. Outside, the darkness is inviting; being trapped inside with her thoughts is far more terrifying.

She slips out the back door, pausing for a moment on the deck. In seconds, mosquitoes descend on her hands, arms, and neck,

extracting the blood meal needed to create offspring. Why had she removed her robe before leaving the house? Perhaps the same reason
she was heading to the carriage house—to punish herself.

This misguided attempt at atonement propels her rubber clogs
forward along the dark path. Even without a flashlight, she doesn't
stumble—almost as if some otherworldly force is guiding her to
the carriage house. After making the bizarre discovery days ago,
she's abandoned her painting.

Though she'd had them removed, the tree stumps that flanked
the front door have left two circular patches of rot, like bruises on
the earth. She grips the knob and twists, a tremor of fear rippling
up her spine. After feeling along the wall for a few seconds, she
flips a switch. Bright light floods the room, and the air-conditioning
unit whirs into action.

She steels herself, then strides across the room to the dark corner, the wall where she'd flung Deja's paw. The empty box is there
but not the appendage. Getting down on all fours, she scrambles
around searching. *Find it. Get rid of it like you should have done in
the first place.* She'd been too much of a coward to handle the matter herself. Instead of cremating the dog, Duncan must have buried the body on the property. Somebody had unearthed it since.
Why? A sick joke or maybe to send a message. Did someone or
something want to discourage her from using her art studio?

For the next hour, she scours the floor, the shelves, upturning
jars, bins, and boxes. There's no sign of the paw. Again and again,
she replays the scene in her head—slicing through the brown packing tape, lifting the box flaps, pushing back the tissue paper, picking up the paw, the smell of ginger and star anise. She holds the
empty box up to the light. No trace of anything. Then she remembers the rusty stains and stray hairs on the dao bào she used to cut
the tape. Scanning the room, she finds the knife on the drafting
table where she'd tossed it that day. She turns it around in her hand,
but there's nothing but metal and a tinge of tarnish.

Delusions? What's wrong with you? Even with the AC on, she feels sweat beading along her temples and hairline. The air inside the carriage house is too close. Then she notices it again. Very faint. Aromatic. Spices. She stumbles out, turning off the lights and shutting the door.

"You're driving yourself crazy," she mutters angrily to herself on the way back. Now that the sun has begun to climb in the sky, she feels silly. She should have gone back to sleep instead of roaming the woods at night. What had she been trying to prove? She'd thought she was being brave—but not finding the paw only proved she was more unbalanced than she previously suspected.

Later that morning, she texts Tabby again.

I'm really sorry. Are you okay? When are you coming home?

But there's no response.

Desperate for some kind of resolution—to anything—she calls Ed Perez. She hasn't heard from either Ed or the police since Detective Harper last questioned her at the station. Nor has there been any breaking news about Byrdie's death.

Ed's words are sober, measured. "No, I haven't heard from Harper either. I'd say that's good news. However, I have fielded a couple calls from journalists. I handled them by giving a refresher course on libel laws. There's no reason for you to worry."

Of course, telling her not to worry has the opposite effect. Should she tell him about the surveillance photos? Maybe Ed could help. All of a sudden, the hairs on the back of her neck stand up. An eerie feeling someone is listening in on their call. "Could I talk to you about something, Ed? Not over the phone, but face-to-face?"

"You read my mind, Annie. I've been worried about you. After we left the police station, you looked so upset, vulnerable, and with Duncan out of town . . . We could grab a cup of coffee or maybe get a drink?"

She's not sure this is a good idea, given the way Ed's looked at her in the past. And even though he has a wife and young son at home, she can't be sure of his intentions. Still, she trusts him and needs desperately to talk things through with someone.

"Coffee sounds good. I do need to clear my head."

"Perfect. I'm booked solid today, but after six I'm yours. My secretary will arrange a car. We can meet at the espresso bar near my office. I can't remember the exact name . . . something Italian . . . Caffè Scuro! It's on the first floor of that new, glass-front hotel. You can't miss it."

When she still can't reach Tabby after lunch, Annie calls Danielle.

"Tabby's fine. She just said you two had a fight. No details . . ." Danielle says. A crosswalk signal beeps in the background.

"I caught her sexting with Austin and overreacted, lost control of my temper." Annie struggles to hide the tremor in her voice.

"It happens to the best of us, babe. Don't beat yourself up too much. She and Aimee are snug at home watching a *Scream* movie marathon. Blows my mind the original came out almost thirty years ago!" Danielle rambles on, but she sounds out of breath. "Listen, I'm late for this big women's healing circle. The hotel elevator was *so* slow. I took the stairs. Ray's meeting me after for a drink."

"I won't keep you, then. I suppose the time away from me will be good for Tabby. Danielle, I can't thank you enough."

Envisioning Tabby tucked away in the Parks' home cinema, Annie's anxieties shift, searching for a new target. It doesn't take long to pinpoint another raw nerve. Faced with Duncan's imminent return, she knows she needs to cancel her assignation with Gabe. It's like she's on a collision course but can't brake.

Bones snap. Steel crunches. The sick thud of a skull slamming against the dashboard. Grasping for control, she picks up the phone, scrolls through her contacts, and presses call.

"Hi! Millie Rae speaking."

Annie freezes. She considers hanging up but doesn't. Confirming Duncan's affair with the young college student will make her night at the whiskey bar with Gabe seem tame by comparison.

"Hello? Who is this?" Millie Rae audibly stifles a yawn.

"Hi, Millie Rae. It's Annie. Annie Shaw. You interviewed—"

"Oh, yes! Hi, Mrs. Shaw. What can I do for you?"

Annie isn't sure what she expected, but Millie Rae doesn't sound guilty—she sounds bored.

"Yes, I wanted to call to thank you for the write-up—" But she stops, remembering she already sent a thank-you note in the mail. "I wanted to thank you in person—er—on the phone."

"That's not necessary. It was my pleasure. My editor loved the piece. Your dog got us a lot of clicks too!"

The mention of Deja stirs Annie. She's done pussyfooting around the question. "I was surprised to see that you and my husband Duncan exchanged several phone calls. Was there a reason the two of you needed to talk?" The other end of the line is silent. "I'd ask him myself but he's traveling."

"Y-yes. We talked about your article. Just some follow-ups after the interview." For the first time, Annie has caught Millie Rae off guard.

"Why didn't you ask me if you had more questions?"

"I-I didn't want to bother you. Duncan said you were going through a tough time with your mother and—"

The mention of her mother, the way Millie Rae refers to Duncan so casually, the fact that the two of them have been talking about Annie privately—all this enrages her.

"What have you been doing with my husband?"

"Doing? I don't like what you're insinuating, Mrs. Shaw. We just talked! Are you okay?"

Are you okay? The question ricochets in Annie's head after she hangs up.

After her shift at the library ended, Anh stood on the curb waiting for her mom to pick her up. She usually heard the hatchback's broken muffler before she spotted the corroded body. To her embarrassment, so could everybody else in town. Mẹ said they couldn't afford driver's ed classes and insurance for Anh, much less a second car. But the seventeen-year-old noticed there was still always money for her mother's junkyard "finds."

Sorting and reshelving books was a boring, solitary job, but Anh was glad to get away from the house, even if she had to hand her paycheck over to Mẹ every week. It was a chance to be separate from her mother; to breathe her own air.

During mandatory break times, Anh had used the computer to print out college applications last fall. Ones her mother didn't know about. She'd also spent her study hall periods in the school cafeteria creating an art portfolio, which she hid in the back of her student locker.

For six days, the acceptance letter to RISD had burned a hole in her jacket pocket. It was such a prestigious school, and the school of Anh's dreams. She'd never even seen the ocean. Her mother would *have* to be okay with it. Maybe she'd even be proud of Anh.

She chewed her lip as the old hatchback pulled into the library parking lot. It slid to a stop in front of her, and Anh climbed in, working up enough courage to take the acceptance letter out of her pocket. She buckled her seat belt—out of habit more than anything else, as the worn nylon was of dubious efficacy—then unfolded the paper and placed it on her lap.

Mẹ didn't notice it at first. She was distracted trying to get the car started again without flooding the engine. She cursed, "Chó chết!" The phrase, literally translated as "dead dog," meant "dammit!" Anh felt her shoulders tighten. She braced herself for another of her mother's bitter outbursts and the humiliation of asking one of the librarians for a jump start. Each tortured choke of the motor tore at Anh's insides. But, eventually, the hatchback sputtered and jolted away from the curb.

Anh breathed a sigh of relief. Resting her cheek against the passenger-side window, she watched as passing trees, dotted with bright green buds, danced in the wind. The lonely rural route had no shoulder, and occasionally a low branch tapped the glass in greeting. She didn't think about the paper on her lap until her mother spoke next.

"What's that?"

Anh's heart jumped. Now doubting the supposition that Mẹ might be proud of her, she considered lying. She could say the piece of paper was a meaningless notice from the library or a school assignment sheet. Maybe she could stash enough money away to buy a bus ticket on her own. That way, she could run away from home and never have to confront Mẹ. But the college required various parental signatures, and she knew her mother would find out where she was eventually. There was no escape. She had to tell her.

"An acceptance letter from a college. The Rhode Island School of Design." Anh rushed to fill in the silence. "It's really hard to get into. I-I'm going."

Mẹ gripped the steering wheel tight. She looked disgusted. She hurled insults at Anh, calling her stupid: "Ngu thế!" Then she reached out and smacked the back of her daughter's head. Hard.

Hot tears sprang to Anh's eyes. She blinked them away, struggling to contain the sobs that were rapidly gathering in her chest, the pressure building so much she trembled.

"So you apply without telling me? How can we afford? We can't afford to eat—to take a shit!" Mẹ spit out her questions, jabbing Anh in the shoulder with each one. "No, you go to community college. Get a good job nearby. Stupid idea. Stupid Anh. Who put this idea in your head? Who tell you to do this? The old witches at the library? You quit! Get a new job."

"It was *my* idea. I want to be a painter." Anh said this so quietly she couldn't be sure her mother heard. But when Mẹ spoke next, it was clear she had—and that her daughter's response had sharpened her rage.

"Oh, you can eat your paintings? Not food? Let me see that!" she said, sneering. Mẹ clutched the wheel with one hand and used the other to snatch the letter from Anh's lap. With barely a glance, she crumpled it up in her fist and threw it out the window, the one that was always open because it was stuck.

Hysterical, Anh shouted, "Stop! That's mine! We have to go back."

But she didn't stop; she hit the gas. Anh swiveled around and watched, powerless as the letter receded into the distance. A piece of her died. The last bit of tenderness she felt toward Mẹ.

All these years, her mother had treated her like an object to be hoarded, controlled. Their home had become a territory her countryless mother had staked out, ruled over. Anh knew she had to break free. And she had to do it now, before she lost her nerve.

Anh no longer heard her mother's taunts over the whoosh of blood in her ears. She grabbed the steering wheel with her left hand. The cracked vinyl slicing into her palm. As blood mingled with sweat, Anh's already tenuous grip slipped away.

Mẹ drew her breath in sharply. Her lips were no longer moving, her rant silenced as she struggled to right the car.

Again, Anh lunged. She held on this time, wincing as her cut palm rubbed back and forth against the jagged vinyl. Anh jerked the steering wheel toward herself, falling back as the car flew off the road. She felt the impact of her cheek slamming into the window as the rocky ground rushed dizzyingly toward them. In the seconds before impact, Anh told herself she was free.

She felt Mẹ's scream pierce her eardrums. An arm shot out across her chest. The front of the hatchback crumpled into the gully. She watched her mother's head bounce off the dashboard, once, twice. Each time releasing a slow-motion spray of dust—and then blood.

Anh looked down at her mother's arm, motionless in her own lap. At the last second, Mẹ had flung out her arm to protect her daughter—instinctively or perhaps in case the threadbare seat belt failed.

The thumping in Anh's ears had quieted. "Mẹ?" She repeated it again and again, holding her breath. Though her mother said nothing, the gash in her forehead gaped red like a mouth. Anh was horrified by what she'd done, but part of her welcomed the silence.

CHAPTER 46

The bonds that once kept you tethered, safe. Later they can strangle you. That was how Dr. Patel described the ties between mothers and daughters. As a daughter, Annie struggled to escape the maternal choke hold. As a mother herself, she is no more free than before. Isolated, suffocating in her own home. Handsome family, big house, enviable profession—*bonds that once kept you tethered, safe. Later they can strangle you.*

All these years she'd mistaken equanimity for control, passivity for peace of mind. She avoided conflict and confrontation, containing her emotions and desires until the inevitable explosion.

Bones snap. Steel crunches. The sick thud of a skull slamming against the dashboard.

Annie knows she shouldn't be here. Not tonight. Not in this hotel lobby. And not waiting to meet him. What she's planning to do will be like taking a blowtorch to her marriage, incinerating her sterile, suburban existence. But at least she'll be the one in control. Not the unseen hand that seemed to be ripping her life apart since her mother's death.

She scans the hotel lobby, but he's nowhere to be seen. Knees trembling, she lowers herself onto a settee trimmed in sapphire-blue velvet. A bachelorette party whirls past, a flash of glittery sashes and short skirts. Annie feels foolish. She doesn't belong—a married, middle-aged mom. Tugging the hem of her slinky black dress, she suddenly wants nothing more than to be at home bingeing

Netflix in her pajamas, tucked under the mustard-yellow throw that she refuses to wash because it still smells like Deja.

Just as she's about to flee, a waiter approaches. The harried young man bears a sleek porcelain bottle and cup balanced precariously on a black tray.

"I didn't order this," Annie says, rushing to correct him as he hastily sets the drink down beside her.

"Compliments of the gentleman," he says, gesturing vaguely behind her, then disappearing.

Annie turns around, searching for a familiar face. She doesn't recognize anyone, but an attractive, silver-haired businessman flashes her an appreciative smile and raises his glass in invitation. She looks away, cheeks burning, heart juddering in her chest. To calm herself, she downs the shot, so nervous she barely tastes it.

"Hello, stranger."

At the sound of his voice, a broad smile of recognition spreads across her face.

"Ike! I'm so happy to see you."

He sits down beside her and, grinning at the empty cup, remarks, "Ah, I see you enjoyed the sake shot."

In college, it had been an inside joke between them. Annie didn't love the taste of alcohol, but, like most undergrads, she welcomed the release of getting drunk occasionally. Lychee-flavored sake shots were her drink of choice. Ike couldn't stand the syrupy sweetness.

"I shouldn't have. My sake days are behind me," she says, blushing as she remembers her booze-fueled kiss with Ike freshman year.

"That's right. You stopped drinking it all of a sudden senior year."

She nods. They're seated hip-to-hip on the tiny settee, and Ike's lime-and-mandarin cologne—the one he's worn since college—envelops Annie. Now that she's more relaxed, the sake's familiar fruity sweetness registers on her tongue. Why had she stopped drinking it so abruptly?

Images stir in the recesses of her mind, not quite formed into a memory but unsettling nonetheless. Geoff's senior project, the portrait of Ike, damaged. Waiting for Ike in his Providence apartment, a pit of jealousy swelling in her stomach. She feels the sake burning her mouth and throat. Her eyes flit from the dark blue velvet settee to her hands, ghostly pale beneath the bright hotel chandelier. Cadmium blue paint smeared across her fingers, the palette knife gripped tight, the ugly sound of canvas ripping. Annie gasps. Feeling lonely and rejected, she *had* stabbed the painting. Afterward, she'd blurred the edges of her memory with more alcohol. The weight of each passing year pushed the truth down deeper and deeper, only resurfacing now with her heightened nerves and the jolt of sake.

Shamefaced, she shoots a furtive glance at Ike. He's too distracted by something on his phone to have picked up on her distress. When he does look up, she forces a tight smile, but inside she's reeling.

She'd rewritten history to downplay her culpability, fully convincing herself she hadn't defaced Geoff's painting. If she'd lied to herself then, what else had she lied about?

GRACE FALLS, 1997

After the crash, minutes passed like hours. Anh sat still, holding her mother's hand and watching as the life slowly drained from her face. What would have happened if a Good Samaritan hadn't spotted their car? Would Anh have run for help? Or would she have escaped by doing nothing and letting Mẹ die?

Suffering only minor cuts, contusions, and a fractured wrist, Anh left the hospital the same day. She was released into the temporary custody of social services. Later, her assigned social worker, a dedicated young woman named Lisa, helped her prepare for RISD. Anh's dream of going to art school, one of only a few wishes she'd been brave enough to share with her mother, was about to happen.

Mẹ hadn't been as lucky as Anh. She'd spent months in the hospital only to be discharged with medical bills she could never pay back. While she was recovering, they'd lost the house, all their belongings hauled to the junkyard. Hysterical, Mẹ called the landlord, but he threatened to sue her for unpaid rent and property damages if she ever contacted him again.

Before leaving for Providence, Anh visited her mother in the first-floor studio apartment she'd rented with the aid of public assistance. Clean and tidy, it was an improvement over their previous living conditions. Anh surveyed the five-hundred-square-foot efficiency feeling a tiny bit better about leaving her mother in Ohio. She opened the sliding glass door, which faced a parking lot and playground. Two little kids took turns pushing each other on a swing.

"It's not so bad, Mẹ. Seems safe," Anh said, breaking the silence.

"Heh. That's what you say. I lose my house, my valuable things. All gone. You do this to me"—Mẹ gestured to the plum-colored scars on her forehead and winced—"then you leave me." She wagged her index finger in Anh's face. "How I give birth to such a selfish thing? You get what you want, huh?"

Anh shook her head, shrinking under her mother's glare. The insults still hurt. Yet the balance of power had shifted irrevocably. *Selfish, stupid, disgusting*—in the split second it took to grab the wheel, Anh had made Mẹ's constant criticisms a reality. She'd managed to wrest control—to physically break away from her mother— but she'd spend the rest of her life bearing the guilt and shame of knowing what she'd done.

In the parking lot, Anh glanced back at the sliding door. She glimpsed Mẹ watching her through the glass. Her mother looked smaller. Just as Anh raised her hand to wave good-bye, the curtain jerked shut.

Suddenly struck by the intensity of her loss, Anh doubled over, resting her palms on her thighs. Mẹ's love had always been conditional. It demanded total loyalty and obedience. *Us or them.* She could never be the daughter her mother expected now. That girl died in the car crash.

PROVIDENCE, 1997

Lively chatter and the occasional hoot of laughter floated through the open window of the registrar's office. A slender boy with teal hair greeted her from behind the tall wooden counter. Smiling shyly at the student worker, she picked up the black felt-tip pen, popped off the lid, then printed and signed her name. A glance over her shoulder revealed nobody else in line, so she took a moment to appraise the signature on the ledger. *Annie.* It looked strange and felt funny to write—but she'd get used to it soon enough.

Annie grabs her cell phone. She starts to dial 911 but stops. *You can't let them trace this back to you.* She picks up the hotel landline instead.

"911, what's your emergency?"

"Harrison Hotel. My—a man—is hurt, dead. I'm not sure."

She surprises herself by having the presence of mind to look at the key card envelope on the nightstand and adds, "Room 929."

"That's good. Now, can you give me the address?"

Pumped with adrenaline, Annie thinks quickly, and she picks up the stationery by the phone. But her eyes can't focus on the tiny letters and numbers. She carries it to the window, squinting in the bright light but finally able to make out the words.

"Tindley Street. D.C. by the Navy Yards. There's only one Harrison Hotel here." *Her breathing is ragged. The adrenaline that had kept her focused now makes her feel sick.* "Can't you just send someone?!"

"Help is on the way, ma'am. I need you to listen carefully. Can you tell me if the man is conscious?"

She forces herself to look at his body, motionless save the grotesque undulation of spiders.

"He's not moving. I don't know what happened! He's covered in bumps . . . spiders." *She's almost too disgusted to say the words.*

"Is he breathing, ma'am?"

"I don't know! How should I know? Please, don't make me look again."

"*I understand, ma'am. Can you tell me exactly what happened?*"

"*No. I mean, I don't know. I must have blacked out.*"

There's nothing more Annie can say. How can she convince this stranger that she doesn't remember? Why would anyone believe she simply woke up inside her worst nightmare?

Alarmed by the blare of sirens, rapidly approaching, Annie drops the receiver. She's overcome by the irrational urge to wash her hands, face, ear—anything that touched the hotel phone. She's losing precious seconds but needs to scratch the itch. Her hands are still wet when she pulls on her dress and grabs her purse. She has to get out. She has to run.

◆

CHAPTER 47

A couple strands of freshly washed hair cling to Annie's cheeks. She dries off her naked skin and slips her arms into a flannel robe. Only then does her body convulse, breaking down into wretched sobs.

As soon as the taxi dropped her off, she raced inside and flung her clothes on the wooden floor of the vestibule. She stood under the shower for over an hour, commanding the voice-activated unit to rise to increasingly hot temperatures, but she couldn't wash away the grisly scene at the Harrison.

Annie had woken up next to the stuff of her nightmares—the disgusting images that plagued her thoughts come to life. No amount of soap or water, no medication, was capable of clearing the murkiness in her brain. What she had seen seemed so real, but her obsessions always did, at least to her.

Twice in quick succession, the doorbell rings. Almost immediately afterward, someone pounds on the glass storm door. Annie freezes. *They know.* She wipes her nose against her sleeve, leaving a snail trail of tears and snot, and hurries to the door. It's Officer Williams, but he isn't smiling this time, his hand resting on his holster.

She cracks the door open just enough to show her face, not enough to let anyone in. "Good afternoon, Officer Williams." She speaks in a stilted voice, using the heavy wooden door as a shield.

Observing Annie's bare legs and feet, the young officer averts his eyes and nervously clears his throat. "Mrs. Shaw. Are you alone in the house?"

"Y-yes."

"Please get dressed, ma'am. We need to take a ride to the station."

◆

She couldn't call Ed this time—and she certainly couldn't call Duncan. Haunted by the image of the disfigured body, Annie vowed not to drag any more innocent people into her mess. *You have to stop hurting people.* But now that she's alone in the frigid interrogation room, all her courage has drained away.

The door swings open and Detective Harper strides in. His expression betrays nothing.

"Mrs. Shaw. How are you? Thank you for coming in." He says this as if she had any control over the matter.

He slides a piece of paper across the table as he lowers himself into the chair opposite her. "An alert came across this morning. Circulated to all law enforcement in the greater DMV area. This is the image that accompanied it. Can you identify this individual?"

It's a security camera still from the back stairwell of the Harrison Hotel. Black-and-white, grainy—*her.* She says nothing, staring at a spot next to the photo where the cheap oak veneer has chipped, exposing the table's pulpy insides.

The detective places three more photos down in quick succession. Annie embracing him in the lobby, her whispering in his ear at the bar, the two pressed against each other in the elevator. "Can you identify these individuals, Mrs. Shaw?"

The sharpness with which he delivers the word *Mrs.* stings like a razor blade dragged across sunburned skin. She was married. If only she'd stayed home that night, nobody would've gotten hurt.

Unfazed by her lack of response, Harper continues. "Did you know that the Harrison doesn't turn on the security cameras in executive-level hallways? Certain influential congressmen rely on

the anonymity. In fact, it's a poorly kept secret in political circles."
His eyes harden on Annie. "But I would wager it's only a matter of
time until DNA results place you in that suite. We *will* find out everything, Mrs. Shaw. It's better for you to talk to us now.

"What were you doing at the Harrison Hotel last night?"

Riddled with doubt, Annie says nothing. Her brain struggles to
piece together the previous evening's events. She hadn't expected
to bump into Ike in the lobby. The pleasure of seeing his friendly
face was fleeting, quickly replaced by guilt when she realized she'd
intentionally damaged Geoff's painting.

Ike had looked at her curiously but was too polite to put her on
the spot. Instead, he filled in the awkward pause saying, "I just met
a friend for drinks at the bar. Well, not a friend, exactly. More of a
fix-up. My cousin thinks she is a matchmaker."

Annie nodded but was too distracted to engage in the conversation. Nor could she tell Ike why she was at the hotel or what she
planned to do. She wouldn't involve him in her sordid affairs. He
seemed to sense her discomfort. "Ah, I am so sorry, Annie. I must
be getting back to the store for tonight's inventory." He made a
slightly exaggerated show of checking his watch. They exchanged
kisses on the cheek and promised to speak soon.

Detective Harper raps on the table to get her attention, the skin
on his knuckles drawn tight, shades paler than the rest of him.

"We're here to work with you, Mrs. Shaw. You don't have to cooperate, but do know that we can legally hold you here overnight
for questioning. If we do not obtain the information we need, we
can secure a warrant to enter and search your residence."

"No!" She can't risk them tramping around inside her house.
Waves of panic flood her brain, crashing into each other, colliding
with her skull. She grips her head, wanting it all to stop.

Having jarred her into a reaction, Harper softens his voice in a
masterful, one-man "good cop, bad cop" routine. "Listen, Mrs.
Shaw . . . Annie. We just want to find out what happened to him."

Her eyes lock on Harper's impassive face, as she drills for answers of her own. "You said what *happened* to him. Does that mean he's dead?"

"I can see you care deeply. This is why it's so very important that you answer my questions, Mrs. Shaw."

Annie's face is red. She's yelling. "You need to tell me! *Is Gabe alive?*"

CHAPTER 48

Harper doesn't answer Annie's question. He crosses his arms and stares back at her stony-faced, waiting for her to speak.

She crumples, her words mixed with choked sobs. "I can't remember. We had drinks, dinner—and then . . ." Unable to finish, she gestures feebly to the elevator photo.

Last night, she'd devoured him, bared every inch of her body. In the afterglow, she murmured, "Why don't we do this every night?" He didn't say anything to reciprocate, just ran his hand from her cheek down to her bare rib cage and hip bone. Did she detect a flash of panic in his eyes or had she imagined it? He was fine when she fell asleep—wasn't he?

"You can't remember? Let's try some easier questions. Maybe they'll jog your memory. Was last night the first time you met Gabriel Correa?"

"No. I first met him during an event at my daughter's school." If only she'd never accepted Danielle's invitation to the spring festival. She'd never have met Gabe and none of this would've happened.

"And I gather your relationship turned romantic?"

"We talked on the phone, had drinks one night b-before . . ." Annie nervously glances across the table at the hotel's stairwell surveillance photo.

"And had you arranged to meet Mr. Correa last night?"

"He invited me to dinner. We agreed to meet at the trattoria on the top floor of the Harrison." Her face flushes as she remembers speaking to Duncan on the phone afterward, as though she hadn't just accepted a date with another man.

"The hotel has confirmed that Mr. Correa reserved the suite in advance. Were you aware of this?"

Annie stammers. "I-I'm not sure. Everything's tangled up in my head—if you're asking me whether or not I wanted to spend the night with Gabe? The answer is yes. I can't deny that!" Realizing she's raised her voice, Annie takes a deep breath before she continues. "But he was fine. We went to sleep, then I woke up and he was like—like that! I don't know what happened, what *those things* were or where they came from. *Is Gabe okay?*"

"Thank you for that information." Harper's amber eyes don't leave Annie's face. "The metro police had specimens delivered to a specialist within the hour, a benefit of being in such close proximity to the Smithsonian. The arachnologist identified 'those things' as juvenile Brazilian wandering spiders." As he checks his notes, the shadow of a smile plays across his face. "—belonging to the genus *Phoneutria*, Greek for 'murderess.'" He now looks directly at Annie. "But *you* would know them by their common name, banana spiders."

"B-banana spiders?"

A vivid memory bolts into Annie's brain, knocking her back in her chair. She'd leaned over the railing to take in the view. The Navy Yard sprawled below, neat rows of shiny new condos lining the banks of the Anacostia. The sulfurous smell of the river mingled with brick-oven smoke, cigarettes, and pot wafted up. A sudden blast of AC as Gabe slid open the door to join her on the balcony.

"Sorry, did I wake you?" she asked.

"Only in the sense that I'm starving. I hold you responsible for working up my appetite." With a hand behind Annie's neck, Gabe guided her mouth to his, his rough stubble rubbing her cheek.

"Mmm . . . but if you're actually hungry, there's fruit." She'd pointed him to a basket of complimentary mineral waters, clementines, and bananas displayed on a low glass table.

Harper interrupts Annie's thoughts. "It's very rare for these neurotoxic spiders to attack a human, much less a human in this geographical region. They inhabit rain forests in Central and South America. Would you care to hazard a guess as to how these specimens ended up in North America, in Washington, D.C., in the Harrison Hotel, and in that exact suite?"

"Of *course* not! What are you asking me?" Annie says.

"As you can see, Mr. Correa's body was covered in spider bites." Gratuitously, Harper tosses photo after photo onto the table. "Notice how the skin has swelled up around each bite, hence the raised bumps. But here," he says, placing another photo squarely in front of her, "in this close-up, fluid has leaked out and the surrounding tissue has started to necrotize."

Annie has closed her eyes, but she winces as another photo drops onto the table. *Plunk!* Like water torture.

"It's very apparent here, in this one"—Detective Harper raps on the table to draw her attention—"that the neurotoxic venom induced priapism—a persistent, intensely painful erection."

Revolted, Annie confronts Harper. "Why are you doing this?"

Harper flips through the papers in his folio, unconcerned with Annie's distress. "Were you bitten as well, Mrs. Shaw?"

"N-no. I guess I wasn't."

"That is peculiar. How? There were literally dozens of spiders in the bed, and you claimed to have been sleeping beside the victim."

Annie's mind races. "I didn't notice the spiders until I lifted the sheet. It must have been tucked under him, separating us."

"Ah, thank you. That's very helpful," Harper says with exaggerated gratitude. "So to summarize, you were conveniently shielded by the sheet and woke up just in the nick of time—to flee the scene."

"Look, I know it sounds like it doesn't add up! But I can only tell you what I saw. I—I don't know anything else." No matter how hard Annie strains, she can't remember what happened after she and Gabe came in from the balcony and had sex again. They lay skin-to-skin, he kissed the top of her head, then nothing. It all went black.

"You underestimate yourself, Mrs. Shaw. It would seem to me that you know substantially more than you're letting on. And as I mentioned, we can obtain a warrant to search your home."

Search your home. Again, the words pump icy-cold terror into her veins. Her ears ring.

From the opposite side of the table, Harper scrutinizes her reaction, the way her eyelid flutters involuntarily, the vein in her temple that seems ready to pop. "We found it more expedient to obtain a different sort of warrant. One to search your browsing history, your cloud, and your electronic drive."

Annie exhales, realizing nobody has entered her house in her absence.

"Though my team is in the midst of reviewing this material, we've already come across an interesting piece of evidence."

Evidence? Annie gapes at him.

"It would seem that some months ago, you developed quite an interest in articles about the Brazilian wandering spider. 'Deadly spiders in banana force family from County Clark home.' 'Dozens of venomous spiders burst out of bananas.' And, from *The Tribune,* 'How neurotoxic spiders found in bananas left man fighting for his life.'"

Annie's head is swimming. "It must be a weird coincidence, I swear. I came across one of those articles online. It's clickbait! Everyone reads them! It actually upset me so much, I stopped buying bananas."

"So you read *more* about the topic that you found so upsetting? Article after article?"

"It's like picking at a scab. I couldn't stop."

"Does that happen often, Mrs. Shaw? That you can't stop? That you lose control? Because I'm starting to believe that the more we investigate you, the more *coincidences* we're going to uncover.

"You don't strike me as a woman who would intentionally hurt anyone, Mrs. Shaw. Yet how would you explain the recent violence befalling those near and dear to you? Byrdie Fenton and now Gabriel Correa. The sudden death of your own mother. Their only connection seems to be their proximity to you."

"Everything is wrong. It's all out of control. I can't explain it. God, I'm so sorry."

Her disgusting thoughts have come to fruition in excruciatingly exacting detail—details that lived in her mind and nowhere else. How could she *not* be responsible?

CHAPTER 49

It's late when Officer Williams drops Annie at home. Appreciating the fresh air after the staleness of the police station and squad car, she settles onto the porch steps. Tilting her head back, she scans the heavens, as if searching for answers. But it's one of those summer evenings when the sun and moon occupy the sky at once, blurring day and night. Everything is careering out of control, spilling out like the horrid spiderlings, seeping across boundaries like the dark pool of decay that had spread around the pasture roses.

Exhausted, Annie presses her thumb to the biometric reader. It beeps, disengages the lock, and she enters. Being home offers little relief. Her jaw doesn't unclench, her fists stay balled up.

After questioning Annie for four hours, Detective Harper provided her with the answer she desperately sought. "I can tell you Mr. Correa is in stable condition but not conscious. Doctors have put him in a medically induced coma to give his body a chance to recover. The neurotoxin induced a blood pressure spike and precipitated a heart attack. Ensuing symptoms, low heartbeat and hypothermia, were so extreme you could easily have mistaken him for dead."

It would all be a waiting game until Gabe woke up and told his side of the story—if he woke up at all. In the meantime, Harper released her with the understanding that she could be called back at any time for further questioning.

Mentally and physically exhausted, she showers, then collapses onto her bed. To Annie's surprise, she's gotten used to having the bed to herself. When Duncan left for Syria, she'd been terrified of being alone, sleeping alone. Now, the prospect of sharing the bed with her husband—the one she just cheated on—fills her with dread. She pulls the top sheet over her head. As her eyelids grow heavy, she glimpses moonlight shining through the weave of the sheet, tiny pinpricks like the ones that pierced Gabe's flesh.

◆

The next morning, Annie is roused from a deep sleep, having the distinct sensation she's being watched. Groggy, she rolls onto her back. A face looms directly over hers. Blinking away the sunlight, Annie makes out the features of her daughter.

"Tabby—Tabitha?"

"About time. I thought you'd never wake up. I slammed the door, clomped up the stairs. I even breathed on your cheek."

"Are you okay, honey? You're back?"

"Uh—yeah. I'm back." She perches on the edge of the bed, eyes trained on her feet. "I'm sorry I ran away. I just needed time to think. I was so mad after—"

"I'm the one who needs to apologize. I should never have raised my hand like that." Shaking her head vigorously, Annie scoots into a sitting position. "I've never told you this, but Grandma hit me sometimes. Not a beating—but just to show she could, I guess. I felt so confused after I found those photos, and I reacted badly. I'm sorry, Tabitha."

Tabby turns a sheepish face toward her mother and catches her eye. Then, all of a sudden, the teenager dives at her, wrapping her in a tight hug. Annie can feel the damp of her daughter's tears on her cheek, soon mingling with her own tears.

A moment later, Annie strokes her daughter's hair. "I'd like to talk about the pictures."

Tabby rolls her eyes and slides off the bed onto socked feet. "I'm just making a pit stop. Remember my class has the end-of-summer trip to Shenandoah?"

Of course, Annie had forgotten about the mandatory team-building activity Park Waldorf scheduled to herald the start of each academic year, but she nods.

"We don't need to talk today, but I want to work on making you feel like we can talk about this or anything else. Even though I've done a piss-poor job of it so far, I need to make sure you're safe. You can't control how these photos circulate. Someone could use them to hurt you, bully you, or even blackmail—" Annie stops, reminded of the photos of her and Gabe outside the whiskey bar. She still doesn't know who sent them to her.

"I know, I know. They do a whole seminar on cyber-safety in school. Every year since sixth grade. I was stupid, but I don't need the lecture." Tabby juts out her chin defiantly. "But I do need to be able to talk to you without every single thing being a big deal."

"I'd like that. I really would. And if you're comfortable with it, I'd like to meet Austin."

Tabby looks away, fighting back tears. "We broke up last night. I don't want to talk about it—other than to say he's a corny loser. Oh, and I made him delete the photos."

"Your father will be happy about that."

"Did you tell him?" Tabby's face clouds. "He still thinks of me as his little girl."

"I haven't said anything, but we'll have to at some point. He'll be back soon."

After a moment's reflection, Tabby nods. "I'll tell him the truth. It'll be okay."

Annie admires the smart, resilient young woman in front of her and silently agrees—everything will be okay as long as she keeps her daughter safe from harm.

CHAPTER 50

After lunch, Tabby hops into a Jeep loaded with tents, sleeping bags, backpacks, and three other girls from her class. Annie waves them off from the front porch, guiltily thankful her daughter will be away on this camping trip. Hopefully, any police matters will be cleared up by the time Tabitha and Duncan return home.

Just as Annie thinks about her husband, her phone dings with a text.

Checked into the Chantilly Airport Motel. Gotta crash. Love you. -D

She shoves the phone into her pocket. Annie has no idea how she'll explain to Duncan what happened with Gabe. Mentally and emotionally exhausted, she just wants to sleep, but as soon as she closes the front door two cars pull into the driveway. Detective Harper's unmarked Crown Victoria and a squad car with Officer Williams behind the wheel.

Why are the police at her house again? What could possibly have transpired between her leaving the station last night and now? Thoughts racing, pulse skyrocketing, Annie steps outside to meet them.

Detective Harper slides out of the sedan, taller in real life than in the surreal interrogation room. "Good afternoon, Mrs. Shaw. We've had a concerning development."

Did Harper's words *concerning development* mean Gabe had succumbed to his injuries? Would she be charged with murder? Suddenly, everything feels like it's spinning out of control again. She feels herself swaying. One of the men supports her with a hand to the back, then guides her by the elbow to the front door. Light-headed, she has no choice but to let them in.

"Gabe—is it Gabe?" she murmurs.

"There's no change in Mr. Correa's condition," Harper assures her. "But we do have additional questions for you."

Quickly, Annie's panic subsides, only to be replaced by nervous anxiety. Facing Harper alone last time just made things worse. For a fleeting moment, she considers calling Duncan. Her husband, holed up in an airport motel, would rush to her side. But it's ridiculous—she's in no state to tell him about being at the hotel with Gabe.

She knows she needs an attorney but feels awkward calling Ed. At the last minute, Annie had gotten cold feet and skipped their coffee appointment. Only later did she get up the nerve to apologize by text, receiving a curt reply of No problem. But glancing now at Detective Harper's somber expression, she knows she needs Ed. "I'd like to call my attorney," she says, directing the two men into the sitting room.

When Ed gets on the line, she apprises him of her last unaccompanied interview with Harper. "Annie, why didn't you call me? I was worried when you didn't show up to our meeting. Just put Harper on. I want to speak to him directly." She brings the phone into the sitting room and puts it on speaker. The concerned, understanding tone Ed used with Annie instantly disappears. "Detective Harper, under no circumstances are you to question my client without an attorney present. I will be there shortly. In the meantime, I've instructed Mrs. Shaw not to answer your queries—should you choose to disregard my advisory."

As they wait for Ed, Detective Harper attempts small talk. "You have a lovely home, Mrs. Shaw." His eyes sweep the room, from the framed family photos on the mantel, to Annie's paintings on the walls, to a traditional ao dai artfully mounted for display. He doesn't touch anything, but his gaze soils the items.

Thirty minutes later, the doorbell rings. Annie throws open the front door, relieved at the sight of Ed's face even though it's pinched with worry. The attorney offers her a brief, reassuring nod. Harper and Williams look on from the sitting room.

Ed and Annie take the wing chairs, leaving the detective and his junior to perch awkwardly side by side on a low love seat. Uncomfortable with the disadvantage, Harper rises to his feet and paces as he speaks.

"As I told Mrs. Shaw, our investigation has yielded some potentially concerning facts."

Eyeing his client's nervous fidgeting, Ed prods the detective. "Can we move on to specifics, please?"

Detective Harper issues a courteous but joyless smile. "As you know, the investigation into Byrdie Fenton's death is ongoing. Given what happened at the Harrison Hotel—and your client's proximity to both victims—my team cross-referenced Mrs. Shaw's whereabouts with any crimes of a similarly unusual nature. We surmised such events would have received extra media coverage at the time.

"Tracing her movements back over a decade was relatively simple, given her limited mobility with her daughter's schooling, and we found nothing out of the ordinary. No irregularities on the occasional trips to the Caribbean, Canada, Hawaii."

Looking the detective directly in the eye, Ed sighs pointedly.

"We were about to abandon this line of inquiry when we discovered a highly unusual incident in Hong Kong in 2002. Mrs. Shaw, you were there on the exact date of the crime and then left abruptly."

"I was in Hong Kong that summer, but I have absolutely no idea what you're talking about." Bewildered, she glances at Ed and notices his jaw twitch.

"The body of a bartender was found decomposing in a hotel trash chute. At first, authorities were unable to identify him. The lower half of his face and hands had been devoured by rats."

"Oh my god!" Annie gasps. "That can't be right. I thought . . ." She stares at Harper now, her eyes imploring him to make sense of it all.

The detective continues, "At the time, two factors led to municipal authorities undertaking, shall we say, a cursory investigation. The powerful hotel and tourism board was extremely sensitive to bad publicity that could scare off visitors, and the bartender himself had known gang ties—first in Penang and later in Hong Kong. Police had no vested interest in interfering."

Ed interjects. "Is this a fishing expedition, Detective? Throw everything against the wall and see if it sticks? You are causing my client undue stress without a shred of real evidence."

"I wouldn't jump to that conclusion, Mr. Perez. I requested the old case file myself and reviewed an itemized list of evidence recovered on or near the body." Detective Harper stares at Annie, trying to measure her reaction to his next words. "Would it surprise you, Mrs. Shaw, that his trousers pocket contained a dozen phone numbers, scribbled on the back of business cards or cocktail napkins? My team discovered that one of these phone numbers was registered to you from 2000 to 2002."

"You don't have to answer that, Annie. A couple of incidents, only tangentially associated with my client, fifteen years apart, hardly constitute a 'pattern,'" Ed says scornfully.

"The connection is stronger than you suggest," Harper says. "Vitreous humor, extracted from the bartender's eye—the remaining one—detected the presence of methanol. Now that brings us back to Pinewood."

"This is a witch hunt," Ed mutters. "Methanol is a widely used industrial chemical—solvents, pesticides, even wiper fluid!"

"Even poison? Methanol is colorless and water soluble with a slight alcohol odor. In Miss Fenton's case, it would have been lost in the harshness and 'kick' of the moonshine. However, the concentration found in the bartender's tissue samples indicates he was forced to drink a substantial quantity of the toxic substance."

Annie hasn't moved. She's physically there, but at Ed's mention of wiper fluid something in her brain clicks. She's floating, peering down at the art supplies in her studio, searching. The shelves are lined with tubs of pigment, brushes, and solvents. On the floor by her drafting table lie folded lengths of canvas and wooden frames. But tucked away in a far corner of the carriage house—three gallons of windshield wiper fluid. The cheap paint medium she's used since college.

Detective Harper brings her back to the here and now. "Mrs. Shaw! Are you even listening? Hong Kong, Pinewood, the Harrison—a reasonable mind would conclude that you, and only you, connect these highly unusual tragedies. Give us an explanation!"

Annie whispers, "How—why—did I do it? Why can't I *remember*?"

PART 3

White tiles cover the walls like in a public high school bathroom. With her head in her hands, Annie hunches over, balanced on the edge of a thin wooden bunk. She's positioned herself as far away from the foul-smelling metal toilet as possible. She tries to imagine herself at home in her bed, but the stench is an ever-present reminder that she is, in fact, in a cell in the county detention center.

"It won't be long. They're just trying to shake something out of you," Ed had said angrily when they met for the last time in the holding room. Then, meeting her eyes for the first time since her detainment earlier in the day, he said, "I'm sorry I can't do more, Annie."

"How long can they keep me here?"

"In order to hold you in custody beyond forty-eight hours, the prosecutor has to file criminal charges." Seeing the panic on her face, he added, "But I highly doubt they'll keep you that long. It's just a tactical maneuver. Harper wants answers. Don't say anything. Not a word." Ed cleared his throat and promised to be back the next day.

Now, Annie clutches her throbbing temples as if to squeeze out the answers that could free her from this disgusting place. For the first time in weeks, she longs for her husband's reassuring presence. More precisely, she longs for the ability to hide behind his privilege. Would they have arrested her if Duncan had been at her side?

In Ed's car, on the way here, she'd broken down and called Duncan's cell phone. It went straight to voicemail. She didn't leave a message—better to let him sleep, oblivious, in an airport motel, while she figured out how to confess about Gabe.

At least Tabby is safe camping with her classmates. A stroke of luck when everything else was going to hell. The thought of being exposed to her daughter as a dirty criminal pains Annie, as if an unseen hand has reached beneath her ribs into her chest cavity, squeezing the muscle of her diaphragm.

She makes it to the toilet just in time to be sick. Knees trembling, she doesn't trust her legs to hold her weight. She has to crawl back to the bunk. The concrete floor doesn't feel rough and dry as it should; instead it leaves a residue on her hands. Years of accumulated filth.

You get what you deserve, Anh.

Just looking at the threadbare wool blanket makes her itch. What if the cell has scabies? A few months ago, she saw a story about a nursing home resident "eaten alive" by the microscopic mites. They burrowed into her epidermis, lived, and laid eggs. Host to millions of mites, the woman's skin crusted over. It no longer served as a protective barrier. Bacteria entered at will, invading her body and eventually causing a fatal sepsis. Annie had punished herself by poring over disgusting dermatological images that showed the patterns of intensely itchy bumps. She told herself she'd never let that happen to her body. She'd drink poison first— kill herself from the inside out, rather than let her skin be penetrated, her body invaded from the outside.

Sour acid rises in the back of her throat. She tries to swallow it along with the remnants of vomit, but her mouth is dry. The room spins, and in her dizzy haze she hears a woman laughing. It's her. She's thinking about Dr. Patel. The doctor would probably call this "exposure therapy" and bill Duncan's insurance for an overnight stay.

The air in the cell is sweltering, but Annie shivers as her mind replays all the terrible things that happened since she found her mother's body in the carriage house.

You get what you deserve, Anh.

"Shut up! Can't you just die? Leave me alone!" Annie screams.

Chatter quiets in the cells around her, but she doesn't notice. Her voice breaks into a choked sob. "Good-bye, Mẹ."

◆

The entire row of cells faces a blank plaster wall. Annie can't see inside any of the other cells, but she knows each one is occupied, some by multiple occupants. She noticed this earlier when an officer escorted her to her own cell. The officer, a heavyset woman with dirty-blond hair and smoker's breath, maintained a constant stream of conversation laden with complaints about overcrowding and being overworked. She spoke with an unabashed racism that she'd probably have censored if Annie had an accent or black or brown skin.

"Used to be decent work. Neighborhood screwups sleeping one off in a cell. Then some asswipe paper-pusher at county decides to make a quick buck by taking overflow from ICE. Now it's a smelly hellhole. We're stuck dealing with it, and most of 'em don't even speak English."

Annie draws her knees up to her chest and rocks back and forth, listening to the hum of voices. One floats above the rest. Higher-pitched, melodic, the voice of a young girl. The child is engaged in rapid-fire conversation with a woman in a language Annie doesn't understand. Her words bounce with excitement while another voice, her mother's perhaps, responds in low tones as though conserving a dwindling supply of energy.

Four decades ago, that had been Annie and Mẹ—with one crucial difference. They'd been welcomed into the safety of a refugee camp, while this little girl and her mother were imprisoned, threatened, and treated like criminals.

Annie listens as the child recites a silly verse in a singsong lilt, maybe a playground chant or nursery rhyme. She and her mom laugh softly at the inside joke. Despite their bleak reality, they are finding a way to survive by creating their own magical world—*just the two of them.*

It's astounding what the brain can do to protect you from harm, especially when you have no control over what's happening. Especially when you've been displaced by bloody wars you're too young to understand.

Mildew-stained tiles cover the walls. The stench of urine mingled with sweat permeates every pore on Hien's body. But she herself does not sweat. She's too dehydrated. In a way, they were lucky their boat was captured before reaching international waters. It saved their lives. There was never going to be enough fresh water to sustain everyone on board.

The jail cell is crowded. She sits with her knees scrunched up, lucky to have a spot against the wall to lean her back. Closing her eyes, she feels the almost imperceptible stirring in her belly. Her swollen stomach prevented her from being taken, used, and never seen again—like many of the other young women. The baby saved her life; now she has to save the baby.

Both of her babies. Her son Bảo rests his head on her shoulder, snoring softly. She almost can't bear to wake him, but she has to. The food cart is coming. Some days it doesn't. Gently, she shakes his shoulder. His eyes fly open. At age six, he's too young to have fear as his first waking emotion.

Hien stuffs a paper bill in his hand. "Go. Go now!" She sees his slim form weave between the legs of the adults and older kids. He must wave the cash between the jail cell bars and get the attention of the Vietnamese woman and her daughter who run the cart. If he does not succeed before the food runs out, she's not sure if the baby inside will survive.

He returns with a packet of rice the size of an orange. She lets him eat first but can't bring herself to stop him. There's barely any left when he's done. Her body heaves with dry sobs. She has to find a way out.

◆

GUAM, TWO MONTHS LATER

Hien shuffles her feet to avoid falling. Her middle is bigger now, making her clumsy. She clutches what's left of her belongings—a small satchel containing two dresses and a knife, and the unborn baby in her belly.

The crowd around her pushes. Officers herd them into the refugee processing center. They will live in tents made of plastic sheeting and boat timbers. And then, hopefully, they will be sent to a friendly country like Canada, France, Italy, or even the United States. Everything will be okay then. She looks at the faces around her. Their eyes are clouded with desperation, death. But beneath this dark cataract lies a glint of hope. They are the lucky ones.

But Hien knows she made her own luck. She had to. For the baby. She traded information, her husband's location, for their release. He is—was—a powerful colonel. She didn't take pleasure in betraying him, but the war forced impossible choices. She chose her children.

Her children—the thought triggers an explosion of laughter. Hysteria. She can't stop laughing, her whole body shakes uncontrollably. The people in the crowd move away from her. They stare but keep their distance.

No, she will never speak of "her children" again. There is only one now. Bảo died last night. Dirty water. An infection. Diarrhea, vomit, until all that was left was spent shell. They told her she couldn't keep him on the boat, but she clung to him. Two men had to unwrap her fingers from his ankles. They tossed him overboard like trash.

Hien wipes saliva from the corner of her mouth and pats her belly protectively. A daughter—she's certain of it. "Anh," she murmurs, repeating the name over and over like a mantra. She will never let this one go. It will be just the two of them.

CHAPTER 52

The crust of drool on Annie's cheek and the stiffness in her limbs are the only indications she slept. She's still exhausted. Her holding cell has no windows. The light, an unyieldingly cold fluorescence, does not betray the time.

Would confessing get her home any faster? She has to be there when Tabby returns from Shenandoah this weekend. The trauma of war had taken something from Mẹ. In turn, her mother had relied on Annie for too much, taken too much of her childhood, too much of her adulthood. Annie is determined not to let her own problems damage her daughter. Still, she knows she can't confess—at least not believably—because for the first time, Annie is certain of her innocence. She failed in some ways as a daughter. She may not be the best mother. She even cheated on her husband. But she is not a murderer.

Harper's interrogation, the disgusting crime scene photos, her imprisonment—all intended to turn Annie upside down, to shake her. And, though she was badly shaken, absolutely nothing had come out. Not a shred of evidence.

She stands up, strides over to the metal toilet, and pees. At this point, she's so dirty—so far gone—that she's free.

◆

A few hours later, a warden leads Annie to a bleak interrogation room. This one does not look like a teachers' lounge, but it does contain the reassuring face of Ed Perez. Annie manages a smile as she lowers herself into the seat beside him. Opposite them, Harper stares pensively into his phone as if he's just received distressing news.

Then he clears his throat and begins his questioning in a voice that's uncharacteristically clipped and tense. "Mrs. Shaw, what can you tell me—now that you've had time to reflect on recent events?

Annie begins to shake her head, but Ed places a hand on her forearm to restrain her. "Detective Harper, my client has given her statement to the best of her ability and still, you detained her."

Harper interrupts: "Mr. Perez, need I remind you your client is a person of interest in not one but at least *three* violent crimes." A muscle at his temple twitches. "And, aside from the victim, she was the only other person in the hotel suite that night."

Detective Harper shifts his attention back to Annie. "I can see this experience has been incredibly stressful, but once you share the whole story with us, the weight of the world will be lifted off your shoulders. Now, this is the time to tell me if you have anything to add."

"Yes," she says before Ed can interject. The attorney's glare bores a hole into the side of her head. A hint of a smile passes over the detective's face.

"Upon reflection, I am absolutely certain I didn't hurt anyone. I'd never hurt him on purpose. I blacked out myself. I must have been drugged too."

"Unfortunately, it's far too late to test for traces in your system," Harper says. "Is there a reason you didn't ask to be tested immediately afterward? Wouldn't it be reasonable for someone in your position to seek medical assistance instead of running?"

Ed asserts himself before Annie can incriminate herself. "This has been asked and answered by my client. We will not be giving any further statement on that point." He gives Annie a cautionary look and continues. "Do you have a new line of inquiry, Detective? If not, I'd like to request my client's immediate discharge."

"Why, yes, there is another discrepancy your client could shed light on," Harper says. He speaks slowly to show he won't be hurried. Again, he is calm and back in command. "The crime scene investigator removed two empty bottles of Corrente, an expensive Italian mineral water, from the wastebasket."

"We both drank one," Annie says, confused.

"The strange thing is that the brand is not carried by the Harrison Hotel. The standard complimentary water bottles were replaced with this more exotic brand. Are you familiar with Corrente, Mrs. Shaw?"

"Yes, I drink it all the time."

"I see. That would explain why we found a case of this expensive Italian mineral water in your pantry," he says, the last part dripping with scorn.

"This is crazy. I drink it because it's certified as pure spring water. A lot of the water bottles you get are just tap water. Who knows what's in there—"

"Yes, anything could be put in bottled water. Isn't that right, Mrs. Shaw?" Harper says.

But Annie doesn't reply, struck by the realization the police have entered her home. They've searched through her things. Her thoughts begin to spiral to all the things the outsiders touched. Her underwear drawer, their dishes, the food in the refrigerator. What if someone used her toilet? Touched the faucet handles?

Fortunately, Ed jumps in. "Detective Harper, my wife drinks Corrente. Do you suspect her as well? This line of questioning is absurd. It's far more likely the housekeeping staff ran out of their standard complimentary water bottles and made a substitution. I guarantee you if I walk into the natural foods market in the Navy Yards, they sell bottles of Corrente water.

"I will be filing for the immediate release of my client. That is, unless you plan to file criminal charges today, which frankly, I don't see happening given the shameful, unfounded speculation and intimidation my client has been subjected to." Having thrown down the gauntlet, Ed leans back and glares at Harper.

Neither flinches, but after a beat, Detective Harper says, "Your client is free to leave at any time. She will be under surveillance," he adds, "for her own safety, of course."

CHAPTER 53

The sun hangs low in the sky as Ed's car climbs the hill toward the Shaw house. There had been paperwork, lots of it, before they were allowed to leave the station.

"Please know I had nothing to do with any of this," Annie says. She spent the forty-five-minute car ride trying to hash out what was going on. The gory homicide fifteen years ago and Byrdie's death were coincidences. If you looked hard enough for connections, you could find them anywhere. The night at the hotel, though—that was very real, and well beyond tragic synchronicity. Someone must have framed her . . . but who?

"Of course. And don't worry, we'll do everything we can to clear this up." Ed sounds confident, but he stares directly ahead, avoiding eye contact.

He promises to call her with any news, and as he's backing out of the driveway, he rolls down his window. "Remember, I'm here if you need me."

After he's gone, Annie lingers on the porch, torn between her worry about the large task of decontaminating her home and her appreciation of her surroundings. In contrast to the rank cell, a warm breeze carries the scent of fresh-cut grass from a neighboring property. The last bits of sunshine illuminate the treetops. Annual cicadas buzz in a frenetic mating call.

As she takes in the view, Annie's smile fades. In the distance, a dark figure takes shape. The scarecrowlike being picking its way toward her—it doesn't belong here. Are her eyes playing tricks on her? Annie shuts them, hoping it will be gone by the time she opens her eyes. But when she does, the figure is closer. Then the light shifts and illuminates the form. Dr. Patel.

The doctor waves and calls out. "Annie, hello! Nobody was here when I arrived, so I took it upon myself to stroll about the gardens to your little carriage house. I hope it's not a problem."

A therapy appointment is the last thing on Annie's mind. She must look a mess after her night in the holding cell, gauging by the quizzical look on Dr. Patel's face as she climbs the porch steps.

"Um—ah—is this a good time?" the doctor asks.

Ignoring the fact that she's in desperate need of a toothbrush, Annie asks Dr. Patel a question. "Where is your car? It's not in the driveway."

Dr. Patel titters. "My speedy driving strikes again. I got here early so I parked on the street a ways back and walked. Need the exercise." Her fingers fly to her waistband.

"I suppose it's as good a time as any," Annie says, too tired to protest. She begins to gesture to the porch bench, then changes her mind. "Would you like to come in?" It almost doesn't matter anymore. Annie is filthy, and Detective Harper's men have already tramped through the house. There is nothing left to keep clean.

Dr. Patel smiles and nods with a mixture of pleasant surprise and mild concern.

"Please have a seat," Annie says, gesturing toward the sitting room. "I'll get us some water." So far, nothing appears to be out of place. Harper's team had been on good behavior. Annie fills a glass from the refrigerator's water dispenser, drinks it greedily, then refills it.

She returns with a cold bottle of water and a tight smile for the doctor, as she recalls their last encounter when Dr. Patel revealed that she and Duncan dated and lived together in college. Why had they kept it from Annie?

She plunks the chilled Corrente mineral water directly in front of Dr. Patel. No flash of recognition on the doctor's face. She simply says, "Delightful! Thanks. It's a bit late, shall we get started?"

Annie sighs, installing herself into a wing chair opposite the doctor.

"How have you been, Annie? I can see you're distressed or . . . um . . . disheveled?"

There's no reason to hold anything back now. Tired and desperate for someone to make sense of the mess, Annie throws caution to the wind. She will tell Dr. Patel everything—the Harrison, Harper's accusations, the night in jail. The story comes out in fits and starts, as Annie stops several times to compose herself. When she describes waking up next to Gabe's ravaged body, her stomach tightens. She takes a sip of water before continuing.

As Annie tells her story, Dr. Patel's usual chipper demeanor transforms into shocked disbelief.

"Have you been able to visit Gabe in the hospital?"

"No. My attorney told me he's heavily sedated, so he's not conscious."

"And what about the other incident the police mentioned, in Hong Kong, you said?"

"There was a bartender. I remember him, but I don't know . . ." she says. Her words come out haltingly.

"Try not to doubt yourself. This is an incredibly stressful situation for anyone. It's important to lean on your support system in difficult times like this. Have you been candid with Duncan about your relationship with Gabe and the recent . . . development?"

"No, I haven't been able to reach him."

At this, Dr. Patel's eyelids flutter, and she purses her lips in what Annie perceives as a sign of disapproval.

"He's my husband. I don't blame him for leaving anymore. I'm the one who blew up our marriage. Honestly, it probably should have been blown up a long time ago," she admits, her voice catching with emotion. Annie stares at a spot on the wall just beyond Dr.

Patel's head. If she makes eye contact, her courage might falter. It's time to speak the truth.

"Why do you think that is, Annie? Your marriage has been strong for well over a decade. Have you always had these unexpressed regrets? Or are they surfacing now because someone else is in the picture?"

"I'm not the first one to have cheated," Annie says defensively. She sees Duncan in the seedy motel room in Hong Kong, the image as vivid as if it happened yesterday. "I mean, it was before we were actually married, but a prostitute was involved. Even though they didn't actually have sex, I was disgusted. I would have—should have ended it immediately, but I found out I was pregnant with Tabby. Then everything just happened. The marriage, all of it, just happened."

"What degree of control did you have in the situation, Annie? Because I'm hearing that you felt powerless. Has there ever been violence in your marriage?"

"No, of course not. Duncan would never hurt me or Tabby. He's always taken care of us all." Annie firmly shakes her head. "Going along with what he wanted was just easier. That way I wouldn't be responsible if anything bad happened. When Tabby was born, you know I had trouble. What if I dropped her or hurt her somehow? I couldn't even get up to bathe, much less take care of another human being. Duncan did *everything*, and he did it better than I would have. He fed her, got her on a sleep schedule, and later, he chose a great school."

Annie buries her face in her hand thinking about how she'd repaid her husband by cheating.

"When I was offered a teaching job in the city, he connected me to Byrdie so I wouldn't need to work away from home, so I could take care of my mom. He was so patient about my mom. I mean, he chose this town for us all, found this house, had it restored for us. It would have been selfish not to go along with everything. It was just better for everyone that way."

"Was it better for *you*, Annie?"

"I don't know. I'd never had to—been allowed to—decide anything until I ran away to college. Then I met Duncan. He was safe, stable, and everything was fine as long as I didn't look too closely. I know it's your job, Dr. Patel, but if you overanalyze things, you'll only see the bad."

"That's actually true. Part of the process is recognizing what's not working in your life so you can take action to fix it. The goal is to focus on what's in your control and let the rest go. OCD doesn't want you to let anything go. It tricks your brain into thinking you can control everything through magical thinking and rituals. But, as I like to say, controlling your own actions is all you can do when circumstances spin out.

"For example, you talked about your mother's hoarding. Her disordered brain compelled her to hold on to things, stake territory, claim loyalties. Her behavior impacted you as a child and beyond. It can be useful to examine that impact, rather than suppress it. Then you can begin the process of forgiveness—for your mother and yourself."

Annie thinks about her night in detention. Hitting rock bottom stripped everything away—the anger, resentment, and judgment she'd held on to for so many years—and made space for a new perspective. She was beginning to view herself and her mother with generosity and empathy. The seeds of forgiveness were beginning to germinate.

"My mother sacrificed. She tried to take care of me, but she was terrified of being alone. She held on desperately to whatever she could—an old coffee can, a rotted banana peel . . . me."

"It sounds like you're starting to examine the causes of her actions—and yours. That's healthy. Locking away painful emotions is how the brain protects itself. The problem is that you can never completely contain the anxiety. Inevitably, it seeps through the crevices and contaminates other aspects of your life.

"Similarly, you might try to bury your marital discontent, but it will inevitably resurface. Everything may seem stable, but then one party has an affair 'out of the blue.'"

"Why now, though? We've been together so long. Why is everything bursting at the seams?"

Tears of frustration have begun to well up in Annie's eyes, but Dr. Patel glances at her phone, distracted. Her reply is jarringly cheerful and pat. "Well, that's certainly something to examine. We've made a lot of progress today and there's a lot to think about. Unfortunately, I'm already quite late for a commitment in the city that I cannot miss. I absolutely cannot."

She stands up and absent-mindedly flicks a cat hair off her navy blue dress pants. "I *am* sorry to rush off like this, Annie. You're going through a very stressful time. We'll resume our discussion in the next session. In the meantime, don't hesitate to buzz me. Leave a message if I can't answer. As I said, don't be afraid to lean on your friends for emotional support! And I urge you to reach out to Duncan again. I know him. He's a good man, a good father, and I *know* he wants to be with you now."

The doctor speaks with a fierce conviction that makes the hairs on the back of Annie's neck stand up.

CHAPTER 54

L *ean on your friends."* That's the advice Dr. Patel had given her. There was something to it, certainly. Annie was accustomed to hiding her pain from others, shoving it back deeper and deeper until it was so far away, she could pretend it never existed. But unburdening herself to the doctor was liberating. She'd begun to put her childhood and marriage under the harsh light of truth and the world had not ended.

She takes Dr. Patel's advice and calls Danielle. Car horns sound in the background. "Hey, honey, can't talk and drive—heck, I can barely drive anyway!"

Annie winces, thankful her friend can't see. She hears a car door slam.

"Just got to Barb's Booty Bootcamp. I'll swing by your place after, and we can talk then. If I can still walk, that is. No promises."

In the sitting room where she was interrogated just the day before yesterday, Annie sets out two chilled bottles of stevia ginger ale and a keto nut mix she knows her friend loves. She catches sight of herself in the wall mirror, surprised to see she doesn't *look* any different. The dark shadows and bloodshot eyes have been there for weeks.

She could even move forward pretending the night in jail hadn't happened. Nobody besides Ed, bound by attorney-client privilege, and Dr. Patel, bound by doctor-patient confidentiality, would know the difference. But part of her doesn't want to do this, and that part has grown strong enough to crowd out the bullies and compulsions that enjoyed free rein for so long. She even managed to clean the house, moving from room to room until she was finished, instead of getting stuck and returning again and again to the same spot. The bandage was ripped off by the police search—but she knows the OCD will still lurk and try to insinuate itself into her life with promises of keeping her safe.

An hour after Danielle arrives, Annie finishes telling her friend about what happened with Gabe and the night in jail. She does not mention the fifteen-year-old murder Harper was trying so desperately to link her to. Hong Kong had nothing to do with her. Ed said they were grasping at straws. And for the first time since Annie's known her, Danielle is speechless. Then she leans over and wraps Annie in her arms. Annie squeezes back and tears spill from both of them.

"Duncan will be back home soon," Annie says. "I've decided to tell him about Gabe right away." Her voice breaks. "There's a chance Gabe might not make it, but even if he does, the affair is over." But, in that moment, Annie considers *not* telling her husband immediately. She remembers what he was like upon returning from his Pulitzer-winning stint all those years ago. Dead tired and uncommunicative, a colorless zombie who lacked the charisma to scare. He'd handle her admission better after a few weeks of decompressing.

A similar thought has occurred to Danielle. "Telling Duncan is the right thing to do, but he'll be gutted. He's devoted to you. It could be better to wait and see what happens with Gabe. This sounds awful, but at least there will be some resolution then and you can tell him the whole story. I mean, this has been a *lot*, even for me. And we don't sleep together, darlin'!" Danielle smiles wryly at her own joke.

Her phone dings and she glances at the screen. "Dammit! I'm supposed to be watching a movie with Ray, like, now," she says, jumping up from the love seat. "Why don't you come over tomorrow night so we can talk some more? It'll just be me and Ray. We'll order in."

"I couldn't impose, and I'd hate to be a third wheel."

Danielle thinks a moment, and then her face brightens. "I'll invite Ike! I haven't seen him in ages. We'll make it a super low-key grown-ups party."

"Sure. That would be nice. What can I bring?"

"Absolutely nothing. Trust me. We're in the middle of a super strict raw food detox. This celeb nutritionist designed it, and I get it delivered from the café in my gym. Everything's guided by probiotics. Ray's even doing it, but I'm sure he cheats all the time."

CHAPTER 55

On Saturday, Annie wakes up early and makes breakfast. Tabby's due back from her camping trip this morning.

The moment Annie got her phone back at the detention center, she texted her daughter.

How are you? I love you.

The reply was typically Tabby:

I'm going to delete this thread, so there's zero chance any of my friends see your message.

But an earnest text followed a couple of seconds later.

We took a night hike yesterday!!! Saw the Milky Way.

Now as she brews tea, Annie smiles at the mental image of her jaded teenage daughter marveling at the night sky. Just then, the front door opens.

"Mo-om! I'm ho-ome!"

Annie races out of the kitchen and catches her startled daughter in a hug.

"Uh—good morning?" Tabby says.

"I made breakfast—charcoal-free this time. Grab a seat in the dining room."

"Ooh-la-la. Aren't we fancy?" Tabby smiles but eyes her mother a little suspiciously.

From the kitchen, Annie regards the back of Tabby's head and a warmth swells inside her chest. Her daughter has grown into a strong, talented, perceptive, kindhearted human. Maybe Annie hasn't always been the best mom, but she's the only one Tabby has.

Annie knows she needs to do better. Trying to construct a contained, controlled world didn't work for Mẹ, and it hasn't worked for Annie either. The ugly side of life always bleeds through whether you wanted it to or not. She owes her daughter the truth.

She carries a big plate loaded with freshly sliced fruit into the dining room.

"Sometimes I love having an Asian mom." Tabby smiles, perched on a chair with her arms wrapped around her knees, feet bare.

As she sits down, Annie playfully grabs her toe. "I remember when you were born, they took your footprint in the neonatal unit. It was so tiny. Your body was so fragile, but I could tell you were strong inside. Daddy said you could handle anything, and he was right. Just look how great you turned out."

Seeing the emotion well up in Annie's eyes, the girl forgoes her usual sardonic retorts. "You okay, Mom? I mean really. You've been, like, distracted with Dad gone."

"I'm okay, yeah." Annie hesitates. It would be so easy to leave it at that, to simply stop talking, but she forges on before her courage dissipates.

"I-I did something, though. Something I'm not proud of." She can't quite look Tabby in the eye as she says, "I went out with someone else. A man. Not your father." She's stammering now and pauses to take a deep breath.

"So you went on a date with a guy who . . . wasn't Dad," Tabby says, her tone even and curious. "What's he like? How did you meet?"

"His name is Gabe. We met at the spring festival. He brought his niece. Looking back, we had this instant . . . magnetism . . . pulling us together."

Tabby snorts at this. "Meaning you wanted to *fuck*."

"Tabby! That's not necessary. Your language." Annie scolds her daughter because she's embarrassed by the truth in Tabby's words. "We really liked each other. Went out a couple of times, and I did spend a night with him." She faces Tabby now, studying her for signs of damage.

"Whoa—does Dad know?"

"Not yet. I'm going to tell him after he files his story. I don't want to hurt him more than I already have." Seeing her daughter's face sadden, Annie reaches out to touch her cheek. "Whatever happens with Daddy and me, we still love you. You know that, right?"

"Uh, yeah. I wasn't worried about that. I mean literally more than half the kids in my class have divorced parents, not to mention the ones from like *third* marriages. You can tell because the dads are geriatric," she says, shaking her head. "I'm not a baby. People get divorced."

"I'm sorry. I know you're not a little kid anymore. You're a smart young woman."

Tabby gives the ceiling a hard stare, but Annie plows on.

"My point is I'm not going to try to put blinders on you anymore. I'll try to show you the good, the bad, and the ugly and trust you to cope."

She takes Tabby's subtle nod as a win. She's finally done something right as a mother. For a few moments, they don't speak. Tabby processes the news and Annie absorbs her daughter's shockingly mature response. Somehow, amid all the craziness, they'd managed to raise a confident, resilient human being.

"That isn't everything, though. Something happened to him. When we were together the other night, he got hurt. I think someone wanted him to die."

Tabby's eyes open wide. "Did he . . . die?"

"No, but he was seriously injured. I don't know his condition now exactly. I haven't seen or talked to him since that night."

"How do you know someone was after him? What actually happened? Were *you* attacked?" Anxiety rises in Tabby's voice. "Did they hurt you too?"

"We weren't on the street. We met in a hotel. We had a room together." Annie feels her face getting hot and turns away to hide it. "He was poisoned. The way it happened, though—it was like whoever did it was inside my head."

"What the hell does that mean, Mom?" Tabby shouts. "You're one step away from saying voices in your head told you to . . ."

"No, Tabby, that's not what I'm saying. I think that whoever did this knows how to scare me. They've been following me, taking pictures."

"Following you?" She swallows. "I'm scared."

Annie presses on. "I was out cold. I think whoever it was must've drugged me too."

"Did you call the police?" Tabby begins shifting nervously in her seat.

"The police are involved, but I'm okay now. Mostly, I'm just sorry if I've hurt you. That's the last thing I want."

CHAPTER 56

Annie brushes her hair, then piles it into a loose knot. Outside, the heat and humidity have returned with a vengeance, and there is the chance Danielle will serve dinner on the patio again. She pulls a simple linen dress from her closet and slips it on.

Tabby went off with her friends a couple hours ago, but not before giving Annie a hug and telling her to "Be safe." After her daughter left, Annie eagerly collapsed into bed, desperate for a catnap. Ed's phone call awakened her from dreamless sleep. He called under the guise of giving her an update on Gabe's condition, but she suspected he was checking in on her more than anything. There had been no change in Gabe, and his brother hadn't left his side. Their mother was too old to travel.

Annie smiled as Ed rambled on, a behavior completely counter to his trademark efficiency. He had been concerned about her and wanted to reach out but was too formal to admit it.

Annie jumped in, "I'll be okay, Ed, thanks in no small part to your support. I probably wouldn't have made it through this far without you. You've been a great lawyer and a really great . . . friend. And, from one friend to another, you don't have to worry about me."

"Don't let my steely calm demeanor fool you. All I do is worry about my clients. *And* my friends." His voice was filled with warmth, and she pictured him smiling on the other end of the line.

Annie gives herself a quick once-over in the mirror and checks her watch. Dressed and ready to go with thirty minutes to spare, she considers stopping by the shop for a bottle of wine but remembers Danielle's strict diet.

Just then, she hears a car pull into the driveway. Tabby must have come back early. Annie skips down the stairs and opens the front door. She doesn't recognize the SUV in the driveway as belonging to any of Tabby's friends. She squints but can't see past the tinted windshield to the driver. The trunk is open.

A familiar voice calls out, but it's not her daughter. "Annie, is that you? I'm home!"

Duncan's beaming face emerges from behind the trunk. He shouts a hurried thanks to the driver and rushes toward Annie, jettisoning his duffel bag on the ground behind him. Soon his tall frame fills the doorway, blocking out the light.

Annie's feet are fused to the ground, her circuitry overloaded with conflicting emotions. She manages to eke out a monosyllabic response. "Hi."

"You . . . don't look happy to see me," he says, half observation, half question. She shrivels as he scans her from head to toe. "You look nice. Sorry, were you going out? I should have called." He doesn't try to mask his disappointment. "I just couldn't stay away any longer, so I checked out of the motel early."

"If I had known . . . I'm just going to Danielle's for dinner."

"Ah—you have on that lovely dress and here I am covered in my own stink. I wouldn't want to hug me either," he says, grimacing. The sunburn on the bridge of his nose has already begun to peel.

Annie softens, recalling how doggedly Duncan worked on deadline, refusing to shower or even to stop and brush his teeth. "I'm sorry. You just caught me off guard. I thought you'd call first. Of course I'm glad you're back. Have you eaten?"

"Don't worry about it. I stopped by the café on the way home. I'm going to hop in the shower so we can still make dinner at Danielle's."

Annie flinches. While she found the courage to be honest with Dr. Patel, Danielle, and even Tabby—she hasn't figured out what to say to her husband. "Oh! Uh, I'm sure she's already ordered, and it's that health food stuff anyway, so you probably wouldn't like it." It's a miserable excuse. Even a passing acquaintance would know Danielle to be spontaneous, a free spirit who'd welcome unexpected guests with open arms and proclaim "The more the merrier!"

"Man, how rude of me. You don't think she'd mind, do you? I should call her. Besides, my system is still so messed up from the time difference I don't think I'll even eat anything. I promise I'll mind my table manners, Annie," he says with a chuckle. Annie lets out the tiniest of sighs.

"Of course. You shower and I'll text her."

"Amazing!" He passes his wife, pausing to give her a kiss on the cheek. His breath smells of stale cigarettes. Annie forces herself not to recoil.

"I know. I'm filthy," he says, staring into her eyes. "I just couldn't wait to see you again."

◆

Showered and changed, Duncan whistles as he fiddles with the radio, one hand draped over the top of the steering wheel. Annie is glad there wasn't time to chat before leaving for dinner. Now that he's back, the real prospect of unburdening herself petrifies Annie.

She'd texted Danielle about her husband's unexpected return. Danielle responded with the scream emoji. Annie's phone dings and she glances at it, careful to angle it away from Duncan toward the passenger-side window.

Did you tell him about HFT?

At some point, Danielle designated Gabe "Hot for Teacher" or HFT in all written communication.

Annie types back,

N.

She's too nervous to write more with her husband sitting next to her. All the bravado she had when he was away has dissipated now that he's here, inches away from her. Telling him about Gabe would be harder than she thought.

"Who's that?" he asks casually.

"Just Danielle."

"Is she mad I invited myself? I shouldn't have. I was just so excited to be back."

"No. You know her. She loves a party."

He chuckles. "That she does. And how's Ray doing? Is he still banging half the PTA?"

"I wouldn't even joke about that. He's up to his usual—and then some."

"Jesus," he says, turning into the private drive that leads to the Parks' house. "You know, I really feel for her. I can't imagine how painful it would be. Of all the people in the world, you choose this one person to be with, to have a child with, and they violate that bond. It's the ultimate betrayal, isn't it?"

She keeps staring out the window but can feel his eyes on her. Has he noticed the flush creeping into her cheeks? "Mind if I turn the AC up?" she asks, fanning herself with a hand. "I'm roasting."

"Sure. I'm numb to the heat right now. After Syria, this place feels like paradise."

CHAPTER 57

They seem okay," Danielle says, returning from the patio door where she'd been eavesdropping on the three men. "Your husband's talking about taking artillery fire and mine's saying he'd choose it over the day he had yesterday. Lost a bundle, but he gets it all back eventually. It's like play money at this point. We have enough."

Flitting about the kitchen in a shimmery kimono-sleeve mini dress, Danielle looks like a butterfly. She prattles on even more than usual tonight, nervously filling in the silent spaces. Edgy, knowing Annie hasn't told Duncan anything about the investigation or the affair. "Ike looks bored to tears. Maybe it was a mistake for me to invite him. I wanted to get his opinion on my latest beadwork, though. It's tribal inspired. Oh god, I meant his opinion as an artist. Not because he's . . ."

Danielle's anxiety is contagious. Annie shoots a nervous glance outside at Ray. Neither Ike nor Danielle knows that Ray was responsible for sending the first photo. But Annie still doesn't know who sent the subsequent photos of her and Gabe. Though Ray denied it, Annie has flip-flopped on whether she believes him. He's capable of blackmail—what else is in his shit-stirring arsenal? It was also possible that wires got crossed and he hadn't called off his man in time.

"Let's not leave them alone too long. Don't want them getting into trouble," Annie says, growing increasingly uneasy as she watches the men standing over the Parks' tiered pool, which features intricately lit grottoes and waterfalls. "Besides, we need to save Ike from the alpha bro banter."

Danielle nods and hands Annie a stack of clean plates to carry onto the patio. The word *patio* seems entirely inadequate as the hardscape white-stone expanse looks fancier than any outdoor restaurant Annie has ever seen. Soft jazz music surrounds them, emanating from some hidden sound system.

Seeing his wife balancing a tray of tall glasses filled to the brim with microbrewed kombucha, Ray wisecracks, "Polishing up your bartending skills, Danny?"

He turns to Duncan for approval, only to find the other man ignoring him. Duncan and Ike have simultaneously leapt up to take the tray off Danielle's hands. There's an awkward moment, but Ike lets go first.

"Ah, so gallant!" Danielle fawns. "Don't fight over me, boys!"

Ray grunts in response. "What are we having tonight, dear?" he asks, rolling his eyes at Duncan while ignoring Ike.

"Pizza!" Danielle grins. "Cashew cheese, veggies on top, and a red pepper flax crust. The best part is, it's all raw vegan, but you wouldn't even be able to tell!"

An awkward silence follows her announcement. Sensing a snide remark from her husband on the horizon, Danielle says, "I have to get some ice. Be right back." She retreats to the house, shoulders slightly slumped.

"Where are you going? The wet bar's six feet away!" he says to Danielle's back, but she ignores him. Even without his wife present, Ray can't help himself. "Trust me, you can tell it's raw and vegan when you're floating air biscuits a couple hours later."

Disgusted, Annie excuses herself, but before she leaves, Ike catches her eye, imploring her not to leave him. "Ike—give us a hand inside?" Without thinking, she winks at him in comradery. Ray tosses a knowing glance at Duncan.

Inside, they find Danielle carefully transferring a carton of jalapeño broccoli balls onto a platter. "Is Ray bitching about the food?" she asks. Not turning around or waiting for an answer, she rambles on nervously, "He just likes to show off. He's such an insecure child sometimes. I wish he were more like Duncan. Are you sure about riding off into the sunset with this other guy, hon?"

Ike clears his throat to announce his presence and, suddenly realizing her misstep, Danielle drops a broccoli ball onto the counter. The three of them watch it roll onto the floor, landing with a dull thud on the marble tile.

Annie turns to Ike. "I-I haven't told you. I haven't even told Duncan. We've been having problems."

"What . . . you guys have been together since Providence! What's wrong?"

Annie struggles with the question. There was never anything *wrong*. Her husband has always been considerate, caring, and a wonderful father. "I don't know if I'm in love with him anymore— if I ever really was." She speaks quietly, almost to herself more than to the others.

"Look, you've been through a lot lately and with Duncan gone . . . maybe he was an easy target?" Danielle asks.

Then, seeing how conflicted and wounded Annie appears, Danielle adds, "Just give yourself a little time. I know you'll do the right thing, whatever that is for you and your family."

"So there's someone else?" Ike asks, staring down at his feet suspiciously.

"Y-yes. I mean there *was*," Annie says, stammering.

"But we shouldn't go into that now," Danielle says, casting a glance outside at Ray and Duncan.

"Well, this is a big decision, and you definitely want to have a clear head. Whatever happens, we're here for you, Annie," Ike says, opening his arms wide. Annie leans into his body and relaxes as he folds himself around her. She exhales, relieved her old friend isn't judging her. But when she looks over his shoulder, her blood runs cold. From the patio, Ray and Duncan are watching them.

CHAPTER 58

"Will we be having drinks?" Annie asks. She could use one. The muscles in her shoulders are balled into tight knots.

"Yes, wine. No spirits because they're distilled. Tonight, everything will be pure, unadulterated, and raw!" Danielle says with forced cheer.

Annie's first glass of chardonnay does nothing to calm her nerves. The second makes her think dark thoughts. Well into the third glass, she's paranoid Duncan will see right through her betrayal. Unable to make eye contact with him, she stares at the plate of cold, uneaten pizza in front of her and downs another gulp of wine.

"Careful, honey. You don't want to set off a migraine," Duncan says with concern.

Danielle chimes in proudly, "Actually, this wine is organic and sulfite-free! See," she says, pointing to the bottle's label, "it says 'hangover-proof.'" Her comment lands with a thud; nobody responds.

Bored with the evening, Ray stretches his arms into the air and leans back with a look of mischief in his eyes. He's been taking surreptitious swigs from a calfskin-coated pewter flask whenever Danielle leaves the table.

"My man, you just came home today, and you guys came straight here? You must be dying. Months surrounded by sand and dudes.

The camels would be looking pretty good to me at that point," Ray says.

"Don't be gross, Ray," says Danielle.

Ray continues undeterred. "I'm just saying, things are gonna be rockin' in the Shaw bedroom tonight. You ready, Annie?" He elbows Ike in the ribs. Ike shudders, embarrassed for Annie.

The thought of sleeping with her husband fills her with white-hot panic. Before Gabe, Duncan was the only man she'd ever been with. What if he can tell now? Does she smell different, feel different?

Duncan saves her. "I'm afraid the only action I'm going to be seeing tonight is my face flat on the pillow. I'm running on fumes. It was all worth it, though, to get to see this face again." He reaches over and strokes Annie's cheek.

"Aww, so *sweet*," Ray mocks, disappointed with his failure to gin up some excitement. "Excuse me if I barf up my broccoli balls." Danielle swivels her head in his direction.

"Fuck, couldn't you just try for once, Ray? The idea was to do this cleanse *together*." She gestures to Duncan's empty plate. "Look, he's jet-lagged and he ate his food without moaning."

"Here we go again. Duncan's a model citizen and I'm *what*, Danny? What?" His nostrils flare with rage. "I can tell you for god-damn certain, I wouldn't leave you and Aimee high and dry for months if you were in trouble and the police were questioning you!"

Ike drops his fork. Danielle's eyes open wide in shocked disbelief.

There it is. Out in the open.

The tension had been stretched taut, but it has finally snapped. Annie feels eyes on her, waiting for her to defend her husband, but her mouth is suddenly dry and chalky. No words come out.

Duncan's amiable nature has soured, and he glares at Ray with pure hatred.

Suddenly contrite, Ray apologizes. "Look, man, I didn't mean it like that. I'm sure you had your reasons and—hey, you'll probably win another Pulitzer. That's cool, seriously. All I do is make money and buy nice shit."

Danielle, ever the consummate host, tries to smooth things over. "Ray didn't mean anything by it. He runs his mouth without thinking. We have *no* right to judge the decisions you make in your marriage," she says, giving her husband a warning look.

Gripping Annie's hand on top of the table, Duncan speaks. "No, I get it, Ray. Really, I do. It might look like that from the outside, but Annie and I discussed it, and it was for the best. Tabby was away all summer anyway." He gives Annie's hand a squeeze as if prompting her to agree, but she says nothing.

She can't feel the blood in her hand anymore. It's gone numb and she's furious. Sure, their daughter had been taken care of and unaffected; Duncan had done what was good for his career. But his decision hadn't been "the best" for her at all. How could he even say that?

He wants her to say it's all okay, and not that long ago she'd have disregarded her feelings and convinced herself it was fine. Now she wants to embarrass him and put a chink in his sanctimonious armor.

"The separation gave me time to work on myself. I started seeing my therapist again," Annie says.

Duncan nods approvingly.

"Did you know Duncan and my therapist dated in college and that they *lived* together?" she says, pulling her hand out of his. "I just found out recently."

◆

"Oh, for the love of— It was *nothing*, Annie." Duncan is unpacking his duffel, carefully putting clothes directly into the washing machine to avoid another showdown with Annie. She'd sobered up on the ride home, but neither of them had spoken. As it had so many times before, NPR filled the voids in their conversation.

"You could have mentioned it *before* I started seeing her as a therapist," Annie says. Her tone is neutral—she isn't angry about Dr. Patel anymore, just confused. She wanted to lash out at Duncan because he'd somehow managed to justify abandoning her. Again, he was the saint, and she was the fuckup needing to be coddled.

Duncan joins her at the kitchen table. He's mistaken her hostility for jealousy, which annoys her even more. "I didn't mention it because it wasn't even worth mentioning. We went out on a few actual dates, but we figured out pretty fast that we were better off as friends. Her parents belonged to the same club as mine. Our personal relationship was insignificant to the extent I even started seeing her for therapy."

"You did?" *Another secret*, Annie thinks. "You never told me you went to therapy. When?"

"It was after that first embed. You were still so early in your pregnancy with Tabby, and I didn't want to burden you with my problems. It was only one or two sessions. Later when you were struggling with PPD, I didn't think anything of recommending her."

Annie—almost desperately—wants her husband to confess to something more. She wants her affair with Gabe to seem less awful by comparison. It's time to play her ace in the hole.

"What about you and Millie Rae? I saw all the outgoing calls you made to her."

To her chagrin, Duncan throws his head back and laughs. "Her? She's not my type, Annie. She wanted some background for the article. We played phone tag for a while."

"That doesn't make any sense. Why wouldn't she call me?"

"Well, I had the distinct impression she was trying to butter me up for a job. A shortcut to a career in journalism—that probably had something to do with her friendliness."

"You never said. How do I know there aren't other things like that you haven't told me? 'Insignificant' things?" She knows she's entering a marital minefield but can't stop.

Duncan reaches over to stroke Annie's cheek, but she pulls away. "Dammit, Annie. I don't know what you want me to say. There are secrets in every marriage, aren't there? You probably have a few of your own."

"What are you talking about?"

"Ray Park seems to think you and Ike are more than friends. I told him that was ridiculous but . . ."

"Nothing happened between Ike and me."

"But would you want it to, Annie? That's almost just as bad."

Her denial comes too quickly, and it's too adamant. She has to change the subject.

"The motel in Hong Kong. I saw you. You said you never actually had sex, but you tried. We never really talked about it after that day. We just ignored it."

The color drains from his face. Suddenly, he's somewhere else.

"Duncan?" Maybe she's been too reckless, dredging up that painful period before they were even married.

He gets up without a word and continues unpacking his duffel. After a couple minutes, he's back from wherever his mind had wandered. There's a hard look in his eyes when he says, "Hong Kong? Why the hell would you bring that up now? You know what you did, Annie."

CHAPTER 59

She listens to his breath. The frustratingly rhythmic inhale and exhale that taunts Annie on those nights she lies awake while her husband sleeps. She watches him, envious of his untroubled descent into oblivion. No guilty conscience tears at him; no intrusive thoughts keep him awake. Some primitive sixth sense alerts him to her scrutiny, and he rolls over, turns his back to her.

All the old wounds were scratched open earlier that evening. *You know what you did, Annie.* Did Duncan somehow know about Gabe? Maybe Danielle let something slip to Ray—the two husbands had been talking alone before dinner—or perhaps Dr. Patel had contacted him and made insinuations. The doctor's loyalty clearly lay with Duncan. Psychiatrists were subject to ethical constraints, but they weren't infallible. Neither were lawyers. Had Ed betrayed privilege in some wayward attempt to get her to separate from Duncan? His lingering gaze, his hand on her back, still made her uncomfortable if she thought about it too long.

She fled upstairs after Duncan's accusation. *You know what you did, Annie.* She can't handle any more truth. When her husband came to bed, she lay on her side, knees curled up into a ball, and pretended to be asleep. It hadn't taken long for him to slip off. It never did. As a journalist, he was supposed to be impartial, but he had his implicit biases that bled into everything from word choice to deciding what to cover and what to ignore. The same way he'd angle a news story to fit his unconscious agenda, he'd rewrite the events of the day to justify his actions.

Now, as on thousands of other nights, he sleeps soundly while she picks herself apart. She waffles over when and what to tell Duncan about Gabe. The affair is over, but she has to ask herself why it happened and what it says about her feelings toward Duncan.

A little after midnight, Annie hears her daughter sneaking home, the door to her room softly closing. Tabby will be elated to see her dad in the morning. Annie doesn't want to spoil the moment for either of them. Maybe she should wait for Gabe's medical situation to *resolve* as Danielle said.

The coldness of the word hurts her, but she can't bring herself to even think the word *die*. If she thought it, there was a chance it could tip the hand of fate. Anxiously awaiting word on his condition, she falls asleep with her phone in her hand. Later, the vibration and flashing screen wake her. Not wanting to stir Duncan, she stuffs the phone under her sleeve, climbs out of bed, and shuts herself in the bathroom before answering.

"Ed? Is something wrong?"

"I'm sorry to wake you, Annie. I thought you'd want to know right away. The doctors decided it was time to take Gabe out of his medically induced coma so they could ascertain how much the oxygen loss affected his brain function."

Annie's heart pounds so loud she can't hear or focus on all of Ed's words. She only understands the broad outline of what he's saying. *Gabe, coma . . . why would he call her so late at night? It wasn't like Ed. Unless—* She jumps at the sound of her husband turning over in his sleep, the bed creaking on the other side of the door.

"Do you understand, Annie? I thought you'd want to know right away."

"I'm sorry, Ed. What did you say?"

"Gabe is awake. He's talking."

◆

Annie takes a few minutes to gather herself after Ed's call. Telling herself she can't hide in the bathroom forever, Annie takes a deep breath, exhales, and opens the door. She marches straight into a wall. The wall is Duncan.

He raises his eyebrow at the still-illuminated phone in her hand. "Who's that? I thought I heard you talking to someone."

"I didn't want to wake you. I was leaving myself a voice memo. So much to do now that you're back home."

"That's sweet." He yawns. "Don't let it keep you up, though. Tabby and I can take care of ourselves." As he says this, he reaches out and pulls her into a tight embrace. The gesture that would have comforted her in the past has the opposite effect of making her feel less secure, even scared. She doesn't know why. A guilty conscience can pervert anything.

CHAPTER 60

Annie wakes to the sound of raised voices. She glances at her phone and sees it's nearly ten. Despite the late hour, she's hardly rested, not having dozed off until dawn. She lies still as the news of Gabe's condition hits her afresh.

Last night, Ed told her Gabe was conscious but claimed to remember nothing beyond falling asleep after they had sex. "Can I talk to him?" Annie asked. On this, Ed had been firm. "There should be no communication between you two at this juncture. The police could perceive that as your attempt at influencing Gabe's recollection of events. It would muddy the waters."

Muddy waters—the phrase brings to mind the image of Byrdie's corpse floating in Lake Gaither. Annie rolls over onto her side, curling her knees to her chest.

The front door slams, and then Duncan's heavy steps thump on the old wooden stairs.

"You're awake!" he says, peeking in.

"I heard voices."

"Oh shit! Did I wake you? Sorry. Jonah's pressuring me to file the last feature by tomorrow."

"I assumed you were done when you checked out of the motel." Duncan's face darkens, so she changes tact. "Jonah is usually so reasonable. You just returned a few days ago. What's gotten into him?"

Duncan is too absorbed in his phone to look up as he mutters,

"People change. I'm sure he has his reasons." He turns and looks directly into her eyes. He seems to see right through her.

With two swift strides he's next to her. He balances on the edge of the bed and strokes her hair as he speaks. "Don't worry. I'm not going to let work take over again. You and Tabby mean the world to me." His nail catches on a snag in her hair, and she winces at the sudden tug and snap of the strand. He doesn't seem to notice. "It's just that I'm under a lot of pressure. I've got to get this piece filed or else all that time, all the sacrifice of being away, will be for nothing. Would it be okay if the three of us have breakfast together and then I go in and do my time at the office?"

She nods, knowing this means he will shut himself into his cubicle until he's done. He's always worked with fierce intensity. She's relieved to have the time to sort out her thoughts and create a plan of action. "That would be great," she says reassuringly. "Tabby will be happy to see you, but by the time breakfast is over she'll be sick of us and ready to jet off with her friends."

Annie's words have the opposite effect on Duncan. He's hurt, not fully coming to grips with the fact that his little girl doesn't need him anymore. His phone rings and he grimaces when he sees it's Jonah.

"Yes." He answers the phone curtly. As he listens, she sees the nerve above his eyebrow throbbing. "Stop with this crap. I'm not some rookie you can bully. You'll have the piece EOD tomorrow. Then you'll have all the time in the world to fuck it up with your edits." This must have appeased Jonah because Duncan says "Bye" in a deflated voice and hangs up.

When he turns to Annie, there's a distant expression on his face. "All these years, I couldn't have done it without *us*. My career, all of it. You and Tabby keep me sane . . . and Annie, I know. I know what kind of a wife you've been to me."

Guilt washes over her. She'd been so selfish. They were a family, and she'd spent the last months focused on nothing but her needs.

She reaches up and touches his cheek, caressing his increasingly salt-and-pepper stubble. He's been good to her, but she's surer than ever she is not in love with him.

◆

"Daddy!" Tabby races down the stairs, leaps into Duncan's arms, and nestles her head on his shoulder. All summer, the teenager's indifference at her father's absence belied her genuine concern. She'd heard stories of journalists killed on dangerous assignments. "You're alive! You didn't get blown up by a land mine."

"Yes, I seem to be," he says, beaming and holding his arms out in front of him. "How did you grow so much in two months?"

Embarrassed, Tabby hunches and retreats back into her sarcastic adolescent shell. "Um . . . hGH? I dunno. We're getting pancakes, right?"

Tabby calls shotgun as she dives into the front seat of Duncan's car. Annie climbs in back, happy to have everyone present and accounted for. One step at a time. It's the only way to get through the difficult task of upending her family. When Duncan finishes his story, there will be plenty of time to talk about both the investigation and their future.

During breakfast at Duncan's favorite greasy spoon, Tabby regales them with outlandish stories of camp cliques and mean girls, and Duncan talks about desert lice and his nightmare flight home. "Why are the people who take their shoes off always the ones you *least* want to take their shoes off?" Conversation comes easily, and the three of them enjoy one another's company in a way they haven't in years.

Still, Annie's thoughts stray to Gabe and the investigation. She'd told the police Duncan was overseas. Detective Harper had been so focused on her, he hadn't inquired again. What if they reached out to Duncan now—before she's had a chance to talk to him?

"Earth to Mom! Hellooo," Tabby calls out, hands cupped around her mouth like a megaphone. "You there?"

Duncan answers, wrapping a protective arm around Annie's shoulders. "Your mom's probably just tired from all the homecoming hoopla." He leans over and kisses her forehead. "Thank god we'll all be staying put for a while. I know I'm not going anywhere."

After breakfast, Duncan drops them off before heading into the office. "It's the final stretch. Gonna pop this baby out tonight if it kills me!"

"Gross, Dad!"

"I'll have my phone on vibrate. I'll try to check it every few hours. Call Jonah if you really need to reach me, okay?" he says, shooting Annie an apologetic look.

"Don't worry. Everything's fine," she lies.

CHAPTER 61

Per Tabby's request, Annie orders a pizza for the two of them. She retrieves the delivery boxes from the porch, noting that the grease has already begun to soak through, and re-arms the Guardian Angel Sentry system. Before she has a chance to set the boxes down, Tabby swipes them from her hands, chanting, "Pizza, pizza, me want pizza!" in a guttural caveman voice.

Annie hadn't heard from Duncan during the day, but she didn't expect to. He'd be knee-deep in work at least until the small hours of the morning, if not longer.

"Why is grease *sooo* good?" Tabby holds a veggie slice above her face and gobbles upward from a thick string of cheese. "Aren't you going to eat, Mom?"

Annie stands, looking out at the black expanse of the backyard and gardens. The few solar lights staked into the ground flicker like real flames yet fail to generate much light. "Not super hungry yet, but you go ahead and start without me."

"Ermh whut? Can't hear you when I'm chewing like this, Mom. Crunchy crust. You're missing out."

Annie smiles to herself. In telling Tabby about Gabe, she'd upturned the boxes of her life and let the contents spill out and intermingle. She'd let things get messy. Yet her daughter still loved her and, if anything, they were closer for it.

She has to tell Duncan next, regardless of whether she'll ever see Gabe again.

Picking up on her mother's preoccupation, Tabby inquires, "Any news on your—er—friend?"

"Gabe's out of his coma. He'll be okay."

"So have you figured out how you're gonna break it to Dad?"

"After he files the story, I'll tell him everything. But to be honest, I don't think there's much left to salvage in our marriage. It's not about Gabe either. That's over. I'm sorry if I let you down."

"You didn't, Mom. I just want us all to be happy, and I can tell you haven't been in a while. It's not like I don't have eyes because I'm a kid. I know you and Daddy were arguing a lot before he left, maybe about him going away.

"But I'm sad for Dad. It's like we're all he's got. Both his parents are gone, and he doesn't talk to the rest of his family. There's his work, but nobody reads long news stories anymore, so that's kinda pointless."

Annie chews her lower lip. "Both your dad and I need to learn how to stand on our own two feet. You won't be around much longer to take care of us." She winks at her daughter, in the process squeezing out the damp that springs to her eyes when she thinks of Tabby going off to college.

"Haha. Is it okay if I'm a total pig and take the rest of this one up to my room? I haven't played Aliens in a week. Can't let my gaming skills get flabby."

Annie agrees, glad to have time to sort out her thoughts. Tabby plants an oily smooch on her mom's cheek, then disappears upstairs to immerse herself in a world of extraterrestrial gore.

Annie disassembles the untouched second pizza, stacking slices on a plate to refrigerate for later, then double-checks the locks and draws the curtains. When she retires to her bedroom for the night, she glances at Tabby's room. The door is closed and it's silent, thanks to Tabby's giant gaming headphones.

Alone in the quiet of her room, Annie considers everything that's happened—Byrdie, Deja, Gabe. She's still certain she would never *intentionally* hurt them. She's not a murderer. But she thinks about the DOPS research supporting the "survival of personality after death." If consciousness is more than a by-product of brain activity confined within our skulls, perhaps it follows that Annie is indirectly culpable. She's agonized about losing control and being responsible for morbid outcomes, painfully ruminating on these thoughts until they eventually escaped into the real world. Worrying about flesh-eating bacteria in Lake Gaither, then seeing Byrdie's decomposing body. Checking Deja's mouth for Asiatic beetles, then seeing them latched on to his corpse. Reading about the banana spiders, then seeing them attack Gabe. The idea that she might have willed these horrors into existence sickens her.

But all this brooding will only make things worse. She decides it's best to shower and rest. As she's undressing, her phone buzzes and Dr. Patel's name flashes across the screen. She slips on a robe before answering as if the doctor can see her nakedness through the screen.

"Hello, Dr. Patel?"

"Annie! I'm glad I caught you. I just wanted to check in with everything going on. How are you doing?"

"Oh, uh . . . thanks. I'm fine," Annie says, her forehead wrinkling. Then she recalls how abruptly their last session ended, and it makes sense the doctor would feel obliged to follow up. Still, Annie pulls her robe tighter and crosses the room to close a gap in the curtains.

"That's good. Great," Dr. Patel says with undue relief.

Did she think I'd jump off a bridge? Did I seem that off? "Well, thank you. Is there anything else I can do for you, Doctor?"

"Nothing. Just, if you and Duncan need to work through anything, I'm always here. I know transitions can be difficult. Getting used to his being back now and dealing with the challenges in your marriage can be stressful—"

Annie interrupts before she can finish. "How did you know he's back?" She replays their last session in her head, certain she didn't tell the doctor her husband had returned.

"W-we've spoken briefly."

"Why? He gets back and you're his first call?"

"I wouldn't say that . . . however, I did speak to him just now, as a matter of fact. Frankly, I'm concerned. He's under a lot of stress, and he doesn't sound like himself."

"Don't you think you should stay out of our relationship considering you dated? It can't be ethical for you to see him as a patient."

"He reached out to me as a *friend*, Annie. I'm a friend of his who happens to be a psychiatrist. There's nothing more to it."

The doctor's words, the vagueness of the situation, all of it bewilders Annie. A troublesome thought gnaws at the back of Annie's mind, slowly worming its way into her consciousness, but not quite ready to surface.

Annie replies with open hostility. "I agree. There's nothing more to discuss. I appreciate what you've done for me, but I think you should just stay out of our lives now, Dr. Patel."

"Wait, Annie! Don't hang up, please. Oh, I'm not expressing myself well at all."

"*Good-bye*, Doctor!"

"You need to be careful—"

"Careful? Don't threaten me, Doctor. You are the one who should watch out. Leave us alone or I'll report you to the medical board." With that, Annie hangs up. She puts her phone on silent. She had a win tonight with Tabby. Dr. Patel just seemed to make things worse.

Annie exhales loudly, slips off her robe, and steps into the smart shower. Her haven. "Set light ten percent bright. Set my shower to one hundred ten degrees. Start my shower." It responds immediately to her command and she's grateful for the lack of complication. As she lathers up, the muscles in her shoulders start to relax.

She's rinsing the shampoo out of her hair when the water runs ice cold. The physical shock triggers a realization. Annie rarely shared details of her childhood and only recently began to open up. Aside from herself, her daughter, and Me, the only person who could possibly know about the charred aromatics is Dr. Patel. Nobody else could have used the intimate memory to gaslight Annie.

"Turn off my shower." But there's no response. Annie ducks under the shower stream and repeats loudly, "Turn off my shower." Again, no response.

It's never malfunctioned before. Maybe Duncan can fix . . . No, she needs to learn not to be so reliant on him. The cold water peppers her back as she steps out. She swoops her sopping hair into a towel and wraps the satiny robe around herself, wishing she'd chosen a thicker one.

The disturbing realization about Dr. Patel has left Annie feeling exposed, vulnerable, and stupid. She should have cut things off with the doctor as soon as she found out about her relationship with Duncan. Annie's mind whirs as she thinks about all the times the psychiatrist adamantly defended Duncan. Were the two of them closer than Dr. Patel let on? Did she still harbor feelings for Annie's husband? And what other personal details had Dr. Patel used against her?

On edge again, Annie crosses the hall to check on Tabby. She opens the door just a crack. She's sitting on the floor, headphones on, oblivious to anything except the aliens attacking from the monitor. And with her back to the door, Tabby won't have noticed her mom anyway.

Annie's about to go back to her bedroom when she hears a scraping noise downstairs. It sounds like it's coming from the kitchen, but she can't be sure. She creeps halfway down the stairs and listens. Silence.

There was a time when she'd have doubted herself, but now she's certain she heard something. She wasn't crazy. The question was no longer "if," but rather *who* or *what* was down there. She doubles back to the landing. She checks that Tabby's door is still shut tight, then grabs her phone and a heavy flashlight as a makeshift weapon.

Making her way back downstairs, she replays her actions from earlier in the evening. She had double-checked each door and armed the security system. If anyone had tried to break in without the code *and* biometric confirmation, alarms would have sounded. She'd have immediately received an alert on her phone and the security firm would already be en route.

None of those things has happened, yet she pauses before reaching the bottom step and grips the flashlight tighter. The sound has resumed, the scratching of metal on metal. Maybe it would be better to turn back and lock herself in the bedroom with Tabby. *Don't be silly. You're not a child hiding under the covers anymore. You can deal with this.*

At the bottom of the stairs, she reaches for the light switch and flips it. Nothing happens. The sliver of moon breaking through the clouds does little to light her way as she pads carefully toward the sound on bare, silent feet.

CHAPTER 62

He has his back to her, focused completely on sharpening the Santoku knife, but he knows she's there. "Hi, Annie."

She stands motionless, paralyzed by confusion. The scene before her, her husband working at the kitchen sink, is all the more sinister because of its banality.

"Did you think I wouldn't get in?" he asks, back still turned away from her. "It's a good thing I keep a key to the master fuse box on my key chain. Can you believe I had to flip a breaker to get inside my own home? The security system is on the same circuit as your fancy shower—sorry about that."

"Wh-what?" Until now, Annie completely forgot that after receiving the photo of her and Ike, she'd called the security company and had them add a secondary verification code. "The PIN code. I had them add it to make sure we were safe while you were gone. Sorry, I meant to tell you."

"Meant to tell me?" He guffaws—his voice is strangled and pained as if he's being forced to regurgitate brambles, thorns snagging on soft pink tissue. He dries the knife off methodically and calmly slots it into the wooden block. "I imagine there are many, many things you meant to tell me, honey. The thing is, it's too late for confessions.

"You see, I heard everything—*saw* everything. If you bothered to figure out how to do anything yourself, you'd know the Guardian Angel Sentry system comes with an optional remote monitoring capability. I upgraded our plan before leaving the country. Worth every penny to see you disintegrate without me—or so I thought."

Hands resting on the counter, he stretches his neck from side to side. Then he turns to face her, and her blood runs cold. There's an ugliness in his eyes she's never seen before.

She'd wanted to tell him everything after his story was filed. But now that she's facing him, her courage drains away like a bladder emptying. She wants to turn and run but her feet don't move.

His eyes rake over her, making her feel dirty. She tightens the sash on her thin satin robe.

"Don't cover up. I can see your nipples are hard. Does this excite you? If I'd known you liked a little danger, we could've gone that way. Is *that* why you turned to him, Annie? Gabe, right? Does he push you around a little? Do you like it?" He takes a step toward her, but the granite breakfast bar separates them.

"How long have you known?"

"*That's* what you ask me?" He's shouting now. "No 'I'm so sorry, Duncan. It was nothing'?" With two swift strides, he sidesteps the bar. "Where is the gratitude? The recognition of everything I've sacrificed for this family? For us? My career?"

"Sacrifice? You won a Pulitzer!"

"That was before we were a family. My career turned to shit after that." He runs a hand through his sandy hair, which has turned cold and gray in the moonlight. "I thought this embed would turn things around. A fresh chance to prove myself. Salvage my career. I couldn't do it."

"But Jonah called. You said you're working on the story."

"I have enough contacts, enough people I can bribe and blackmail for intel. The prick will have a story tomorrow. I have to get rid of these distractions first."

"Where have you been, Duncan? What have—"

"I turned back after a week. Never even made it to the post. Spent a week drinking in Croatia until I got in some trouble. Then made my way back to Munich. I thought about how my career was shit, my marriage was shit, my little girl was basically gone . . . and I realized who was responsible." His ice-blue eyes lock on hers, seeing right through, and in one stride he closes the distance between them.

In a voice that is suddenly quiet and emotionless, he says, "My pretty little compulsive mess." He strokes her cheek, but she flinches and turns away. He grabs her chin and jerks it upward to look at him. He's yelling again. "I was so fucking patient all these years trying to get you help. How did you think it made me feel when you looked at me like I was a monster because I wore shoes in the house? Or didn't wash my hands? I adapted and learned to handle your insane rituals. I put up with your mother, all of it, so we could be a family." His thumb stabs at his chest as he says, "*I* am the one who took care of this family." Then, jabbing his index finger into her chest, "*You* were a mess. *You* were the one who destroyed our family."

Through tears, Annie begs, "Please, please, lower your voice! Tabby will hear."

"I saw through the window that she's gaming. She won't hear anything until she reaches level seventeen or whatever nonsense. I don't blame her for taking her aggressions out in violent video games. She's an angry child, Annie, and it's your fault for being such a god-awful mother."

"No, no, *no*! Don't say that," she sobs, pushing Duncan away with both her hands to his chest. He doesn't even budge. Instead, he returns the shove, and it sends her flying into the wall by the mudroom.

He advances, towering above her and shutting out any slivers of moonlight. "How do you like that, Annie? Do unto others as you'd have them do unto you."

When she hit the wall, the impact made her teeth snap down on her tongue. She's shocked by the taste of blood in her mouth. The mix of blood and saliva drips down her chin, and she's sure her husband will realize what he's done and be sorry. "Look what you've done, Duncan. You've hurt me."

"Poor little Annie. Let me kiss it and make it better." He jerks her up like a rag doll. She squirms, turning her head away from him, but he grabs her jaw with one hand and pushes his lips onto hers. He forces his tongue into her mouth. He tastes like stale cigarettes, coffee, and alcohol.

The violent intrusion nearly causes her to throw up. He pins her tight against the wall and she can feel him getting hard. It disgusts her. *He's getting off on hurting you. Controlling you.* He pulls his mouth away for a moment and she gasps for air. *"My* wife. *My* family."

When he fumbles to undo his belt buckle, she realizes there will be no regretful apologies—that he intends to complete his invasion of her body. She's disgusted by his clammy hands on her thighs. She could go along with it and retreat into the safety of her thoughts. Her body would take the punishment, but her mind would be immersed in the blue skies and bougainvillea of the French Quarter photograph in *National Geographic* . . . then she could shower it all away afterward.

When he jams his tongue inside her mouth again, a switch inside her flips. She isn't going to retreat into her world of magical thinking. She remembers Dr. Patel's words: *Controlling your own actions is all you can do when circumstances spin out.*

She doesn't deserve this, so she bites down *hard.* Even when she tastes his blood, she doesn't unclamp her teeth. His eyes open wide in confusion and for a moment he flails.

She doesn't let go until specks of light float across her field of vision and she realizes his hands are wrapped around her throat.

"You ungrateful little bitch. I never should have helped you."

That was always how it was in his eyes. Looking down, he'd helped her, taken care of her. It made him feel big. For a time, she'd wanted to be taken care of, but now—she's realized she wants more. Maybe a part of her always has.

Before he can push his way inside her, she turns her hips slightly, maneuvering for some space. Then, using the wall at her back for leverage, she strikes him in the groin with her knee. Twice. He recoils in pain, giving her just enough time to run into the mudroom and out the back door.

She pauses on the patio. *What if he goes back for Tabby?* She has to keep him engaged to draw him away from the house. "Why . . . why did you have to hurt Gabe? Is it because I fucked him or because you knew I couldn't wait to do it again?" Then she runs, barely escaping Duncan's lunging grab.

He's bigger, faster, but she knows the woods better. Quickly, she abandons the manicured garden pathways. Jagged rocks jutting from the clay soil claw at her bare feet. Brambles rake against every inch of exposed skin and snag the delicate silk of her robe. Yet she's oblivious to the pain, concerned only with surviving. In an evasive maneuver, she doubles back quietly and crawls into a small gully, flattening herself under a fallen tree trunk.

She hears his boots crashing through brush in the opposite direction.

"Did you think I wouldn't find out about him? I'm a journalist. Surveillance, investigation—it's not exactly a challenge when the subject is as incompetent as you, Annie. You don't even clear your browser history.

"You know I tried other ways. I'm not a violent man. I thought texting you those photos would send you into a tizzy. That you wouldn't leave bed for a month. I thought it would be enough to keep you out of trouble. But I underestimated your commitment to being a *whore*, Annie. You can't blame me for miscalculating since you haven't had much of an appetite for sex with *me* lately."

He stops moving and listens. "I may be a professional failure now, but you have to admire the beauty of my recent work. You're an 'artist,' after all. It wasn't easy orchestrating that night at the Harrison.

"Even just acquiring the spiders—I had to call in a favor from a source, a drug trafficker in Costa Rica. He said it would be less hassle to ship me a kilo of cocaine, but I insisted. I saw to everything myself, including the roofied bottles of Corrente, every detail designed to make Gabe uniquely revolting to you. The bite of just one adult spider could kill him—but that wouldn't have been any fun. I needed dozens of young ones in order to poison *and* maim him.

"You'd be so disgusted by what you saw that you'd stay away from him—or he'd die. Either way, win-win. The police would suspect you, or maybe we'd have to have you committed, then you would've needed me more than ever."

He's walking again, but this time his steps sound like they're receding. "Believe it or not, I still held out hope you wouldn't go through with it. I staked out a spot and observed from a vacant loft across the street. Do you know how much it hurt when you did?

"After, it was easy getting into the room. Don't even know why hotels give out key cards—the *illusion* of security, I guess. I confess, I stayed to watch for a minute after releasing the spiders. Passed the time while I ate the banana and tossed the peel in the trash. I mean, I had to make it look real. I'm a perfectionist."

She lies motionless in the gully, heart pounding. As long as he talks, she knows she's safe. A barn owl calls out right above her, causing her to jump involuntarily. Maybe the leaves rustle, but she doesn't think so. She listens but he's gone quiet. No more shoes breaking sticks. No more hurtful words. The air is still. She presses down flatter into the mud and feels its silky batter squish between her toes.

Then everything goes black.

CHAPTER 63

When she opens her eyes, the interior of the carriage house gradually comes into focus. She struggles to get up off the floor but falls over onto her side.

"Don't move or that's gonna leave a mark," he says, gesturing to the rope that tightly binds her ankles and wrists. "I like to use duct tape but had to improvise." He roughly tips her back so she's sitting up again.

The movement makes her nauseated. There's a stabbing pain in the back of her head. "It hurts . . ."

"You might not feel well. I know you're prone to migraines and a heavy branch to the skull doesn't help. I'll untie you soon, just try to calm down."

"You don't have to do this, Duncan. Gabe isn't dead. It won't be murder! We can explain it to the police."

"You know I was going to give you yet *another* chance? When I came back, and we had dinner at your friend's house, I reconsidered. But this evening, it was too much. Even for me. And I'm a patient guy! Here I am at the office, dealing with the pressure of writing—well, constructing—a story on deadline, and I overhear you and Tabby chatting about your betrayal. Casual, like you're talking about changing a toilet paper roll. And the way you both acted like I was pathetic. *You* pitying *me*?"

"I didn't mean for that to happen. Tabby loves you so much—the affair was my mistake. Please, Duncan, this doesn't have to go any further."

Annie's pleading seems to go unheard. Duncan paces the room, staring blankly into the distance, running his hand through his hair over and over. "I'll have to get Lily Patel to attest to your twisted state of mind, but that'll be easy. Old girl doesn't have a clue about me, never has. Should stick to her test tubes and cats." He stops, opens a drawer, and rifles through the contents before continuing. "Now, let's see what we can say. Poor, poor Annie feels so guilty. Depressed *again*! The police are on to her. They even know about Hong Kong. What can she do?"

"Hong Kong?" She realizes too late she's talking out loud. The two words snap him out of his daze, and his eyes focus on her as though seeing her for the first time.

There's surprise in his voice. "Did you really not know? Part of me always hoped you knew and loved me anyway."

He flashes a wicked grin and snickers as though he's telling a story by the office water cooler. "When you saw me in that motel window, I thought you'd realize how fucked up I was after Kabul. But you only cared about yourself. How it made *you* feel." He crouches down next to her, his face serious again. "I could never cheat on you. I couldn't even get it up after what I saw in Afghanistan. When I came back I was 'Blood and Guts' Shaw, remember? Wars pervert people, Annie. You know that, seeing how it made your mom a nutcase."

Putting his hand to his heart in mock solemnity, he said, "It's true, though. I confess. I thought fucking a hooker might help me. Help us. But I couldn't do it. Then, after forty-five awkward fucking minutes, her lowlife pimp started banging on the door saying I needed to pay if I wanted more time. Fucking humiliating.

"But you know what was *more* humiliating? Seeing you all over that greasy bartender. Letting him look down your top. After you left the hotel, it was easy to chat him up. Guy had no filter. I had to listen to him brag about 'the one' he had lined up for later that night."

"No, Duncan. Stop. I don't . . ."

"Yes, Annie. You will listen to what *you* made me do. Though I can see why you might not want to know how much better I felt after I poured wiper fluid down his dirty mouth. You know, it always irked me how you kept using that stuff, even though I had plenty of money for professional supplies. Afterward, I pushed him into the trash chute. I felt like a fucking hero, cleaning up the world one lowlife at a time." He beats his chest and grins.

Annie shakes her head in disbelief. A sharp pain shoots through her skull. All these years, Annie saw what she wanted to see. Now the mask has fallen, and the man in front of her disgusts her. She looks away.

"I can see you're worried. Tabby won't know I've taken care of you. We'll do it so it looks like you killed yourself with the same wiper fluid you used to poison the others. That way I can help our daughter through the mourning period and see her off to college. Really, we'll be better off without you. Just the two of us."

She can't leave her daughter alone with him. She has to get help. The carriage house is set back from the road, but there's a chance someone would be driving past, a chance someone could hear, so she screams. She releases all of her repressed demons, all of the pent-up anxieties, in one long, bloodcurdling, animalistic wail.

Quickly, he jams a rag into her mouth, and she gags, but maybe someone heard.

"Nobody can hear you anyway. That's why you stuck your mom out here, isn't it? To contain all the mess—the disordered thinking— in one place, so you could have your neat gardens, fancy dog, and picture-perfect life."

He disappears to the adjoining room, calling over his shoulder, "We need a pen and paper for your suicide note. Don't get up, though, I'll find them."

From somewhere outside, the beam of a flashlight plays quickly across the wooden floor, then evaporates. *Someone heard her call for help.*

CHAPTER 64

D uncan returns, humming and holding a stubby sketching pencil and a sheet of newsprint. It doesn't seem as though he noticed the flashlight beam.

"Let's untie your hands so you can write, but I have to leave your feet tied and your gag in because I can't trust you. You understand that, right, Annie? I can never trust you again."

His expression is so cold and full of hate, she can't comprehend how this is the golden knight in shining armor she met all those years ago on the College Green. Whatever he'd seen in his first stint in Afghanistan had broken something inside him. Or maybe this had always been in him, a seed of abject cruelty waiting for the right conditions to germinate.

He wraps her fingers around the pencil, but she lets her hand go slack and the pencil drops to the floor. He sighs and stoops over to pick it up.

"Look what you've done. You've broken the tip. We're going to have to do something about that." He scans the room. His eyes stop at Annie's drafting table, landing squarely on the dao bào.

"My god. You kept something of your mother's after all. No burial, nothing. I thought maybe you didn't have a nontransactional bone in your body, Annie." Duncan picks up the Vietnamese cooking knife and strokes the five-inch blade against her cheek. "Be good now, okay? I don't want to hurt you until I have to."

He crudely sharpens the pencil using the peeler set in the middle of the blade. Then he rewraps Annie's fingers around the barrel. This time he doesn't let go, nearly crushing her hand in his.

She gapes at him, trying to speak, but her words are stifled by the gag.

"I can't understand you now . . . or ever, I suppose," he says with a snort. Then he yanks the bloody rag out of her mouth, making her cough.

"B-Byrdie? Did you kill her?"

"I poisoned her—slipped a teensy bit of your wiper fluid into her moonshine. Enough to damage without being detected." He laughs, then seeing the horror on Annie's face, adds, "Hey, you helped— leaving that key in the catch-all tray. But the stubborn biddy just kept hanging on, so I got impatient. Dumped her in the lake."

"But you were the one who introduced me to Byrdie . . ."

"She was supposed to throw you a couple of bones, so you wouldn't take that teaching job way back when. You couldn't see it, Annie. You couldn't see how that job would have taken you away from your family." He shakes his head. "Byrdie kept you just busy enough, but things got out of control, didn't they? Old girl landed you that magazine interview.

"Thankfully, Millie Rae thought she could butter me up for a journalism job. Practically begged me to help her with that silly article. She was going to portray you as some serious artist, but I told her how much you loved that schnauzer painting—'dogs and babies, *that's* her passion,' I said. She even sent me a few layouts and let me choose.

"But as soon as I dealt with the article, Byrdie got you worked up about painting murals for the entire garden club. You were gone for hours and hours at a time. I could already feel you slipping away from me after your mom died." The last words he says in a near whisper as if unable to accept their truth. "I thought replacing your sertraline with placebo pills would be enough to make you fall apart, to keep you at home." Seeing the shock in Annie's eyes, he continues. "Placebo pills are incredibly easy to get—prop sites sell them down to the exact milligram."

When Annie first started taking the prescription, Dr. Patel cautioned her about the potential side effects of abruptly stopping the medication. Withdrawal could include *digestive symptoms*—nausea, appetite loss, vomiting; *sleep problems*—vivid nightmares, unusual dreams, insomnia; *mood swings*—anxiety, panic, anger; *strange sensations*—prickling, tingling skin, hypersensitivity to sound, dizziness, and brain zaps, like an electrical shiver in your brain.

Annie had associated these experiences with her mother's death, her ghost. In reality, the explanation wasn't supernatural—it was withdrawal. She had only started to get a grip on her symptoms once Dr. Patel prescribed the new dosage, which was delivered to her home in a fresh bottle.

"But even without the prescription, you still didn't appreciate how much you needed me. You forced me to keep going. I took care of the dog but kept a little memento for you."

Deja's paw! Thinking about her friend rekindles Annie's defiance. "I won't write a note," she says in a small but steady voice. "Tabby can't think I did these things."

"Well, it would be worse if she knew *I* did these things. I'd have to go to jail and then she'd be left with you. You're incapable of taking care of a fly, Annie. You'd find some way to fuck it up, I'm sure. No, it's much better this way."

Once she writes the letter, her fate is sealed. He won't need anything else from her. She has to stall for time. The person with the flashlight will go get help.

She forces herself to turn her head and look him in the eye. "What *happened* to you, Duncan?"

The question enrages him. "*Me?* This isn't about *me*, Annie! Can't you see you're the problem and I'm the one *fixing* the problem? That's what our relationship has always been, right from the start. Me taking care of you. Fixing everything for you."

"I think—I think we loved each other once."

"That ended when you fucked someone else."

"No, it ended a long time before that. Hong Kong. Ever since you came back the first time."

"Don't you dare pin this on me!" he shouts. He slaps her across the side of her already concussed head.

"Daddy, no!"

Tabby's voice paralyzes them both. Annie's stomach sinks. Help is not on the way—and now her daughter is in danger too.

CHAPTER 65

Tabby flings the door open and throws herself onto Annie, wrapping her arms around her mother protectively.

"Don't hurt her." Horrified, she touches her mother's bloodied temple. She clearly can't believe this is real.

"We're just playing a game, honey. How long have you been out there?" Duncan asks in a disquietingly calm voice.

"I heard everything. Don't . . . don't lie to me." The child spits the words out between sobs. "The back door was open. Mom was gone. I came out to look for her. I heard what you said. I *heard* you!"

"I need you to understand, Tabby, your mother is responsible for all of this. Not me. I've only tried to take care of this family. Being your dad is the only really good thing I've ever done. I'm so proud of you." He reaches out and tries to stroke his daughter's shoulder.

She squirms to avoid his touch. The rejection wounds him and he recoils.

Then Tabby stands up, hands balled into fists. "*You're* the one who hurt those people. Look what you've done to Mom. You're not my father. You're—you're a monster!"

He lunges forward, desperate to hold her in his arms and comfort her, but she cowers, shielding her head with her slender arms. "Don't ki . . . kill me," she pleads.

"What? Baby—my little girl—I would never." Stunned by the fear in her eyes, he retreats backward, muttering, "No, no . . . no . . ."

His gaze falls on Annie, bloodied and bound at the ankles, as if he's seeing her for the first time.

Wordlessly, he swivels around, picks up a gallon of wiper fluid, and unscrews the top. He brandishes the poison high in the air like a pistol.

"Don't hurt us, Duncan. You don't have to do this," Annie pleads.

"But I have to do it. It's the only way to clean up this mess."

Tabby screams and lunges at her father, hands balled into tight fists. "Stop it, Dad! *Daddy*, don't!"

Reflexively, Duncan extends a stiff arm, but the defensive action is enough to send the girl tumbling. There's an audible thump as her head hits the wooden floor.

Annie and Duncan gasp. He drops the gallon of wiper fluid and rushes to Tabby's side. In seconds, he's cradling her head in his lap. "Oh my god. Tabby, I'd never hurt you. My baby." He presses two fingers beneath the child's jaw, desperate for the reassurance of a pulse. His shoulders fall as he breathes a sigh of relief. "You've just passed out."

Delicately, he examines his daughter's head. "I can't believe she did this to you. Your own mother." He shakes his head. "No blood. You'll be okay. I'm here. I've got you."

Gently, he strokes Tabby's coppery hair as though nothing has happened, as though he's tucking her into bed. In a distant, sing-song voice, he chants his daughter's favorite nursery rhyme:

> "Ladybird, ladybird, fly away home,
> Your house is on fire and your children are gone,
> All except one,
> And her name is Ann,
> And she hid under the baking pan."

Hearing the nursery rhyme sparks something inside Annie.

He'll never let Tabby go. You have to save your daughter. You have to try.

With her right hand, Annie begins to loosen the ties on her ankles. They weren't that tight to begin with, since Duncan hadn't anticipated his wife putting up much of a fight, much less being able to overpower him.

Even though her husband is bent over Tabby, Annie takes care not to make any sudden movements that could catch his eye. Methodically, her slim fingers work at the knot, gradually teasing it loose. She nearly has it undone when Duncan, still rocking their unconscious daughter in his arms, speaks.

"She could wake at any time. We have to do this *now*. No note."

All of a sudden, a spray of red, red blood shoots across Tabby's face. Individual ruby droplets cling to the downy peach fuzz on her cheek. Slowly they merge, sliding together into one dark pool.

CHAPTER 66

Will she be okay?" asks Detective Harper. He gestures to Tabby, who has been balled up in the back seat of his car sobbing hysterically for the past hour. The child services representative nods and rubs her eyes, having been summoned in the middle of the night. "Losing a parent—there's no denying the trauma. It will leave its mark but, in my experience, kids are surprisingly resilient."

"She hasn't said a word, though. Just keeps rocking herself back and forth crying. She seems to feel safer in the squad car."

Detective Harper observes a silver Mercedes pulling into the drive. His eyes narrow, then relax in recognition. He waves a hand. "Mr. Perez, over here!"

Ed joins them, shaking his head in disbelief at the scene teeming with police and bound by yellow crime scene tape. "My god. I came as soon as I got the call." He appears curiously fallible in jeans without his suit-and-tie armor.

"I had no idea things were this bad. Are you sure it was suicide? Was there a note?"

"Not in the main house, but my team's still looking. The kid's too dazed, but we have the eyewitness account. The body was recovered from an outbuilding, her art studio, but everything there is too fried to be of much use," Harper says.

Ed coughs and covers his eyes as a gust of wind hurls smoke and char in their faces.

"Is she okay?" Ed asks.

"Tabitha's in the car. Just some bruising. Poor thing is traumatized."

"I actually meant—" He stops midsentence, interrupted by someone calling his name.

"Ed! Ed!" From the back of an EMT van, Annie emerges. Her head is wrapped in gauze, and she clutches an emergency foil blanket around her shoulders. Woozy from a hefty dose of painkillers, she stumbles toward him.

"Easy! Careful." Ed rushes over and takes her forearm. "Annie, I'm so sorry. It never even crossed my mind Duncan could be dangerous. He seemed so devoted to you guys—"

"Tabby rejecting him was too much." Annie takes a deep breath. "Once he was exposed, his entire self-image came crashing down. There was no way to pretend anymore. He couldn't stand not being seen as the good guy. He killed himself . . . I barely had time to get Tabby out of there."

Ed observes Annie's bruises and the dried blood crusted on her collarbone. "He did this to you. I can't believe it."

"He was in pain for a long time, even though he didn't show it. My affair fueled his conviction that I was the problem. In some ways, I was. We were both guilty of avoiding reality, thinking we could control everything. When I let go—blew it all up—I felt like I was reborn. It made him angry, desperate—he needed me to stay weak for him to feel strong."

"I always thought he was one of those guys who had it all going for him," Ed says, looking at her wistfully. Annie turns her eyes away, breaking the spell.

"I have to check on Tabby. They just finished stitching me up when you came." Distracted, Annie glances over at the squad car.

"Go. I'll take care of the paperwork."

She thanks him and makes her way down the drive, numb to the gravel beneath her still bare feet. When she knocks on the front passenger-side window, Tabby looks up, wide-eyed with fear.

"It'll be okay, honey. Unlock the door. It's your mother."

CHAPTER 67

Annie has one chance. One chance to strike before Duncan leverages his size and strength to squash her. She's not sure if the knot on her ankle is loose enough to give—or if it'll hold and she'll fall on her face—but there's zero time for rumination and doubt. Instead, with a clarity and focus she's only ever employed in the two-dimensional world of painting, Annie springs to her feet and snatches the dao bào from the drafting table where Duncan so casually tossed it.

At once, she's standing over her husband and daughter.

One chance. One second. One sweeping stroke. Blood sprays, then gushes from his throat, splashing on Tabby's cheek. He slumps, his hands go slack, and he releases the girl from his grip.

Annie dives toward her daughter. She hooks her arms under Tabby's armpits and slides the girl, heavy and unconscious, out of the carriage house into the cool quiet of the night.

Then, knowing what she has to do, Annie squares her shoulders, turns, and strides back inside the carriage house.

Duncan has collapsed onto his side, his sandy hair turned to rust. Carefully, Annie approaches what she can only hope is his dead body. The figure that loomed so large over most of her adult life is now crumpled, still. His skin has taken on a pale, bluish tint—at one with his cold blue eyes. Wide open, staring, they belie the fatal gash on his neck. As Annie watches in horror, Duncan's eyes fix on her. They harden into an expression of pure, cold hatred.

One last burst of life, then death.

Finish it. Save yourself.

Annie digs her hand into Duncan's back pocket and slides out the Zippo lighter she'd hoped would be there—he had resumed his pack-a-day habit despite turning back before reaching the post in Syria. She picks up the dropped gallon of wiper fluid. Half of it has streamed across the floorboards in pinkish rivulets. The rest, she pours over his body.

Her thumb flicks the metal wheel. She drops the lighter and runs.

◆

With the dew-laden fronds of a wood fern, Annie strokes Tabby's cheek, reviving her and washing away her father's blood. The child's eyelids fly open.

"Mom! Where's Daddy? What . . ."

A loud crash cuts through the sleeping woods. The T-beam has collapsed, the roof caved in.

The girl sits up. The burning carriage house casts a flickering orange light over her terrified face.

"Can you get up?" Annie asks. "We've got to go *now*."

CHAPTER 68

THREE MONTHS LATER

Annie swirls her drink, watching as sweet, cheap whiskey coats her glass. For a moment, she says nothing, then shifts in her chair.

"Tabby's staying with Aimee's family for a while. She's getting her learner's permit. I'm nervous about that, but I also know it's for the best. And she's in therapy, trying to process how her 'hero' dad betrayed us all. She hasn't forgiven me entirely either. She thinks I should have run for help, that I could have tried to save him, instead of watching over her until she woke up. But she's coming back to me, I feel it."

"Give her time. Let it happen on her schedule," Dr. Patel says. She studies Annie intently from across the glass tabletop. "*Could you have saved—*"

Annie cuts her off. "We all know there were missed opportunities. None of us knew the extent of Duncan's trauma. After he came back from assignment early, you said he called you secretly for advice, that he seemed despondent and angry."

Shamefaced, Dr. Patel lowers her head. "It happens. I should have insisted he see a therapist. Our friendship blinded me. To reassure him you were making progress, I repeated the lovely memory you shared about your mother and the charred ginger and star anise. I-I never dreamed he was a danger to himself or anyone else."

Annie frowns, recalling how Duncan had overseen the installation of the new HVAC system in the carriage house. He'd know exactly how to disseminate the aromatics.

Dr. Patel lifts her chin and squares her shoulders, moving on from her professional error. "No more private patients for me anyway. Strictly clinical research trials."

Annie nods. She's forgiven the doctor for her indiscretion. Duncan preyed on damaged, socially inept women. It was his specialty.

Dr. Patel glances at the surrounding tables before leaning forward and whispering, "I assume you've been cleared of all charges in the case of the murdered heiress?"

"Yes! I shared Duncan's confession with Detective Harper. The police examined his car. The GPS tracking proved he'd driven to Pinewood and Lake Gaither that night." Smug in the belief that someone of his social stature and repute would not be suspected—and he wasn't—Duncan didn't try very hard to cover his tracks. Evil hiding in plain sight. "If anyone checked, he'd just say I took his car. Who would believe me over him?"

"How dreadful!" Dr. Patel exclaims. "It's all so much to take in. Do you have a support system in place, Annie? Where do things stand with Ike? Gabe?"

"Old habits die hard, don't they, Lily. We're not in your office, and I'm not your patient. You and I are two friends drinking underneath a heat lamp, on the rooftop patio of a cheesy sports bar in downtown Arlington."

Dr. Patel flushes. "I told you I don't get out of the clinic much. I thought this place seemed hip." Just then, a goofy beer commercial with a yodeling goat appears on the TV screen above their table, and they both chuckle.

When a waiter approaches with the bill, Annie shoos Dr. Patel's hand away. "You can get the next one. Believe it or not, Byrdie

Fenton left me and Ike each a small sum in her will. He's going to put his toward his master's in architecture."

"So you and Ike have stayed in touch." Dr. Patel glides her fingertips over the silky cat sleeping in her lap. She'd adopted Shug months ago. The Siamese quickly became her favorite—though she'd never admit to having one. She'd told Annie that Dirk was learning to deal with his jealousy.

"Ike's driven out to see me a few times. Last Saturday we cooked dinner together, which was really nice—the house is so empty. And I'm going to be helping out at the store a couple times a week, so he can study for the GRE."

"That's wonderful news. I am so very happy to hear that," Dr. Patel says with genuine enthusiasm. "And Gabe? Rest assured, I'm asking strictly as a nosy friend."

"Rushing into that relationship was an impulse, my way of grabbing the steering wheel, convincing myself I was in control when I was really being reckless. Like that bartender in Hong Kong. People got hurt."

Annie thinks about how this was all too apparent the last time they spoke on the phone. Gabe still lay in his hospital bed—each word a painful struggle, his throat raw from the recent intubation.

"I can't tell you how sorry I am," Annie said. The police had already explained to him that it was her husband who had hurt him.

"Confession. I lied too," he said in a strained, gravelly voice so unlike his own. His words were followed by a coughing fit that wrenched at Annie's insides.

"What—what do you mean?"

"I'm five-seven . . . but my team did win the championship in the Arlington Rec League."

Annie smiled. Despite everything, she would've liked for it to be more than a one-night stand. But they haven't spoken since, and Annie doubts they ever will. "It's for the best—I don't know if either of us could get over what happened with Duncan."

At the mention of his name, the warmth drains from Dr. Patel's face. "You didn't answer my question before. If you had run for help, could you have saved Duncan?"

Annie imagines the look of disgust on her daughter's face if she ever found out the truth. Like her own mother, Annie had sacrificed her husband to protect her child. She shakes her head. "He wanted us all to die together in the fire but didn't realize how much wiper fluid had splashed onto his sleeves and pants. His clothes caught fire as soon as he flicked the lighter. I barely had time to get Tabby out of there." Her words are false, but the stench of her husband's burning flesh and hair seems so real. It haunts her during lonely moments. It invades her nostrils now.

Annie stares past the doctor's shoulder, to where a wet snow has begun to collect on the nearby rooftops. She shivers. "No. I couldn't have saved him. It was out of my control."

EPILOGUE

Annie concentrates on the road, where a gentle spring rain has begun to glaze the asphalt. She hazards a nervous glance across the car at her daughter, who is surprisingly sans earbuds. They're on their way to meet Aimee and Danielle at the Park Waldorf spring festival. Annie was relieved to hear Ray wouldn't be attending the event this year, though she's heard he's been getting treatment for his sex addiction and hasn't fallen off the wagon.

Suddenly, Tabby shrieks, "Did you see that?"

Annie's eyes dart frantically across the road. She glimpses the tail end of a plump ginger cat waddling into the underbrush.

"It was massive. Bright orange like Garfield." Tabby laughs.

Annie grins. She hasn't seen the sixteen-year-old laugh like that in a while. Tabby just moved back home last week. In typical teenage fashion, since then she's spent most of her time either out with friends or sequestered in her room. But the adjustment has been easier, for both of them, than Annie anticipated.

Just then, a dark cloud passes over Tabby's face. She clears her throat, hesitating before speaking. "It's weird. The spring festival always reminds me of Dad in the dunk tank. And that makes me smile, but then I immediately feel guilty for smiling. Like, I should hate him, right? I-I mean, he was a mur—"

"He was your father, and he loved you," Annie says firmly. "Nobody's all good or all evil. Hold the happy memories close to your heart—that's how you keep the good part of him alive."

"Thanks . . . I really needed to hear that from you," Tabby says, quietly exhaling.

Annie's heart soars. She's reveling in the newly open lines of communication with her daughter. And in just a few months, they'll be embarking on college tours together. Right now, Tabby's set on studying environmental science at Brown, and she can certainly afford it.

Unbeknownst to Annie, Duncan adjusted his will a month before leaving for Syria. The bulk of the Shaws' sizable inheritance will go to Tabby, held in trust until her twenty-first birthday. Ed advised Annie to contest the will, explaining that Virginia law makes it virtually impossible to entirely disinherit a surviving spouse without an ironclad pre- or post-nuptial agreement.

But she has no desire to challenge the document—Annie's never really felt like a Shaw anyway. She goes by her maiden name now, and her career is thriving. Though she still accepts commercial work—the pet and baby portraits—she also has a show coming up at a small gallery in D.C. The series, titled *Bloodlines by Annie Le*, explores the themes of hereditary trauma and maternal bonds. Unlike her earlier work, the style is abstract. Breaking out of the controlled world of realism has allowed Annie to birth a new style—gloriously unorthodox and unique. She's dedicating the show to Mẹ.

Just as they pull into the school parking lot, she spots Danielle's high, swishy ponytail in front of the gym. Annie's excited to share her good news—the gallery owner agreed to display some of Danielle's beadwork in the lobby.

"Can you drop me off right there?" she says, pointing at her friend. "Thanks for the ride and congratulations on the license. You're a fine driver, Tabby." Before the engine's off, Annie is halfway out the door.

ACKNOWLEDGMENTS

Every good book is the result of a successful creative collaboration. I'm indebted to my editor, Lindsey Rose. Like a gifted choreographer, she helped me to organize the movement of the story, to develop my ideas, and to transform my words into the finished "performance" you see here. Bravo, Lindsey!

Thank you also to the entire team at Dutton, including art director Christopher Lin, cover designer Vi-An Nguyen, production editor LeeAnn Pemberton, copy editor Amy Schneider, and editorial assistant Charlotte Peters. Special thanks to Amanda Walker and Isabel DaSilva for sharing this story with as many readers as possible, and my deepest gratitude to Christine Ball for believing in this book.

To my agent, Stefanie Lieberman, and the stellar team at Janklow & Nesbit Associates, including Molly Steinblatt and Adam Hobbins: Thank you for your guidance, your determination, and your unwavering commitment to excellence.

To my early readers—Helen Gaughran, Stephanie Huszar, Patty Miller, Isabel Frabotta, Jessica Nguyen, Molly Frabotta, Erica Curtis, Karen Mejia, and Lucy Lee—thank you for your wonderful suggestions and encouraging words.

To Richard Levine, MD, at the Berkeley Therapy Institute: I am eternally grateful for your life-changing OCD diagnosis and treatment plan.

To my friend, fellow author, and the best mindset coach in the business Camille Pagán: You taught me how to show up for myself, how to take control, and how to create my own success. This book—and the books to follow—are a direct result of that, and I can never thank you enough.

Finally, thank you to Alex for over two decades of love, adventure, endless patience, and unlimited support—and especially for being my krav maga partner; not all husbands are brave enough to risk getting kicked in the groin.

ABOUT THE AUTHOR

K. T. Nguyen is a psychological thriller author and former magazine editor. Her features have appeared in *Glamour*, *Fitness*, and *Shape*. She grew up in a small town in Ohio and currently lives in a small town in Maryland. She loves native plant gardening and scruffy terriers.

Visit K.T. online and sign up for email updates at
ktnguyenauthor.com

 /K.T.Nguyen.Books
 KTNguyen_Author